MW01140414

Running Towards the Abyss

David Spell

Volume Four of the Zombie Terror War Series

This is a work of fiction. Any similarities to events or persons, living, dead, or fictitious are purely coincidental. Some actual locations are used in a fictitious way and the descriptions included here are not meant to be accurate. No part of this publication can be reproduced or transmitted in any form or by any means, electronic or mechanical, without permission in writing from the author.

Copyright ©2018 by David Spell. All rights reserved. Published in the United States by DavidSpell.com.

ISBN: 9781983225239
Imprint: Independently published

To my grandchildren: Micah, Lyla, and Knox
You are each my favorite and I'm excited to watch your lives unfold!

“The godly has perished from the earth, and there is no one upright among mankind; they all lie in wait for blood, and each hunts the other with a net.” (Micah 7:2)

“Contend, O Lord, with those who contend with me; fight against those who fight against me!” (Psalms 35:1)

“I fear not the man who has practiced 10,000 kicks once. But I fear the man who has practiced one kick 10,000 times.” Bruce Lee

“I would like to see every woman know how to handle firearms as naturally as they know how to handle babies.” Annie Oakley

Table of Contents

Chapter One

A Dark Road

Sixty miles Northeast of Atlanta, Monday, 1700 hours

The tall, muscular man in dark clothing, arrayed in tactical equipment, moved quickly but cautiously down the deserted street. The winding, two-lane road ran parallel to Interstate 85. Chuck McCain had found a trail that led from the interstate into the woods, dumping him out at the empty street he found himself on, continuing his journey north. He had been eating up the miles on I-85 throughout the day, but night was falling, the temperature was dropping, and it was time to find a place to bed down for the night. The clouds had been progressively getting darker and he knew that rain or worse was coming.

McCain hadn't seen any moving cars or any other signs of life all day, but he had seen plenty signs of death. He had shot a group of eight decaying, infected people who had been lingering around a car crash on the interstate a few hours before. Bodies, blood, and gore littered the scene, most of the destruction caused by zombies and not the vehicle accident itself.

Further on, he had entered the woods next to the highway,

skirting around two other car crashes. A few more zombies had been standing in the roadway, not moving. Thankfully, Chuck was able to get by these undetected. His right hamstring was still bothering him and he didn't feel like running.

A large redbrick house with white columns appeared as he rounded a curve. He left the roadway for the cover of some trees, pulling out his binoculars. The front door stood open, an invitation and a threat. All of the windows were covered with plywood and the grass was over a foot tall in the front yard. There were no vehicles in sight, but it looked like the garage was on the other side of the house, out of his view.

Chuck moved deeper into the woods, parallel with the two-story residence, until he could see the backyard. A swimming pool sat unattended, full of green water. The windows on the backside of the house were also boarded up and the back door was closed, probably secured from the inside.

McCain knew that he only had about half an hour of daylight left and it looked, and felt, like it was going to start raining, maybe even snowing, any time now. He checked the flashlight mounted underneath his suppressed Colt M4 rifle. He flicked it on and off, confirming that the batteries were still strong, and moved towards the open front door. He paused at the dark entrance, listened, and sniffed. Nothing. He moved the fire selector on the rifle to "Auto."

Chuck was a federal police officer and, until recently, working for the Centers for Disease Control's Enforcement Division. He and his men had been on the front line of the fight against both terrorists and zombies. When confronting the infected, all of their shooting was done in the "semi-automatic" mode to help them accurately make head shots, the only way to ensure a zombie was stopped for good. Here, trying to survive by himself and not knowing what dangers might await him inside, however, he wanted to be able to get a lot of rounds downrange quickly, depending on the type of threat he encountered.

He entered the house, moving to the left so he wouldn't be silhouetted in the doorway, scanning over the top of his rifle, and finding himself in a small corridor. A large formal living room ran off of it to his left. A stairway to the second level was up ahead on his right.

McCain moved through the living room, using his gun-mounted light to illuminate the dark house. The living room connected with the dining room and then a big, open kitchen back to his right. A large patch of dried blood was visible on the tile floor where it looked like a body had been dragged to the back door.

Chuck continued through the kitchen, the rifle still at eye level, and into a small sitting area with a large window that would have overlooked the backyard if it hadn't been covered with plywood. A leather armchair was laying on its side, while more dried blood stained the hardwood floor. A small bar in the corner beckoned him to come back for further investigation after he finished clearing the house.

The rest of the lower level was empty and he started up the stairs to check the second floor. His ears picked up the sound of movement and something thudded to the floor in the first room on the right, just at the top of the stairway. The floor creaked and whatever or whoever was inside was coming towards the door.

Chuck raised the rifle to his shoulder and sniffed the air but didn't pick up the smell of death. He hadn't heard any growling yet, either. Maybe it hadn't smelled him. The floor creaked again and a large black cat's eyes glowed yellow in the light from the flashlight as it padded into the hallway.

Seeing the intruder, the cat hissed, running down the hallway, away from him. McCain let out his breath and took his finger off of the trigger of the M4.

"Your lucky day, kitty."

The upstairs was clear of both the living and the dead. If he could secure the front entrance, this would be a good place to spend the night. With both small and large groups of infected wandering around, along with the human predators, you didn't want to get caught outside after dark.

A closer check of the front door revealed that it had been kicked in, the frame shattered. The good news was that the hinges were still intact. Chuck took off his backpack and was about to pull one of the heavy leather couches over from the living room. It would keep the door closed against all but the biggest groups of infected and it would slow down human criminals long enough so that he could deal with them, too.

The dark clouds blocked out the moon and the stars. It was cold and Chuck knew the temperatures would be below the freezing mark tonight. January in Georgia could mean sub-freezing temps for a couple of weeks or just as easily have spring-like weather. The approaching winter storm looked like it was going to be nasty and he was thankful that he had found this house to pass the night in.

As he started to drag the sofa across the floor, the sound of voices came from the street. It was almost completely dark by now and McCain stepped closer to the door to listen. A woman's and a man's voices were moving down the road, back the way that Chuck had come. They need to shut up, he thought, or they won't get to wherever they are going.

And where could they possibly be going in the dark? He hadn't seen any survivors in days. And the survivors that he had encountered were as dangerous as the zombies. Good luck, whoever you are. He quietly closed the door.

A baby's cry, however, made him open it again. He didn't want to get involved. In this strange, new world he was hesitant to trust people or to try to help them. The woman tried to quiet the baby, but the crying only got louder. It sounded like they were right in front of the big house.

McCain slipped out the door and used the darkness to sneak up on the people. It was tricky because he didn't want to surprise them and have them pull a gun on him. At the same time, he wanted to check them out before offering to help them.

As he approached, he realized that they had stopped and appeared to be debating whether or not to seek shelter in the large structure. The rain started and helped them to make up their minds. They turned and started in the direction of the front door.

Chuck illuminated them with his gun light. "Stop," he said, softly. "Keep your hands where I can see them."

The woman screamed, jumping backwards at the sight of the big man pointing a rifle and shining a light at them.

"You need to be quiet," McCain told them, quietly. "I heard your voices and the baby crying as you were coming down the street. You're welcome to join me in the house. It's pretty big and I think we'll be safe for the night."

As a career policeman, Chuck knew how to read people. He was already getting a bad vibe off of this couple. The tall, skinny, white male had the pockmarked face of the meth users he'd dealt with over the years. A black duffel bag was slung over his shoulder.

The girl was tall, as well, and had probably been attractive at one time. Judging from her looks, Chuck assumed her parents had been a mix of black and Asian. Her eye sockets were hollow and she also had the appearance of a drug user. Maybe a prostitute? he wondered to himself. But she was holding a baby carrier containing a crying baby with a diaper bag draped over her shoulder.

The male spoke up. "We don't know you, man. How do we know we can trust you?"

Chuck kept the rifle pointing down but left the flashlight on so that he could see them.

He shrugged. "You can keep walking and try to find another

place to spend the night. But I came from the way you're going and there isn't a lot to choose from."

The woman looked over at her companion and said, "I think we should stay here. We can't be out walking around at night. It's too dangerous."

"What are your names?" McCain asked.

"I'm Tonya. This is Greg," the woman answered.

"I'm Chuck. You guys are safe with me, but I'm going back in and securing the door so you need to make up your minds fast."

Suddenly, loud growling came from nearby. Infected had either been following Greg and Tonya or had just heard or smelled them.

Greg swallowed hard and looked at Chuck. "Thanks for the offer. We'll stay here, too."

"You guys go on in. I'll take care of these before they can alert any more of their friends."

The couple hurried towards the front door, the growls closer now. McCain's rifle light illuminated the four zombies, just twenty yards away. Chuck left the flashlight on and let the rifle hang from its sling across his chest.

He quickly drew his 9mm Glock 17 pistol and pulled the suppressor off his belt, screwing it onto the threaded barrel. The suppressed 9mm was much quieter than the M4. The pistol was also equipped with a flashlight mounted under the frame.

He thumbed that light on, also, and saw that three of the four infected were badly decomposed, a light breeze hitting him in the face with the nauseating smell of death and decaying flesh. The fourth one must have been recently infected. She had been an attractive twenty-something girl, wearing sweat pants and a Clemson t-shirt at the time of her infection. She suddenly began to sprint towards McCain, snarling at what she hoped was going to be an easy meal. The pistol coughed and a 9mm hollow point bullet punched into her left eye, spinning her around and dropping her onto her back.

The three decomposing zombies kept shuffling forward, growling and snapping their teeth together. Chuck made three more quick head shots, and then shone the light on the four bodies to make sure they were all down for good. He did a three hundred and sixty degree scan, making sure the area was clear, reloading his pistol with a full magazine. McCain stood in the light, icy rain for another minute, listening. Satisfied that these were the only zombies in the immediate area, he retreated to the safety of the house.

In the White-Columned House, 60 miles Northeast of Atlanta, Monday, 1900 hours

Chuck got Greg to help him shove the sofa against the front door. They dragged another couch over and placed it long ways to the entrance to the living room. If any infected managed to get inside, this barrier would give McCain a few extra minutes to pick them off.

Tonya pulled a plastic yellow flashlight out of the diaper bag she was carrying. She sat on the floor nursing the baby with Greg sitting near her. Chuck held a small flashlight of his own that he carried on his belt. Between the two of them, they had enough light so that they could all see each other.

McCain took off his body armor plate-carrier and eased himself to the floor with his back to the wall and looked at his three guests.

"So, where are you guys coming from?" he asked.

Greg looked at Tonya. She answered for them.

"We're trying to get to some friends' house a few miles further down the road. Our car broke down earlier today so we've been walking."

"Where do you live?"

Chuck saw her glance at Greg again.

This time, Greg answered, "We live up near Carnesville. It's a small town, maybe twenty miles north of here."

Chuck nodded. "These must be good friends you're going to visit. It's really dangerous to be out moving around. Do you guys have any guns?"

The couple looked at each other. It was clear to McCain from conducting so many suspect interviews over the years that they were not being truthful. They kept looking at each other to make sure they didn't contradict the story they were having to fabricate in the moment.

Greg answered, "No, but we need some. We need to be able to protect ourselves."

"Where do your friends live?"

"They're on the other side of Braselton," Tonya said, looking down at the nursing baby. "How much farther is that, Chuck?"

"At least fifteen miles. That's a lot of walking with a baby."

Tonya started crying and looked at Greg. "What are we going to do? We're almost out of food. That's a long walk and I'm scared." She wiped her eyes with her hand. "Sorry," she said, making eye contact with Chuck so he could see her tears.

"I understand," replied McCain. "These are tough times for all of us. So, do you know that your friends in Braselton are OK? The zombies came right through there."

They both shrugged. "We hope so. We don't really know if anyone's still alive or not with the phones being down," Tonya answered.

Probably the first thing they've said that was true, Chuck thought. But why would they be making this trip into such a dangerous area?

"I'm just glad we found this place where we could hole up and ride the night out," added Greg. "Thanks for letting us share it. The biggest problem for us is that we don't have many supplies, and without a car, we're in a bad spot."

"Well, I'll be leaving in the morning so you can keep the house," McCain told them. "I can't help you with supplies, though."

"What about you?" Tonya asked. "Where are you going?"

"I'm trying to find my daughter. With the power grid and satellites down, I haven't heard from her in months."

"Where's she at?"

Without getting too specific, he answered, "Up near the South Carolina line, maybe another thirty or thirty-five miles."

Greg nodded at McCain's rifle, leaning against the wall, next to the CDC officer. His eyes looked over the big man's helmet, armor and attachments laying on the floor, and then his backpack and holstered pistol.

"That's some nice gear you have."

"Yeah, it is."

They chatted a bit more and McCain sensed that there was a lot more to this young couple that they weren't telling him. No problem, he thought. Everybody is entitled to their own secrets.

Chuck decided to take his things upstairs and turn in for the night in one of the bedrooms. In the low light, though, he noticed that Greg and Tonya appeared to be having a conversation with their eyes. The baby was finally asleep and she gently laid him in the carrier.

The two of them made eye contact again and Tonya took a deep breath, nodding almost imperceptibly to her companion. Greg nodded back at her, and glanced at Chuck in the dim light. McCain knew then that things were not going to end well. Let's go ahead and get it over with, he thought.

"I'm going to scout around a little bit and see if there's anything valuable in the rest of the house," McCain said, climbing to his feet.

"Good idea," Greg nodded, a little too enthusiastically.

McCain picked up his rifle and left the room. He had wanted to check out the bar that he had seen earlier, anyway. When he got out of sight of Greg and Tonya, he set the rifle down on the floor, quietly drew his pistol, and screwed the suppressor back on.

Behind the bar, besides cobwebs, he found a number of empty bottles. He got down on his hands and knees and shone his light on all the shelves. God loves me, Chuck thought. In a dark corner, hidden behind several empties, was an unopened bottle of Evan Williams Kentucky Straight Bourbon Whiskey. He sat it up on the top of the bar, picked up an empty Jack Daniels bottle, and walked back out to the living room.

"Look what I found," announced McCain, holding up the empty bottle in his right hand.

Chuck's pistol was in his left hand by his side, concealed behind his leg. In the light of Tonya's flashlight, he saw that she was standing with her back to him. She spun quickly, pointing a small revolver at McCain.

Greg was still seated on the floor but his hand was under his shirt, near his waistband. This wasn't going the way that he had pictured it. McCain never imagined the woman would be the one to try and rob him.

"Sorry, Chuck," she said. "We need your guns and stuff. Nobody needs to get hurt. Just drop your pistol belt and you can leave."

"You're just going to take my equipment and kick me out? That's it?"

"That's it. I've got to take care of my baby and we need better weapons."

Climbing to his feet, drawing a small pistol, Greg said, "Thanks for helping us out tonight. It's nice to know that there are still good people like you in the world."

"No problem," McCain said, letting a tremor of fear sound in his voice. "I don't want any trouble."

A look of relief crossed Tonya's face. McCain suddenly

underhanded the empty bottle at her and stepped to his right, firing a back-fist into Greg's face. The whiskey bottle hit Tonya in the chest and she jerked the trigger of the revolver, firing a shot that struck the floor where Chuck had been standing. From a distance of ten feet, McCain raised the Glock, firing two shots into her chest and then a third that struck her in the forehead. Blood erupted from that wound and she collapsed to the floor.

The strike to Greg's face snapped his head back and knocked him five feet across the room and into the wall. He crumpled to the floor, stunned, but somehow still holding onto the pistol. Chuck swung around and sighted in on the pockmarked face.

"Don't do it."

Greg's face registered shock, blood dripping out of his damaged nose. The gunshots had awakened the baby, who began to scream. Greg stared at McCain, realizing that the big man was about to shoot him in the head, and let go of his gun, raising his hands over his head. The gun clattered to the floor beside him.

"Face down on the floor, hands behind your back," Chuck ordered.

He continued to cover Greg with his Glock but the priority now was to quiet the baby. The shots and the screaming would attract any Zs in the area. He saw a pacifier laying in the child carrier next to him. Chuck grabbed it with his right hand and slipped it into the crying infant's mouth. He finally calmed down as Chuck rocked the carrier for a couple of minutes.

McCain stepped over to Greg and said, "Don't move. I'm going to handcuff you and search you."

The stunned man was breathing hard, his face hurt, but he still hadn't said a word after watching Tonya get gunned down. He finally found his voice.

"You just...you just killed her. You murdered her," he managed to say.

"The problem with pulling a gun on somebody is that sometimes they pull one, too," replied Chuck. "And the problem with shooting at someone is that sometimes they shoot back."

He slipped metal handcuffs on Greg's wrists and searched him for additional weapons. He had a folding knife in his right front pocket and an extra magazine of .380 ammo for the Bersa pistol he had dropped.

"What are you going to do with us?"

McCain ignored him and went over to Tonya and knelt beside her bleeding corpse, her lifeless eyes staring at the ceiling, the bullet hole in her face still dribbling blood.

"Why would you do that?" he asked her. "I tried to help you and you turned on me."

He shook his head and searched her, finding nothing of use. Her revolver was a Smith & Wesson Air Weight in .38 Special and Chuck put both of the guns, the knife, and ammo in his backpack and then searched Greg's duffel bag and the diaper bag.

Thankfully, the baby had gone back to sleep. He was so little, maybe a year old, McCain guessed. What was his life expectancy?

Greg's duffel bag contained the drugs. Two ziplock baggies of meth with two balls in each. The four 'eight balls' together were about fourteen grams of methamphetamine. That was a lot of dope for one guy to be carrying around. The street value was around a thousand dollars before everything had fallen apart.

More digging uncovered two more plastic bags, each containing an ounce of marijuana. The value on that had been around six hundred dollars before the zombies showed up. McCain found fifteen extra rounds for Tonya's revolver, which he kept. The duffel bag also contained their meager food supplies, a few packets of trail mix, some beef jerky, and a can of peanuts. The trail mix packs and the beef jerky hadn't been opened so McCain threw those into his backpack.

“Where were you taking the drugs?” he asked Greg.

“Man, the world is ending and you’re asking me about some dope? You don't know what you're dealing with here. The guy those drugs belong to is going to be really pissed.

“And Tonya worked for him and you just gunned her down. He’s going to come after you and cut you up into little pieces. Or maybe the people we were supposed to be delivering to will come after you. Either way, you’re a dead man.”

“We’re all dead men, Greg. Some just sooner than others.”

Chuck shook his head and changed the subject. “What’s your baby’s name?"

“It’s not my baby, but his name’s Jeremy. Tonya never told me who the dad was. If I had to guess, the baby’s daddy is the same man who owns those drugs. And you murdered her. I wouldn’t want to be in your shoes, man, when he catches you.”

“Well, Jeremy is your son now or you can take him to his dad.” said McCain.

South of Commerce, Northeast of Atlanta, Tuesday, 0630 hours

Chucked dozed fitfully with his pistol at his side. He left Greg handcuffed, even when he said he needed to use the restroom. Eventually, he peed on himself during the night.

Jeremy slept until 0500 hours. McCain woke up before he started crying too loudly. There was a good supply of baby food and formula mix in the diaper bag. Thankfully, there was a bottle of milk in the bag and Jeremy sucked on it gratefully.

As he checked his equipment, reloaded all his magazines, and prepared to continue his journey, he couldn’t help but stare at Tonya’s body. With her dead, now he was worried about what would happen to Jeremy. Meth-head Greg didn't strike him as Dad of the Year material. Chuck ate his own breakfast, a cold Meal Ready to Eat pouch of hash brown potatoes with bacon. He washed it down with some water, saving the coffee packet for later in the morning when he took a break from walking.

When he was ready to leave, McCain crouched next to Greg. He made a point of holding the Glock next to his head as he unscrewed the suppressor and secured it on his belt. Greg stared fearfully at the gun, not knowing if the man holding it was going to execute him now or not. Eventually, Chuck slipped the pistol into its holster.

"Greg, I'm going to take the handcuffs off and then I'm leaving. You had better take care of that baby or I'll track you down and kill you. Really, you just better hope you never see me again." McCain stared into the other man's hollow eyes.

Greg couldn't hold his stare, looking away. "I will, I'll take care of him, I promise. Are you going to leave me a gun?"

"No, I'm not leaving you a gun. You tried to rob me, remember?"

"But, those things are out there. It's dangerous not to have a gun."

"You didn't seem to have a problem with trying to take mine from me and throwing me outside in the middle of the night. Just remember these wise words, 'You reap what you sow.' And, here are some more wise words. Don't try and follow me."

When the cuffs were off, Greg rubbed the circulation back into his wrists. Jeremy had finished his bottle and was ready for something else to eat. Chuck backed away from him, shouldered his pack and slung the M4 across his chest. He pulled the sofa back far enough so that he could slip out the front door.

As he started walking north in first light of dawn, Chuck saw a light coating of snow from the previous night's storm. The sky was still overcast and the temperature felt well below freezing. Hopefully, the storm will hold off until I make some progress today, he hoped.

The events of the previous night played through Chuck's mind. The police officer shook his head in disgust. He had tried to help those people. In reality, with those Zs so close behind them, he had probably saved their lives, yet they had still tried to rob him. You've got to mind your own business, McCain, he told himself. You can't save the world and you need to find Melanie.

After traveling for about a mile, McCain stopped and pulled the methamphetamine out of his backpack. He opened the baggies and dumped the contents into the snow and slushy mud on the side of the road, grinding the drugs into the ground. A little further on, he did the same with the marijuana.

He continued moving north on the deserted, two-lane road until it curved sharply to the right, and began taking him to the east, away from where he wanted to go. Chuck left the blacktop and cut through the woods for almost a quarter mile until he was again staring at the never-ending, empty interstate. He set his mind to walking so he could get to his daughter as soon as possible.

North of Commerce, Northeast of Atlanta, Tuesday, 1630 hours

McCain hadn't been able to move as quickly as he had hoped. He figured that he'd only covered around fifteen miles walking north on I-85. Groups of infected had forced him to take wide detours through the woods to get around them. His goal on this trip was to always avoid contact, even if it slowed his pace down.

The Commerce exit had been more exciting than he had planned for. It was a large interchange with outlet malls, a large truck stop, restaurants, and gas stations, all close to the interstate. There had been no wooded areas to duck into and he simply had to keep moving north, shooting at least twenty Zs scattered along the road.

There were abandoned vehicles parked on the shoulder and even left in the middle of the interstate, both north and south of the bridge. McCain knew that once he got past this exit, he would have the safety of the woods again if he needed them. Fortunately, most of the lingering zombies in this area were seeking victims around the business district of the small town of Commerce.

As he walked, Chuck had a lot of time to think about the events of the past three months. America, and specifically the east coast, had never really recovered from the last attacks. The three simultaneous car bomb detonations combined with the three suicide bombers in Atlanta, Washington, D.C., and New York City had been devastating for those key cities and beyond.

The explosives that had been packed into the three vehicles and into the three suicide vests contained a deadly mixture of the zombie virus and radioactive waste. These dirty bombs killed and infected thousands in the three metropolitan areas. The packs of infected had immediately begun to move deeper into their respective cities and then, using the interstate system, had marched out into the suburbs to find living food.

The radioactive materials combined with the zombie virus that Iranian operatives had brought into America had created some zombies with superhuman strength. At this point, however, with the governmental breakdown, there were few resources being used to study the phenomenon. Like it really mattered, Chuck thought. The zombie virus was the most deadly bio-terror weapon ever invented.

After the CIA discovered that Iran had been responsible for releasing the weaponized virus throughout the United States over six months earlier, the President had declared war, unleashing the full military might of America on that rogue nation. Within just a few weeks, Iran was a smoldering pile of ruins.

Iranian operatives, however, had already infiltrated the United States through Mexico and had continued to launch multiple attacks at civilian targets. Many of these strikes had involved spreading the zombie virus, while others had been more conventional terror attacks. All were deadly.

Chuck McCain and the officers of the Centers for Disease Control Enforcement Unit had been some of the first to encounter people infected with the bio-terror weapon. CDC teams throughout the US had been the tip of the spear in the fight against the zombie hordes. McCain's teams had also taken out several of the key terrorists behind the attacks.

A Presidential Executive Order that allowed the CIA to keep their hand in the war on terror had created the CDC Enforcement Unit. The Central Intelligence Agency is forbidden by law from working or conducting operations on American soil. The executive order, however, allowed the CIA to stay on the forefront of the fight by covertly funding and supporting these new federal police officers. CDC Officers operated in every city in the US where the Centers for Disease Control had an office and they had jurisdiction throughout America.

McCain and his men had battled both foreign-and-domestic-born Islamic terrorists and had done their part to eliminate thousands of people infected by the incurable zombie virus. Three months ago, however, everything had started to come unraveled. Chuck's two teams, along with a handful of local police and a few FBI agents, faced off against a surging mass of thousands of zombies after the simultaneous car and suicide bomber attacks in downtown Atlanta.

The American President, flush from his military victory over Iran, had accepted a bad policy suggestion from his advisors. The

President listened to an idea that originated from an undercover Iranian operative who had managed to infiltrate the FBI and connect himself with the Deputy Director of the Mass Weapons Directorate.

The policy idea presented to the President was that the United States, after thoroughly defeating Iran, did not need to use its military forces to combat those whom had been infected and turned into zombies in America. Federal and local police would be able to handle the thousands of new zombies without any outside help. It would be an international public relations victory for the United States to defeat the Zs without having to unleash the American military on American soil.

This turned out to be a devastating mistake that allowed multiple thousands of zombies to steamroll over police roadblocks and barricades and continue to march in search of other victims. There just weren't enough police officers to stop the thousands of Zs who had been infected. By the time the President rescinded his order and released National Guard units, it was too late. The entire east coast was now considered a danger zone.

The roadblock that McCain and his men had manned, just north of Atlanta was a perfect example. They had fewer than a hundred law enforcement officers trying to stop thousands of zombies. Three Islamic terrorists had also managed to attack the police from behind while they were fighting the Zs, only intensifying the devastation. One of Chuck's men and many of the police officers were killed. McCain and several of his other agents were wounded, barely escaping with their lives.

After the subsequent failure of the power grid, people had begun to flee to "safer" states. The problem was that every state in the union had been impacted, to some degree, by the virus. The CDC teams had continued working for the next two months, conducting rescue missions inside zombie-occupied regions around the Metro-Atlanta area.

With the government being run from underground bunkers, law and order had eroded to the point of anarchy. With the collapse of the power grid, communications had soon followed suit. It was presumed that these breakdowns were the results of additional terrorists' plots, either cyber-attacks or through the bombing of key targets. Without the internet or ability to watch the news, however, no one knew for certain.

Chuck attempted for over a week to contact the Assistant Director of Operations for the CIA, Admiral Jonathan Williams, without any success. McCain had some big decisions to make and he needed the input of his boss. With their support system no longer in place and with no way to communicate with Washington, Chuck had made the difficult decision to send his agents home to look after their own families.

The CDC was still functioning as best they could in a rural fifty-acre facility east of Atlanta. Some of their best researchers were committed to trying to find a vaccine that would work against the zombie virus. As long as they had fuel for their large generators, the site had electricity, and the epidemiologists could work.

This location was well away from the path of the zombies, hidden from view by a fence and the dense forest that surrounded the facility. Four of McCain's officers and two civilian security guards had chosen to stay behind to guard the facility and the scientists. All of his other men had packed their vehicles and moved their loved ones to safer locations or were undertaking similar journeys to his own, trying to locate family members.

The temperature was dropping again and Chuck had been watching the clouds getting darker and heavier. It felt like more snow was coming, letting the police officer know that it was time to look for a place to camp out for the night. Those dark clouds also mirrored the darkness that hung over Chuck's soul, he realized, wondering if he would ever be able to shake it off.

Hopefully, tonight he wouldn't have to deal with another Greg and Tonya. This particular stretch of I-85 was barren, but McCain could see an overpass in the distance. Maybe there would be some place that he could get in out of the cold.

He increased his pace as the wind picked up, cutting through his layers of clothes. The pain in his right hamstring was a dull throbbing. He had popped some Tylenol earlier and kept walking. When the snow finally started to fall, Chuck was still a half-mile from the bridge. At least I don't see anyone who wants to eat me, he thought. This snow was mixed with freezing rain, a Georgia specialty, McCain noted.

As the big man made his way up the exit ramp to Old Federal Road, he was conscious of how exposed he was, being out in the open. He eased to his right into the small copse of pine trees that paralleled the ramp. He scanned the area on the west side of the interstate with his binoculars. A large truck stop on the left side of the street and a smaller one on the right. Several tractor trailers were parked or abandoned at both businesses.

He didn't see any people, living or dead, which was good news. Those stores would be worth investigating another time, he thought. The vehicles in the parking lots, however, might mean Zs inside. He'd try to find a house to use for the night.

Chuck turned east onto Old Federal Road and stayed on the shoulder, close to the trees running along the roadway. A convenience store was just ahead of him, siting on the right side of the street. A few cars were scattered around the parking lot here, too. The snow and sleet continued to come down, the snowflakes increasing in size by the minute.

McCain crouched, moving closer, until he could see the front of the convenience store. He felt himself shudder: only two hundred yards away, a group of twelve zombies clustered near the front door, their faces pressed against the window, peering inside. What had their attention? he wondered. If there was someone inside the store, the Zs would normally be banging on the glass until they shattered it. At least their attention is away from me, he thought.

A sign on the left side of the road advertised new homes a mile further down Old Federal Road. Chuck stayed low, crossing the street, and slipping into the woods across from the store with the Zs. He moved quickly but carefully in the direction of the housing development. After a quarter of a mile, the woods gave way to an open field. There was no sign of any infected and Chuck moved back to the roadway, walking as fast as he could on the snow blanketed ground.

Chapter Two

Savior

South of Carnesville, Northeast of Atlanta, Tuesday, 1705 hours

Chuck couldn't scout the neighborhood as thoroughly as he would have liked. The builder's sign in front of the subdivision advertised "Homes for Sale," but all the houses that McCain saw appeared to have been occupied before their owners had fled the flesh-eating zombies that swept up the interstate. He had less than a half hour of daylight left and was shivering as the wintery mix of precipitation continued to fall on his wet clothing. He needed to find shelter before hypothermia took hold of him.

He chose a house in the middle of a cul-de-sac near the entrance to the subdivision. The short side street ran directly off of the main road that led into the neighborhood. The doors and windows appeared intact, a big plus. He cautiously circled the gray, two-story frame house, rifle pressed into his shoulder, as he listened for any signs of life.

The doors were locked but he found a lower level window in the rear that wasn't. Chuck eased it up and listened some more. He sniffed inside and was pleasantly surprised to only smell the musty odor of an abandoned house. McCain was a solid six feet two, two hundred and twenty pounds, and maneuvering through the window wasn't easy or safe since he hadn't cleared the inside of the residence yet.

Thankfully, he was able to get inside without hurting himself or making too much noise. He closed and locked the window behind him and slowly searched the residence. The more he searched, the happier he became. This is really nice, he thought. Unlike the abandoned house that he had shared with Greg and Tonya the night before, this one didn't appear to have been visited by the virus. There were no bloodstains on the floors or walls and it hadn't been ransacked.

Most of the homes closer to Atlanta had been broken into and looted already. Here, Chuck got the feeling that the residents had packed up and gone on a trip and could return at any time. He knew that probably wasn't true but he was thankful to have a relatively warm, dry place to rest and wait out the winter storm. The homeowners had even left a few clothes and some canned goods behind. His own food stores were getting low so this find was a pleasant surprise.

Something caught his eye as he cleared the kitchen. A thermometer hung outside the window over the sink, attached to the glass by suction cups. There was just enough light that he could read the red temperature line. Twenty-four degrees. It would not be a good night to sleep outside. Thank God I found this place, McCain mused, still shivering in his soaked garments.

He had no idea if there were any other survivors hiding out in the neighborhood or not. He doubted it but knew it was possible. There were plenty of people who had chosen not to evacuate as the government had ordered. For most of those, however, things had not turned out well.

McCain also had no idea if there were any infected lurking in the subdivision. He had seen the group up the road in the convenience store parking lot and couldn't take a chance on lighting a fire to warm himself or to dry his clothes. It might attract both the living and the dead.

Now it was time to get his wets clothes off. Chuck stripped off his body armor and jacket. He had on several layers of shirts, all of which were soaked to his skin. After stripping to the waist, he grabbed a dry t-shirt and a long sleeve thermal top out of his backpack, shivering as he pulled the shirts on, thankful to feel mostly dry again.

He pulled a fresh pair of socks out of his bag and set them on the coffee table next to the couch. They would be going on in just a few minutes. After spreading his wet garments over the dining room chairs, he scrounged around in the closets upstairs to see what else he could use while his clothes dried out. He only had the pants that he was wearing and just one more shirt tucked inside his pack. A few more layers of dry garments would be nice.

The man of the house was not as big as Chuck and wore medium size shirts. At this point, however, anything would do. Even a University of Alabama sweatshirt that he found folded on the top shelf of the master bedroom closet. "Roll Tide," McCain said to himself as he tried to force the sweatshirt on over his broad shoulders.

A car engine roared as a vehicle sped into the neighborhood and skidded to a stop nearby. Chuck dropped the too-small sweatshirt to the floor, quickly making his way down to the living room and peeking out of the closed curtains. Men's voices filled the air. He could see them, three houses down from him. A white SUV had pulled into a driveway and several men were struggling with something in the backseat.

Another sound cut through the evening silence. A girl's voice screaming, "No!"

A shiver went down McCain's spine and it had nothing to do with the cold. The men laughed and two of them reached into the vehicle for her legs. Suddenly, one of them recoiled backwards, screaming and holding his face.

"She kicked me in the nose! I think the little bitch broke my nose! I'm gonna kill her right now," he yelled, drawing a knife from his belt and starting back towards the car.

A tall muscular man grabbed him and held him back as the other men laughed.

"Not yet, you aren't," an authoritative voice boomed. "We'll all get to have some fun with her and then you can kill her, Larry."

Two other men grabbed at the girl from the opposite side of the car. She fought back with everything she had, flailing at them with her fists, screaming for them to stop, but a big, balding man drew back and punched her in the face. The sound of his fist impacting her head carried all the way to the end of the cul-de-sac and McCain's ears.

A sick feeling dropped into Chuck's stomach as he saw the girl go limp and dragged out of the SUV. The man who had punched her tossed the small body over his shoulder and they all walked towards the front door. Three of the men had long guns, Chuck noticed, one of them the distinct shape of an AK-47.

Without consciously thinking about it, McCain had already thrown on his modular lightweight load-carrying equipment (MOLLE) plate-carrier. Weighing around thirty pounds, the carrier contained heavy front, rear, and side armor plates, pouches for rifle and pistol magazines, an individual first-aid kit, a Glock knife, and a CamelBak hydration system attached to the rear. He slung his rifle over his chest, snapped on his black kevlar helmet, and rushed towards the back door.

The snow wasn't falling as heavily now but the freezing rain continued to pelt him, threatening to soak his dry shirts. At least two inches of snow and ice already covered the ground. It would soon be dark and Chuck didn't want to be outside after nightfall. With all the noise the newcomers had made, there could already be Zs moving into the area.

The good news was that he had the element of surprise. They had no idea that anyone else was around and they clearly only had one thing on their minds. The bad news was that there were four of them and four to one were never good odds.

McCain used the two adjacent houses for cover as he maneuvered next to the target house. It sounded like all four of the men were inside with the girl. They still were making no effort to be quiet as their loud laughter carried through the thin walls. Do these clowns not realize that hungry zombies will come running to all the noise that they were making?

Of course, Chuck hadn't been able to recon the house so he had no idea of the floor plan. At the same time, he wasn't going to stand by and watch a girl be murdered by these animals. He paused for just a moment and thought about how things had changed. A few months earlier, he would have tried to arrest these men. Now, he realized, that was the furthest thought from his mind.

South of Carnesville, Northeast of Atlanta, Tuesday, 1725 hours

Her head and face hurt really bad and she was so cold that she felt herself shaking. Who was laughing? Was she back at the school?

Elizabeth Benton tried to open her eyes but even that effort brought sharp pain. She suddenly realized that she didn't have a shirt on. No wonder I'm so cold, she thought. Benton shivered as she tried to cover herself with her hands, the laughter only growing louder.

Elizabeth finally forced her eyes open but then wished that she had kept them closed. She was lying on a couch in the middle of a living room and the big bald creep was standing over her, leering down as he took a drink from a bottle. In his other hand, he was holding Elizabeth's red flannel shirt and her bra. Another man, maybe in his forties, with greasy hair, stepped into view. He was holding a bloody cloth to his nose as he glared down at her.

"You're gonna regret kickin' me, little girl, I promise you. You're gonna regret it."

The room was illuminated by three candles flickering on the counter that separated the living room from the kitchen. The other two men were standing behind the couch, looking down on her. She couldn't see them clearly because of the low light and because of the pounding in her head. It didn't matter. Their faces were etched into her mind forever.

The skinny guy with the long, stringy hair and yellow teeth. The fourth man was the one the others had called, "5-0." He was big and muscular, with a bushy mustache. He hadn't said much but the other three deferred to him. Elizabeth had watched in horror as 5-0 had shot all three of her friends in the head and then stuck a pistol in her face less than an hour before. She had expected him to shoot her as well, but he'd changed his mind.

What could she do? She couldn't fight all four of these animals. They had already said they were going to kill her. Her head continued to throb, but suddenly, a sound track began to play in her mind. It came from several years before when she had taken a women's self-defense class. She heard her instructor's voice. "Don't give up. Don't ever give up. As long as you're breathing, keep fighting."

"Give me a drink of that, Bobby," a voice demanded.

Bobby handed the bottle to 5-0 and said, "I say we get this party started," dropping her clothes to the floor and reaching for his belt. "Get her pants off, Larry."

Elizabeth decided that they might very well rape her, but she was going to be dead first. She squinted as Greasy Hair reached for the button on her blue jeans and she launched a kick at his groin. Her heel caught Larry full in the testicles and he grunted in pain, stumbling backwards.

Without warning, a crashing sound froze Bobby and his friends in place. They all turned towards the back of the house, not sure what was happening as the double French doors burst inward. There was a loud pop and Bobby's head snapped back, blood spurting out of a hole in his forehead.

Chuck stood to the side of the rear entrance and did a quick peek through the back doors. The four kidnappers were standing around a couch, looking down and laughing at something. He couldn't see the girl but that had to be who they were staring at on the sofa. The bald guy reached down where McCain guessed she was lying and after a minute, stood back up holding a red shirt and a bra. This elicited more laughter.

A middle-aged man with a bloody nose was standing next to the bald man and leaned down, saying, "You're gonna regret kickin' me, little girl, I promise you. You're gonna regret it."

McCain was formulating his plan. The two men on the other side of the couch were standing in the shadows. One of them was the biggest of the four, probably close to his own size. He was the one Chuck had seen carrying the AK. Nice mustache, McCain thought.

Chuck couldn't hear everything that was said inside, but he did hear, "Get her pants off, Larry," and knew that it was time for him act.

Suddenly, the man with the bleeding nose recoiled and bent over in pain as a small foot collided with his groin. That little girl has a set, Chuck thought. Let's go while they're distracted. He reared back and kicked into the center of the double French doors, shattering the frame and sending them flying open.

He started shooting as he burst through the doorway, his first shot hitting Bobby in the head. McCain continued moving, stepping to the right and putting a shot into Larry's chest and another into his face.

Stringy Hair managed to draw a pistol and was raising it as Chuck swung his muzzle back to the left and fired again, the two 5.56mm rounds ripping into his sternum. A third bullet punched through his yellow teeth and exited out the back of his head.

McCain's movement had brought him far enough into the room to where he could see the girl lying on the couch. She was shirtless and trying to cover herself, pulling her legs up into a fetal position.

"Get on the floor!" he yelled towards her.

She didn't move but Mustache Man suddenly came up from behind the couch firing his AK. It felt like someone had hit Chuck in the chest with a baseball bat. The breath was driven out of his lungs and he felt his knees buckle. A second shot from the AK whizzed by Chuck's left ear as he took a step to the right, trying to get out of the line-of-fire. McCain managed to fire his M4 twice at the man and was rewarded with hearing a grunt of pain and seeing wooden splinters explode outwards from the front of the AK.

Chuck's first round had struck the man's left hand that was wrapped around the front wooden hand guard, shattering fingers and destroying the rifle. McCain's second shot had hit his attacker in the center of the chest, eliciting another gasp. Mustache Man dropped the broken weapon, rushing to his right to clear the couch as Chuck fired twice more and missed. The bullet to Chuck's sternum had slowed his reaction time and he realized too late that he couldn't track his target.

Mustache Man charged, knocking the muzzle of McCain's rifle to the side with his left forearm and throwing a straight right punch that caught Chuck on the left side of the face. McCain rolled his head with the blow, but still felt his adversary's power. His muscular attacker continued forward, grabbing Chuck around the waist, shoving him backwards across a coffee table that was next to the sofa, and falling on top of the intruder who had just killed his three friends.

The table collapsed under the combined weight of the two men. Chuck's attacker was top of him, punching him again in the face with his right hand and reaching for his throat with his left hand. McCain saw an explosion of light from the fist to the head, taking the full impact of the punch. He knew that another strike like that would knock him unconscious, leaving both Chuck and the girl defenseless.

The attacker's right hand wrapped around McCain's throat, Mustache Man's eyes full of hatred as he tried to choke the life out of the man beneath him. The round that hit his AK-47, however, had destroyed three of the fingers on his left hand, and he wasn't able to grip Chuck's neck with both hands.

McCain was an MMA fighter and had fought professionally for several years while he was a police officer. Even though Chuck had wrestled in high school, he always preferred to fight standing up. As a cop and as a pro fighter, however, he understood the importance of having a good ground game. His head had started to clear but his chest still throbbed. Chuck had no idea how badly he was hurt from the gunshot, and with Mustache Man on top of him and clearly intent on killing him, McCain needed to end this now.

From his back, Chuck viciously slammed both open palms onto his attacker's ears, bursting the eardrums. The man on top of him cursed in pain and instinctively reached for his own head. McCain shot the heel of his right palm under his opponent's chin, snapping his head back, as Chuck's left hand grabbed a handful of hair on the back of the man's skull.

The body always follows the head and Chuck twisted the

kidnapper's head to the side, quickly reversing their positions, rolling the muscular man onto his back, mounting him, and dropping heavy, thudding elbows onto his head and face. Normally, after a few of these strikes, the referee would pull him off, signaling the end of the fight. There was no referee here, though, and Chuck needed to make sure that Mustache Man was never going to be a threat again, slamming powerful elbow strikes into his skull, over and over, until his foe was not moving.

After it was clear that his opponent was unconscious, Chuck rolled him over, drew his Glock knife, and shoved the blade into the base of his attacker's skull. He wiggled the handle until he was confident the kidnapper was dead. McCain thought that he had struck his adversary in the chest with a shot from his rifle. When he searched him, he felt the heavy body armor, similar to what McCain himself was wearing, and saw where his own 5.56mm round had impacted the center of the ballistic vest.

Chuck glanced over at the girl on the couch. She had sat up and was watching him, her mouth hanging open. She appeared to be having trouble focusing as she looked at him with fear-filled eyes. She pulled her legs up under herself and backed to the far end of the sofa. The left side of her face was swollen and her left eye was almost closed. Her bottom lip was busted, with dried blood around her mouth.

"We need to get out of here," he said, trying to bring his breathing back under control. Chuck yanked his knife out of the dead man's head and cleaned the blood off on Mustache Man's shirt, and re-sheathed it. "I don't know if there are any zombies around here but that shooting may bring them in."

"Who…who are you?" the girl asked quietly, wrapping her arms around her knees.

"My name's Chuck," he answered, forcing a smile. "I was in the neighborhood and it looked like you could use a little help. I've got a house just up the street where I was going to hole up for a couple of days."

McCain realized three things. He was still sitting astride the dead man, the girl still didn't have a shirt on, and something wet was running down his lower back and legs. Chuck tried to avert his gaze as he reached beside him and picked up her flannel shirt and bra.

"Here, put your clothes on and then we need to go. I'm going to search these guys and take whatever they have that we can use."

Chuck got to his feet, removed a glove and probed around his lower back. There was no pain, but his hand came back wet. His flashlight revealed that it wasn't blood, he saw gratefully. His sternum really hurt but he would check it and his back later.

The girl was having trouble getting her shirt on so Chuck reached over and helped get her arm in the sleeve.

"What's your name?" he asked, gently, trying to gauge how bad she was hurt.

"Elizabeth Benton," she answered. "Are they all…dead?"

"Good question. Let me check." A moment later, he said, "Yep, they're all dead. Now, let's get out of here."

He reloaded his rifle and searched the four bodies. Mustache Man had been a cop. I never would've expected that, Chuck thought. Mike Carter had worked for the Franklin County Sheriff's Department according to the badge and ID he was carrying. Not much protecting and serving out of him, McCain thought, shaking his head and slipping Carter's ID card into his pocket. Chuck stood and started to gather their weapons into a pile.

The AK-47 that Carter had used was damaged by Chuck's round but he found an AR-15, a Mossberg .12 gauge shotgun, a .40 caliber Glock Model 22 pistol, and a Taurus 9mm pistol, stacking them next to the front door. Another AK, two more ARs, three scoped hunting rifles, and six other handguns were in one of the bedrooms. McCain also located extra magazines and a few boxes of ammunition to go along with the firearms. In another bedroom was the real jackpot: ten boxes of canned food, freeze dried meals, bottled water, several cases of beer, a few bottles of wine and two unopened bottles of whiskey. These guys had quite the stash here, McCain thought.

"Where are you taking me?" Elizabeth asked, as he came back into the living room carrying some of the supplies.

"Like I said, I found a house where I was going to wait this storm out. You'll be safe with me. I think that punch to the head gave you a concussion."

Chuck looked out the front windows but didn't see any movement. Maybe there are no Zs in the area, he hoped. He still needed to check his chest. It was really starting to throb with pain, but he was breathing OK and didn't think the round had penetrated his body armor. He'd get to it later.

The car keys were in Stringy Hair's pocket on a heart key chain with the name "Elizabeth" printed across it.

"Is that your car they were driving, Elizabeth?"

She nodded and looked at him, her eyes still not focusing. "Yeah, they killed my friends, grabbed me, and took my car."

The reality of what she had just said brought the emotion to the surface and she started crying. Elizabeth Benton has had quite a day, McCain thought.

Chuck made nine trips to the Jeep Cherokee carrying the weapons and supplies that he had discovered inside the house. There was even a large black hoodie and another t-shirt that would fit him. McCain saw that there were already several guns and more cardboard boxes of canned goods in the back of the Cherokee. Score, he thought. He would do a more thorough inventory later.

After a last look through the kidnappers' house, it was time to go. Elizabeth's shirt had been ripped open and the buttons torn off of it, so she held it closed against her body. McCain found a gray down jacket in one of the bedrooms that was too big for her but would do for now. Her fingers fumbled with the zipper and Chuck knelt in front of her zipping the jacket up to her chin.

As he helped her up off of the couch, she swayed as a wave of dizziness and nausea swept over her. Elizabeth turned to the side and vomited. Thankfully, it missed Chuck but coated Larry and Bobby's bodies.

"I'm sorry," she apologized.

"No problem. Come on, I'll help you out to the car."

Elizabeth was unsteady on her feet as Chuck helped her to the front door. He supported her with his right arm, holding his rifle in his left hand. The area still looked clear as they stepped outside. Just as they got to the Cherokee, however, the sound of growling came from nearby.

It was almost completely dark and Chuck activated the rifle's mounted flashlight to illuminate up the scene. As the group of ten infected shuffled towards them, McCain felt fear but his training kicked in, calming him. They were still at least twenty-five yards away, moving across the front yard, all of them growling and snarling in unison. He hurried around to the passenger side, helping Elizabeth into the vehicle.

"Stay in the car," he told her, closing the door.

The zombies were inside fifteen yards now, all of them appearing to have been infected for a while. The decomposition of their bodies gave them a ghastly appearance while the stench was almost overpowering. There were five men, three women, and two children in the group.

He raised his rifle and started shooting, exploding a head with each shot. The last one, a young girl, dropped right at his feet on the driveway. Thankfully, these Zs didn't move very fast, he thought. After scanning the area to make sure it was clear to move out, he reloaded, stepped around the bodies, got into the SUV, and drove up to the house that he had commandeered.

In a perfect world, he would get out, go into the house, open the garage, and drive the Cherokee inside. With Zs in the area, however, he wasn't going to attempt that. He activated four-wheel drive, turned up the driveway, and maneuvered around the house through the snow and ice-covered yard, until he came to a stop on the patio next to the back door.

At least here, the car was hidden from the street. As he got out of the Cherokee, McCain felt the snow coming down again, the large flakes falling heavily. Hopefully, the snow would cover their tire tracks, he thought, as he assisted Elizabeth Benton into the house.

Abandoned house, South of Carnesville, Northeast of Atlanta, Tuesday, 1810 hours

Chuck had to let go of Elizabeth so he could close the door once they were inside. She immediately felt the room spinning but the big man caught her, wrapping his strong arm around her, before she could fall.

"What's wrong with me?" Elizabeth gasped.

"Your brain got rattled when that scumbag punched you and now you've got a concussion," he said, helping her upstairs and into the master bedroom. "The vomiting, dizziness, the slurred speech, those are all symptoms. I'm going to give you some Tylenol and some ice to put on your face. The main thing you need to do now is get some rest."

"Are you a doctor?" she asked, slurring her words but trying to smile.

"No, but I used to be a fighter and I saw a lot of guys and girls get their brains rattled. You'll be fine in a couple of days."

Elizabeth sat down on the bed and Chuck could see that she was shivering. She suddenly remembered something, putting her hand on

McCain's arm.

"A couple of days? No, I need to get back to the school now and tell them what happened."

Chuck handed her the Alabama sweatshirt that hadn't fit him. "Why don't you put this on? It's gonna be a cold night. I'll be back in a couple of minutes with some ice."

Using his flashlight, he found a plastic ziplock bag in a kitchen cabinet and then walked over to the back window, peering out into the dark night. He didn't see or hear anything as he quietly eased the rear door open, suppressed pistol in hand. Snow continued to fall, leaving a thick white blanket over everything that he could see.

Satisfied that it was safe, McCain knelt, scraping some snow and ice into the plastic bag, then withdrew back into the house. He locked the door and pushed the dining room table up against it. A leather couch was shoved long ways against the front door. McCain opened his backpack, digging around until he found the container of pills and a bottle of water that he took upstairs with the ice pack.

Chuck stopped outside the bedroom door. "Hey, it's me," he called, softly. "I've got some ice for your face and some Tylenol."

Elizabeth was a small shape in the king size bed. Chuck turned his flashlight on and saw that she had gotten the sweatshirt on over the top of her flannel shirt. She was still shivering, though, the temperatures inside the house being only slightly warmer than outside.

McCain had no idea what the girl had been through and tried to speak calmly and quietly to her. "I'm going to shine my light on your face. I want to see how bad the swelling is."

His light illuminated a very pretty, young woman. Maybe late twenties, he thought. Her eyes were green and her light brown hair was a tangled mess from her ordeal. The left side of her face was already bruising. Her left eye was partially closed from the swelling and her bottom lip was busted and bloody. She reached up and felt of her injuries.

"It really hurts. How bad is it?"

"There's a lot of swelling around your eye. That's why we need the ice. You're gonna have a nice black eye but it doesn't look like any permanent damage. And I don't think that cut on your lip needs any stitches."

"What was your name again?" she asked him, taking the four tablets and swallowing them with water from the bottle he handed her.

"Chuck. Chuck McCain. Now, I'm going to put this icepack on your face. Can you hold this on your eye? We need to get that swelling down. Tell me again what your name is."

He remembered but wanted to see if she did.

"Elizabeth Benton. Are you OK?" she asked, concern in her voice, and pointing to his throat. "You've got blood on your neck."

McCain took off his glove and felt the area she had pointed out. The right side was sticky from where Mustache Man had attempted grab him with the remains of his left hand.

"Yeah, I'm good. It's the other guy's blood. I'll go clean it off in a minute."

Benton nodded. "I really need to get back to the school, Mr. McCain. They don't know what happened."

She started to sit up but gasped from the pain in her head. Another wave of dizziness hit her and the young woman fell back onto her pillow, crying.

"I'm sorry, Elizabeth," Chuck said, sitting down next to her. "We aren't going anywhere tonight. It's too dangerous to travel when it's dark. Plus, it's snowing again and the roads are going to be impassable for a couple of days. I don't want to take a chance on getting stranded out in the middle of nowhere. And, you're hurt.

"Sleep tonight and we'll talk about it tomorrow and figure out what we need to do. You're safe with me. I promise. I'll let you have this room and I'll keep watch downstairs in the living room. If you need anything, just call me. I'm a light sleeper."

The girl nodded at the big man as tears seeped out of her eyes, her small frame shivering in the cold house, her breath visible with each exhale.

"Okay, but it's so cold. Can you help me get under the blanket?"

Chuck tucked her under the covers and went looking for more bed linens. He was also going to need to wrap up himself. McCain found additional blankets in the hall closest and a pillow on one of the other beds. He removed the last dry shirt from his pack and brought it and another blanket to Elizabeth.

"Here's another blanket and one of my t-shirts. It hasn't been washed in few weeks, but it's dry and the more layers you have on the better."

"Thank you for what you did, Mr. McCain. Thanks for everything," she said, quietly.

The room was still spinning, but she could feel the Tylenol starting to kick in. When he left she managed to get the black shirt on and wrapped the extra blanket around her small frame. The shivering finally stopped as her body started to warm up.

Even in her dazed and confused state, Elizabeth understood the stranger's words and knew he was right. For some reason, she trusted this man and knew she was going to be OK. Yes, he'd rescued her from those animals who had killed her friends, but it was more than that. She sensed that this was someone who would do what he said and he had promised to protect her.

What had he gotten himself into now? Chuck wondered, as he walked down the stairs. He watched and listened at the front window for several minutes and then repeated the process at the rear of the house. Satisfied that they were safe for the moment, McCain stripped off his body armor and shirts.

He shivered, standing half-naked in the cold house, stepping into the half-bathroom connected to the living room. Chuck needed a mirror so he shut the door and shone the small flashlight onto his chest. There was a two-inch red circle just to the right of his left nipple from the 7.62x39 AK-47 bullet. It was already starting to turn purple. Chuck moved his fingers around the area. It hurt to touch but nothing felt broken.

"Thank God for that armor," he mumbled.

He shone the light so he could see his face and neck in the mirror. His left eye would be black by tomorrow but the swelling was minimal from where he had been punched. McCain used his fingers to feel around on his face and the side of his head. The area around his eye was tender, just like the old days after a fight.

Wearing four ounce mixed martial arts gloves, it was almost impossible to compete and not get marked up. His police co-workers got used to seeing him report for duty with black eyes, stitched up facial cuts, and other assorted injuries. This one was nothing.

There was a large amount of dried blood on his neck and he used some water from a plastic bottle to wash it off. The cold was bad enough but now being cold and wet was just miserable. He walked into the kitchen and found a hand towel with which to dry himself off.

McCain quickly put his clothes back on, including the extra t-shirt that he'd found in the kidnapper's house. He picked up the black hoodie, noticing the NASCAR logo on the back. It didn't smell very good but it would keep him warm until his own garments were dry.

His black, kevlar-lined cargo pants were still damp but he didn't have any others to put on. He should've taken a pair of jeans off of one of the dead guys but he hadn't thought about it and sure wasn't going back to that house tonight. McCain still had not changed out of his wet socks. He found the dry pair still laying on the coffee table, took his combat boots off, and soon had warm, dry feet again.

After getting as comfortable as he could, the federal police officer shone the light on his black plate-carrier. He touched the hole where the rifle round had hit him, inserting his finger and feeling the indention in the metal plate, thanking God his attacker had been a good shot and hit him center-mass. When he flipped the carrier around, he found where the mystery liquid had come from. The combined four hundred and fifty pounds, he estimated, of himself and the dirty cop he'd been fighting had crushed that wooden table, sending several pieces into his CamelBak, puncturing it.

McCain unsnapped the hydration device and removed it, tossing it to the side. Well, that's a few less pounds I'll be carrying, he thought. He still had two liters of water in his pack and plenty of water treatment tablets. He had also taken two twenty-four packs of bottled water from the kidnapper's house.

With the end of the couch pressed against the front door, Chuck stretched out with his feet facing the exit. He wrapped up in the hoodie and a thick blanket, and laid his rifle beside him on the floor, holding his suppressed Glock across his chest.

Back to my original question, he thought, as he lay there shivering. What have I gotten myself into with this girl? He had to get to Melanie. That was his only mission at the moment. He didn't mind helping other people when he could, but his primary responsibility was to get to his daughter.

A conversation from months earlier popped into his mind. He and Rebecca Johnson were driving back to the Centers for Disease Control Headquarters in Atlanta. Chuck and his team had just been involved in encountering and shooting the first people on American soil to be infected with the zombie virus. Rebecca was in charge of the Atlanta CDC enforcement office, but McCain had fallen in love with her the first time they had met, when she came to his house to recruit him. Always the professional, however, Chuck had managed to keep his feelings concealed.

As they drove she had asked him, “Do you know what your calling is, Chuck?”

Something about Rebecca had made Chuck answer honestly, even though he thought it sounded a bit cheesy.

“I don’t know that I've ever really thought of it as a calling,” he had said, “but I suppose that's what it is. A cop, a soldier, a Marine, a fireman. Those jobs really are all callings. No one gets into this line of work for the money or for the perks. So, yeah, I guess I do know what my calling is. It sounds corny, but 'To Protect and Serve' is what I'm called to do.”

McCain had tried to help Greg and Tonya, only to have them turn on him. Now, he was caring for a girl he didn’t know after risking his life to save her from a certain death. He hadn’t been able to save Rebecca, though. The familiar stab of pain dug deeply into his heart.

He sat up on the couch and reached over into his backpack, removing a bottle and a black stocking hat. Who would leave behind an unopened bottle of Evan Williams? he wondered, pulling the hat over his head. Maybe someone who had gotten infected with the zombie virus and only had a taste for flesh now?

Would he ever get over Rebecca’s death and his feelings of guilt for not protecting her? He sipped the bourbon, enjoying the burn as it went down his throat. That fateful day, he and Rebecca had been having such a nice time with Melanie and her boyfriend, Brian, on the University of Georgia campus, where the young couple were both studying to become teachers.

Just a few weeks before that, Chuck had finally gotten the courage to ask Rebecca out for dinner, fully expecting her to turn him down. Instead, she had said, “Yes,” and they had begun dating. Eventually, Chuck had invited her to accompany him to Athens to meet Melanie and Brian on the UGA campus.

After a nice lunch, Mel had surprised him with tickets to the Bulldogs' home opener football game. The four of them were just about to enter Sanford Stadium when gunshots erupted and Amir al-Razi burst out of the Tate Student Center across the street. Al-Razi was an Iranian intelligence agent who had launched several terrorist attacks around Atlanta using the bio-terror virus.

In the ensuing gunfight, Chuck had killed al-Razi, but not before the Iranian had managed to fire two shots, one of which struck and killed Rebecca Johnson. McCain had played it over and over in his head. If he hadn't tried to get the terrorist to surrender, if he'd just shot the armed man in the back, Rebecca would still be alive.

Chuck knew that in reality, it wasn't that simple, nor could he change the past. He took another couple of sips of the whiskey, closed the bottle, and then lay back down. He had been planning to tell Rebecca that he loved her on the ride home after the game.

Instead, being pursued by Zs, he had carried her dead body in his arms away from the scene and watched it get zipped up inside a black body bag. Chuck and his team had managed to rescue around sixty people from the UGA campus and had killed hundreds of zombies. Thousands of other people were killed and infected with the virus, in and around the stadium and the student center. McCain wondered if the university would ever reopen.

In their last conversation, Brian's dad, Tommy, told Chuck that they would take care of his daughter. Melanie had assured her dad that Brian and his family were really looking after her. Since that phone call, however, he hadn't talked to Mel in three months. After the power and communication grids stopped working, he'd been unable to get in touch with her.

Brian's mom and dad were lay pastors in their local church and Brian seemed like an honorable young man. So, at least Melanie was with good people in a safe place. The problem now was that Chuck wasn't even sure where she was. Brian's family, the Mitchells, lived in Hartwell, near the South Carolina border with Georgia.

That last time Chuck had spoken with them, Tommy had informed him that his parents had a small farm in the mountains near Hendersonville, North Carolina. He told Chuck they were leaving immediately since thousands of zombies had surged out of Atlanta and were moving up the interstate. Melanie was going to send her dad the address for the Mitchells farm but then everything had stopped working. Power, internet, and all other communications had just shut down.

McCain did have the address for their home in Hartwell and that was where he was heading. He was hoping and praying that Melanie or Tommy had left him their new whereabouts or some clue as to where they might be. But, before he could do that, he had to figure out what to do with Elizabeth Benton. She had said something about a school. Maybe tomorrow she would be feeling better and could tell him her story.

Abandoned house, South of Carnesville, Northeast of Atlanta, Wednesday, 0730 hours

They sat in Elizabeth's room sharing a packet of beef jerky and some trail mix that Chuck had taken from Greg and Tonya, sharing a mug of hot coffee. Benton's back was against the wooden headboard in the bed. McCain had pulled a rolling chair over from a small desk and sat next to the bed.

Daylight illuminated the room and Elizabeth could see that while it had finally stopped snowing, the sky was gray and threatening. Other than a lingering headache and the pain from her badly bruised face, Benton was feeling much better this morning and was now able to get her first clear-headed view of the man who had saved her life.

She had awakened with the stranger's scent in her nostrils. At first, she was disoriented and couldn't remember where she was and why she was alone. Then, the events of the previous day came rushing into her mind, as well as a blurred image of the stranger who had brought her here. The shirt that he had loaned her was warm but it was saturated with his scent. It was a nice smell, she thought. Musky and masculine.

The next aroma that her nose had picked up was of coffee. My brain really must have gotten rattled, she thought. I know there's no Starbucks around here. The sound of footsteps coming up the stairs startled her and McCain had come in carrying the food and a steaming cup.

"How about breakfast in bed?" Chuck said, smiling and holding up the beef jerky and trail mix bags. "I'd planned on whipping us up some pancakes, eggs, bacon, and grits but, you know, the zombie apocalypse and all."

In spite of everything, she laughed, the pain shooting through her head causing her to immediately regret it. How long has it been since I've laughed out loud? she wondered, putting her hand to her forehead.

"Oh, don't make me laugh," she said, smiling back at him. "My head's still pounding. Is that coffee?"

"It sure is. I hope you don't mind sharing," he replied, handing her the warm mug. "That was the only coffee cup that I could find downstairs."

Elizabeth held it in both hands and let the hot steam rise onto her face. She closed her eyes and sipped the liquid. Another sip and she handed the cup back to Chuck.

"That's the best coffee I've ever tasted. How did you do that? I mean that's hot," she said, surprised.

McCain chuckled. "I don't think I've ever seen that reaction to MRE instant coffee before but I'm glad you like it. The MREs, that's Meal Ready to Eat, comes with a chemical pouch to heat the food. They call it a flameless ration heater and it works great without giving your position away."

Benton examined the man in front of her and couldn't help but notice his size. Chuck McCain was a big man. His shoulders were broad and his arms bulged underneath the black hoodie. His dark brown hair was hidden under the black stocking cap and his face was covered with the beginnings of a beard. His blue eyes were clear and she could see in them sadness, intelligence, compassion, and danger.

She wasn't good with ages but she guessed Chuck was around forty years old. He was a nice looking man, she thought, for a guy that old.

There were old scars around both of his eyes but the area around the left one was bruised with some redness and swelling.

"What happened to your face?" she asked, pointing to the damage. "How'd you get hurt?"

Chuck touched his left eye and shook his head. "I must be losing my touch. That last guy managed to shoot me, punch me, and tackle me."

"He shot you?" she asked, surprised at this revelation.

"Oh, yeah, and it hurt really bad," he admitted, handing her the coffee mug and pulling up his shirts to show the now dark purple mark that the AK round had left behind on his chest. "Thankfully, he hit me in the body armor."

"But you killed all four of them. I don't think you're losing anything," Elizabeth commented. "What are you? Some kind of special forces solider?"

McCain smiled. "No, I was just a police officer near Atlanta for twenty years. Later, I went to work for the CDC Enforcement Unit, trying to control the outbreak of the zombie virus. Obviously, we didn't do a very good job."

He left out the part of his career where he took two one-year contracts with the United States Military. After his early retirement from the police department, Chuck had been hired as a police liaison officer with an army Special Forces A team. Working with the SF soldiers had sharpened and developed the skills he had gained as a SWAT officer. It was after these two contracts in Afghanistan that he came back to the US and was recruited by Rebecca Johnson to come work for the CDC.

Chuck and Elizabeth sat in silence for a couple of minutes lost in their own thoughts, sharing the last of the coffee.

"How'd you find me yesterday?" the young woman asked, quietly.

He shrugged. "There's not much to it. I'd been walking all day, heading north. I got off at that exit, the one with the truck stops and convenience stores, but I didn't want to take a chance on camping out there."

McCain saw recognition and pain cross Elizabeth's face when he mentioned the truck stops.

"I saw the sign advertising this neighborhood," he continued, "and hurried over here. I was wet and freezing by the time I found this house. My clothes were soaked and I was shivering. I'd just gotten a couple of dry shirts on when I heard a vehicle on the street.

"Those guys weren't even trying to be quiet. I was just gonna watch them through the window and hope they didn't attract any zombies. I wasn't looking for any trouble and just wanted them to stay down there and quit making so much noise.

"But then I heard you scream and saw you kick that one prick in the nose. You were fighting and screaming and I saw the bald guy punch you. You looked like you needed a little help."

Benton reached up and touched her swollen face again and fingered the cut on her lip. Chuck could see that she was processing all that he said. He needed to know more about her, though, to decide what kind of help that he would give her.

"I'd love to hear what happened and how you ended up with those losers?" he asked. "You said something last night about your friends and a school."

After several more moments of silence, McCain said, "If you don't want to get into it now, I understand." He started to stand.

"No, wait," she told him. "I need to talk about it. Just give me a minute."

"Take your time," he answered, settling back down and looking out the window at the snowy landscape. "We're going to be here a while."

The Northeast Georgia Technical College was fifteen miles up the road, near the small town of Lavonia. Elizabeth was on staff there as a Career Counselor, and also worked closely with the president of the school on special projects. It was a small college and she filled several roles, but guiding students down their best career path was her main passion.

After hundreds of zombies were spotted heading their way up I-85 a couple of months earlier, most of the students had fled for their homes or any other safe location. However, some faculty and students had decided to stay on campus, thinking they'd be safer together. The school was several miles off the interstate and located outside of the city limits, surrounded by trees in a secluded area.

Elizabeth had also chosen to stay because she, too, felt a sense of responsibility to look after the students who had remained. And, the campus had become her home. She lived in one of the dorm rooms, serving as a Resident Assistant. The rest of the faculty knew her background and went along with allowing her to live at the school.

Seventy-five students, faculty, and family members were hunkered down on the small vocational college campus. The college police department had been composed of seven officers. Five of them had fled the approaching zombie horde to get their own families to safety. The other two, Officers Tina Miles and Jason Storey, stayed to protect those who remained behind.

As the zombies swept up the interstate, the estimated numbers grew to over a thousand. These had been infected when a suicide bomber abandoned his car bomb just off of I-85 in downtown Atlanta. The bomb in the car and the suicide vest both contained high explosives, shrapnel, the zombie virus, and radioactive materials.

This was the dirtiest of dirty bombs and the same scenario had been repeated in Washington, D.C., and New York City. Those who were infected when the bombs detonated created a domino effect, passing the virus to thousands in their zest for flesh. These, in turn, migrated through Atlanta, using the interstate system to go in every direction.

It took the infected a few days to reach the Lavonia area and by that time the number of Zs had continued to swell. Most of the residents had fled, heeding the Governor's order to evacuate, but others tried to stand and fight. Local police, aided by a number of well-armed civilians, shot and killed over three hundred of the zombies, but vastly outnumbered, all of those police officers and civilians were overrun. They were all either killed and devoured, or returned as zombies in a bizarre twist of fate. There were just too many infected and too few defenders.

The Zs swept through the small town, forcing their way into homes containing survivors, which spread the virus even further. After they ran out of victims, most of the zombies continued up the interstate towards South Carolina, while hundreds wandered around the countryside. Thankfully, the technical college was in a rural area, nestled behind several hills, and only accessible by a long driveway.

Mr. Nicholson, a member of the faculty and a military veteran, had taken charge of the group's security. He and Officers Storey and Miles organized the defense of the campus and created a schedule so that several sentries were always on duty, keeping watch. Nicholson taught a commercial vehicle driver's course and automotive repair.

He used one of the long, fifty-three foot semi-trailers, which he trained his tractor-trailer students on, to set up a barricade, blocking the entrance leading into the school. Wrecked vehicles from the collision repair course shop were added to the barricade, creating a formidable roadblock that was manned around the clock by armed student sentries.

This barrier was designed mainly to keep human invaders out but would slow down zombies, as well. The roadblock was set up so that two vehicles could be quickly moved to let cars in or out if the need arose. The trailer was an excellent position to keep watch from, and its height would keep the sentries safe from the ever-reaching hands of attacking Zs.

Mr. Nicholson also set up roving patrols around the campus. There was no fence around the college and infected or human invaders could gain access to the school if they were willing to fight their way through a dense forest. Because she was on staff of the college, Elizabeth had sat in on the security planning meetings. She had heard Nicholson say more than once that their biggest challenge was a lack of firearms.

The first Zs showed up at the school, walking down the main driveway, a week after their attack on Lavonia. Everyone not on defense hid in the dorm or other reinforced buildings. The sentries lay quietly on the ground or on top of the barricade hoping the infected would not see them and move on.

The zombies' sense of smell, however, alerted them that fresh flesh was nearby. The twenty-five infected began growling, rushing the roadblock, and shoving up against the vehicles. Mr. Nicholson had two of the students boost him up onto the roof of a wrecked van, wedged in next to the big trailer.

Armed with a small rifle, the faculty member climbed from the van onto the top of the eighteen-wheeler and began shooting the Zs in the head as fast as he could pull the trigger. Officer Storey clambered up with Nicholson, using a pistol to help eliminate the Zs.

Elizabeth had sat in her Jeep Cherokee as the middle-aged man and the campus police officer had killed every single zombie. She and one of the campus maintenance trucks were parked nearby, engines running, facing back towards the campus as escape vehicles in case the zombies broke through or somehow got around the barricade.

After waiting for an hour to see if any more infected would show up, Nicholson directed some of the male students to load the bodies into the back of the maintenance pickup and haul them to the backside of the college grounds. They were dumped out of sight of the campus, in a thick wooded area.

The group at the college had had little contact with the outside world after communications broke down. Two weeks after they had killed the group of Zs, Mr. Nicholson called a meeting with everyone and said that the food supply was dwindling and they were going to need to send out foraging teams to find supplies. They began sending out four-person teams once every week or two.

The teams were usually composed of one of the campus police officers and three of the other campus residents. Everyone was supposed to take a turn going out but priority was given to those with prior military service or those who were comfortable handling firearms. Their goal was to not use their weapons, but unfortunately they'd had to shoot infected people almost every time they left the safety of the college grounds.

So far, they had been able to gather supplies from businesses in and around Lavonia. They had even picked up a few more survivors and brought them back to the campus. The forage teams usually drove one of the campus pickups or a student's or faculty member's SUV. On each trip, they loaded up as many supplies as their vehicle could carry from the local supermarket, convenience stores, and even some homes that had been abandoned.

The need for a constant supply of food forced the looting teams to travel farther and farther from their sanctuary. The previous day, Elizabeth had volunteered to take the foragers in her Jeep Cherokee. As one of the key faculty members she didn't have to go, but felt that she needed to carry her weight. The team was composed of her, Officer Storey, Margo and Lamar. Margo was in the Air Force National Guard as a military police officer and Lamar was in the Criminal Justice Program at the college.

Mr. Nicholson had recommended that they go further south to see if there was anything left at the truck stops and stores at the Old Federal Road exit. It was the furthest away from the campus that any of the teams had ventured out but they were starting to have trouble finding food around Lavonia. Elizabeth drove, Jason the police officer rode shotgun, with Lamar and Margo seated in the back.

Elizabeth had a 9mm pistol that Mr. Nicholson had handed her. She had never shot a handgun but he had patiently walked her through how to use it, giving her an hour of familiarization. Jason Storey had strapped his police-issue gun belt over his blue jeans and was also carrying a shotgun. Margo cradled a military-style rifle across her lap and Lamar had both a black assault rifle and a pistol.

Up to this point, all of the people that the foraging teams had encountered had been friendly. Fifteen additional people had accepted the invitation to join the group at the technical school campus. Looking back, Benton knew that they had grown complacent.

There were two truck stops at the exit on opposite sides of the street. On the other side of the interstate was a convenience store. Their plan was to search all three businesses, taking as much as they could pack into the Cherokee, and then get back to the campus before dark. Driving on the interstate was possible but dangerous. Zombies still lingered on both the north and southbound sides so the mission to the truck stop had consisted of a roundabout route using back roads.

The trip had been uneventful until sleet and snow had begun raining down on them just as they had approached the first truck stop. There were a couple of cars and a few tractor-trailers scattered around the parking lot but they didn't see any people, living or dead. Elizabeth backed her SUV up to the front of the business, a high overhang protecting them from the worst of the freezing rain.

Officer Storey cautiously pulled the door of the store open and listened for movement. The flashlight mounted on his shotgun swept the interior. Satisfied, he turned and motioned for Margo to join him. The civilian police officer and the military police officer disappeared inside the truck stop.

Their standard operating procedure was to always try and make contact with whoever might be hiding inside. If the business owner was present, they would pay for their supplies. If no one was there, they would take as much as they could and inventory it when they got back to the campus. After things got back to normal, Mr. Nicholson would make sure that every business owner was repaid in full.

Elizabeth and Lamar stood on the sidewalk next to the rear of the Cherokee keeping watch, shivering as a cutting wind whipped across the large parking lot. Lamar held his rifle loosely while Elizabeth's pistol was still tucked into her waistband. She turned the collar of her black leather jacket up as the large snowflakes and freezing rain continued to fall.

Without warning, gunfire erupted from multiple weapons inside the store, followed immediately by a woman screaming out in pain. Elizabeth and Lamar both jumped but the young criminal justice major recovered quickly, running and jerking the door open, and raising his rifle to point inside.

A man's voice cried out, "Stop the bleeding! Help me, 5-0, you've got to stop the bleeding!"

The darkness inside the store combined with Lamar's eyes not having adjusted to it blinded him and he couldn't see anything.

"Officer Storey? Margo?" he called, tentatively.

Suddenly, more gunshots came from inside the business and Lamar collapsed in the doorway, blocking it open. The young man groaned loudly, gasping for air, struggling to breathe. And then there was silence again.

Elizabeth's feet were frozen in place. She reached for her pistol but it got tangled up in her shirt and jacket, clattering to the pavement. She knelt, grabbing for the gun.

"Don't move," a menacing voice said.

Benton looked up at a balding man who was pointing a black rifle at her. She froze, her eyes locked on his. The man's gaze took all of her in as he nodded slightly, a wicked grin on his ruddy face. He turned his head slightly to speak to someone behind him.

"Look what we have here, Larry. Cover me while I go grab her and check their car."

An older man with oily hair and a scraggly beard stepped over Lamar's body as the bald man walked towards her. Everything inside of Elizabeth screamed at her to run away but she couldn't get her feet to move. Larry was holding a pistol and kept it pointed at her. He reached down and picked up Lamar's rifle.

"Did you see this, Bobby? This is a nice AR. I think I'm gonna keep this one for myself."

Bobby lowered his gun and stopped in front of the terrified girl. Without hesitation, he slapped Elizabeth in the face, snapping her head back. He grabbed her and spun her around, shoving her against the side of the Jeep. He searched her for additional weapons, his hands lingering over her breasts. He pulled her leather jacket off and threw it to the pavement.

"You're not gonna need that in a little while," he whispered in her ear while pressing his body against hers. "I think you and me are gonna be real good friends."

"Please don't hurt me," she whimpered. "Just let me go and you can have my car."

She felt blood dripping down her chin from a busted lip. The man's hands were still on her and she began to shake, causing him to laugh.

"I think we will. And I think you're gonna come with us," he laughed.

Bobby reached down and picked up Benton's pistol, tucking it into his waistband. He did a cursory check of the Cherokee making sure that it was empty.

"Come on," he ordered the girl. "Let's go back inside and see what 5-0 wants to do with you."

"I know what I want to do with her," Larry said, licking his lips.

The bald man grabbed her arm and pulled her roughly through the open door. Blood had pooled around Lamar and she stepped in it as Bobby forced her inside. Her friend's lifeless eyes looked up at her, emphasizing her own weakness, as she stepped over him, a numbness settling over her.

Twenty feet inside the store, three additional bodies were sprawled on the floor, illuminated by flashlight beams. A skinny man with stringy hair and a pasty face was holding a pistol and kneeling beside a short, fat man lying in a puddle of blood that encircled him. A large, gaping wound on his right leg appeared to be where the blood had come from.

"He's dead, 5-0. I think he bled out," Stringy Hair said, his voice trembling as he looked up at the large man standing next to him.

5-0 was tall and muscular with a thick mustache. He looked down on their dead companion without emotion, but shook his head.

"I never liked Jerry much anyway," he grunted. "He was always complaining about something and was always hungry. It does piss me off that these guys shot him, though."

As Elizabeth's eyes adjusted, she realized that Officer Storey was lying on his back, just to her right, not moving. She had seen that he was a wearing a bulletproof vest but it clearly hadn't worked. There were several bleeding wounds on his chest, arms, and one through his throat. Margo was on her side a few feet to Benton's left, groaning softly, clutching her stomach.

The one they called 5-0 had a rifle on a sling but he drew his pistol, walking over to Storey and shooting him in the head, the loud shot causing Benton to scream. He repeated the process with Margo and Lamar and then walked over to Elizabeth, pointing his pistol at her forehead. She saw his finger on the trigger, starting to tighten.

"No, please," she pleaded. "We were just looking for some food."

Bobby cleared his throat. "5-0, she's got a car outside. I was thinking maybe we could take her with us and have a little fun, if that was OK with you."

Benton's eyes were glued to 5-0's trigger finger. He finally let the pressure off but kept staring at her. His eyes burned with hatred, but he nodded and lowered the gun, putting it back into his holster.

"Grab their guns and load up with some supplies and let's get back to the house," 5-0 ordered. The other three men jumped into action, leaving Elizabeth standing next to 5-0.

"You are a pretty little thing," he whispered, as he ran his hands over Elizabeth's body, causing her to cringe. "I bet a little slut like you really knows how to make a man happy."

She knew that if she tried to run, this man would shoot her in the back. Maybe that would be better, she thought. She knew that what they had planned for her was going to be worse than death. And how bad could it hurt to get shot and die? She couldn't bring herself to do it, though, hating how weak and helpless she felt.

The skinny guy drove and 5-0 sat in the front with him. Bobby and Larry sat in the back with Elizabeth between them, reaching under her shirt and groping her all the way back to the house. From their conversation, she gathered that they had been at this house for a few days and were using it as their base. She heard them say something about their truck having run out of gas and were thrilled to be able to ride instead of walking through the snowstorm.

The four men talked in graphic detail about what they were going to do to Elizabeth. She kept her eyes closed as they touched her and she began to pray for the first time in a long while. She hadn't been to church in several years and, if she was honest, would say that she had walked away from her faith. However, during that miserable car ride back to the kidnappers' house, Elizabeth Benton made peace with God because she knew that she was about to be raped and murdered.

"And then you showed up," she finished, smiling at Chuck, tears glistening in her eyes. "God answered my prayer. I don't know how to say 'thank you.' There's no way I could ever repay you, but thank you. You didn't have to get involved. You risked your life for me and…" She started crying.

McCain didn't know what to say but got up from the chair and sat next to her on the bed, putting his hand on her shoulder. She fell into his arms and buried her face in his chest, her loud sobs continuing for several minutes. Chuck let her cry herself out, just holding her. She had been through so much and he had no idea how to comfort her other than just giving her a shoulder to cry on.

When Elizabeth recovered her voice, she said, hanging her head, "I feel so guilty. Officer Storey, Margo, Lamar, they're all dead but I'm still alive. It doesn't seem right. It doesn't seem fair."

"I understand," Chuck nodded. "They call it survivor's guilt. I have my fair share, too."

The girl looked up at him, surprise in her eyes, still wet with tears. "You do?"

"Oh yeah. Let's take a break. I need to take a look outside and make sure everything is still quiet and then I'll tell you a little of my background."

Abandoned house, South of Carnesville, Northeast of Atlanta, Wednesday, 1000 hours

The neighborhood was quiet and Chuck didn't see any signs of life as he peered outside. Looking down the street, he saw snow covered mounds indicating the final resting places of all the Zs he'd shot the night before, strewn around the yard and driveway of the kidnappers' house. The low, gray clouds hinted at the possibility of more snow. There was no way he would take a chance driving on these icy streets. The thermometer in the kitchen window showed twenty-seven freezing degrees outside and it wasn't much warmer inside.

With the government shut down, no one was clearing the roads and the thought of getting stranded somewhere, miles from any kind of safe shelter, was not an option. Plus, there were roving packs of zombies, not to mention gangs of robbers and murderers lying in wait for unsuspecting victims.

When McCain went back upstairs to check on Elizabeth, he found her lying on the bed with her back to him. Thinking that she was resting, he turned to leave. Her voice stopped him.

"You can come in. I'm not asleep," she said, quietly.

He really wished Elizabeth had been sleeping. Chuck had already decided that there was no way he could tell her everything about his life. He would tell her about some of his battles and about some of the men that he had lost but he couldn't talk about Rebecca. That was too deep, too painful, and too personal. He needed to keep that door shut and locked. That pain was for him and for him alone.

McCain laid his rifle on the foot of the bed and sat back down in the chair next to where Elizabeth was lying. She still had her back to him, curled up in a ball and it was evident that she was still crying.

"I didn't tell you everything," she confessed, sniffing.

Uh-oh, he thought. Where was this leading?

"We all have our secrets," he said.

"You saved my life and I think I owe you the rest of the story. You might not want to help me anymore after you hear this but I need to talk about it before I lose my mind."

"Okay," he told her, "but I'm not a priest or a counselor. I think we're all just trying to do the best we can in this crazy new world."

Benton sat up in the bed and wiped her eyes on her sleeve. She sat with her back against the wall, looking straight ahead, not making eye contact with McCain. She took a deep breath.

"The reason I'm living on campus at the college is, well, it's my parents. I killed them."

As a police officer, Chuck had mastered the art of concealing his emotions. In his mind though, his first thought was, she doesn't look like a psycho-murderer but appearances can be deceiving.

"I was their only child and I still lived at home. They loved me and were fantastic parents. We had a great relationship. I was at work about six months ago when I got a call from my mom. I answered but there was nothing, just the sound of someone breathing and then a crash like she'd dropped the phone.

"She was having problems keeping her blood pressure down and I was taking her to the doctor the next day to get it checked, so my first thought was that she was having a medical emergency. I called 911 and asked for an ambulance. I left work and drove home as fast as I could. I beat the ambulance there and rushed inside. Daddy's car was in the driveway so I figured she must've called him, too.

"When I opened the door, I heard this terrible growling noise. Then I saw Momma on top of Daddy in the living room, eating him. She'd ripped his throat out and there was blood everywhere. I started screaming for her to stop and ran over to pull her off of him, but then Momma came after me, growling and trying to bite me. She got between me and the door and I didn't know what to do.

"Her face was covered with Daddy's blood and she was just about to grab me and I saw this big, heavy glass vase on the table beside me. I'd given it to her as a Christmas present a few years earlier. I'd even given her the flowers that were in it the week before. I didn't even think about it, I just grabbed that vase and smashed it over her head. I killed her," she said, glancing over at Chuck. "I killed my own mother.

"But then Daddy started moving. I thought that he was going to be OK so I rushed over, but he started growling and snapping his teeth together. I yelled at him, trying to let him know that it was me, his daughter, Elizabeth.

"He rolled over and started crawling towards me, trying to grab my leg. I backed up and tripped and landed on my back. Daddy reached for my ankle but I managed to snatch it away before he could bite me. I jumped up and ran out the back door.

"The ambulance and a police car were just pulling up. I told the officer what had happened and I think he was about to throw the handcuffs on me. But then Daddy stumbled out the back door making those terrible noises. He was covered in blood and you could see where Momma had bitten him on his arms, his face, his throat.

"Daddy started running up the driveway towards us and the police officer told him to stop. Daddy just kept coming and the officer started shooting. He must've shot him five or six times in the chest but it didn't even slow him down. But just as Daddy got to him, the officer shot him in the head and that was it."

Elizabeth was breathing hard, her eyes squeezed shut, the memory vivid in her mind. After a few minutes, she continued.

"I killed my mother and I was responsible for Daddy getting shot and I feel guilty every single day. That's why I live on campus. I never went back to my house again. I had some friends go pack up my things and bring them to me. The president of the college told me that I could live in one of the guest rooms in the dormitory if I would serve as a Resident Assistant.

"And now, Jason, Margo, and Lamar, they're dead and I'm alive. I didn't even try to save them. I don't know what I could have done differently, but I should have done something. I failed my parents and I failed my friends."

Elizabeth's voice had gotten stronger as she had talked and it appeared that she'd cried all that she was going to cry. That's a lot for anyone, but especially a young woman, McCain thought. Now, she just looks sad with no light in her eyes.

Chuck nodded. "I'm sorry you've had to go through all this and I'm really sorry about your parents. How do you think your mom got infected?"

Benton looked at McCain and sighed deeply. "I heard on the news that some people got infected through their medicine. Is it possible she could've gotten the virus like that?"

"Very possible," he answered. "Months ago, that was the first part of the bio-terror attack. Some of the Iranian terrorists were able to get jobs at pharmaceutical warehouses and infected hundreds of prescriptions with the virus and then mailed them out all over the country. I'm guessing your mom was on medication for her blood pressure?"

"She was," Elizabeth replied. "And I know she got her prescriptions sent to her through the mail."

"We were able to intercept some of those bad drugs but not all of them," Chuck said, looking into her eyes. "I'm sorry. I know that nothing I say is going to make you feel any better, but you can't keep beating yourself up.

"There was nothing you could've done to help your parents. Nothing. Obviously, your mom was a victim of those tainted drugs, she turned on your dad because he was there, and unfortunately he also became a victim. Ultimately, your folks were killed by the terrorists who used a bio-terror weapon. You were fortunate to escape with your life.

"And as for your friends at the truck stop, they were ambushed. Again, there was nothing that you could've done. These were really evil people that killed them and kidnapped you. But, I know that really doesn't help with the guilt. Why were you spared and why were they killed? I've asked myself that same question for a while now."

Chuck saw Elizabeth give a slight nod as if he had read her mind. The big man sighed, looking straight at this girl not much older than his daughter, and decided to dive in deep. He told Elizabeth about his failed marriage many years before.

Sadness flooded his heart as he talked about Rebecca Johnson. McCain told Benton how much he had loved Johnson, but how he'd been unable to protect her, and how she had died in his arms after being shot by one of the terrorists involved in spreading the zombie virus. McCain talked about the pain and the guilt that he carried with him every day and the nightmares that sometimes still came to him in the night.

He shared about the remorse he felt from not telling Rebecca that he loved her before she had been murdered. Chuck had had the courage to face down criminals, terrorists, and packs of zombies intent on killing and eating him, but hadn't been brave enough to tell the woman he loved his true feelings.

Rebecca's death had been formally reviewed and Chuck had been cleared of any fault in the incident. That didn't take away his self-reproach, though, or make him feel any better. He knew that he had failed her.

Chuck told Elizabeth about the guilt he carried for not being with his daughter, Melanie. Chuck was comforted knowing that she was with good people and was safe, but he could not get past the feeling that he had let her down by delegating her well-being to other people. He also confessed his fear of not being able to locate Mel and Brian's family.

McCain even spoke of Greg, Tonya, and baby Jeremy. He'd had no choice when he shot Tonya, but he felt a tremendous sadness for Jeremy. What kind of world was he growing up in? Would he even get a chance to grow up? Chuck didn't trust Greg to do the right thing but there was no way that McCain was going to bring the child with him. What terrible choices people were having to make in a society where law and order had broken down.

By the time McCain had finished talking, he was emotionally drained. He felt the tears flowing down his face and turned away, embarrassed. Elizabeth climbed off the bed and stood next to Chuck, putting her small arm around his broad shoulders. She pulled him close, holding him as he cried.

"I'm sorry," she whispered.

Chapter Three

Heart Issues

Abandoned house, South of Carnesville, Northeast of Atlanta, Wednesday, 1600 hours

Both Elizabeth and Chuck felt better, somehow lighter. Neither one could explain it but opening their hearts to each other, sharing their similar pain, confessing the guilt they carried, had started the healing process in both of them. Elizabeth could never remember pouring her heart out to anyone like she had just experienced with Chuck. There was a comfort level with this virtual stranger that she had not felt with a man in a long time.

And after hearing how he had lost the woman that he'd loved, Benton now understood the sadness she had seen in his eyes. McCain had been carrying his own load of anguish for a long time. And yet, he had chosen to risk his life to save hers, and was treating her with the utmost courtesy and respect as they huddled in an abandoned home in the Georgia blizzard.

This Chuck McCain was a complex man, Elizabeth pondered. He was a killer; she had seen him in action, but at the same time, he was gentle, letting her cry herself out as he held her and told her it was going to be OK. Elizabeth could feel herself being pulled into this man's orbit and she didn't understand it.

He's so much older than me, she thought. Maybe I just feel this way because he saved my life and I'm so grateful for that gift. Plus, we're stuck together inside this freezing house. Or maybe it's because we're both hurting that I'm feeling drawn to him.

Don't let your emotions get away from you, Elizabeth told herself. You've just seen three of your friends murdered, you were beaten and had your brain scrambled, kidnapped, and then rescued by a stranger in a hail of gunfire. Of course you're emotions are going to be out of whack. And Chuck has bigger things on his mind than me, she reasoned. I'm just a little blip on Mr. McCain's radar.

McCain was embarrassed that he had lost control of his emotions with this young woman whom he didn't even know. At the same time, though, he had to admit that it had felt good to open the door on some of those feelings that he had tried so hard to keep bottled up. It touched him deeply that, even in her own pain, Elizabeth had held him while the tears had rolled down his face. Chuck wasn't a crier and it hadn't lasted long, but the human contact, the physical touch, meant a lot. And coming from a pretty, young woman was a nice added benefit.

The swelling on Benton's face had gone down by the afternoon. McCain was happy that the ice compresses were doing their work, and that her headaches were not as severe. The area around her left eye was purple and would be sore for several days. McCain's face had taken so much punishment in his fighting career that his own black eye wasn't even something that he thought about.

While Elizabeth napped, Chuck worked out on the carpeted floor of the living room. Since the homeowner didn't have any exercise equipment, McCain started with ten sets of twenty-five pushups. Then he elevated his feet onto a chair, performing ten sets of twenty decline pushups, interspersing those with ten sets of fifteen unweighted squats. He finished his training with crunches until he could do no more, finally lying back on the carpet to catch his breath.

"Pretty impressive," Elizabeth commented, watching from where she was perched at the top of the stairs.

"Thanks. The end of the world has made it kind of tough to stay consistent with my workouts." That one is sneaky, Chuck thought. I didn't know she was there until she spoke.

"We've got a nice gym at the college that you can use."

He glanced at her and saw a hopeful expression on her face. He sat up and began his stretching routine.

"Do you use the gym much?" he asked.

"Not really," she admitted. "I like to run. I've done a couple of half marathons but never got into weight training."

Benton walked down the stairs, seating herself on the couch as McCain continued stretching on the floor. She wrapped his blanket around her shoulders, her breath visible with every exhale in the cold house.

"What are we going to do, Chuck? I know we can't leave until the temperature rises and melts the roads, but when that happens, what were you thinking?"

McCain shrugged. "We'll get you back to your friends at the college and I'll keep going. I'll head over to Brian's house in Hartwell and see if Melanie left me an address where I can find her in North Carolina. All I know is that she said it was near Hendersonville."

"Okay," said Elizabeth, "but if you want to stay with us for a few days at the campus, we have a generator that we turn on three days a week to take hot showers and wash our laundry. We also try to have one hot meal a day in the cafeteria. How does that sound? A hot shower, clean clothes, a few hot meals. And, don't forget the gym. Plus, I'm sure we can give you some food to take with you when you leave."

It sounds like she's trying to sell me an apocalyptic time-share, he thought. Chuck quickly did the math in his head. It would be almost a full day's walk from Lavonia to Hartwell, maybe longer depending on his route or if he had to evade Zs and/or living predators.

When he didn't answer right away, Chuck saw disappointment on Elizabeth's face. She really wants me to stay, he realized, surprised at the revelation. To be able to take a hot shower and wash his meager wardrobe did sound amazing. And he couldn't remember the last hot meal that he'd had.

"You sure I wouldn't be a burden? It sounds like you guys have enough mouths to feed as it is."

The young woman's face lit up. "No! You saved my life, Chuck. It's the least that I can do. Plus, I know that you and Mr. Nicholson will enjoy talking. Maybe you could take a look and make sure our defenses are strong enough?"

"Okay, I'll stay for a day or two. That sounds like a good idea. But speaking of defense," McCain said, "tomorrow, I want to work with you on your weapon skills. I'm going to show you how to handle your pistol and then I'm going to teach you how to use a rifle. It's just you and me on the drive back to the school and if we get attacked, two guns are better than one."

Benton nodded slowly, the events of the previous day still fresh in her mind. She had no desire to ever touch a gun again but, in this new world, she knew that knowing how to shoot was a very important skill to master. Elizabeth had seen McCain in action, and even what she had witnessed in her dazed state let her know that she needed to learn everything she could from him.

She swallowed and said, quietly, "Sure. You're right. I don't have much experience with guns but I'm willing to learn."

Chuck nodded. "Good enough. You don't have to become an expert but give me a couple of hours tomorrow and I'll help you develop some skills that might save your life or my life. And it's not like there's whole lot else to do."

After a few more minutes of stretching, McCain got to his feet and said, "I'm going to go take a look outside. If everything's clear, I want to do an inventory of what's in those boxes in your car. It looks like the guys who kidnapped you had already loaded some supplies into the back and I didn't get a chance to dig through all the stuff that I took from their house. I also want check out all the guns and ammo I took from them. Maybe there's even something good in one of those boxes that we could have for dinner."

An hour later, they sat on opposite ends of the couch eating cans of cold beef stew and drinking cold beers. Chuck was tempted to light a fire in the fireplace but he knew that it would be a mistake. He had seen first-hand the strong sense of smell which the infected possessed. And for any roving bands of criminals, smoke out of a chimney would be a red flag announcing the presence of victims waiting to be attacked.

McCain had gone through all the boxes in the Cherokee, finding a variety of both industrial-sized cans of food for use in a restaurant and smaller ones for individual family use. The truck stop had a diner and the kidnappers had raided the kitchen as well as the shelves of the store. There were main dishes, like the beef stew they were eating, along with vegetables and soups.

The criminals had also loaded up on bottled water, beer, wine, and cigarettes. Chuck had been pleasantly surprised to find an unopened bottle of Jack Daniels Tennessee Whiskey and another of Johnnie Walker Black Label Scotch in one of the boxes from the house. Of course, these were now safe in the back of Elizabeth's SUV.

The sizable weapons and ammo cache in the vehicle included the firearms the gang had stolen from Elizabeth and her friends, the guns the kidnappers had used, and the stash at their house. Benton pointed out a 9mm Springfield XD pistol as the one she had been carrying. Chuck brought it and one of the AR-15s into the house.

As they ate, Benton asked McCain questions about his law enforcement career and his fight against the zombie virus. She was also curious about Melanie and wanted to know all about Chuck's daughter. As they talked, Elizabeth realized that by learning about Melanie, she was learning more about her father, too.

After they finished eating, Elizabeth carried their trash into the kitchen and came back with two more beers, handing one to Chuck.

"Have you got a boyfriend on campus who's worrying about you?" McCain asked.

She took a drink before answering. "No. I'd just broken up with a guy I'd been dating when the situation with my parents happened. Now, there's someone at the school who thinks we're dating but I can't convince him that I'm not interested. I made the mistake of having lunch with Bradley one time in the meal hall and now he thinks we're a couple."

Elizabeth shook her head and continued. "He follows me around. I catch him watching me when I'm outside or even from the other side of the cafeteria. He's several years younger than I am, he's a student, and isn't even on my radar of guys I might be interested in."

Chuck smiled. "That sucks. You've got a stalker on a campus where you can't get away."

"I've told him over and over that I'm not looking for a relationship right now but he doesn't want to take 'no' for an answer."

"I could have a talk with him," McCain suggested, sipping his beer. "I can be pretty persuasive when I need to be. Remember, I have a daughter not much younger than you and I had several heart-to-heart conversations with some of the boys who came sniffing around."

"I don't want to make him feel bad," Benton said. "I just want him to leave me alone. Honestly, I haven't felt like being with anyone since Momma and Daddy died.

"I've really been a loner for the last few months. I would stay in my room or in my office, trying not to interact with anyone unless I absolutely had to. A friend of mine on the faculty teaches nursing. She confronted me one day and told me that I was depressed and offered me some medicine."

"What did you do?" Chuck asked.

"I didn't take the medicine but I did start running again a few weeks ago. There's a track at the school and I've been running every day. The exercise has helped, plus I've been trying to get out of my dorm room more and to be a little more sociable. Even volunteering to go out on the mission was a big deal for me because I'd been so reclusive. I think I was starting to get better but this morning was a real turning point."

"How so?"

"When we talked and you let me cry on your shoulder, it was like someone lifted a thousand pound weight off of me. I'd been carrying the guilt of my parents' deaths around for all of this time. You didn't judge me even though I've been judging myself. You affirmed me and helped to see that whole situation in a different light. I think the black cloud is finally lifting off of me."

McCain saw the smile light up her pretty face as she spoke. He was glad that the young woman was feeling better but he had not had so many touchy-feely conversations in years. She had experienced some devastating losses, though, and he was glad that he'd been able to be a positive influence in her life. And, if Chuck was honest with himself, he felt better after opening up to her, too. He needed a drink.

They sat on the couch in the cold house as the sun went down, the room starting to get dark. It had not snowed anymore that day but the temperatures had stayed well below freezing. Chuck reached into his backpack and pulled out his bottle of Evan Williams.

"Do you like bourbon?" he asked.

"No," the petite girl answered, "these two beers are about my limit. I'm already feeling light-headed."

McCain took a swig straight out of the bottle. "The problem with not having any power this time of year is that it's dark at 6:00 in the afternoon. It's too early for bed and there's nothing on television."

As the darkness settled in, Chuck stood and closed the living room curtains all the way. They had been open about a foot to let the light in. He had a couple more sips of the whiskey and put the cork back in the bottle, feeling much warmer.

"Can I have a sip?" Elizabeth asked.

"You sure?"

"My teeth are chattering, I'm so cold. Maybe it'll help me warm up."

He handed her the bottle and leaned back on the sofa. Elizabeth coughed and cleared her throat after she sipped the whiskey.

"That's really strong," she commented, tilting back the bottle for another drink.

"It is but it's one of my favorite bourbons. I found it in that abandoned house where I had the run in with Greg and Tonya. I needed a drink after that, too."

Chuck motioned for the whiskey and had another swallow. After a minute, he felt Elizabeth's hand touch his arm.

"Maybe just a little more," she slurred, taking a deep drink, holding on to the neck of the bottle. "It's not like I'm going anywhere tonight. Unless you want to take me out somewhere nice."

McCain laughed. "Let's survive the end of the world first. Maybe one day I can take you and Melanie out for dinner."

"That would be nice," Benton said, her voice slowing down. "I'd like to meet her."

She handed the bottle back and Chuck closed it, setting it on the floor. After a few minutes, he felt Elizabeth getting to her feet.

"I guess I should go and get some sleep since you're going to turn me into a Marine tomorrow."

As she stood, however, the room started spinning and she sat back down on the sofa.

"Then again, I may be sleeping on the couch with you," she said, giggling. "I told you I was a lightweight. Can I have a little more? After you get past that first swallow, it's really good."

Chuck handed her the bottle but said, "This is it, though. I'm cutting you off after this drink."

She gave him the whiskey back and mumbled, "No problem, Mr. McCain, I don't think I need any more bourbon tonight."

Benton slid over on the sofa until she was right next to McCain and whispered, "It's cold in that big bed by myself. Can I stay down here with you?"

"Uh, sure, I guess." Chuck doubted the wisdom of this idea but realized they probably did need each other's body heat in the cold house. "It'll be tight on this couch but we'll be warmer snuggling up."

"Oh, warm and snuggly sounds nice," Elizabeth replied, a bit tipsily, wrapping her arms around the big man. "I think I'd like to snuggle. I think I like to snuggle with you, Chuck."

"Well," McCain said, feeling uncomfortable, not sure where this conversation was heading, "you're safe with me. I won't do anything to you, but I don't want to see either of us freeze to death, either."

"Maybe, I want you to do something to me," Elizabeth purred, playfully, pressing her body against his. "Maybe, I want to do something to you. Maybe, I want us to do something together."

Lead us not into temptation, deliver us from evil, McCain prayed. How long had it been since he'd had a gorgeous young woman throw herself at him? He stretched out on the couch and let Elizabeth lay up against him. He wrapped the blanket around both of them.

When Chuck didn't make a move to take advantage of her offer, Elizabeth mumbled, sounding disappointed, "It's OK. I'm sure a big handsome man like you gets girls a lot prettier than me."

How do I even respond to that? he wondered.

"Beth, I don't want to take advantage of you. Plus, I'm old enough to be your father."

"But you're not my father. Nobody ever calls me 'Beth,'" she said, quietly, continuing to slur her words. "But it sounds sweet coming from you. I like it when you call me 'Beth.' That's nice."

Her head rested on his chest, with her body against his, and Chuck was already much warmer than he had been the previous night. Yep, it had been a long time since he'd had a beautiful girl resting against him. This is really not a good idea, he thought. Beth got quiet and McCain hoped that she'd fallen asleep.

"Nobody's ever called me 'Beth,'" she said again, after a few minutes. "But you're not a nobody," she slurred softly. "You're a somebody. Chuck McCain, you are a somebody. You're a hero. You're a superhero. You're my superhero."

Chuck smiled, making a mental note not to offer Beth any more alcohol.

"Thanks for the vote of confidence. But first, let me get you back to your friends at the college, safe and sound."

"Right. You drop me off and then you ride off into the sunset like a superhero. I bet you forget about me by the next day."

McCain had forgotten how emotionally draining it could be dealing with the opposite sex. The two beers and the little bit of bourbon that Beth had consumed had lowered her inhibitions and loosened her tongue. Chuck was at a loss for what to say.

There was no doubt he was ready to get her back to her people and continue with his mission of locating Melanie. At the same time, if he had to be stuck inside of a house in a winter storm during the zombie apocalypse, Beth was pretty good company, even after a few drinks.

"You're going to forget about me," he heard her say again, very softly. A few minutes later, she was asleep.

McCain woke to the sound of vehicles moving outside. The luminous dial on his watch showed 0150 hours. Car tires driving over the icy streets got louder as they got closer. Elizabeth's face was pressed against his chest with Chuck lying on the front edge of the couch. He kissed her on top of the head and slid out from under her to the floor. Why did I kiss her? he asked himself.

Headlights lit up the living room curtains. They're on our street, he realized, feeling a stab of fear and quickly grabbing for his rifle. A peek through the curtains showed three sets of headlights pulling into the driveway of the kidnappers' house. Chuck quietly put on his body armor and pistol belt. The voices of the vehicles' occupants carried loudly through the dark night as they exited two pickups and a passenger car.

Chuck sat down on the sofa next to Elizabeth and gently shook her shoulder. He put his mouth to her ear, speaking softly, "Beth, wake up. There are people outside."

The girl sat up slowly, pulling the blanket around herself and wiping the sleep out of her eyes. McCain told her what he had seen and asked her to go upstairs. He loaded Benton's 9mm Springfield pistol and handed it to her as she stood up.

She leaned in to Chuck and asked, "Did you kiss me on top of the head or was that a dream?"

"We'll talk about it later. Please go upstairs," he answered. Why did I do that? he wondered.

Kidnappers' house, Thursday, 0155 hours

Joey Lester turned into the icy driveway of the safe house and bounced over something. His passenger wasn't wearing a seatbelt so his head hit the roof of the black Ford F-150 pickup as they lurched to a stop.

"Ouch! What did you hit?" Joey's bigger, but younger brother, Don, asked, rubbing the top of his head.

"I don't know. Something laying on the driveway. I hope I didn't mess up my truck," he said, as the two men exited the vehicle.

A silver four-door Toyota Tundra and a blue Chevrolet Malibu pulled into the driveway behind the Ford. Joey withdrew a three-cell Maglite from under the seat to see what he had run over. The beam of light illuminated the small figure of a snow-covered child underneath his truck. His gasp brought Don over.

"Look, Don. We ran over a kid. A zombie kid. Looks like 5-0 or one of the guys shot her in the head."

Don looked around nervously. "Man, I didn't think there were anymore zombies around here."

The driver of the Toyota, Hoss Harper, walked up holding a flashlight of his own. His three passengers started unloading boxes from the bed of their truck. Hoss and Don had anchored the offensive line of the Franklin County High School football team several years earlier. After getting arrested for stealing cars, however, they had both dropped out of school and had been pursuing a life of crime ever since.

Hoss shined his light around the driveway and front yard, excitedly pointing out several other suspicious mounds. He kicked the snow off of the closest one and found the decomposing body of a woman. She had a bullet hole under her left eye and the back of her head was missing.

“Looks like the boys had a fun time of it,” Harper commented. “Let’s go wake ‘em up and see what they’ve got to drink.”

Wesley Maddox, the driver of the Malibu, popped the trunk and his two passengers started unloading, as well, carrying supplies towards the front of the house. Curses and yelling suddenly came from inside the residence. Bo Harris was the voice that carried the furthest. He had ridden with Harper and had just wrangled a large box of canned goods through the front door.

Joey and Hoss both drew pistols from their belts. Don reached inside the Ford and grabbed his .12 gauge Benelli M4 shotgun. Wesley pulled an AR-15 rifle out of the passenger compartment of his car and the four men cautiously entered the house.

Bo was on his knees, crying beside two figures on the floor. His flashlight lay beside him providing the only illumination in the dark room. One of the other men pulled out a cigarette lighter and lit the candles that had been left there earlier.

“Somebody killed my daddy!” Bo wailed, grabbing at Larry’s dead body and shaking him.

Joey put his hand on his friend’s shoulder and shone his flashlight around the carnage in the living room. Bobby and Larry were clearly dead. Bobby had been shot in the center of the forehead, while Larry had a bullet hole in his chest and another above his right eye. And to make it even worse, someone had vomited all over both bodies. The smells of death and puke were making Joey feel nauseous.

Joey’s light illuminated another figure lying in the remains of a coffee table a few feet away.

“Is that 5-0?” he exclaimed. “Guys, I think 5-0 is dead!”

All talking ceased. Even Bo quieted down for the moment at that revelation. How was that even possible? 5-0 was one of the few people whom Joey Lester had feared and respected. And now he was dead?

Lester's flashlight illuminated the smashed and broken features of the muscular man's face as he knelt beside him. Joey rolled him over and saw an apparent knife wound to the back of his head and the bloody damage to his left hand.

"Ronnie's dead, too," Wesley said. "He's over here behind the couch."

"Where's Jerry?" Hoss asked.

"You guys check the rest of the house," Joey ordered.

Several of the men spread through the residence, Don leading the way with his shotgun. They returned a minute later reporting that it was empty.

"There's no sign of Jerry," Don announced, "and everything's gone. The guns, the food, the booze. Somebody cleaned us out, Big Brother. What do we do now?"

Wesley spoke up, "We need to get out of here. Whoever did this might come back."

"Shut up, Wesley!" Bo yelled, spittle flying out of his mouth, climbing to his feet. "I hope they come back. I'll kill every one of them."

"Bo, you've got to quit yelling," Hoss said, stepping over to his much smaller friend and putting a big hand on his shoulder. "Man, we're sorry about your dad. We all liked Larry and we'll try to find out who did this. But we don't need any more zombies over here. There's already a bunch of dead ones in the front yard."

"I'm sorry, Hoss. It just hurts so bad. I want to make 'em suffer," he replied, starting to cry again, his fists balled up at his sides.

"What now, Joey?" asked Wesley.

He and Joey were best friends and looked more like brothers than Joey and Don did. While Don and Hoss were both six foot three and weighed around two hundred and sixty pounds, Joey and Wesley were both around five foot ten and weighed a solid one hundred and eighty pounds. The two friends even sported matching mullets. They enjoyed lifting weights together at Maddox's house when they weren't out breaking into other people's houses.

Joey Lester realized that everyone was looking at him, waiting for some direction.

"Give me a minute to think," he answered, stepping towards the shattered back door.

He shone his light through the opening, looking for clues on the back deck. The snow had covered any footprints that might have been there. Something reflected light back at him from the living room floor, just inside the doorway.

Lester knelt down and picked up a piece of brass. 5.56mm. He saw several of those scattered around the room. So, the gang that hit us is probably carrying AR-15s. That means they're well armed.

Joey walked over to the backside of the couch and saw stringy-haired Ronnie lying on his back. He had been shot in the chest and face. A few feet to his left lay an AK-47, or at least what was left of it. He recognized with a start that it was 5-0's gun. The front stock had been shattered, with the bullet also striking the barrel, and ruining the firearm.

A couple of empty 7.62x39 pieces of brass lay a few feet away. So Ronnie or 5-0 had managed to get a couple of shots off but it didn't stop whoever had raided their safe house. These guys had even taken the magazine out of the AK. They had left nothing behind.

He stood back up and crossed the room to where 5-0's body lay. Joey bent down to take a closer look at the man who had taught him how to be a professional criminal. They were never really friends but in a warped sort of way, the corrupt police officer was the father figure he and Don had never had.

Their business relationship had been a profitable one. If he was honest, the only reason that he wasn't in jail or dead was because of Mike Carter's influence. Even Don, as big and tough as he was, always showed respect towards the big man.

How many people had it taken to kill the big sheriff's deputy? Joey shone the light over 5-0's body again. Three of his fingers were all but gone, hanging by exposed tendons and skin. His face looked like it had been pulverized and his nose had been flattened. His right eye and the bones around it were destroyed, and to finish him off, someone had stabbed him in the base of the skull. It must have taken four or five big men to take 5-0 down and kill him with a knife.

And where was Jerry? he wondered. He knew that Jerry and 5-0 didn't get along but he couldn't picture Jerry doing this. He wasn't capable of it. He was a strong back and he knew how to use a gun but there was no way he could have pulled this horrific scene off on his own.

Plus, he was as scared of 5-0 as the rest of them. No, this had to be a rival gang. Maybe they took Jerry with them for some reason or maybe he'd escaped. Whoever this other group was, they were a force to be reckoned with. They had killed at least four of his people, including their leader, and there were a bunch of dead zombies outside, as well. Had the other gang killed the Zs or had 5-0 and his guys?

Joey stood up. "Wesley's right. We can't stay here. Take the stuff that we just brought back to the cars and let's go over to the truck stops at the interstate. That was the last place these guys were supposed to hit. Maybe there'll be a clue or something. We can spend the night there and head for one of the other houses tomorrow."

Within minutes, the vehicles were on the road. With the icy conditions, what would normally have been a five-minute trip took almost twenty. Joey was still trying to wrap his head around the fact that his criminal mentor was dead.

Carter had recruited him and Wesley six years earlier, when they were both nineteen. Joey had managed to graduate from high school but just couldn't hold a job. Instead, he and his buddy, Wesley, were breaking into one or two homes a day in and around Carnesville, Lavonia, and Hartwell.

They were careful to only pick empty houses in which the homeowners were at work. The two young men stole jewelry, guns, cash, and other items that they could quickly pawn or sell to their friends. Joey loved the adrenaline rush of breaking into someone's home, digging through their possessions, and then taking what he wanted.

The Lester brothers had both been arrested and served time as juveniles for burglary and car theft. Don, younger than Joey by a year and a half, wasn't quite as smart as his older brother and was back in jail almost as soon as he became an adult. Don and his best buddy, Hoss, were stopped by the Georgia State Patrol, driving a stolen car and in possession of a stolen firearm. A short stint in a medium-security prison convinced the two big men they didn't want to go back there.

Joey and Wesley were childhood friends. They both considered themselves smart, as well as cautious, having pulled off over a hundred successful burglaries. Until 5-0 stopped them.

They'd had a good day, hitting two houses several miles outside the city limits of Lavonia in Franklin County. Both of the homes sat way off the road and the burglars had followed their familiar routine. Wesley drove his Malibu up the driveway and parked. Joey would ring the doorbell or knock on the door.

If someone answered, he asked them if they had any scrap metal they wanted to get rid of. The usual answer was "no" and the two thieves would leave the area, driving into neighboring Hart County and taking the long way home. Any contact with a resident signaled the end of their day. They always assumed that person would call the police on them for suspicious activity and they did everything they could to avoid contact with the local authorities.

Today, however, they had been lucky and no one had been home at either location. Joey and Wesley took turns kicking in the back doors. They had loaded the trunk of the car with five guns, some nice jewelry, an iMac computer, two iPads, a forty-two inch flat screen TV, some high-end liquor and various other odds and ends that they could turn quickly. After splitting their stolen cash, each man also lined his wallet with three hundred and twenty dollars before they had even tried to fence the stolen property.

Maddox took a roundabout way back to town, utilizing several dirt roads just in case someone had seen them and alerted the police. The dirt road that they were on would soon dead end into Highway 17, which would take them back into Lavonia. Joey and Wesley were talking about what they were going to buy with their latest windfall of cash and stolen property when the sound of a siren and the flash of blue lights in their rear view mirrors got their attention.

"What do I do?" Maddox asked, panic in his voice. "Should I run?"

Lester thought quickly. Very few people actually escaped the police. "You might outrun the one but you weren't going to outrun the radio," the saying went. And Wesley wasn't known for any NASCAR driving skills.

"Go ahead and stop but play it cool. Maybe he's just getting you for speeding or something."

Wesley slowed down and pulled to the side of the narrow dirt road. A large figure emerged from the Franklin County Sheriff's car and slowly walked up to the Malibu.

"It's 5-0!" Wesley whispered loudly to Joey as he glimpsed the deputy's face in the mirror, his eyes concealed behind mirrored sunglasses, his big biceps stretching against the polyester uniform shirt. Deputy Mike Carter had a reputation among the local toughs as a no-nonsense officer who wasn't afraid to use force to arrest people.

He lifted weights daily at the Fitness Plus Gym in Lavonia and there were rumors that he was involved in the local steroid scene.

Big Don Lester had made the mistake of smarting off to the deputy one night after being caught drinking underage with Hoss Harper in a school parking lot. Don woke up in the back of the police car, on his way to jail. Hoss told him later that Carter had a thrown a single punch that had knocked him out.

"Well, well, what do we have here? Mr. Maddox and Mr. Lester. It's been a while since I've seen you boys. What're y'all up to today?" the deputy asked, standing next to Wesley's open window. Carter's hand rested conspicuously on his holstered Glock.

Wesley and Joey both tried to answer at once, nervously talking over each other. 5-0 cut them off with a wave of his hand.

"Turn off the vehicle," he ordered, "and hand me the keys." Wesley quickly complied.

"Step out of the vehicle, Mr. Maddox."

As soon as Wesley's feet hit the ground, the deputy spun him around, handcuffed him, searched him, and walked the young man back to the patrol car.

Over his shoulder, Carter said, "Mr. Lester, don't you move a muscle, do you hear me?"

"Yes, sir," Joey answered quickly. How did he catch us? he wondered. It doesn't really matter because as soon as he sees all the stolen property in the trunk, we're going to prison for a long time.

Deputy Carter appeared at the passenger door, opening it, and motioning for Joey to get out. In moments, the process was repeated and Joey was secured in the back of the police car with his friend.

"Did he say anything to you?" Wesley asked.

"Nothing, what about you?" Joey answered.

Maddox just shook his head as they both watched Carter searching the interior of the Chevrolet Malibu. He appeared to be taking his time, letting the two prisoners watch him, just waiting for their stash to be uncovered. After a few minutes, the policeman walked to the rear of Wesley's car and leaned against the trunk as if he was thinking. He made eye contact with the two men in the back of his cruiser and smiled an evil smile.

Slowly and deliberately, 5-0 turned around and used Maddox's key to open the trunk. The two thieves could see the deputy shaking his head as he dug through the stolen property. After letting them sweat for a while, Carter walked back to his police car and opened the rear door on the side where Joey was sitting.

"It looks like we have a serious problem here, boys."

Joey and Wesley hung their heads. They had been caught red-handed with thousands of dollars worth of stolen goods and didn't even try to deny it. Both of the men had been to jail before as juveniles and as adults. Since turning eighteen, however, their arrests had been minor and neither had served any time in prison. They knew that was about to change.

"Here's the deal," the police officer stated. "I've been watching you fellows for a while and compiling a file on you a mile long. Today wasn't your first rodeo and I've got enough evidence to link y'all to at least another fifty burglaries. That's a lot of jail time, boys."

Wesley finally found his voice. "Deputy Carter, I know this doesn't look good but..."

"Shut up, Wesley," the deputy ordered. "I'm the one talking right now. Yep, it certainly looks like you two are about to be exposed to a whole new level of the criminal justice system."

He let that thought hang in the air for a minute before continuing, staring intently at both of the young men. "That is unless we can reach some type of agreement."

Maddox and Lester looked at each other, thinking that their ears were playing tricks on them. Were they being offered a lifeline? They both knew that the police would sometimes turn criminals into informants in exchange for keeping them out of jail. Neither man wanted to become a snitch.

Joey's mouth was dry and he stammered trying to speak. "What…what kind of agreement, Deputy Carter?"

"I'm glad you asked, Joey. It's pretty simple. You boys start working for me. I run this county and oversee several enterprises.

"You'll keep doing what you're doing, taking from the rich and giving it to the poor. Only we're the poor." He laughed loudly at his own joke and continued. "You fellas have some talent but you're not very sophisticated. I know for a fact that if you keep doing things the way that you have been, you'll end up as a play toy for somebody named 'Bubba' in one of the state prisons.

"Here's our deal and these things are non-negotiable." Carter removed his shades, bending down so they could see his eyes, and counted off on his fingers as he gave instructions. "Really, it's just three simple little things. Number one, I'll tell you who to sell your stuff to. Pawnshops are a no-go.

"The GBI and most police departments have detectives who do nothing but drive around checking pawn records all day. You'd be surprised how many burglars are entertaining Bubba in jail right now just because they sold stolen stuff to a pawnshop. I'll send you to some people who are safe to deal with. We won't make quite as much money but there's a whole lot less risk involved.

"Number two, I get a third of everything you sell. I like cash and you'll pay me regularly. Don't try to screw me over and we'll have a long and prosperous business relationship.

"Number three, you will never, ever mention my name to anyone. Like I said, I'm involved in a variety of activities here in Franklin County and even some of the surrounding counties but I stay under the radar. This is our little secret.

"I'd actually like to see you boys expand your operation and add some more teams so we can all make more money. You can bring on whoever you like as long as you can trust them. But, my name and involvement is never to be mentioned to any of your other friends.

"Now I like being upfront with people so let me just say right now, if you try to cheat me or if you mention my name to anyone or if you ever have thoughts of turning me in, I'll kill you. Plain and simple. No loose ends. Of course, that would never happen with you fellows. I try to screen my associates ahead of time and you two seem to be levelheaded and dependable.

"A while back, though, I did have an associate go rogue on me. Y'all may have heard about Tyler Monroe. He decided to change the rules that I laid out and it didn't go so well for him."

This got the desired reaction from Joey and Wesley as their mouths fell open. They had both known Tyler. He had bought stolen property from them on several occasions. A month earlier, they had driven over to Monroe's house to sell him some guns and jewelry. As they got close to where he lived, Joey pointed out smoke rising into the sky.

When Wesley turned onto Tyler's street they could see the smoking ruins of his house. There were several police cars, fire trucks, and other emergency vehicles parked around it. Joey heard later on the news that the medical examiner's report had shown that Tyler Monroe had been hacked to death and then his house set on fire. After finding narcotics in the crime scene, the Sheriff's Department was calling Monroe's death "a drug deal gone bad."

Lester and Maddox looked at each other. Had 5-0 just admitted to them that he'd killed Tyler Monroe?

"Now, here's what my business partners get from me," the deputy continued. "First of all, I'll keep the heat off of you. I'll feed our investigators some bad intel and keep them looking in other directions. Now, of course, I can't do much for you if you get arrested in another jurisdiction, but here in Franklin County, I should be able to cover for you.

"Another thing I'll provide are some good leads. I'm friends with all the local gun store owners and some of the other businesses. I can make sure that the houses you're hitting have stuff worth stealing. 'Work smarter, not harder', is what I like to say," he concluded, chuckling at his own wit.

Joey and Wesley stared at Deputy Carter in disbelief. Was he trying to set them up? No, that couldn't be it. He already had them dead to rights. They were caught. The trunk of Wesley's car was open and the stolen property was right there, staring out at them.

"Can we have minute to talk, sir?" Joey asked.

"One minute and that's it. I need to get out of here so talk fast and figure out what you want to do. Just remember that Bubba is waiting to make your acquaintance."

The deputy closed the back door of the police car and let the two friends talk. He rummaged around in Wesley's trunk, pulling out a .40 S & W Glock 23 pistol. After admiring the gun for a few minutes, he walked back to the police car and opened the rear door again.

"Well, boys, what's it going to be?"

Joey spoke for them. "We'd love to work for you, Deputy Carter."

Abandoned house, Thursday, 0215 hours

McCain breathed a sigh of relief as the three vehicles backed out of the driveway and left the neighborhood. He had watched them carry boxes inside but their yells and screams had carried up the street when they had found their dead friends. A few minutes later, they brought the boxes back out, loaded them into the two pickups and the passenger car, and then sped off on the snow-covered roads. Chuck counted nine men, whom he hoped would not be back now that they knew their safe house was compromised.

He climbed the stairs and stopped outside of the master bedroom. "Elizabeth? They're gone now. May I come in?"

"Please," she said, quietly. Benton was sitting on the floor next to the bed, a blanket around her shoulders, holding her pistol, and looking terrified. McCain sat down beside her on the carpet.

"What happened?" she asked, and Chuck told her what he had seen.

"So we can leave tomorrow, please?" she pleaded, her face a mask of fear. "If those guys were driving, the roads are OK, right?"

"No, the roads are still bad and covered with ice. The temps haven't been over freezing for two days. Those guys are idiots for driving now, plus they have a three-car convoy. If one of them gets in trouble, they can take care of each other.

"Now if it warms up later today, I'd love to get out of here. But, I need you to trust me on this. I've been by myself for the last few weeks and it's a very dangerous world out there right now."

Elizabeth laid her head on Chuck's shoulder. "You think those guys are hooked up with the ones who killed my friends and kidnapped me?"

He put his arm around her, trying to comfort her. "They have to be. That group didn't just randomly pick that house in the middle of the night. They had a lot of stuff stored in there that I took when we left. It's almost like that house was a storage facility for them. But after seeing their buddies dead inside, they took off. I don't think they'll be back."

"You promise?" she asked, softly.

"No, but I promise to protect you until we can get you back to your people."

She took a deep breath and held him tightly. "Why'd you kiss me earlier?"

"I don't know," he said, after a moment. "I woke up with you lying on top of me and it just seemed like the natural thing to do. I'm sorry if I offended you, Beth. I didn't mean anything by it. You're a beautiful girl, but I don't want you to think I'm trying to take advantage of you."

Elizabeth didn't say anything for a long time as they sat holding each other in the dark, cold room.

"You think I'm pretty even with my face all beaten up?"

"That's especially cute," he answered with a smile. "Remember, I was a fighter, so to me, that's just a mark that you weren't afraid to mix it up. I think you're tougher than you realize."

Benton continued to hold onto the big man, as if she was afraid he was going to leave without her.

Finally, McCain sighed, "We probably should try and get some sleep. Why don't you sleep up here where you can have a little privacy?"

"I don't want to be by myself, Chuck. I'm not a scaredy-cat but if there are more of those guys out roaming around, I'd rather stay close to you. Can you please stay up here with me? I may have said some things earlier that made you uncomfortable and I'm sorry for that. I told you I was lightweight when it came to booze. Please, just don't leave me alone."

After taking a quick peek out all of the windows, McCain returned to the bedroom and took off his plate-carrier, pistol belt, and boots. He climbed into the king size bed, lying right on the edge. It wasn't that he didn't want to be close to Elizabeth. His problem now, he realized, was that he did. He also knew that he had to stay focused on the mission at hand so that he could keep them both alive.

Beth's back was to him but Chuck sensed that she was awake. He started to ask her if she was OK but checked himself. He considered reaching over and touching her but realized that would not be a wise move, either. Some things were better left alone and he eventually drifted off into a fitful sleep.

Truck Stop, South of Carnesville, Northeast of Atlanta, Thursday, 0230 hours

The scene inside the truck stop was almost as confusing as the one back at their safe house. Don's flashlight illuminated a young black male lying just inside the door. He had been shot several times in the chest and abdomen. Another bullet had struck him on the side of the head.

Further inside the business, they found Jerry. He had taken a close range shotgun blast high up on his right thigh. The wound was gaping and the surrounding floor area was a frozen pool of blood.

Opposite Jerry lay a white guy wearing soft body armor with several holes in it. Joey speculated that it was probably 5-0's AK-47 that had done the damage. Soft body armor would never stop an AK round. This dead man also had a hole in his head.

A few feet further to their left they found a light-skinned black female, on her side in the fetal position. Joey rolled her over, noting the wounds to her stomach and chest. He normally would not have wanted to touch her dead body but the events of the previous months had hardened all of them. Frozen blood pooled around her as well, and there was also a bullet hole behind her right ear. Empty brass casings and shotgun shells littered the scene.

"This one was a cop," announced Hoss. He had pulled Officer Jason Storey's badge wallet out of his rear pocket. "His ID says that he was a Campus Police Officer at The Northeast Georgia Technical College."

"Don, check that dead guy by the door and see if he has any kind of identification," said Joey, digging through the dead girl's pockets, pulling out a student ID card from the same school where the cop had worked.

"He's got a student ID from that technical school, too!" Don called over, holding up Lamar's laminated identification card.

Joey turned the information over in his mind. He sensed that there was a connection between what had happened at their safe house and the dead bodies here, but he just had no idea what it was. Mike Carter would have been able to put the pieces together but now Joey's friends were looking to him for guidance.

"What do you think, man?" asked Wesley.

"I think we're going back to school," Joey finally answered.

Chapter Four

Survival

Abandoned house, Thursday, 1000 hours

Elizabeth held the Springfield XD pistol in the solid two-handed stance that Chuck had taught her. She was a quick learner, he noted approvingly. Mr. Nicholson had given her a lesson on gun handling the day before her team's ill-fated journey to get supplies. Now, McCain spent over an hour working with her on her stance, grip, use of sights, and movement to cover.

Beth then practiced dry firing for another hour. Dry firing or firing the gun without ammunition is a great way to train one's fundamentals when live fire is not an option. A good trigger pull is an essential skill for using any firearm. Jerking the trigger pulls the muzzle off of the target and can cause a miss. Chuck patiently cocked and recocked the pistol as Elizabeth worked on pulling the trigger correctly.

"Okay, that's enough for now. Good job," said McCain. "Let's take a break and then come back in a little while and work on using a rifle."

Benton made a face at him. "My shoulders and back are sore. This is a lot of work."

"True story. You're using some muscles you haven't thought about for awhile. Hopefully, you'll keep practicing what I teach you and become a deadly weapon. These are dangerous days we're living in, Elizabeth Benton, and I want you to be able to protect yourself."

"Did you teach Melanie to shoot?" she asked.

Chuck smiled at the memory. "I sure did. I was known as the cool dad because I would take her and her friends shooting when they were teenagers. As Mel got older, I tried to take her to the range regularly. Of course, she lost interest and didn't want shoot as much as I did. I'd have to bribe her by taking her out to a nice restaurant after we left the range.

"When she started dating Brian, it turned out that he was a gun guy and loved to shoot. On one of their first dates, he took Melanie shooting at range near the UGA campus. She told me later that she outshot him with one of his own guns."

"Nice!" said Elizabeth, approvingly. "I hope I get to meet her one day."

A cloud passed over Chuck's face but he forced a smile. "I'm sure we'll cross paths again. Remember, I promised to take you and Mel out to eat."

McCain walked into the kitchen to check the temperature. It was a sunny day and the skies were clear for the first time in almost a week. Thirty-nine degrees. We're getting there, he thought. Maybe tomorrow, Beth and I will be able get out of here. I can return her home, stick around at the college for a day or two, and then be on my way.

Firearms instruction can be a very hands-on process. The instructor will often need to help the student make small adjustments in their stance or grip. Chuck was a very good firearms instructor but he found that being so close to Elizabeth was a definite distraction.

He spent a much longer time teaching her to use the AR-15 rifle because it was a more complicated gun. He taught her how to load the weapon using an empty magazine for safety, as well as how the long gun functioned. Then he had her stand up and worked on her grip, stance, and aiming the rifle.

As Chuck stood behind her with his arms reaching around the young woman to adjust her grip, Beth leaned into him, looking into his eyes, and smiling sweetly. "If you wanted to hug me, you should've just said so. This gun is getting heavy."

"You've got to take this seriously," he said, his eyes twinkling. "Plus, it's not nice to tease an old man. It's not good for my heart. Now come on, let's work this."

"Hang on," she said, lowering the AR-15. "How old are you? I'm guessing forty."

"Bless you, my child," McCain replied. "I'm forty-four. And I'm guessing you're all of twenty-seven?"

"Close. Good guess. I'm twenty-eight."

"Okay, now that we've established that I'm old enough to be your father, let's get back to work."

Abandoned house, Thursday, 1600 hours

Chuck had kept an eye on the thermometer throughout the day and knew that it was forty-three degrees outside and the sun was starting to do its work. The snow on the driveway was thawing and the snow in the yard was turning back into water. He could see the ice on the street in front of their house becoming slush.

He began mentally planning the drive back to the Northeast Georgia Technical College. It was approximately a fifteen to twenty mile drive, depending on their route. That was a lot of driving in a world where bands of robbers or Zs could be waiting around any corner to ambush them.

The interstate was close by, but he had seen and experienced first-hand the dangers of using it for travel. The surface streets presented their own set of dangers but were a better choice. When the thousands of zombies swept up the interstates leading out of Atlanta weeks earlier, they had left destruction in their wake. Sections of the interstate were completely impassable, with hundreds of abandoned and wrecked vehicles, as well as the remains of the victims. Many zombies still lingered, watching and waiting for their next meal.

From what McCain had seen, the side streets would give them a better chance of success. He wished he had another of his shooters with them in the car to even the odds. How great would it be to have Andy or Scotty with him? Or Eddie and Jimmy or any of the other CDC agents? But, they were taking care of their own families and loved ones. Chuck and Elizabeth would have to do the best they could.

"Really?" Beth squealed, throwing her arms around his neck and hugging him tightly when Chuck told her of his plan to leave the next day. He hugged her back, enjoying the moment.

When she finally released her grip and stepped back, McCain saw tears in her eyes. Her left eye was still bruised, matching his own black eye, but most of the swelling on her face was gone. And it was such a pretty face, he thought, staring at her. Beth looked up at him, gazing into his eyes, a sad smile on her face.

"It's been a traumatic few days, hasn't it?" he asked her, sensing what she was feeling.

Elizabeth nodded her head, wiping the tears off her face on the sleeve of the University of Alabama sweatshirt she was still wearing.

"What do I tell them at the school? How do I explain why I'm alive when everyone else got killed? I guess I still feel guilty." She hung her head.

Chuck nodded, putting a hand on her shoulder. "Remember what we talked about. Feeling guilty is normal but it wasn't your fault. I'm going back with you and I'll help you tell them what happened. I think everyone's going to be so glad to see you. And I'm holding you to your promise. You promised me hot showers, hot chow, and clean clothes."

Benton managed a grin, the torrent of emotions flowing through her now including feelings for the big man standing in front of her.

"I'm glad you'll stay for a few days. I want everyone to meet you so I can tell them what a superhero you are."

Chuck laughed, embarrassed. "Okay. Right now, I'd like you to practice some more with your rifle and pistol. We have a long drive through hostile territory tomorrow and we may need your gun fighting skills before the day is over."

For the next hour and a half, Beth practiced her weapons handling with a newfound intensity. Chuck didn't try to overwhelm her with knowledge. The main things he stressed were getting the gun on target quickly, focusing on the front sight, and not jerking the trigger. These skills were just scratching the surface of what she really needed to know but, for now, they would have to do.

Their dinner consisted of more cold canned meals. Elizabeth had chicken vegetable soup, while Chuck found a can of beans and franks. They enjoyed a bottle of California Chardonnay, sharing the only drinking glass Beth could find in the kitchen. She'd insisted on the wine, telling McCain it was their last night together in the cold house and promising not to drink too much.

"What do you think is going to happen tomorrow?" she asked him, as the sunlight began to wane, and the living room darkened.

"Hopefully, nothing. Maybe we'll just drive straight through and get to the college without incident. But we do have to be prepared in case we lose the vehicle."

"Lose the vehicle?" Benton repeated, the alarm evident in her voice.

"Remember, the guys that got you also took your car. I didn't tell you before, but I lost two vehicles the first two days after I started my trip."

"What? How did you lose two cars in two days?" she asked, incredulously.

Chuck lived east of the small town of Dacula, in what was still a somewhat rural area northeast of Atlanta. McCain had bought his house twelve years earlier, just as Metro Atlanta exploded with growth. His quiet neighborhood was just one of many that had sprung up.

When Chuck had started his journey three and half weeks earlier, he'd left his personal Chevrolet Silverado locked in the garage at his house. Instead, he took one of the gray Nissan Armadas his men had rented after losing their government issued SUVs during the fight against the zombie hordes in Atlanta a few months earlier.

One of his teammates, Scotty Smith, along with his paramedic girlfriend, Emily, had been staying with McCain since the zombies had overrun Atlanta. Smith's apartment was near ground zero where the dirty bombs had detonated, while Emily lived west of the city, eliminating the possibility of either going back to their homes.

Chuck had told them to stay as long as they needed a place to live, but he was leaving to find his daughter. With the communication grid down, he hadn't spoken to Melanie in months and he had to know that she was OK. Scotty felt an intense loyalty to Chuck, the kind of loyalty that comes when men experience battle together. Emily, however, was planning on traveling to her brother's house near Gatlinburg, Tennessee, where her parents had managed to escape to. McCain could see that his friend and teammate was torn between wanting to help him or staying with the woman with whom he had fallen in love.

"Scotty, Em needs you more that I do," McCain said, loading his supplies into the Armada.

"I know, Chuck, but it's going to be dangerous out there on the road by yourself. Man, I'm sorry. I feel like I'm letting you down," the former Army Ranger sniper said, hanging his head.

"You've never let me down, Scotty. You take care of that girl and secure my house when you leave. I left the gun safe open. Take whatever you need and lock it up, too."

"Do you think Andy and Eddie and Hollywood are going to be OK over there at the CDC site?"

Chuck shrugged. "I hope so. I gave them the option of leaving but Eddie and Andy didn't want to risk their families' safety trying to get to their relatives. Eddie's people are in Illinois and Andy's are in central Florida. Those are both long drives with zombies and bad guys along the way. Hollywood has stayed in close contact with his folks in LA until things fell apart and California wasn't affected as much as we were on the east coast. Jimmy told me he may try to get to Athens to find Grace."

Andy Fleming, Eddie Marshall, Jimmy Jones, and Alejandro "Hollywood" Estrada were a part of the CDC Enforcement Unit. Fleming and Marshall were both team leaders, and Estrada was on Eddie's team. Jimmy was Eddie's assistant team leader. Dr. Charles Martin, the Assistant Director of the Office of Public Health Preparedness and Response at the CDC, had agreed to allow Fleming and Marshall to house their families inside the CDC compound if the two men would oversee the security of the facility. Jones and Hollywood were both single and had also volunteered to stay at the rural location, assisting in keeping it safe.

"I'm proud of them for staying," Chuck continued. "If it wasn't for Melanie, I'd stay, too."

Smith grabbed his boss in a bear hug. "I'll see you soon."

Emily came out of the house as Chuck was preparing to start his journey. She embraced him tightly and said, "Thanks for taking care of us, Chuck," kissing him on the cheek.

Em had been the paramedic who had patched up Scotty and Andy, after they were both shot and wounded in a gunfight with terrorists trying to spread the zombie virus in the initial bio-terror attacks. Smith had convinced the young woman to give him her phone number and they had been dating for a couple of months.

McCain smiled at her. "You look after Scotty. Good luck on getting to your parents and remember, you're welcome to stay here as long as you want."

He left his house at 0800 hours, saying a silent prayer for protection for himself, Melanie, Scotty and Emily, and all the men who had worked for him. Chuck had heard reports of homes being broken into by roving bands of thugs. Some of Atlanta's notorious gangs had fled into the suburbs when the Zs took over the city.

As criminals moved into the affluent suburbs, citizens attempted to protect their homes. In many cases, the second amendment worked as it was intended to, and residents were able to protect their families and property by shooting these intruders. In other cases, criminals with no concern for human life slaughtered innocent victims who had something that they wanted.

The reality was that, for the moment anyway, society was breaking down. Very few, if any, police officers were working anymore, so no one was left to keep the peace. With the breakdown of the power and communications systems, most officers had decided to abandon their posts and focus on getting their own families to safety. McCain couldn't blame them.

He and his two CDC teams had worked as long as they could. They had performed a number of rescue missions around the city, saving people who were trapped in their homes when the zombies came through. Once Chuck lost contact with the Department of Homeland Security and the Central Intelligence Agency, however, he had sent his men home for the last time with orders to get their families somewhere safe. He allowed them to keep all their weapons and equipment and got each team member to write down their escape locations so he could get in touch with them later.

As zombies and gangs continued to wreak havoc, National Guard troops were finally released to supplement the local police in killing the Zs and curbing the lawlessness. In reality, the Guard did not have the training or skill sets to be effective. Zombies or criminals easily overran roadblocks manned by troops.

Citizen soldiers operated under very strict rules of engagement when dealing with living, breathing people. The roving gangs did not have any rules of engagement, ambushing the roadblocks, killing the soldiers, and stealing their vehicles and weapons. In other cases, robbers simply waited until zombies overran National Guard positions and then just walked in and took the equipment they wanted.

Chuck's house was over ten miles east of the interstate. His plan was to take surface streets that paralleled the highway for his trek northeast to Hartwell, but he wanted to at least scout out I-85 and see how it looked. Georgia Highway 20 was a large interchange where the interstate crossed the four-lane road. McCain intended to take the ramp up to the interstate and see if it looked passable. He didn't want to get stuck on I-85 but if it was reasonably clear, he might use it to go north as far as he could.

There were cars scattered all along most of the surface streets the closer he got to the interstate. Partially eaten bodies were becoming a common sight, as well. He saw several small groups of infected loitering on the side of the road and in the parking lot of a convenience store near the interchange. As the big Nissan SUV rumbled by, the zombies heard the noise, and began to follow.

The overpass was only about a quarter of a mile away and Chuck's senses went on alert as he scanned the area looking for threats. Just as he started to turn up the northbound entrance ramp to I-85, he saw movement on the bridge. Three figures and the glint of sun off glass let him know that things had just taken a turn for the worse.

To his right, McCain saw that a tractor-trailer and four passenger cars blocked the ramp. He might have been able to get around it but the heavy bang of a bullet impacting the front of his Armada urged him to find cover fast. The sound of the gunshot was followed by another, this one punching a hole through the middle of the windshield, shattering it, and striking the passenger door.

McCain accelerated towards the closest safe place, under the bridge. The overpass was close now, just a hundred yards away. Another bullet thudded into the metal hood of the Nissan, sparks shooting into the air. Two other weapons joined the shooting now, their bullets striking the engine compartment and the top of the SUV. Chuck jerked the steering wheel to the right and to the left, trying to throw off their aim. A rifle round found his left front tire, deflating it immediately, making the vehicle difficult to steer.

Red emergency lights began flashing on the dashboard. Just a little further, he thought. He smashed down the power button praying that his window would go down in time for him to get off some shots.

Thankfully he was left-handed, and drawing his Glock, McCain quickly fired ten shots in the direction of his attackers. Another bullet smashed through the roof of the Armada, just missing his head but striking his headrest as he fired out the window. The attackers' gunfire ceased as the smoking SUV rolled to a stop underneath the bridge.

Chuck did a quick reload of his pistol as he was exiting the vehicle. He grabbed his backpack and his rifle and ran across the oncoming lanes of the highway. The big man scrambled up the bridge embankment and hid behind one of the concrete pillars on the opposite side of the road. The zombies that had been following him were over five hundred yards away, still shuffling in his direction, the gunshots agitating them, and making them growl even louder than normal.

Two minutes later, McCain heard voices and saw three figures cautiously maneuvering down the embankment on the far side of the roadway. The three men were all in their twenties, all carrying long guns. One of them was heavyset with long brown hair and a full beard, carrying a bolt-action, scoped hunting rifle. Another had a shaved head and goatee and was armed with an AR-15. The third man was thin but carried himself with a military bearing. He was carrying an AK-47 and wore a chest rig with extra magazines.

Their voices were amplified under the bridge. The man with the AK was clearly angry. "I told you not to shoot the engine, you dumb ass. The goal was to kill the driver, not the car, so we'd have a ride."

"I'm sorry, JT," the larger man with the hunting rifle said. "I think my scope got knocked out of whack when I dropped it. Those shots weren't even close to where I was aiming. I know I hit him, though. That last shot probably got him right between the eyes."

"Well, let's see what he's got and then get out of here before those zombies get to us."

Chuck waited until they were all the way under the bridge and almost to the Armada. AK Man and Fat Man were on the driver's side, with Baldy approaching from the passenger side. As the leader got to the driver's window and looked in, McCain leaned out from the left side of the pillar, putting the red cross of the EOTech sight on the side of his head.

"Right between the eyes, huh?" AK Man said, turning from the empty vehicle to berate his companion.

Chuck squeezed the trigger. The suppressed shot was louder than normal under the bridge as the man crumpled to the asphalt, blood splattering the side of the vehicle. A slight shift to the right and two more shots hit Fat Man in the chest. The hunting rifle clattered loudly to the pavement, its owner falling backwards against the side of the Armada, and sliding to the ground.

The AR-15 of the bald man fired, the bullet impacting the concrete embankment five feet to McCain's left. Chuck slid to the right, peeking around the other side of the pillar. Baldy was leaning over the hood of the SUV, waiting for Chuck to expose himself again. When he glimpsed McCain, now on the other side of the pillar, it was too late. The bandit's eyes were wild with fear as he tried to swing his rifle over but he had no chance.

Chuck squeezed the trigger twice, heard a gasp of pain, and watched his adversary fall. He glanced at the other two men whom he had shot and saw no movement. A look back up the road, though, and he saw that the pack of Zs were inside four hundred yards now. McCain slipped his backpack on and hurried down the embankment towards the Armada. Smoke and steam were still pouring out from under the hood and it was clear that this SUV wasn't going any further.

AK Man was dead, the round having exited out his forehead. Chuck quickly unloaded and field stripped his rifle, throwing the pieces in different directions. The dead man had a Kimber compact .45 ACP pistol in a holster on his belt. Chuck stuffed it and an extra magazine of ammo into one of his cargo pockets.

Fat Man was alive but probably wouldn't be for long. McCain pulled the bolt out of his hunting rifle, throwing it away. On the opposite side of the truck, the other thug was groaning. Chuck had aimed at and hit AR Man's right shoulder and his right side. Normally, from that distance he would shoot center-mass or make head shots on human targets. Not today, though. He needed this guy alive.

McCain cautiously approached, pointing his rifle at the downed man. Baldy was writhing in pain and was in and out of consciousness. The 5.56 mm round had shattered his shoulder and collarbone. The other bullet had punched a hole lower, on the same side, destroying ribs, and possibly collapsing a lung.

Chuck picked up his attacker's AR-15 and removed the magazine, putting it into one of his pockets. The police officer pulled the bolt to the rear, ejecting the chambered round. He then pushed the takedown pin out and the rifle opened up. He snatched the bolt carrier out of the gun and tossed it away. The thug had an extra loaded thirty-round magazine in his back pocket that McCain took, as well.

The zombies were now inside two hundred yards and closing fast. Chuck dragged the wounded man ten feet beyond the rear of the vehicle, into the path of the oncoming Zs. Fat Man was still moaning softly, but he could stay where he was.

"What…what are you going to do to me?" Baldy asked weakly.

McCain ignored him and checked the interior of the Armada, grabbing a few things but leaving so much behind. He made sure that his backpack was secure, quickly reloaded his rifle, and started running away from the scene.

The wounded man lifted his head and saw the group of twenty-five zombies running towards him and began yelling at Chuck.

"No, you can't leave me here! I'm sorry, man. Please! Don't do this to me."

As McCain ran out from underneath the overpass, the piercing screams of the zombies' newest victim filled the air and echoed in Chuck's mind. He turned to the right, using the extra time that the wounded man's death had bought him, and ducked into the tree line, running north while paralleling the interstate.

Abandoned house, Thursday, 1900 hours

Chuck and Elizabeth sat on opposite ends of the couch in the cold, dark house, finishing their bottle of wine.

"Why didn't you tell me this before?" Benton asked, wrapping the blanket around herself.

"I'm not proud of what I did," McCain answered, looking over, barely able to make her out in the darkness. "You've been through a lot. I didn't want you to know that you were stuck in this house with a monster."

The girl did not respond for several minutes. McCain expected her to be shocked by what he'd done and knew that she would never view him in the same way. He didn't even see himself as the same person he'd been just a few weeks prior, he'd changed so much. Survival is not a polite game and he was a little surprised at how quickly he had adapted to the new normal.

Chuck felt movement as Elizabeth got to her feet. She probably doesn't want to be around me anymore and is going upstairs, he thought. I understand how she feels.

Instead of leaving, however, Beth came and sat next to him. She pulled the blanket around both of them and wrapped her arms around the big man.

"I don't think you're a monster. You didn't have to get involved and help me but you did. Monsters don't risk their lives for other people. You got shot in the chest saving my life. I don't know if I would've jumped in to save me. You're a good man but I think that all of us are finding ourselves doing things we never imagined we were capable of."

McCain digested what she had said. He didn't feel guilty that he had used a wounded man as bait for zombies so that he could escape.

That guy had just tried to kill him, after all.

For Chuck, it was more of a shock that he'd done it without even thinking twice. Elizabeth was right, though. In this strange new world, survival involved making decisions and doing things that, a few months before, would have been unheard of. Beth and Chuck sat in the silence of the quiet house, listening to each other breathe.

"You said you lost two cars. What happened to the other one? Or do you not feel like talking about it?" she asked, her head leaning against his shoulder.

McCain smiled. "There isn't as much to that story. After I hit the woods, I walked for a few miles before I finally came out of the brush, moving along the shoulder of 85. It was quicker walking that way but I was close enough that I could duck back into the woods if I needed to.

"I didn't see any Zs for the first couple of miles and then, they where everywhere. One or two here. A few there. And wherever they were, there were usually bodies. It really slowed me down because I had to hike quietly through the undergrowth so they wouldn't see me or smell me.

"I had to sleep out in the open that first night. I found a secure place a couple of hundred yards off the highway, up on an embankment, but it was a cold and miserable night. The next day I decided to try to find another car.

"After walking for an hour, I came up on several vehicles that had been wrecked or abandoned along the road. There were bodies and the remains of bodies scattered everywhere but no Zs in sight. I saw a black Honda Civic that didn't look damaged. The keys were in it and it started on the first try.

"I drove around a few small groups of zombies and managed to make it almost five miles before I got to an overturned tractor-trailer and a big pack of Zs about two hundred yards in front of me. This was one of the biggest groups that I'd seen so far on the interstate, maybe fifty. I stopped because I knew I couldn't get around them, not in a Civic anyway. Then I looked into the rearview mirror and saw another group of around twenty coming out of the woods a hundred yards behind me."

Chuck felt Beth's arms squeeze him even tighter. I'm really going to miss her, he suddenly realized.

"What happened? How'd you get away from them?" she asked.

McCain wrapped his arm around his companion, pulling her a little closer, and laughed. "Adapt, improvise, and overcome. I held the horn down for a couple of seconds to really get them fired up. Then, I aimed the Civic at the group in front of me, reached in and put the gear shift into 'Drive,' and ran as fast as I could into the woods."

Chuck felt Elizabeth relax and heard her laugh softly. "Did you get any of them with the car?"

"Thankfully, that stretch of highway was straight and flat. That little car plowed right through the middle of them and took out fifteen or twenty. The group behind me, though, was another matter. They'd seen me run into the woods and most of them followed me. I spent the rest of the day going deeper and deeper into the forest trying to evade zombies. They just kept coming.

"There was a big creek, almost a river, that I crossed, figuring the more barriers between me and the Zs, the better. The problem was, I stepped into a hole in the middle of the creek and fell down, getting completely drenched. So, now it was getting on towards evening and the temperatures were starting to drop. I couldn't start a fire so I just kept going.

"I finally came to a two-lane road and found an abandoned house where I could rest and dry out. The next day, I couldn't move. I'd pulled a hamstring with all my running through the woods and almost drowning.

"It took a couple of days to heal up but after that, I decided to give up on trying to find another vehicle. Cars are big targets, so I just kept walking. I'd go as far as I could each day and then find a place to spend the night.

"And speaking of night," McCain yawned, "we need to get some sleep. Tomorrow's going to be a big day."

"Yeah, good idea," Benton said, standing. She reached down and took Chuck's hand and said, "Come with me?"

McCain swallowed hard, stood up, and peeked out all of the downstairs windows. After satisfying himself that they were safe, he followed her up the stairs, cupping his hand over his flashlight, just illuminating their steps in front of them. He repeated the process, looking out all of the upstairs windows before retiring to the master bedroom. How was he going to navigate this situation?

Beth was already under the covers, huddled in the middle of the big bed, he noticed. Chuck took off his boots and got under the blankets fully clothed. The temperatures had remained above freezing all day, and the sun had melted much of the snow and ice.

It was still cold, however, with the temperatures in the thirties, and Elizabeth slid over next to him. He could feel her shivering even with several layers of clothing on, her small body against his, her arm draped across his chest. They lay in a comfortable silence for several minutes, warming up under the covers.

"Can I ask you a question? A really personal question?" Elizabeth's voice was timid, as if she wasn't sure she should broach this subject.

Chuck lay on his back with the beautiful twenty-eight year old girl next to him. He had already bared his soul to her like he had done with few others. What was she going to ask him now? Part of him was ready to be by himself again and another part of him knew that, somehow, over just two days, he had come to care about Beth deeply.

"Sure. Go ahead," he answered.

There was a long pause. "Why haven't you tried to have sex with me? I know you're a gentleman and I appreciate that, but you haven't even asked. And if you had asked, I would've said, 'Yes.'

"I mean you've already seen me mostly naked and I practically threw myself at you last night. You saved my life and that seems like a way that I could show my appreciation. Most of the guys that I've dated, we go out once or twice and then they're ready to hop into bed."

"In case you haven't noticed," McCain replied, "we are in bed."

"You know what I mean," she said, laughing and lightly slapping his chest. "Am I just not your type? Or, well, I know I'm not as pretty as a lot of other girls, but we've been together for two days and I guess I'm just surprised."

Chuck laughed quietly. "You aren't afraid to deal with the elephant in the room, are you? First, let me say that you're very beautiful, inside and out. As for whether or not you're my type? I could fall in love with you very easily, Beth, but I'm not foolish enough to think that you'd be interested in a man who's sixteen years older than you.

"But, the real answer to your question is pretty simple. I'm a Christian and I try to live by God's Word. I believe the Bible and it teaches that sex outside of marriage is wrong. Now, that doesn't mean I don't have feelings and desires, and lying here this close to such a pretty girl, just the two of us, all alone in a big, cold house, requires an infinite amount of self-control."

She accepted his answer and thought about it. "Okay, but please don't get mad at me, I'm just trying to understand. The Bible also says we shouldn't kill and, well, I know you've killed some people. I'm not criticizing you; I'm just trying to figure out if one commandment is more important than the other. It seems like not killing would be a bigger deal than not having sex."

"That makes sense except the Bible never commands us not to

kill," Chuck said. "It commands us not to murder. There's a big difference between the two. Maybe I should, but I don't regret any of the people that I've taken out. I even let that one guy, Greg, who I told you about, live. If it hadn't been for the baby, I would've killed him, too.

"Now I know everybody doesn't believe the Bible and even those who say they do, often don't live by it, me included. But the Book teaches that sex is one of God's greatest gifts to us, but it's to be expressed in the context of marriage. After my divorce, years ago, I dated and slept with a lot of women, and enjoyed every second of it. I was young, single again, and girls were turned on by the uniform.

"I was living it up, thinking that life couldn't get any better. Then one Easter, another police officer, a good friend of mine, invited me to church. I hadn't been to church since my wedding and before that, I don't think I'd gone since I was a child.

"My buddy told me his kid was in a production that they were putting on for the holiday and I thought, why not? I wasn't into religion but I'd go because my friend invited me. Well, that morning, my life changed. I didn't go to church looking for anything. I wasn't having a crisis. I really thought my life was great.

"But while that pastor preached his Easter message, something happened inside of me. It was like all of a sudden I knew that what he was saying was true and I needed to give my life to Jesus. That day was kind of like a new start for me."

McCain laughed softly at a memory. "I had a date that very evening and we spent the night together. The next morning, I felt so guilty. I can't even explain it; I'd never felt guilt over my sex life before, but I knew that God was speaking to me.

"That morning I promised him, among other things, that I'd keep myself pure until I got married again. As hard as it is, I've been able to keep that promise. I'm sorry if that comes across as weird. You probably think I'm a freak."

"Wow," Beth said, "that's amazing, and no, I don't think you're a freak. Like I told you before, I was a Christian, but now I'm trying to find my way back to God. I admire your discipline, but I'm not sure if I understand or even agree with that whole waiting-until-you-get-married idea. But I really appreciate your honesty and sharing that with me. I didn't know there were any men like you left in the world."

"I'm nothing special, Beth. I was in the right place at the right time to help you. I'd do it again; I'd just try not to get shot or beat up the next time I save your life," he said, with a chuckle. "But you don't owe me anything and I don't want either of us to do something that we'll regret later. I've really enjoyed meeting you and hanging out, and I hope you meet a great guy who'll take good care of you."

Elizabeth was quiet for a few minutes and then softly asked, "Did you really mean what you said? About how you could fall in love with me?"

Oh, no, McCain thought. What have I done? At least she isn't laughing at me or calling me a dirty old man. She'll probably tell me that she's flattered or something like that.

Chuck sighed. "Yeah, I meant it, but I'm sorry if I was out of line."

"Don't be sorry, Mr. McCain. I think I could fall in love with you, too."

Neither one of them knew what to say next. Chuck turned towards Beth and their lips met, electricity shooting through both of them. After another, longer kiss, Chuck wrapped his arms around the young woman, holding her tightly. Within minutes, they were both asleep.

Northeast of Atlanta, Friday, 0700 hours

Chuck had awakened with the first hint of sunlight coming through the bedroom windows. Beth was still lying up against him, her body draped over his. He watched her sleeping for a few minutes, saying a silent prayer of thanks that he'd been able to rescue her from her kidnappers, but wondering what the future was going to hold for them. I could get used to waking up in bed with her, he realized, the thought surprising him. Gently, he leaned over, kissed the young woman on the forehead, and crawled out of bed.

It was so cold in the house that McCain wondered if he would ever be warm again. The thermometer in the kitchen had good news, though. It was already thirty-five degrees and the sun was shining brightly. That would keep thawing everything out and hopefully allow them a safe, ice-free ride back to the technical school.

And then what? he wondered, staring out the kitchen window at the melting snow and ice in the back yard. Deliver Beth to her friends, stick around for a day or two, and then keep trying to find Melanie? How was he going to feel leaving Elizabeth? Would he ever see her again? What would happen to her? What would happen to him as he continued his journey? So many questions, but if there was ever a time that he needed to be mission-focused, this was it.

He heard footsteps behind him. A small pair of arms reached around and hugged him tightly.

"So, what's the plan?" Elizabeth asked him.

"Let's share a cup of coffee, eat, and hit the road?"

Twenty minutes later, after another meal of beef jerky and trail mix, washed down by hot MRE coffee, Chuck started putting on his equipment. He snapped his gun belt on and slipped his kevlar-lined jacket over the three shirts he was wearing. The black Nascar hoodie went over the jacket, and he pulled on his heavy body armor, adjusting the velcro straps until it was comfortable.

He had Beth layer up with all the clothes she had, including the shirt from Chuck that she had been wearing. Her next mission was to go through the house one more time, looking for anything that might be useful to them. Any and all food items, especially, needed to be brought along.

McCain checked his weapons and magazines, and then looked out all the windows to make sure there were no surprises waiting for him. He stepped out into the back yard carrying his kevlar helmet, placing it in the backseat of the Cherokee where he would be sitting. He quietly rearranged boxes of canned goods in Beth's SUV, transferring several to the front passenger seat, creating a buffer that would stop bullets.

Chuck wished that he'd kept his soft body armor for Beth to wear. That had been one of the things that he had been forced to leave behind in the shot-to-pieces, Nissan Armada. A few more boxes of food went into the backseat of the Cherokee. He pushed several against the left rear passenger door, stacking them so they stopped just below the window frame. They would provide a layer of protection against rifle fire but he couldn't stack them any higher because he needed to be able to fire out the windows.

One more thing, he realized, checking his work. Walking back inside, he found Elizabeth watching him through one of the kitchen windows. Her Springfield pistol was tucked inside her waistband and her rifle was laying on the counter next to her.

"Are your guns loaded and ready to go?"

"I think so," she answered. "Would you check them for me?"

The 9mm pistol had a loaded magazine in it but did not have a round chambered. He showed her how to pull the slide to the rear and release it to chamber a bullet, making the gun ready to fire. Her AR-15 was in the same condition, so he showed her how to put the weapon into battery and had her click the lever on the side of the long gun to 'Safe.'

"I'll be right back," he said, opening the door from the house to the garage.

After rummaging around for a few minutes, he was back holding an almost square piece of plywood, roughly two feet by three feet. That should do what he needed it to do.

McCain had briefed Benton over breakfast about her role on the drive back to her school. It was a simple plan with few moving parts. She was to drive in the middle of the road whenever possible. She wasn't to stop or leave the roadway unless Chuck told her to. McCain made it clear that she wasn't to exit the vehicle unless he indicated that it was safe to do so. And, lastly, she wasn't to use her weapons unless it was absolutely necessary. He wanted her to focus solely on piloting the SUV.

The piece of plywood went between the center console and the front passenger seat of the Jeep to prevent the canned goods from shifting and hitting Beth while she drove, keeping the boxes in place to ward off any stray bullets that penetrated the car door. It wasn't perfect and bullets could still come flying through the windows but the makeshift barriers that McCain had in the front passenger seat and in the backseat with him would offer at least a little protection.

Chuck took a deep breath and glanced at his watch. 0900 hours. We should be at the Northeast Georgia Technical College in plenty of time for lunch, he thought. It was only a fifteen-mile drive but in this strange new world, that was the equivalent to a hundred miles.

Beth was looking at him expectantly. She had been very quiet this morning, which in the short time that he had known her was uncharacteristic. He looked into her eyes and saw fear. I understand that, he thought.

Her left eye was black and blue, the eyeball slightly bloodshot. Another few days and that eye will be fine, he thought. That is, if we live through today.

McCain forced a smile and winked at her. "So, you ready to go home, Beautiful?"

She looked down and nodded. She stepped towards him and they embraced. He sensed that she wanted to say something.

"Hey, its OK. I'm scared, too," he said.

"Yeah, but now I'm afraid of losing you," she replied, quietly.

Her words struck a chord inside of Chuck and he held her close. What's happening to me, he thought? I can't believe the feelings I'm having for this young woman. He prayed a silent prayer for protection. He squeezed Beth and released her, taking her face in his hands, and kissing her softly on the lips.

"I hope I'm not being too forward, but I'd like another one of those when get to the school," he said, looking into her eyes and smiling. "Come on. Let's go."

Chuck sat in the middle of the back seat with both windows down while Elizabeth drove. His rifle hung from the sling across his chest, pointed to the right since he was a lefty. The Glock, suppressor attached, lay next to his left leg. Inside the tight confines of the vehicle, it would be easier to grab the pistol to engage threats on the driver's side rather than trying to swing the rifle around.

The plan was to drive north on Highway 59 as far as they could. Beth had grown up in the area and knew other back roads but those would take them on a much more roundabout trip. Highway 59 was two-lane state highway that paralleled I-85. If they didn't run into any problems, the route would take them almost the entire way to the college.

The first three miles were smooth sailing. The blue skies were clear and the road was mostly ice-free. There were none of the abandoned or wrecked vehicles that Chuck had encountered on the interstate. They passed house after house, sitting isolated off of the road, not seeing any signs of life. It was cold riding with all of the windows down, but they needed to be able to fire their weapons without shooting the glass out.

As they drove around a slight curve, however, McCain picked up movement next to a house ahead of them on the right side of the road. Elizabeth had to slow down because of a large patch of ice just as two white males stepped out from behind a brown van parked next to the house. The men aimed long guns at the Cherokee from a distance of around seventy yards.

"Guys with guns to our right," he told Beth. "Watch the road and drive."

He flipped the selector of his M4 to "Auto," raising the rifle to his shoulder just as the two attackers fired. Benton screamed as a heavy bullet slammed into the rear of the Cherokee. She shoved the accelerator to the floor as Chuck squeezed the trigger twice, firing two full auto bursts at their attackers.

One of the men spun around, dropping his gun and collapsing as one of McCain's rounds hit him in the abdomen and another struck him in the chest. The other shooter threw himself facedown in the grass as more of Chuck's bullets struck the van behind which the two men had been hiding.

There were no more shots from behind them as Beth drove around the ice and sped away. Chuck continued to scan the area, looking for additional threats while he swapped magazines in his rifle.

"You can slow down now. We're out of their line of sight."

McCain saw the white-knuckle grip that Beth had on the steering wheel and could see the speedometer was at seventy-five miles an hour. He reached over the seat and gently touched her shoulder.

"It's OK now. You need to slow down."

At his touch, he felt her relax and she took her foot off of the gas pedal.

"What just happened?" she asked, looking at him in the rearview mirror. "Those guys just started shooting at us! For no reason! They just started shooting!" She was almost yelling.

"I don't see any houses on this stretch of road," Chuck observed. "Stop for a second and let me check where we got hit."

The Cherokee slowed to a stop in the middle of the road. Chuck slid the boxes out of the way so that he could exit the vehicle. A single bullet hole had penetrated high on the passenger side rear quarter panel, piercing the metal and entering the storage compartment of the Jeep. He got back into the SUV and rearranged the boxes next to the door.

"Do you smell that?" McCain asked Beth.

"It kind of smells like spaghetti," she answered, sniffing the air.

Chuck turned around, checking the items they had stored behind them. Thick red liquid was dripping from a bullet hole in a cardboard box.

"Well, now I'm pissed," he said. "Turn around and take me back so I can kill that other bastard. He shot one of our big cans of tomato sauce."

"I hope you're kidding about going back," Beth answered, nervously, trying to smile.

McCain laughed. "He definitely deserves to die for his crime, but someone else will have to do it. Let's keep going."

"I got a glimpse of two guys back there," she said, as the Jeep started forward again. "Did you see any more?"

"No, just those two," Chuck replied, "and I got one of them. Hopefully, the other one will have a 'Come to Jesus' moment with himself and see the error of his ways."

Four miles down the road the houses and businesses were closer together, indicating their approach into the city limits of Carnesville. The small town presented a new set of challenges to Elizabeth and Chuck as they passed through.

Beth pointed out her window. "Right up here on the left is a grocery store, a Dollar General, and a Family Dollar store."

"So, a lot of high-end shopping in Carnesville, huh?" McCain quipped.

"Yeah, right? But those businesses are pretty much cleaned out. We've sent looting teams down here before. Their last trip, though, they almost got overrun by zombies. They pulled up to the grocery store, and saw the front doors were propped open. Then this big group came charging out after them, and our guys just barely got away."

As they passed the small shopping center on their left, Chuck saw what Beth was talking about. The doors of the Market Place grocery store were still propped open. All of the glass had been smashed out of the front of the Dollar General. Three figures stumbled out of the grocery store, running towards the roadway and the passing vehicle. Additional Zs poured out of the other businesses at the sound of the car driving by. McCain could see the blood and gore that covered them.

"And speaking of zombies…" he muttered.

The small downtown area was just two hundred yards ahead of them now, but several vehicles were parked lengthwise across the road, forming a makeshift barricade, blocking their access into town. Beth braked to a stop, not sure what to do. There did not appear to be anyone manning the barrier. McCain, his head on a constant swivel scanning the area, looked to the rear and saw at least fifteen zombies now coming towards them from the area of the shopping center they had just passed, most shuffling slowly, decomposition making their movements sluggish. Two of the pack, however, were overachievers and started to run towards the SUV.

"Keep moving forward and see if you can drive around on the shoulder," Chuck told Beth, pointing to the two cars and the pickup blocking the road. "We can't sit here."

McCain guessed the town had been abandoned if there were still groups of zombies in the area. Elizabeth pulled up to the vehicles, parked end-to-end across the two-lane road. There was a narrow sliver of snow-covered shoulder that she thought she could squeeze through. Benton steered around a white Ford F-150 pickup truck bearing a "City of Carnesville" placard on the side.

The soft, muddy ground caused the Cherokee's tires to lose traction, though, and Beth found herself spinning the wheels on the soft shoulder. A glance to the rear told Chuck the Zs were less than a football field length away, the two runners even closer. Beth began to panic, holding the accelerator to the floor, causing the tires to spin faster, the vehicle still stuck in the mud. The back end of Jeep started to swing around.

"Stop!" Chuck ordered. "Put it in four-wheel drive."

"Right," Elizabeth said. "Sorry. How close are they?" she asked, trying to look out the rearview mirror.

"Just focus on driving. We're good," Chuck answered.

We really aren't good, he thought. The two runners were inside fifty yards.

With the four-wheel drive engaged, the Jeep's tires got some traction and Benton was able to drive around the barricade, getting them back onto the dry pavement. Chuck glanced at the remains of four bodies that had been torn apart, lying next to the vehicle barrier.

"Leave the four-wheel drive on and let's get through town," he said.

Elizabeth nodded and kept the SUV moving. The pursuing zombies kept coming but Chuck wasn't worried about them as long as their vehicle kept going forward. They had just passed the Franklin County Courthouse on their right and were almost clear of downtown Carnesville when a surging pack of thirty zombies suddenly rushed off a side street, directly in front of McCain and Benton, less than a hundred feet away. As one, they surged towards the Cherokee, blocking the entire road.

These Zs were a mixed group. There were bloody men in business suits, growling women wearing dresses, two decomposing Hispanic women wearing aprons, and lots of infected children. At least half of this group of zombies looked like elementary school age kids.

In an instant, McCain took all of this in. These people had been infected for a while, he realized. Their bodies were in various stages of rot and decay.

"What do we do?" Beth screamed.

"Hang on a sec," he said, calmly leaning out of the left side window with his pistol, exploding the two heads of the running zombies who were about to reach their vehicle from the group coming up behind them.

There was no place to go, he realized, pushing the power button to put the windows up.

"Chuck?"

The pack about to converge upon their vehicle was only twenty feet away.

"Put your windows up and pull to the left and drive through those small ones. Gun it and let's go!"

"But they're children!" she exclaimed.

"Now!" he ordered. "Do it or we die."

Elizabeth hesitated, their vehicle sitting motionless. McCain grabbed the door handle and was about to dive out of the Cherokee and start shooting Zs. If he could get them to chase him, Beth could get away, he thought. Just as he tugged the handle, he was slammed back into the seat as Elizabeth shoved the gas pedal to the floor.

Several zombie children were on the far side of the pack that was almost to the vehicle. As she accelerated and steered to the left, the SUV ran over three small boys, two girls, and a grown man. There were several seconds of sickening bumps as the Cherokee slammed into and bounced over the infected children. The impact of the SUV on the man knocked him up onto the hood and into the windshield, face-first, cracking it and leaving a bloody trail on the glass and down the front of the Jeep. He slid off to the right and Benton realized that she was free and clear, the zombies all behind them.

Three miles outside of town, Chuck asked her to stop the vehicle so he could check it for damage. He also needed to check Beth and make sure she was good to keep driving. It's not every day that you intentionally drive through a pack of children, zombies or not.

McCain scanned the area through the windows and then exited and walked around the Jeep. The front was coated with blood and gore. The right headlight was smashed out and there was damage to the fender, the grill, and the bumper. Blood covered the hood and the windshield would need to be replaced.

Elizabeth sat in the driver's seat, holding onto the steering wheel, staring straight ahead, tears streaking down her face. Chuck walked around and opened her door, taking her hand, gently helping her out of the Cherokee. She fell into his arms and started crying. He let her sob for several minutes, standing in the middle of the road, while constantly looking around them for threats.

"Hey, we need to keep moving," Chuck said. "Are you going to be OK?"

"No, I'm never going to be OK after that. I just ran over a bunch of kids. I'm going to see their faces forever."

McCain continued to hold her, stroking her hair. "My new favorite person told me recently that 'all of us are finding ourselves doing things that we would never have imagined we were capable of.' Beth, no matter what it looked like, those were not children. They were dead bodies that were only functioning because of this evil virus. You did what you had to do and you saved both of our lives. I'm proud of you. You're a pretty good driver, too."

"Really? You think so?" Her voice was quiet, her face still buried in his chest.

"Yeah, you can be my driver anytime we're going to have strangers shooting at us or we're being chased by zombies."

The rest of the trip turned out to be anticlimactic. They spotted a group of Zs in the parking lot of a large factory as they drove past. Another handful of the creatures were milling around a Kingdom Hall of Jehovah's Witnesses. There has to be some irony there, McCain thought.

The road was clear and Elizabeth had her head back in the game. It's good to see that she recovers fast, Chuck noticed. Deal with the trauma, cry it out if you need to, and then move on. Whenever things got back to normal, though, therapy and counseling were going to be lucrative fields, Chuck mused.

Chapter Five

Home

The Northeast Georgia Technical College, Lavonia, Georgia, Friday, 1110 hours

"We're here," Elizabeth announced, the relief evident in her voice.

Chuck saw the sign identifying the school as the Cherokee turned off of the main road onto a long, winding drive. After a half mile, a formidable roadblock loomed in front of them. With slight embankments of dark red clay rising on either side of the narrow road, the trailer and the vehicles completely eliminated the possibility of any unauthorized cars getting onto the campus.

Two young men, one black and one white, both holding rifles, were sitting on top of the trailer, their legs dangling. The sight of the bloody SUV prompted both of them to stand and aim their guns at the vehicle. The black guy took a step back, knelt, and picked up a phone that was laying on top of the trailer, speaking into it, and then hanging it up.

Benton stopped fifty feet before she got to the barricade and put the car in park. She stepped out with her hands up and waved.

"Hey, Todd and Jermaine. Can you let me in?"

"Miss Benton? We thought something bad had happened to you guys!" Todd answered, clearly excited to see Benton's familiar face.

He slung his scoped, bolt-action rifle over his shoulder.

Chuck saw the young African-American man pick the phone back up, say a few words, and then watched both men scramble down to make an opening for Elizabeth's Jeep, moving two vehicles so that she could drive through. They quickly reblocked the hole in the barricade and walked over to the stopped Cherokee. Jermaine carried his AR-15 with the muzzle pointing towards the ground.

The young men observed the damaged and bloody hood, the cracked windshield of the SUV, and then looked inside the Cherokee expecting to see their friends. Instead they saw a big, heavily armed stranger staring back at them. Confusion was evident in their eyes.

"We got ambushed at one of the truck stops. Everybody's gone," Elizabeth told the two students, motioning towards the backseat. "This is Chuck. He saved my life and he's going to stay with us a couple of days."

Jermaine found his voice. "So Margo, Lamar, and Officer Storey are…?"

"They're all dead, Jermaine," she said, quietly. "There were a group of men waiting for us inside the first truck stop that we went into for supplies. We'll have a community meeting later and I'll tell everybody everything. Right now, I need to go find Mr. Nicholson."

Benton drove away from the stunned sentries and McCain saw what was probably the main administrative building a few hundred feet beyond the barricade. As they got deeper into the campus he could see other buildings spread out over the hundred-acre compound.

"We'll stop here first," she told him, pulling up to the administrative building. "We just call this 'Admin.' My office is here along with Mr. Nicholson's.

"He usually hangs out here unless he's out patrolling. He rigged up a phone system that connects to different points on the campus for the sentries to call in. Mr. Nicholson calls his office 'the command post,'" she said with a chuckle. "The dining hall is right behind this building so we can drop off these boxes of supplies before we go over to the dorm."

As Beth pulled under the overhang in front of Admin, she drove by a firing position made out of two layers of sandbags. It would allow someone to step out the front door of the building and in two strides be in a position of cover to engage any attackers. A stocky, ruddy-faced, sandy-haired man exited the front door and was waiting for them when the vehicle stopped. Chuck saw his eyes take in the appearance of the Jeep, Elizabeth, and him.

The man was wearing wire-rimmed glasses, clothed in khaki cargo pants and a green polo shirt. The shirt was tucked in, the pants looked like they had been pressed, and he had on black boots that must have been polished that morning. McCain saw a full size .45 automatic pistol in a holster on his side. Chuck also noticed that he had a strange cadence to his walk, as if he'd had an injury to one of his legs.

Chuck took off his helmet and got out of the vehicle, leaving his rifle and body armor behind, but keeping his pistol belt on. Beth had already gotten out and was speaking softly with the man. The ruddy face softened as Elizabeth spoke and the two embraced. McCain saw him speaking quietly to Beth as they hugged. After a moment, Elizabeth turned towards Chuck and motioned him over, wiping her eyes with the sleeve of her sweatshirt.

"Chuck, this is Mr. Nicholson. Mr. Nicholson, this is Chuck McCain, the man who saved me."

"Jake Nicholson," he said, sticking out his hand. McCain took it.

"It's nice to meet you. Beth said you've done a great job securing this campus."

Nicholson sighed. "Thanks. It hasn't been easy but I think it's as safe as we can make it with what we have. Elizabeth told me a little of what you did. I'd like to hear the rest of the story later, but thanks for bringing her back. She's very special to us."

Jake looked Chuck over and cocked his head. "Military?"

"No, I used to be a SWAT cop but I did do a couple of tours with a Special Forces A team in Afghanistan as a police advisor. My last job was with the CDC Police. You?"

"Marines. You were with the CDC? You guys were right in the middle of this whole zombie virus, right?"

Before McCain could answer, the door behind them opened and a forty-something, redheaded woman, came out. She was wearing blue jeans, a green sweatshirt with the school's logo, and a navy blue jacket with campus police patches on it. Her black leather utility belt held a 9mm Sig Sauer pistol, extra magazines, handcuffs, pepper spray, and a collapsible baton.

"Elizabeth! We've been so worried," the newcomer said, grabbing and hugging the younger woman.

Nicholson motioned at the redhead and spoke to Chuck, "This is Officer Tina Miles. She was the other campus police officer who stayed to look after these kids when the zombies swept through."

Miles looked at Chuck, the empty SUV, and scanned the area. "Where's everybody else?"

Beth didn't answer right away. Jake stepped over and put his arm around Tina.

"Tina, this is Chuck McCain. Elizabeth and the team got ambushed. Everybody else was killed. They kidnapped Elizabeth but Chuck was passing through and was able to rescue her."

Tears began to flow down Tina's face as she struggled to control her emotions. Jake kept his arm around her, comforting her.

"I'm so glad you're OK, Elizabeth. I'm sorry for the others but I'm thankful that you made it back to us," Tina said. The two women hugged again.

Jake looked around and then spoke quietly to Chuck, "Are you a smoker, McCain? I haven't had a cigarette in weeks and I sure could use one now."

Chuck smiled. "Hang on a minute."

He walked to the rear of the Cherokee and opened the cargo door. He reached inside, rummaging through a couple of boxes before finding what he was looking for. McCain walked back over to Nicholson and handed him a carton of Marlboros.

The man's eyes lit up. "I think you and me are going to be good friends."

Ten minutes later, Benton's Jeep Cherokee was backed up to the main entrance of the cafeteria. After gawking at the blood-covered and damaged front end of the vehicle, a group of chattering students started unloading the boxes of food and supplies. Word had spread quickly across the small campus that Miss Benton was back and all the residents flocked to the dining hall.

Both students and faculty alike were delighted to see Elizabeth, wanting to hug her and ask her about what happened. She asked them all to wait until the vehicle was unloaded, saying that she would speak to everyone inside the large room about what had happened to her and the team. McCain stood off to the side watching Beth and observing how much everyone loved her. She was clearly in her element here, confident, with a smile and a kind word for just about everyone she encountered.

Jake and Tina stood outside in front of the dining hall smoking their Marlboros, savoring every puff. A slim young man, his hair pulled back into a man bun, walked up to the two of them and spoke in a chastising tone, "Mr. Nicholson, Officer Miles, this is a smoke-free area. You're not supposed to be smoking here."

Chuck had just come back out to talk with Jake and get a little more information on how secure the campus really was. He heard what the student had said and saw Miles turn away, trying not to laugh. Nicholson ignored the interruption, continuing to enjoy his cigarette, staring out across the campus.

When the student didn't take the hint that he was being ignored, Jake turned towards the young man and exhaled smoke in his direction, causing him to cough.

"Bradley, go away. In this day and age, I'm much more likely to die from getting eaten by a zombie than I am by lung cancer."

As Bradley stomped angrily into the dining hall, Jake nodded at Chuck and smiled. "That was Bradley. He's the student body president and he's got the hots for Elizabeth."

"Right," said Chuck. "She told me about him."

Interested in seeing the interaction between Elizabeth and Bradley, McCain strolled back inside just in time to see the student body president trying to hug Beth. She didn't hug him back, keeping her arms at her side and just said, "Hello, Bradley. Good to see you, too."

Unlike everyone else, Bradley did not get a smile.

"I was so worried. I'm glad you're OK. Maybe we can hang out later?"

"No, we can't. Look, I'm kind of busy right now."

Not taking the hint, Bradley released his hug but kept standing too close to Elizabeth for her comfort. She took a step backwards as the student kept talking.

"Did you know that Mr. Nicholson and Officer Miles are smoking right outside that door? And who's Mr. Seal Team Six over there?" he asked, glancing over his shoulder at Chuck.

McCain made eye contact with Benton and smiled at her, walking across the room to stand next to her. She looped her arm through his and said, "Chuck, this is Bradley Thomas. He was the student body president here. Bradley, this is Chuck McCain. He saved my life."

Chuck did not offer his hand to the young man, merely nodding at him.

Beth walked away from Bradley, taking Chuck with her. "Thanks for coming over," she said, quietly. "I was trying to figure out how to get away from him."

An attractive woman in her mid-thirties approached the pair. "Karen!" Elizabeth exclaimed. The two threw themselves into each other's arms.

"You had us all so worried, Elizabeth! What happened?"

Ignoring the question, Beth said, "Karen, I want you to meet Chuck McCain. You'll hear more about him in a few minutes."

"Chuck, this is Karen Foster, our campus nurse and my good friend," Benton told him. "She's the one who told me I was depressed and helped me get started on the road to recovery. Karen has done an incredible job of keeping us all healthy and has put together a team of EMTs and nurse trainees that look after us."

McCain and Karen shook hands. "It's nice to meet you," Chuck said.

He saw the other woman's eyes looking closely at Elizabeth, taking in the damage to her face. Karen's eyes then lingered over him, noting the bruising to his face, as well. This must be some story we're all about to hear, Karen thought to herself.

"It's good to see you smiling, Elizabeth. We've all been busy worrying about you but it looks like you've been hanging out with a good-looking man for a couple of days," Karen said, both ladies giggling.

Five minutes later, everyone was in the big room and Elizabeth began relating her ordeal. She gave a sanitized version of what had happened to Officer Storey, Margo, and Lamar. She started crying but regained her composure and talked about how the four men had kidnapped and beaten her. Her face still carried the bruises so everyone could see some of the evidence. Chuck saw a number of people in the dining hall wiping the tears from their eyes as Benton talked.

"And just when I thought I was dead, this man," she said, pointing at Chuck, "broke into the house and rescued me. He didn't know me but he risked his life to save me, even getting shot in the process. Thankfully, his body armor saved him."

Everyone broke out in applause except Bradley. He merely stared at Chuck. He had already seen how Elizabeth looked at the big man. He shook his head, wondering what he would have to do to gain Elizabeth Benton's love.

After the clapping died down, Beth continued, "In just a minute, I'm going to let Mr. McCain share a few words. But before I do that, I want to say that I'm so sorry about Jason, Margo, and Lamar. I feel like I failed them and I failed you," she said, bursting into tears.

Several voices said, "No way. You haven't failed anybody, Miss Benton."

Elizabeth held her hand up with a slight smile, "Thanks for that. Chuck and I talked about how it's normal to feel guilt after going through something like this. But I just felt like I had to say 'I'm sorry.'"

The tears were pouring down Beth's face as a stunning young African-American woman walked up to the front and put her arm protectively around the crying woman, leading her off to the side of the group. Chuck quickly stepped to the front of the room to take some of the attention away from Elizabeth so she could compose herself.

"I told Beth that she doesn't have anything to feel guilty about. This was a terrible crime committed by evil people. These criminals ambushed your group and there was nothing she could've done to stop it. And I want to say how sorry I am about your friends who didn't come home. We've all lost people we love but it's never easy."

Oh, its "Beth" is it? Bradley thought. He just meets her a few days ago and now he thinks he can call her "Beth?" He shook his head again.

McCain continued, “I’d like to let you know what a tough girl Elizabeth is. Before I could even get to her, the kidnappers were trying to drag her out of the car into their house and she kicked one of them in the face and broke his nose. Later, while I was looking in the window and trying to figure out the best way to get inside the house to rescue her, I watched her kick one of them in the…well, in the groin area.”

Elizabeth was smiling broadly through her tears and the group laughed loudly, happy for something to cheer about.

“It’s OK to say ‘balls’ Mr. McCain,” shouted a girl seated on the back row.

“Okay,” said Chuck, grinning, “Beth kicked the guy in the balls and that created enough of a distraction so that I could get in and get her out.”

Beth interrupted Chuck. “Mr. McCain is being very modest. He killed all four of the men who murdered our friends and kidnapped me. Then when he was trying to get me out of that house to a safe place, pretty much having to carry me, we got attacked by a big group of zombies and he killed all of them, too.”

The crowd buzzed at the revelation that the man in front of them had not only rescued Elizabeth but had also eliminated the people who had slaughtered their friends. The audience nodded appreciatively. McCain spoke for a few more minutes telling them what he knew of the outside world. While there were still groups of zombies in the area, he stressed that the biggest threat now appeared to be the breakdown of society and the roving bands of criminals.

So this McCain guy is tough and knows how to kill people, Bradley pondered. But he’s old enough to be Elizabeth’s father. There is no way that she’s fallen for him. She’s just being nice to him because he saved her. And McCain better not be trying to put the move on her. He needs to find someone his own age.

Chuck answered a few of the students' and faculty's questions and then Benton stepped back in, her composure now intact.

"Mr. McCain is only going to be with us for a few days. He has a very important mission of his own that he'll be continuing," she said, looking into McCain's eyes. "He put his life on hold to help me so I promised him some hot showers and several hot meals before we send him on his way."

Elizabeth held Chuck's gaze for a moment. Even as she smiled at him, he saw the sadness in her eyes. He looked away, flooded with his own emotions. Would he ever see her again after he left this place?

After the meeting wrapped up, Chuck saw Elizabeth speaking with Mr. Nicholson, who was smiling and nodding. Benton then turned and spoke with two younger women. After a few minutes, they hurried off, clearly on a mission.

Nurse Karen rushed over to McCain and grabbed him, hugging him tightly. "Thank you for what you did," she said, looking into his eyes, tears dripping out of her own. "Elizabeth is such a special person." The nurse lowered her voice and said, "And you made her smile again, even after everything she's been through." Karen hugged him again and hurried off.

Chuck walked over to Jake and Tina, just as the former Marine was sending a student off with some instructions.

"I just told him to go fire up the generator so you can have some hot water. In fifteen or twenty minutes, you'll have a hot shower," Nicholson told him.

"That'll be great, thanks!" said McCain. "I can't even remember my last one. Officer Miles, I have a question for you."

"Please, call me 'Tina,' and ask away."

"Do you know any of the Franklin County Deputies?" He handed her Mike Carter's ID card.

She looked at it and said, a hint of disgust in her voice, "Oh, sure. Mike. They call him '5-0' from his time in narcotics. Where'd you get this?"

"He was one of Beth's kidnappers. He's the one who shot me and gave me this," he said, pointing at his still-bruised left eye. "I killed him and found his police ID when I searched him.

"Beth didn't share with the group a part of her story that she shared with me. She told me that after your people got ambushed and had already been shot, Carter went around and put a bullet in everyone's head. He was going to shoot Elizabeth, too, but one of his guys talked him into taking her along so they could have some fun with her before they killed her. What do you know about Carter, Tina?"

The campus police officer's eyes had grown large at these revelations. "He hated us campus police, that was for sure. I get it. We're kind of like babysitters with guns, but every now and then we'd have something that we needed help with and we'd request the county to send us a backup unit.

"Whenever 5-0 showed up, he always made it clear that he didn't think we were real cops, and he always talked down to us. Some friends of mine who worked with Carter at the county told me there were rumors he was into some shady stuff, but their internal affairs could never build a case against him. Plus, he supposedly had dirt on the some of the brass over there at the SO."

"What kind of stuff do you think he was into?" Chuck asked.

"My friends heard he had his fingers in a lot of pies: drugs, prostitution, stolen property. The biggest rumor was that he ran a big network of burglars and thieves who gave him a cut of their take to keep the heat off of them."

McCain nodded. "We may have a problem," he said.

He told Jake and Tina about the three carloads of suspicious people who had shown up two nights earlier at the kidnappers' house.

"There's no doubt in my mind that they were connected to Carter and his people. The question is, can they connect the dots back to here? If those three carloads of guys found their dead friends in the house and then retraced their steps to the truck stop where their guys ambushed your people, is there any way they might find a connection to the school here?"

Tina nodded. "I'm sure Jason was carrying his police ID. And Margo and Lamar probably had their student ID cards with them. So yeah, it wouldn't be too hard to put the pieces of the puzzle together."

"How many people did you see in that convoy?" Jake asked Chuck.

"I counted nine males. It was dark and I was only able to see in the light of their car headlights so I could've missed a couple. How many folks do you have on campus here?"

"We've had a few more join us since this started. We were up to ninety but we just lost three so make it eighty-seven. Now, not all of those eighty-seven are fighters. I'd say maybe a quarter to a third could be depended on in a fight."

"I can't imagine nine guys trying anything unless they have a lot of reinforcements," McCain observed. "I think we're OK. It might not be a bad idea, though, to beef up your security patrols for the next couple of days. How are you set for weapons?"

Tina and Jake looked at each other and shrugged. "Not so good," Nicholson answered.

"I might be able to help you out a little with that," McCain told him.

Before he could elaborate, a pretty girl with almond-colored skin walked up to the three of them. Chuck recognized her as the young woman who had comforted Elizabeth while she was talking to the group.

"Hi, Mr. Nicholson, Officer Miles. Mr. McCain, I'm Miss

Benton's assistant, Alicia. She asked me to drive you over to the dorm and show you to your room. She left a little while ago with some of her friends. She asked me to tell you that she'll see you later but she really needed a shower," Alicia said, with a beautiful smile.

Chuck sensed that there was a toughness to Alicia that wasn't too far below the attractive surface.

Tina looked at Jake and said, "I'll go double-check the patrol schedule and see how we can add some more manpower. From here on out, we need to have the supply teams leave their school IDs behind. I hate the idea that some gang might try to attack us here."

To Chuck, she said, "Good to meet you, Chuck. Thanks for bringing Elizabeth home. I look forward to talking more. I'll see you guys later." She turned and was gone.

Chuck noticed the way Jake and Tina looked at each other. They were about the same age, mid-to-late-forties, and it was obvious that there was some chemistry there. Good for them, he thought. If you have to be stuck on a technical school campus out in the middle of nowhere, waiting for the world to end, you might as well be stuck with someone who loves you.

"Jake, you look like a man who appreciates a drink from time to time," Chuck said, after Tina had walked away.

"That I am," Nicholson nodded, "that I am, but you'll have to forgive me for my lack of hospitality. The zombie apocalypse has made it kind of tough to keep my bar stocked."

McCain smiled. "Come see me later, wherever Alicia is taking me. You bring a couple of glasses and I'll provide the bourbon. I'd love to talk and see how we might be able to help each other."

At the mention of bourbon, Jake's eyes lit up. "Sounds good. I'll see you after while. Enjoy your shower."

Alicia had been standing by Chuck during the whole exchange with Tina and Jake, waiting patiently. He smiled at her and said, "Lead on."

The Northeast Georgia Technical College, Lavonia, Georgia, Friday, 1215 hours

"So how long have you worked with Elizabeth?" Chuck asked Alicia, as she steered Beth's Cherokee out of the dining hall driveway and turned right. He noticed the jailhouse tattoos on her hands, wrist, and forearms as she drove.

Alicia saw Chuck looking at her tattoos and then turned her attention back at the road. "I've worked with her for three years and I owe her everything."

Chuck was listening but turned to look out the window at the beautiful campus. After a long pause he looked over at his driver to see that she was crying. He waited until she got her emotions under control.

"Miss Benton told me that you were a police officer. I hope you won't judge me. I showed up here four years ago, a week after getting released from the county jail. Part of my probation was that I had to get my GED and get a job. I'd dropped out of school at sixteen and had been in and out of lock-up for one thing or another," she said, smiling wanly.

"The college here offers the GED so I came to apply. Miss Benton was one of the first people I talked to. I didn't realize that I was going to have to pay for the prep classes and the testing, though, so I got up and walked out. I'd just got out of jail and I didn't have any money.

"Miss Benton followed me out the door and asked me if I wanted a job. Mr. McCain, I was nineteen years old and I'd never had a job before. My mama and my grandma have lived off welfare their whole lives. Miss Benton told me that they had an open position in the cafeteria and that school employees didn't have to pay for their GED course.

"I didn't want to work in no cafeteria, serving food to people who probably thought they were better than me because they were in college. But, I heard myself say, 'Yes ma'am, I'd like a job.' She told me that she knew I'd do well there and she promised that she'd help me study for that GED test."

Alicia had pulled up in front of a long, two-story brick building. The sign identified it as the "Student Residence Hall." She put the gearshift into park and turned the engine off but made no move to get out.

"I found out later from another faculty member that the school doesn't give free tuition to employees. It's discounted but not free. Miss Benton paid for it out of her pocket. And she helped me study. I wouldn't have passed if she hadn't helped me.

"After I got my diploma, Miss Benton asked me to apply as a student at the college. I started to walk away again. I didn't think I could afford it. I didn't think I was smart enough or that I'd fit in. You know Miss Benton is a career counselor so she asked me to take this test to figure out what I was good at.

"Mr. McCain," she said, glancing at him, but not making eye contact, "I didn't think I was good at anything. I'd never had anyone, in my entire life, who believed that I was smart or talented or had said anything positive to me. Miss Benton came back with the results of my test and said that I had an aptitude for business administration. I laughed! I didn't know anything about business but she handed me the test and that's what it showed."

Chuck listened intently to this story, amazed at what he was learning about Elizabeth Benton.

"So she told me that I needed to enroll in the Business Administration Program. I told her I couldn't do it. I thanked her but I knew there was no way I'd make it through that course. Miss Benton just smiled and said, 'Of course, you'll make it. I'm going to help you.'

"I'd been working in the cafeteria for about year by then and Miss Benton said she needed an assistant and offered me the job. I didn't know what an assistant did or was supposed to do, but I took the job and started learning everything I could from her. She taught me how to dress professionally, how to answer the phone, how to talk to people, and she helped me get my Associates Degree."

By now, the tears were pouring down Alicia's face as she looked over at Chuck. "Mr. McCain, I cried myself to sleep every night while she was gone. I didn't think she was coming back. Miss Benton may only be a few years older than me but she's more of a mother than my own mom. She's not the nicest white person I've ever met, she's the best person I've ever known. Period."

Alicia wiped her face, took a deep breath, and regained her professional composure. "I apologize for taking up your time, sir. I just wanted to let you know how Miss Benton has influenced my life. I'll get you inside to your room now, and have a couple of our security team unload all those guns in the back."

Alicia led Chuck into a two-room suite at the end of the first floor hallway. Turning left inside the dorm room took him into the bedroom. Two male students carried in all of the guns that McCain had recovered from the kidnappers. Chuck had made sure they were all unloaded and clear before anyone handled them. The firearms were deposited on the extra single bed in his room.

Alicia thanked him again for bringing Miss Benton back and shook his hand. She handed him the key to his room and left, shutting the door behind her. As Chuck stripped out of the clothes he had been wearing for days, he looked around the small room. It was devoid of decor except for the two beds, a dresser, a small table with a lamp on it, and several cardboard boxes stacked in a corner. The other room contained a small sitting area with a couch, chairs, dining table, and a small kitchenette.

Between the two rooms was the bathroom. It contained a bar of soap, a towel, and a razor. He turned the shower on and for the first time in months, felt hot water. He soaked, lathered, rinsed, and repeated. The soap also worked as shaving cream and he scraped his hairy face clean.

Chuck took entirely too long in the shower and enjoyed every second of it. He walked out of the bathroom, clad only in his black briefs, drying his hair with the towel. The sound of someone clearing their throat startled him and he almost dropped the towel.

"Sorry, I knocked but you were in the shower," Elizabeth said, smiling and looking him over. "The nice thing about being an RA is that I get a master key," holding it up for him to see.

She was sitting on the empty bed with her legs crossed, her wet hair wrapped in a towel. She was wearing clean jeans with a tight pink sweater and had even put on some makeup and lipstick. Beth blushed when she realized he had caught her staring at him and laughed with embarrassment.

"That's a sight I could get used to," she admitted.

"Well, hi there to you, too. Don't you look gorgeous? I'm glad I had my underwear on," Chuck said, grinning at Beth. He was glad to see her, even though they had only been apart less than hour. "I missed you. Where's your room?"

"Hey, you got to see me mostly naked, so fair is fair. My room's right across the hall. I hope that's OK but I wanted to be close to you."

"Three days stuck in a house together and you still can't get enough of me," he said, smiling. "What's the dining schedule?"

"We only eat twice a day to conserve food," she answered. "We have breakfast at 9:00am and dinner at 4:00pm."

"Sounds good," he replied, even though his stomach was already growling.

He finished running the towel through his hair and tossed it at

Beth, who giggled and caught it. McCain picked up his cargo pants off the floor and started to put them on.

"Did you say I could get some laundry done?" he asked.

"Here, I brought you some clothes." She reached behind herself and handed him a stack of garments. Chuck took them and found gray sweatpants, a green t-shirt, a green sweatshirt, and a pair of black athletic socks, all of them bearing the school's logo.

"Brand new from the school store and I'll make sure all your laundry gets done, don't you worry."

"These are perfect, thanks," Chuck said, putting the clothes on while Beth watched him.

"You don't get embarrassed having such a young girl watch you get dressed?" she asked, playfully.

He laughed. "No. When you get to be my age you don't worry about it and just enjoy the attention. I'm not in as good of shape as I was fifteen years ago plus my hair's turning gray and starting to thin out."

Beth shook her head, watching him pull the t-shirt on over his broad shoulders and muscular chest. The sleeves of the shirt looked like they were going to rip trying to contain his arms.

"I can't imagine you being in any better shape fifteen years ago," she commented, getting to her feet and standing in front of him. "You look pretty good to me right now."

Elizabeth stepped closer to Chuck and reached up, putting her arms around his neck, looking into his eyes. "You said you wanted one of these when we got here but I forgot. Sorry."

His arms went around her waist and pulled her into him while they kissed. When they came up for air Chuck said, "Since you forgot, I think you owe me another one as interest."

As they continued to kiss, they both felt their passion rising, not wanting to break their embrace. Chuck pulled the towel off of Beth's head, running his hand through her damp hair, savoring her scent. A knock at the door startled them and they stepped back, out of breath. They looked at each other with wide eyes and a realization that they really cared for each other.

Elizabeth took a deep breath, walked over, and opened the door. Jake Nicholson was standing there, holding two glass tumblers in one hand and a rolled up pair of blue jeans in the other. He was surprised to see Elizabeth, breathing heavily with a flushed face, standing in Chuck's doorway.

"Hi, Mr. Nicholson, come on in." Beth took his arm and led him inside. "I was just taking Chuck's clothes off for laundry," she told him, blushing again. "No, I mean, he just needs a few things washed and I was going to make sure it got done."

Jake gave a wry smile, noticing how flustered she was. "You feel better after a hot shower, Elizabeth?"

"So much better. Thanks for getting them to turn the generator on. I know it was off-schedule but much appreciated."

"You know I'd do anything for you," Jake said, softly patting her shoulder.

Beth smiled back at him as she bent down, picking up McCain's dirty garments. Chuck reached into his backpack and pulled out several other shirts and things that needed to be washed.

Jake handed Chuck the blue jeans he was holding. "I see Elizabeth brought you some fresh clothes, but here's a pair of jeans I pulled out of lost and found that I think will fit you. And that's really a nice shade of lipstick you're wearing, McCain," Nicholson said, nodding at the big man's face.

Now it was Chuck's turn to blush. He wiped his hand across his mouth, trying to get rid of Beth's lipstick.

"Thanks for the jeans," he managed to say.

Beth giggled, hurrying for the door, saying, "It'll probably be tomorrow sometime before your laundry is dry. I was thinking, maybe after dinner, we could take a walk and I could show you around the campus?"

"I'd like that," Chuck answered. "Let's plan on it."

"Well, I'll let you two talk and I'll see you at dinner." Beth smiled at the men as she closed the door behind herself.

Jake nodded at Chuck, a slight grin on his face. McCain smiled and shrugged.

"Come on into the sitting room," Chuck said, pulling the bottle of Evan Williams Bourbon out of his backpack.

Nicholson's eyes took in the arsenal of weapons laying on the unused bed and he let out a low whistle. "That's a lot of guns."

"It sure is," McCain agreed, thankful to change the subject. "Some of them came from your people. The others belonged to their killers. Most of those were in the house where I rescued Beth. Of course, you can take the ones that are yours, but I have a proposition that I think you'll be interested to hear."

Jake's eyes showed interest and he nodded, following Chuck into the adjacent room. McCain again noticed the other man's odd gait as he walked. Nicholson eased into a brown leather chair opposite of McCain on the matching leather couch. The Marine placed the two glasses on the small table between them and the federal police officer poured a healthy amount of whiskey into both tumblers.

Nicholson closed his eyes, held the glass up to his nose, and inhaled. He took a drink, smiling at McCain. "It's been a long time."

Jake put the glass down and looked at Chuck. "I want to hear what happened out there with Elizabeth and I'd like to talk to you about our security here. But, first, I want to know up front, are you and Elizabeth sleeping together?" Nicholson held out his palms. "I know it's none of my business, but hear me out.

"I don't have any kids of my own but Elizabeth's like a daughter to me. She's been through a lot and I feel very protective towards her, as well as all the other kids on this campus. Most of the boys that we have here are good kids but they're still boys, and we have a lot of attractive young women, as well. I'm sure there's a lot going on behind closed doors that I don't know or even want to know about.

"And I understand that Elizabeth isn't really a kid. She, Tina, Jason, and I've been the ones in charge but, really, Elizabeth is the one we all defer to. She's the highest ranking faculty member to stay behind and she's a natural leader."

As Jake had started talking, McCain felt a flash of anger that this stranger would ask such a personal thing. If the roles had been reversed, however, Chuck would have felt the same way. He was always overly protective of his daughter and even some of her friends who didn't have an involved father.

McCain looked Nicholson in the eye. "No, we haven't had sex. We did sleep together, clothed, trying to stay warm when that snowstorm came through. The offer was made, but I turned it down. She'd just been through something very traumatic and I didn't want to take advantage of her in such a vulnerable state. Plus, I'm sixteen years older than she is."

Jake took in this information, picking his glass back up. "You've got more self-control than most men would've had. Either way, she's different now. She's not the same girl who left on that foraging trip."

"What do you mean?"

"McCain, I haven't seen Elizabeth smile or laugh in months. After the incident with her parents, she withdrew into a shell. She still functioned, as we've all tried to get through this crisis, but she didn't talk any more than she had to and stayed in her dorm room or her office for hours at a time.

"We all knew she was depressed, but none of us knew how to help her. Now she's back, acting like her former, happy self. I can't remember the last time she was so…bubbly," Nicholson said, finding the word he was looking for, and motioning with his glass to the other room where the three of them had just been.

"And for what it's worth," Jake continued, "all the students noticed the difference at the meeting. Alicia even told me, 'I don't know what that big man did to Miss Benton but I hope he keeps doing it.'"

Chuck smiled and looked out the window, melting snow still on the ground. This really is a beautiful campus, he thought, looking at the trees surrounding it.

"If I'm honest," McCain said, looking back at Nicholson, "and if she's honest, we do have feelings for each other. But I'm planning on leaving in a couple of days. I've got to find my daughter."

Jake listened as Chuck told him of his search for Melanie and what his plans were. McCain also told him a little more of how he came to be in the right place at the right time to rescue Beth. Chuck didn't need to embellish the details. Any way you looked at it, one man taking out four armed men was pretty impressive. The very fact that McCain put his life at risk to rescue someone he didn't know told Nicholson a lot about Chuck McCain.

They were both on their second tumbler of bourbon when Chuck asked, "What about you? You said you were a Marine. How'd you end up teaching here?"

Nicholson grunted. "I was planning on being a lifer and had just made E-6 after nine years. I was in Combat Logistics. That's Marine-speak for a transportation unit. We supported the front line troops. I made sure my Marines not only knew how to drive and pack those big trucks, I also made damn sure they had all the tools and skills to repair those beasts. The long stretches of desert road in Iraq were not a place where you wanted to be broken down.

"My last convoy, we were transporting supplies and a new rifle company to a FOB, a forward operating base." Jake's eyes looked past Chuck to a spot on the wall. McCain had seen that look on more than one veteran's face as they relived a memory.

"We got ambushed," Nicholson continued. "I was riding shotgun in the lead truck and an RPG slammed into us, just up from the driver's door and blew it off. It killed him instantly and knocked me halfway out of the cab. The insurgents had done what they intended: hitting us first and blocking the road.

"When I came to, I heard the bullets pinging into the body of the truck where they were trying to shoot me. I was hanging out of the vehicle by the remains of my right leg but thankfully, they're crappy shots. More RPGs and small arms fire were raking the convoy. Then I heard this voice ordering his Marines to 'get into the fight and start killing those bastards.'

"The rifle company we were transporting dismounted and started returning fire. All of a sudden, this streak came running towards me from the rear of the convoy. I don't think I've ever seen a human being run that fast, and he was shooting while he ran. He got to me and I saw that it was the young second lieutenant whose platoon we were transporting.

"He pulled me free from the truck and laid me on the ground. That was when I realized my right leg was mostly gone at the knee. It was just being held on by a little tissue and muscle."

Jake pulled his right pants leg up to show Chuck the prosthetic. McCain nodded. The odd gait now made sense.

"So this LT put a tourniquet on me but I'd already lost a lot of blood. When I started fading, he slapped me in the face and told me that he was ordering me to stay alive. He'd yell at me to stay with him and squeeze off some suppressing fire.

"He got real excited after he picked off one of the bad guys who was getting ready to fire another RPG at us. His Marines started moving forward and within minutes they had killed or run off all of the insurgents. They called in a chopper to medevac me and the other casualties out of there."

Nicholson pulled himself out of the memory and took a drink of his bourbon. "I'd love to know whatever happened to that lieutenant.

There's no doubt in my mind he saved my life."

McCain smiled. "Well, if that was a Lieutenant Jimmy Jones, I can tell you exactly what happened to him."

Jake's eyes opened wide. "That was his name! How in the world did you know?" he demanded.

"I am or was, depending on how this thing plays out, the OIC of the Atlanta unit for CDC Enforcement," Chuck answered. "Jimmy's one of my guys and I read his file. He was awarded the Bronze Star with the Combat V for his actions that day.

"His CO recommended him for the Silver Star but it got downgraded. His men stopped the ambush and killed seven of the terrorists. Your driver was the only KIA. You and two others were wounded."

Nicholson nodded. "I didn't know that he'd been decorated. Good for him. He definitely deserved it. I'm surprised to hear he left the Corps. He seemed like a good officer with a promising career ahead of him."

McCain nodded. "He made captain and did a second tour in Iraq. Then his mom was diagnosed with terminal cancer and he got out to be with her during her last year.

"After she passed, he became a cop in Alabama for a few years and then decided to go federal and joined us. He's a good one. I'll hook you guys up after, well, if things ever get back to normal."

"That'd be nice. Anyway, after that I was medically discharged. I was living over in Greenville at the time and was looking on-line for jobs and saw the listing for teachers in the "Commercial Truck Driving," and "Automotive Technology" courses. They must've not had many people apply because they hired me," the Marine chuckled.

They sat in a comfortable silence, sipping their drinks.

"Elizabeth told me that she thinks you can help us with our defenses here," Jake said, his tone flat, clearly not excited by the idea.

Chuck shook his head. "No, from what I've seen you guys have everything under control. Remember, my background is mainly law enforcement. Perimeter and site security is more of a Marine's sweet spot.

"Now, if you'd like, I'd be happy to let you show me around and see what I can see. Sometimes a pair of fresh eyes can notice things that you might've missed. Plus, the army SF guys that I worked with did show me a few tricks."

Jake grunted, satisfied with Chuck's answer. In some ways, McCain was still an unknown entity and Nicholson did not need him just showing up, trying to change things. In reality, though, Jake knew Chuck probably could help them. Nicholson had trained their sentry teams, teaching them all he knew but, even though he was a Marine, he'd seen minimal combat.

"What about all those weapons?" Jake said, motioning towards the other room. "You said something about a proposition?"

"They're all yours. I've already pulled what I wanted and I figure you guys need them more than I do. I'll just need some things in return."

Jake's eyes lit up. "That's a big help, McCain. We only have weapons for about a quarter of the people here. That should put us closer to thirty-five or forty percent of our residents armed."

"How are you set for ammo?"

"Pretty good. The campus police have a stock of 9mm, 5.56, and .12 gauge."

"Great," Chuck replied. "I need some 9 mil and 5.56 to restock my supply. It's been a rough month. I also need a vehicle. Have you got something I can have? Preferably something you don't need back."

Nicholson sat silent for a moment and then nodded his head. "You can have one of the campus maintenance trucks. It's a few years old but it runs great. I teach some of the classes in the automotive repair section and we use the school's vehicle pool to practice tune-ups and oil changes. It should do you good."

"Perfect, thanks. So, Jason and Tina were the only two campus police officers to stick around?" Chuck wondered.

"That's right. This was Storey's room," Jake answered, motioning outward with his hands. "Elizabeth sent a couple of students over here to pack his stuff up before Alicia brought you over."

That makes sense, Chuck thought. Those are his things in the boxes in the other room, stacked in the corner.

"He and Tina didn't have any relatives in the area and so they chose to stay. And, especially lucky for me because Tina and I have gotten really close," Jake smiled. "It's funny. I don't think we ever had a conversation before the zombies showed up but now, let's just say we spend as much time together as we can."

"Nothing wrong with that," McCain said. "She seems like a super person."

Nicholson nodded and asked, "What else?"

"How are y'all set for food? You've got a lot of mouths to feed."

"You and Elizabeth brought us a big load of supplies. With what we already had, we're good for a few weeks. As you'll see at dinner, no one's going to get fat here, but we're all surviving. A couple of our students are hunters and manage to take down the occasional deer and small game. I figure I'll give it two weeks and then we'll need to send another team out."

After another sip of his drink, Jake asked, "Is Elizabeth going with you when you leave?"

Chuck was surprised at the question. "No way. It's too dangerous and she's no cop or soldier. She told me you gave her a little weapons familiarization and I worked with her some, as well, but I don't want to see her get hurt. No, it's better if she stays here."

Even as he said it, Chuck felt conflicting emotions. He was beginning to think that he had actually fallen in love with the girl and couldn't bear the idea of seeing her get hurt again. After Rebecca's death, he didn't think he would ever be able to love again. I guess I was wrong, he thought.

Jake nodded but said, "I saw the way that she looked at you. That's going to be a tough sell."

Outside of Lavonia, Georgia, Friday, 1300 hours

Joey Lester and Wesley Maddox sat at the kitchen table in Wesley's home, several miles east of Lavonia. They were each holding a lit cigarette, with two open bottles of beer leaving rings on the table in front of them. Conversation from the rest of the house carried into them as the crew talked, drank, and smoked weed.

The two men had just walked in the door from their reconnaissance of the Northeast Georgia Technical College. Don and Hoss had accompanied them but had stayed with the trucks while Joey and Wesley slipped into the woods. The gang leaders had learned that you always took at least two vehicles when you had to go somewhere, since you never knew when you would encounter zombies or people with guns. A second vehicle increased your chances of getting away alive.

All of the men had grown up in Franklin or Hart Counties and were familiar with the school. The college was in a remote area, seven miles southeast of the small town. There were scattered homes along the way but Joey and the others had searched them on other looting trips and knew that they had all been abandoned.

Lester had turned into a dirt driveway a quarter mile before reaching the school's entrance, pulling up next to an old, gray doublewide mobile home. Harper followed and they turned both trucks around for a quick escape. This vacant home bordered the college campus, with the school only six hundred yards through the woods.

Several months earlier, right after the zombies had swept through the area, Joey had taken his team down the long driveway to the school. His plan had been to see what had been left behind. He'd had no idea that people were still on campus until he saw the barricade a few hundred feet in front of him and two students pointing guns at them.

Joey and Wesley, along with most of their gang, made their living as burglars. They did have a few car thieves and armed robbers among them, as well, but Lester and Maddox always tried to break into homes and businesses when no one was there. They didn't want to get shot or have to shoot anybody. The last thing that Joey wanted was to be involved in a firefight so upon seeing the armed roadblock at the entrance to the college, the thieves had immediately turned their vehicles around and left quickly. Since then, they had steered clear of the technical school, not knowing how many armed people were on the campus.

Now, however, they wanted to get some payback. All the evidence pointed to people from this school as having been the ones to kill Jerry at the truck stop, and if Joey was right, they were also connected to the deaths of Bo's dad, Larry, as well as Bobby, Ronnie, and 5-0.

The whole gang wanted vengeance but Joey had wanted to do a little recon first. His 9mm Beretta was in a hip holster and he carried a Saiga-12 .12 gauge semi-automatic shotgun. Wesley carried a .45 caliber Glock Model 21 in a shoulder holster and had an AR-15 on a sling across his back. Lester and Maddox both had on camo clothing and waterproof boots. All of the equipment that the crew used had been stolen in residential break-ins.

The burglars didn't know if the college had security patrols but had to assume they did. Their plan was to approach as quietly and as stealthily as possible. If spotted they would retreat to their vehicles and get out of there. If they had to fight, the goal would be to disengage and escape.

After moving slowly for four hundred yards, the two men stopped on a slight ridge overlooking the front of the campus. They went flat on their stomachs next to a massive fallen pine tree. There was a gap of over a foot where the tree was hung up on its stump allowing them to peer under it, hidden from view. Joey pulled out a pair of binoculars and scanned the buildings within his sight line. It was 11:00am but there was no activity at the moment.

Off to their right, Lester spotted movement. A young man and a young woman, both carrying long guns, were walking down a sidewalk behind a large brick building, possibly containing classrooms, Joey thought. They were talking and laughing as they walked, never even glancing towards the wood line off to their right.

"Not the best security I've ever seen," Joey said, softly, passing the binoculars to Wesley. They watched the pair disappear deeper into the campus.

A few minutes later, the sound of a vehicle came from the direction of the driveway into the school. The two men couldn't see the barricade from their position on the ridge but they knew it was a few hundred yards further to their left. Soon, a white Jeep Cherokee drove into sight and pulled under the overhang at the administrative-looking building near the front of the campus.

Joey watched through his binoculars as a girl got out of the driver's seat. An older man, maybe a teacher, met her and they talked and hugged. Wesley took a turn with the glasses. When the girl turned, letting him get a glimpse of her face, he let out a low whistle.

"Whoa! I've haven't seen a girl that good-looking in a long, long time."

Maddox observed a muscular man dressed in black climb out of the backseat of the SUV. He took off a tactical vest and left it inside the vehicle. Wesley handed the binos back to his friend.

"Look at this, Joey!" Maddox hissed. "That guy's wearing 5-0's NASCAR hoodie. You think he was the one who killed him?"

Lester examined the man through the binoculars, noticing his large, muscular frame. His face even had the same "Don't mess with me" attitude that 5-0 always had. Looks like he's got a Glock on his waist, Joey noticed.

"And that jacket the chick is wearing looks like the one Larry had," Joey noted. "Remember? Gray and puffy, we used to call him the Michelin Man."

Wesley got the binos back and took a look. "Yeah, I think you're right. It just don't make sense. That little hottie and that big guy couldn't have taken out 5-0 and all the others. There had to be more of them. We counted, what, three dead ones with school ID on them at the truck stop? I don't get it, man."

Maddox peered closer at the white SUV and saw the many boxes stacked inside of it. He handed the binoculars back to Lester.

"They were the ones who robbed us, Joey. Look at all our stuff in the back of that Jeep."

Joey could see what Wesley was talking about and shook his head. How did these two people pull off such a stunt? Well, they were going to pay for it, that was for sure, Lester thought.

A red-haired woman joined the three people outside the building. There was some hugging and crying between the two women that the burglars could see. A few minutes later, the girl and the big man drove around behind the building they had been stopped at. Wesley could see the damage to the windshield and the blood on the front of the Cherokee. The vehicle left their line of sight but they watched as people excitedly started congregating back there.

Joey tried to count the gathering crowd but he didn't have a good angle to see the structure that everyone seemed to be converging on.

Voices and laughter carried across the campus to the two burglar's position, letting them know that something was happening behind the administrative building. At 11:30am, Lester and Maddox started their withdrawal, crawling slowly until they were out of sight of the campus. By 11:45am, they had reached their companions and started for home.

"So, what are we going to do, Joey?" Wesley asked, taking a long drink of his beer and finishing it. He stood and walked to his back door, opening it and tossing the empty bottle into the backyard. He reached into a cooler sitting just outside and pulled out two more Budweisers, handing one to Lester.

Joey stubbed out his cigarette and quickly lit another one, taking a deep drag. He finished his beer and opened the fresh one that Wesley had just given him. Maddox could see that his friend was nervous. They had worked together for a long time and Joey was always the one who stayed cool when the police got behind them in traffic or if a homeowner pulled up while they were inside ransacking their home.

When the zombies invaded the area, 5-0 had walked away from the Sheriff's Department and given up any pretense of being a cop. Most of the other deputies had left to look after their own families, but Carter abandoned his post to fully immerse himself in the dark side of the law.

He began spending more time with Joey and Wesley and letting them know the full range of criminal activities with which he was involved. They found out that Carter ran prostitutes, oversaw a thriving drug business, and had a number of groups of thieves, besides their own crew. 5-0 had introduced the two men to many of his other team leaders.

Carter explained that with communications being down, it was important that they all have the ability stay in touch. The only way that was going to happen was face-to-face and knowing where each other lived. The members of all the different gangs understood that 5-0 was in overall charge but men like Joey and Wesley ran their own teams, making sure the Boss got his cut of the earnings.

Now, Joey realized that none of Carter's other team leaders even knew that he was dead. He and Wesley would need to make contact with and recruit as many of these other criminals as they could before they launched their attack on the college. They were going to need all the firepower that they could get.

"You know we have to do something," Maddox said. "The guys want revenge and they'll get it with or without us. They'll follow you but we need to come up with a plan."

Lester sighed. "I know. I don't like going in there not knowing what we're up against. I counted about fifty people but I may have counted some twice and there could've been others I couldn't see. We know they have security at that roadblock and we saw those two who looked like they were more interested in each other than patrolling the campus. Have you got any ideas?"

"How many more guys do you think we can round up?" Maddox asked.

"Maybe seven or eight, maybe a few more than that. 5-0 didn't introduce us to everybody and it's hard 'cause we just can't call 'em up. We've got to go try and find them. We could start this afternoon and check on a couple of the boys that live close. Tomorrow we can try and track down a few more, but it ain't gonna be easy. We'll see who we end up with. Even if ten more of 5-0's guys went with us, that's nineteen of us against, what? Fifty, sixty people? Do you like those odds, Wesley?"

Joey took another drink of beer, shaking his head. "I want payback, but I don't want to die getting it."

Wesley nodded. "You're right, but you're forgetting one major ace-in-the-hole we have. We're really good burglars. We've made a nice living getting into people's homes and businesses and haven't got caught since we were kids. Those people we saw at that school didn't seem like they were expecting any trouble.

"I think we can get in easy enough. That's what we do. I'll admit, it might get a little dicey, but if we can get in there late at night, I think we can do some damage and get out. I guess the big question is, 'What message do we want to send?'"

Joey grunted, stubbed out his latest cigarette, and lit another one. "Whaddya think? Somebody's gotta die so we can avenge 5-0 and the other guys. I say we kill the big dude and the hottie, then steal back our supplies and whatever they're guarding at that school."

"Or kill the man and take the girl with us. I think the boys would enjoy gettin' to know her," Maddox winked wickedly at Lester. "But even if we kill her, let's keep it simple. It'd be great if we had enough people to go in there and just take over the place but I don't see us doing that with the few guys we have."

Lester looked more relaxed now. "I like it, Wesley, I like it a lot. Let's nail down some of the particulars and then talk to the guys."

The Northeast Georgia Technical College, Lavonia, Georgia, Friday, 1615 hours

Elizabeth and Chuck walked to the dining room together, her arm looped through his. McCain enjoyed the normalcy of a sidewalk stroll under the tall oak trees with this beautiful woman at his side. He couldn't remember the last time that he'd been able to relax. Beth pointed out several of the buildings and told him what they were used for, chatting away for the entire walk.

McCain had on the jeans that Jake had given him and the t-shirt and sweatshirt that Elizabeth had provided. He had left his long gun and body armor in his room but had on the pistol belt containing his Glock. Chuck had seen a number of other people wearing pistols on the campus but the only ones carrying rifles or shotguns were those on sentry duty.

"Do they have a public display of affection policy on this campus?" McCain asked Benton, smilingly putting his arm around her shoulders and pulling her close.

"Probably, but who's going to enforce it?"

"Do you care if anyone sees us together like this?"

She reached up and clasped her fingers through his hand draped around her shoulders. "I probably should, but we don't have that much time and I want to make the most of it. Plus it's not like we're doing anything, Mr. Celibate," she said, laughingly, giving him a hip bump.

When they walked into the cafeteria, Alicia was waiting for them. "Hi, Miss Benton, Mr. McCain."

"Alicia!" Beth said, smiling and hugging her assistant. "I didn't get a chance to thank you earlier for coming up and standing with me while I was talking to everybody. And thanks for getting Mr. McCain settled. I don't know what I'd do without you."

"Thanks Miss B," her assistant replied, embarrassed but returning the smile. "We're just so glad you're back."

Elizabeth leaned over and spoke into the younger woman's ear. Alicia smiled and nodded. Benton turned back to McCain, touching his arm.

"Chuck, Alicia will take you through the food line and help get you situated. I need to make the rounds and speak to as many people as I can. I want to make sure everybody's OK after losing Officer Storey, Margo, and Lamar. I'll see you in a few minutes."

Beth left them, going around to all the tables, talking to the students, faculty members, and other residents. Chuck noticed again how everyone's face lit up when she spoke to them and how she made a point of not rushing as she conversed with each one individually. Most of the residents got up from their meals to hug

Elizabeth as she came by their tables.

Alicia cleared her throat and said, "Mr. McCain, if you'll come with me, I'll help you get some dinner."

As they walked across the large room, Chuck said, "Alicia, thanks for telling me your story earlier. That was very personal and it meant a lot that you'd trust me with it. It was actually very inspiring and I hope many other people get an opportunity to hear it."

Alicia looked at Chuck's face and into his eyes. Very few people, and even fewer men, had spoken such kind words to her. Sure, many men had commented on her looks or said things to try and get her into bed, which sadly, too often had worked.

Elizabeth had coached Alicia on developing her self-esteem over the last few years but she still had trouble discerning what was sincere encouragement and what was flattery to get her clothes off. Even at the end of the world, there were men and boys on this campus who had made a pass at her. Mr. Nicholson had been very protective and had had several serious conversations with those who had tried to take advantage of her. Nicholson was one of the few men whom Alicia felt she could trust.

As she looked into McCain's eyes, she saw nothing but sincerity. Did he really mean what he said? she wondered. My story inspiring and maybe even helping other people? She had never even thought of that.

Alicia looked down, self-conscious. "Thank you, sir. That's very nice of you to say that. I didn't meant to dump all of that on you, but I guess I got kind of emotional after hearing what Miss Benton went through and about how you risked your life to save her."

"Well, I'm serious about what I just said," Chuck replied. "Your testimony will inspire and encourage a lot of other young people, especially young women, that no matter where we've come from, we always have the opportunity to start over."

As they went through the food line with a number of other campus residents, everyone wanted to thank Chuck. The men shook his hand and all the women wanted to hug him. Dinner was spaghetti with some kind of meat, along with canned vegetables. Alicia led him towards a round table where Jake and Tina were already sitting.

Before they got there, McCain leaned in close to his guide and said, "And you've probably noticed by now that Elizabeth and I kind of like each other, so what you told me gave me a lot of insight into what a special person she really is."

Alicia didn't answer but smiled broadly at Chuck's confession, putting her plate down, sitting to McCain's right, across from the Marine and the campus police officer.

"Hey, Tina. Hey, Jake." McCain nodded at his new friends. "This looks like some awesome chow."

"It's not too bad," said Nicholson. "In honor of having Elizabeth back, I had them to throw in the last of our venison. This cold weather has helped us a lot. One of my students killed a nice deer on the back side of the campus almost two weeks ago and with the freezing temps, the meat hasn't spoiled. Now we just need him to kill another one."

"What do you guys cook with?" McCain asked.

"Propane. One of the things that we always want our scavenger teams to bring back are propane canisters. One of our industrious welding students rigged the big commercial stove back there in the kitchen so we could attach gas canisters to fire up the range once a day."

"Sorry we didn't bring any back with us."

Jake dismissed the idea with a wave of his hand. "Don't worry about it. You and Elizabeth had bigger issues to worry about. We have enough gas to last us a few more weeks if we don't go crazy with it."

The dining room was abuzz with conversations and laughter.

Chuck noticed that Beth had finally made her way through the food line and was approaching their table with her plate. She greeted everyone and set her plate down next to Chuck on his left, promptly removing an extra chair between herself and Nicholson to an adjacent table. As she seated herself beside McCain, he noticed Jake and Tina exchange knowing grins.

"McCain, you want me to take you around the campus tomorrow and show you how our defenses are set up?" Nicholson asked. "I was thinking after breakfast?"

"Sure, that sounds good. And Elizabeth said that you guys have a pretty good gym here. I'd like to get in a few good workouts before I have to head out. My body's getting soft."

"For sure," Jake replied. "Make yourself at home."

Bradley Thomas walked over to their table, placing his food in the empty space on Beth's left side. He looked around for the chair that had just been there, a confused look on his face.

"I could've sworn I saw an empty seat here," he observed.

"Someone else must've needed it, Bradley," Tina said, keeping a straight face.

Not to be turned away, he grabbed a chair from another table and sat down. Bradley leaned in and was just about to say something to Elizabeth but Nicholson beat him to the punch.

"Bradley, I'm putting the next team roster together to go gather supplies. I noticed you still haven't gone out, so I'll put you on the next trip."

"Oh, r-right, Mr. Nicholson," Thomas stammered. "I've been busy with a lot of stuff on campus. And I figured that there were a lot of people who would rather go in my place. You know, people who are better with guns and stuff."

"A man's got to know his limitations," McCain deadpanned, in his best Clint Eastwood impersonation.

Bradley glanced over at the stranger, not sure if he'd been

insulted or not.

"That's nice, Bradley, that you'd think so much of others," Jake continued, "but Elizabeth managed to go out and she practically runs this place."

"Definitely. Please put me on the schedule," Bradley said, smiling weakly at Beth. "I certainly want to pull my weight around here."

Alicia spoke up. "Mr. Nicholson, if you need to add me to a supply team, go ahead. I don't know much about guns either, but if Miss Benton can go, I'll sure follow her example."

"Thanks, Alicia," Nicholson answered, smiling at her, "but I'm not putting any more ladies on the schedule. Thank God we got Elizabeth back but I'm making a command decision that from here on out, we're only sending men. Don't you agree, Bradley?"

Thomas had become very interested in his food and was regretting his decision to sit at their table.

"I'm not so sure," he finally answered. "Women have fought for years to gain equality. I thought that one of the planks of the feminist movement was that they can do whatever a man can do."

"So you want another woman from this school to suffer what Elizabeth went through, is that what you're saying, Bradley?" Chuck asked, staring into his soul.

"That's not what I said," he snapped, glaring at McCain. He quickly looked away from the intensity in the big man's eyes.

Chuck shrugged. "Mr. Nicholson is trying to protect the women in your community. That sounds like a pretty good idea to me."

"Have you thought about when you'll leave, Chuck?" Tina asked, diffusing the tension. "We'd love to have you stay as long as you can, but I know how it feels when you're separated from your kids."

Chuck saw the pain in her eyes. He wondered where her kids were and if she would ever see them again.

"I'll head out on Monday morning," he answered. McCain felt Beth stiffen at the news that he had set a day to leave. She knew that he wasn't staying long, but hearing it still caught her by surprise.

"Now that I have some transportation," Chuck went on, "I'm feeling a lot better about getting over to where my daughter was staying in Hartwell."

"Transportation?" Elizabeth repeated.

"I'm letting him take one of the school's maintenance trucks," Nicholson explained. "That's the least we could do for him after rescuing and bringing you home. And Chuck's added substantially to our firearms arsenal."

"I'm not sure that's a good idea, Mr. Nicholson," Bradley spoke up. "That vehicle belongs to the college and we need to go through the proper channels."

Jake sighed and shook his head. "I don't remember asking for your opinion, Bradley."

The young man started to protest but Tina cut him off, "And after you go to Hartwell, what then, Chuck?"

"That's the question," Chuck answered, looking down. "Hopefully, Melanie left me directions for where they were going. If she didn't…I just don't know."

"It'll be OK. I know you're going to be able to get to her," the police officer said, reaching out and patting one of Chuck's hands.

"Thanks, Tina."

McCain looked at Beth who was staring at her plate with a blank look on her face.

"How's everybody doing?" he asked her. "It was nice watching you work the room, sharing your special brand of sunshine."

She forced a smile, locking eyes with Chuck. He saw a river of emotions flowing inside of her.

"Everybody seems to be doing surprisingly well," Elizabeth finally answered, looking across the table to Jake and Tina. "What do y'all think of having a memorial service on Sunday during our regular chapel?"

"We have a service every Sunday morning," Benton explained to McCain. "One of the faculty members who stayed is a pastor and he leads it. It's amazing how a zombie apocalypse gets people interested in getting closer to God."

"A memorial service is a great idea," said Tina.

Jake nodded. "Yeah, good thinking. We could have a few students share about each person we lost. Let's do it."

Elizabeth turned to Alicia. "Can you help us put it together? We'll need to ask a few people ahead of time who were close to Margo, Lamar, and Officer Storey."

"Yes, ma'am. I'll get right to work on that."

Chuck saw Jake make eye contact with Alicia and give a slight nod of the head towards Tina.

Alicia understood. "Officer Miles, would you like to say a few words about Officer Storey at the service?"

Tina's expression became somber. "I'd be happy to do that, Alicia. Thanks for asking."

Bradley finally saw his opportunity. "I'd love to help you plan the service, Elizabeth. Would you like to meet tomorrow?"

"No, Bradley, I'm not meeting with you. Alicia will let you know if there's anything that you can do."

"I was just trying to help," he said, angrily getting to his feet. He softened his voice, not wanting Elizabeth to see him losing control of his emotions. "I'll see you guys later." He took his empty plate and walked off.

"That boy just doesn't take a hint," Nicholson commented, shaking his head.

Thirty minutes later Chuck and Beth walked out of the dining hall, hand-in-hand. Benton had gotten quiet after she and her co-workers had discussed the memorial service. He knew that she was upset but wasn't sure what he could say to make her feel better.

"So, did you still want to show me around the school?" Chuck asked, looking down at Beth and slipping an arm around her shoulders.

"What do you want to see?" she asked, softly.

"Or we could just find a quiet place to talk?"

She looked up at him and nodded. Beth led him back towards the dorm building but turned down another sidewalk that led into a secluded spot where several park benches were spread out under the large oak trees. She seated herself on the closest one, pulled her feet under her, wrapping her arms around her knees. Elizabeth lowered her head to her chest, closing her eyes.

McCain could feel the temperatures dropping and knew they couldn't stay out here too long. It did feel good to be outside, though. He sat down on the bench, putting his arm back around Elizabeth, enjoying being close to her. For several minutes, neither one said anything. She finally leaned towards the big man, laying her head on his shoulder.

"I've enjoyed watching you interact with your family here," Chuck told her. "These folks really love you."

"Yeah, these are great people. They've all worked hard to build a community here. It's been special to be a part of it." She paused, taking a deep breath, and then continued. "I'm sorry I'm kind of in a funk. When you said you were leaving Monday, I felt like I'd been punched in the stomach."

"We talked about this. You knew it was coming," he said gently.

"But that doesn't make it any easier!" she snapped, pulling away from him. "What am I supposed to do? You go riding off into the sunset and what, I never see you again? I won't know if you've been killed, eaten, or turned into a zombie! Or maybe you find Melanie, which I pray you do, but then you forget about me?"

Beth closed her eyes again but Chuck could see the tears leaking out. A flashback suddenly hit him in the face. The last time that he had been walking around a beautiful college campus with a beautiful woman was that terrible day, months earlier at the University of Georgia. Melanie, Brian, Rebecca, and Chuck had had a wonderful time. They had eaten at one of the best hamburger joints in the small town of Athens.

After lunch, they had strolled through the downtown area and enjoyed a coffee at the Zombie Coffee and Doughnuts. The name had made them all laugh, especially since Chuck and Rebecca were in the middle of fighting zombies and the terrorists who would spread the bio-terror virus. After their coffee and desert, Mel and Brian had guided them around the beautiful UGA campus, ending up in front of Sanford Stadium. That was where Melanie had surprised her dad and Rebecca with tickets for the football game.

The four of them were just getting ready to enter the stadium when McCain had hung back, confessing to his daughter that he was in love with his gorgeous blonde boss. Chuck was planning to share his feelings with Rebecca on their way home from the game. Before they could get into the stadium, however, the zombie virus attack was launched on the unsuspecting university, turning it into a killing field. Within minutes, Rebecca was dead.

In a moment, this memory swept through McCain's mind as he stared off into space. He turned and saw Beth staring at him, the tears still in her eyes. She'd seen the shadow go across his face but then, just as quickly, it was gone. Chuck knew he had screwed up before. He wasn't going to make the same mistake again.

"Elizabeth Benton," Chuck said, sucking in a deep breath, taking both of her hands in his, "I love you. I really, really love you. We don't know what the future holds but I believe that we're supposed to be together. I'm leaving Monday, but I promise you, I'll be back."

He paused, shaking his head and sighing. "Here I am, trying to be all serious, and I end up quoting a line from 'The Terminator.'"

Beth giggled, wiping her eyes. "I don't think I ever saw that movie," she admitted.

"What? You've never seen The Terminator?" he asked, incredulous. "That's an American classic! It's Arnold as the bad guy, terminating everybody. But it's also a nice love story about a man who comes back from the future to save an important woman and ends up falling in love with her. And I'm going to come back for you, well, that is if you want me to."

Elizabeth threw her arms around Chuck's neck and hugged him tightly. "I love you, too, Chuck McCain, and you better come back for me."

After a few minutes, Chuck gently kissed her soft lips. "I have a present for you," he said.

"A present? Really?" she asked, excitedly.

"Yep. I wish I could say it was flowers or expensive chocolates but I still think that you'll like it. The only thing is, it's in my room so you'll need to come with me."

"I see what you're trying to do. I've heard about men like you who lure young women into their room," she said, standing and pulling on his hand. "Come on, lure me."

Outside of Lavonia, Georgia, Friday, 1900 hours

Joey and Wesley had little to show for their recruiting mission that afternoon. Mike Carter's network of criminal associates had not heard that he'd been killed, and they were all shocked at the news. At the same time, however, they weren't shocked enough to volunteer to be a part of the boys' planned attack on the technical college.

When Joey stopped to think about it, he understood. The other teams had nothing to gain by joining them, and much to lose. Of course, if Lester could have promised them a big payday, he knew that they would've jumped right in. If they had enough manpower to take over the entire campus, others would want to participate.

Instead, this was just a revenge hit. Sure, everyone was upset that 5-0 was dead, but most of these guys were thieves, not killers. There was nothing in it for them. Plus, they all realized that they were now free to keep all their profits since their boss was no longer in the picture.

They had visited four of Carter's people today. Only Neil Dodd committed to being a part of the raid, promising to be at Maddox's house by midday Sunday. Dodd had a reputation among all the gangs as 5-0's primary enforcer. If Carter felt that one of his people was holding out on him and he didn't feel like dealing with it himself, he sent Neil Dodd. Neil was visibly angry to hear of Carter's death and seemed to want revenge as much as Lester and Maddox. Dodd also promised to bring some people with him.

All nine of Joey and Wesley's gang sat around the living room drinking and passing around a bong. Candles illuminated the room as they discussed their plan for getting vengeance. At this point, they needed some extra bodies if they were going to successfully get onto the vocational school campus, kill the big man wearing 5-0's hoodie, and kill or snatch that woman. Tomorrow they would visit seven more of Carter's criminal associates, hopefully with better luck.

"When are we going in, Joey?" Don Lester asked his brother.

"I was thinking Sunday night. How does that sound?" The mixture of weed and alcohol had calmed Joey's nerves. "It'll take all day tomorrow for us to go out and try to round up some more of 5-0's guys. I hope we can do better tomorrow than we did today. We got Neil, but other than him, today was a total waste.

"After we figure out who all's going with us, we need to talk about it some more and come up with a good plan. The main focus of the mission needs to be: get in, pop the big dude, grab the girl, and get out."

The much bigger Lester brother took a deep hit of the marijuana, holding it for a few seconds before exhaling a cloud of smoke.

"The problem with weed is, it makes me even hungrier than normal. That dude and his little chick really cleaned us out over there at that safe house. We had some good supplies locked up safe and sound there. Now, my stomach is growling because our stores are low."

"I bet they've got a lot of food over at that college just waiting on us," Hoss chimed in. "If Joey and Wesley saw fifty or more people, they're keeping 'em fed somehow."

"Yeah," replied Don, angrily. "They're eating good 'cuz they cleaned out our safe house. I think we need to load up while we're there and restock some of our supplies."

"Look," Joey cut in, taking another puff off of the bong. "We've got to stay focused here," tilting his head back and blowing the smoke towards the ceiling. "We're going to be outnumbered real bad. I think we stick to the plan of getting in, taking out that guy, and grabbing the hot chick. If she resists, we kill her, too, and then bug out.

"We can grab whatever's close, but they have a security team and they aren't going to just let us walk in there, kill one of 'em, kidnap a girl, grab a big load of supplies, and then leave. And we don't know if anybody else besides Dodd is going to join us or not. Hopefully, we'll have better luck tomorrow when we visit some more of 5-0's people."

"What do we do if we strike out again tomorrow?" Wesley asked.

Bo Harris spoke up. "We're still going whether we get anybody else or not, right, Joey?" The statement was as much of a challenge as it was a question. "That man killed my daddy and I'm gonna kill him. And that girl you two saw needs to pay as well, but we can let her pay on installments."

Several of the other gang members laughed at Bo's crude joke. Joey looked around the room and saw everybody staring at him. Was he tough enough to keep leading them? This seemed to be the unspoken question. He took a swallow of beer and made eye contact with Bo.

"Oh, yeah, we're going. Sunday night. And if it's just us, we'll do the best we can. You guys need to know, there's a lot of people on that campus. Like I said, I counted at least fifty and there's probably more than that. We're really going to have to figure out the best way to get in, and we're going to need to be really sneaky.

"They're going to have us outgunned but I reckon those college students ain't never seen any real action. We'll go by one of the other safe houses beforehand and make sure we've got plenty of firepower and ammo. Plus, we need to restock our food," he said, nodding at his brother.

Bo sat back and nodded, satisfied, enjoying another pull on the smoking bong when it was passed to him. He hoped that he was the one who got to put a bullet into that big bastard's head for killing his old man. And he planned on being the first one to enjoy that sweet girl. Maybe they could even grab a couple more of those little college cuties while they were at it.

The Northeast Georgia Technical College, Lavonia, Georgia, Friday, 1930 hours

They had started in Chuck's room. Beth had lit the three candles that were in the sitting room. In the candlelight, Chuck handed Elizabeth her present. It was a 9mm Glock 19 pistol. He gave her three magazines, ammo and a holster to go with it. He had found the gun in the stash at the kidnappers' house, no doubt stolen off of someone else whom they had ambushed.

"I want you to wear this or carry it on you all the time. I know you guys have a security team, but I'd feel so much better knowing you have a firearm to protect yourself. It's a little bit different from that Springfield that you were carrying, but we've got two days for me to give you some lessons."

Beth's eyes lit up. "Oh, I'd like you to give me some lessons, Mr. McCain. Up close and personal, just like last time? Yes, please!"

He laughed and said, "I bet you would. I'd offer you a drink to warm you up but the only thing I have is some bourbon and we both know that you and whiskey don't mix so well."

Now it was her turn to giggle. "You're never going to let me live that down, are you? I'm not even sure what all I said."

"Trust me, it was memorable."

"Well?" she grabbed at his ribs, trying to tickle him. "Aren't you going to tell me? How about if you come over to my room? I have a nice bottle of Cabernet Sauvignon that I've managed to hoard and I'd love to share it with you and maybe loosen your tongue up a little."

"Do you think we need a chaperone?" he asked. "I don't want your neighbors spreading rumors about how you were spending time alone in your room with a strange man."

Benton chuckled. "If you knew all the hanky-panky that's happening in this dorm, you'd be shocked. I mean think about it. There isn't a lot going on and entertainment options are limited.

"I'm just hoping no one ends up pregnant. We don't have any doctors here and I don't know if Karen has ever delivered any babies. That would create a whole different type of campus drama."

They sipped their wine in the flickering candlelight of Beth's small living room. Elizabeth was feeling better now and both of them enjoyed sitting, talking, and continuing to get to know each other better. Chuck had shown her how to wear the Glock after attaching the leather holster to one of her belts. The gun sat perfectly against her right hip. McCain planned on working with Benton as much as he could over the next two days, helping her to become familiar with the pistol, teaching her how to draw and fire it.

After several glasses of wine, Chuck knew he needed to go back to his room and get some sleep. Before he could get up, though, Elizabeth set her glass down, moving onto Chuck's lap, straddling him. They kissed for several minutes until Beth finally laid her head against his chest.

"Take me with you when you leave," she said, quietly. "I can help you."

He didn't answer her right away. McCain had known this conversation would come and he wanted to handle it correctly. He kissed her on top of the head and said, "No, I can't do it."

"Why not?" she asked, pleading. "You know you need a driver. You saw how well I drove on the way up here. It's dangerous out there for one person on their own."

"I know, but there are two reasons why I'm not taking you," Chuck answered. "Number one, these people all need you here. You're one of the primary leaders and they're looking to you for guidance. You know that your place is here, at least for now.

"Number two, I love you and I can't bear the thought of you getting hurt. There are no guarantees that I can protect you where I'm going. I'm not even sure I can protect myself. If I end up having to worry about you out on the road, I might get both of us killed, and the thought of that scares me more than us being apart. Stay here. You'll be safe and they need your leadership."

"Okay," she said, resignedly. "I won't argue with you, but you're wrong about one thing. My place isn't here anymore. My place is with you. Even while we're apart, my heart will be with you, so you'd better hurry back to claim it!"

Chapter Six

Evil Intentions

The Northeast Georgia Technical College, Lavonia, Georgia, Saturday, 1000 hours

Chuck and Jake walked across a wet, grassy field towards the edge of the technical college's campus. With the daytime temperatures in the mid-forties, most of the snow had melted, leaving just a few patches where the sun had not yet reached. Back to their right was the main driveway coming into the campus, as well as Admin and several other buildings.

McCain was wearing his pistol belt, his body armor over his sweatshirt, and his rifle slung across his chest. Nicholson was similarly attired with a Sig Sauer Sig516 rifle slung over his shoulder. His Kimber pistol was secured in a holster on his side and a lit cigarette hung from his mouth.

"That's a nice .45 you've got," Chuck observed.

"I love my Kimber. I've always been a big fan of big bullets. What about you? Are you really a 9 mil fan or is that just what you had to carry for work?"

"I guess it's both. This is my issued Glock 17, but I like the .45. I even carried one early in my police career. But I know for a fact that if hadn't been for the high capacity of my Glock I wouldn't be here. Starting off with eighteen rounds before I have to reload has kept me from getting eaten by zombies several times."

"Fair enough," Jake shrugged. "Whatever works. When the first wave of Zs came through here, me and Jason put them down with .22s. I had a Ruger 10/22 rifle and he had a Browning Buckmark pistol. We both had other guns with us but we wanted to see if the little bullets would work."

"It sounds like they did," Chuck commented.

"Mostly. We used the .22s because we didn't have any idea how many zombies were in the area and we didn't want the sound of our shots to carry. The main problem we saw with the little bullets was it occasionally took two or three shots to put one down. Those rim fires didn't always penetrate the skull as well as I would've liked, but yeah, they worked."

Nicholson actually moved quite well on his prosthetic leg over the large field surrounding the campus. The school had open space of several hundred yards from the college buildings to the forest that encircled it. This was a large buffer zone for sentries to pick off Zs or criminals who tried to cross during the day. Of course, at night it would be a different matter entirely because no one on campus had night-vision goggles.

"How'd Elizabeth take it when you said you were leaving Monday?" Jake asked.

Chuck shook his head. "About as well as could be expected. You saw her at dinner. When she heard what I said, she looked like she was going to be sick."

"I told you it was gonna be a tough sell. That girl's in love with you and I hope you don't break her heart."

"Man, I already feel bad enough. I've fallen in love with Beth but I don't want to see her get killed. It would just be too risky to take her along."

Nicholson nodded. "You're right. It's dangerous out there. I've got her Cherokee over at the shop where we teach auto repair and some of my students are going to fix it up for her. You guys had an eventful ride. A bullet hole, a damaged front end, a smashed windshield, and a really nice coating of blood and gore."

They were almost to the edge of the forest, when Jake paused and turned to McCain.

"For what's it worth, we'll take care of Elizabeth for you. I'm not letting her go out on any more raids. I didn't want her to go on that one but she insisted, saying she needed to lead by example. She has nothing more to prove and, like I said last night, I'm not sending any more of our women out. There are plenty of other ways to keep them busy around here."

McCain was thankful for Nicholson's words. Beth did not need any more adventures.

Chuck had asked for the walk around the edge of the forest so he could look for likely entrance points. With only one driveway, there was a real possibility for intruders to sneak in through the forest. McCain wanted to see how good Nicholson's security measures were on the far edge of the perimeter.

"We really have two perimeters," Jake said, stopping and pointing at the edge of the woods. "This is the outer one. We've got trip flares set up ten feet inside the wood line on anything that even looks like a trail or an access point."

"That's cool. Where'd you get the flares?" McCain nodded, peering intently into the woods.

"I've always loved this kind of stuff. I'm a Marine, after all. I already had some but we looted an Army-Navy Surplus Store a while back and found all kinds of useful items."

"Have you ever had animals trip them?" Chuck could see that the undergrowth was not very thick here, making it easy to see almost a hundred yards deep into the hardwood forest.

"Maybe it was an animal. We had one go off in the middle of the night a month or so ago. We got into position and waited. One of my security guys fired a couple of flares up into the air to illuminate the area, but we never saw anything.

"We did have zombies trip some flares one night not long after we killed that first batch at the barricade. Eight of those nasty things came stumbling through the forest one night at 0200hrs. Tina was in my office manning communications and I was actually sleeping in my own bed for a change. I heard the whistles, which is what we use to call everyone to action, so I jumped up, threw my stuff on, and got there before the shooting started.

"It was good that I was there. When those kids started shooting, they couldn't hit crap. We threw up some flares and killed all of them inside fifty yards. After the last one fell, I looked down and realized I'd forgotten my pants. I'd put my leg on, thrown on my web gear, grabbed my rifle, but I forgot my pants and showed up in my boxers."

McCain laughed. "I bet that made a lasting impression on the guys."

"It would've been OK if it had been guys, but most of the security working that night were girls."

Chuck smiled and shook his head. "And you've got the trip flares around the entire campus?"

"Mostly. We started running short so we didn't rig the areas where the forest is the thickest behind the school. So, yes, it's not as secure as I'd prefer but we only have so many flares. We put a couple back there, just not many."

Jake started walking again, wanting to continue the tour. McCain was still staring into the forest.

"What's on the other side of these woods, Jake?"

Nicholson stopped when he realized McCain wasn't following

him. "Nothing really. Adams Farm Road is the main road in front of the school. Why?"

"How far through the woods is that road?"

"A few hundred yards, I guess."

"Can you show me where the flares are so I don't trip them? I want to take a look at something."

Jake hesitated. "Sure. I was wanting to walk you around the rest of the perimeter, though."

"It's probably nothing," Chuck said, "but I want to check something out. I want to see how easy it would be to get through these woods. If you want to wait here, no problem. I can catch up with you later if you don't want to go."

"I'll come with you; I need to show you where the flares are anyway," Jake responded, hearing the slight challenge in Chuck's voice.

Nicholson guided the two of them around trip wires until they were inside the woods.

"Now what?" he asked.

McCain didn't answer as he stepped past Nicholson, concentrating on the ground in front of him, moving deeper into the forest. Ten minutes later, Chuck stopped suddenly and knelt down, pointing to fresh footprints making a trail towards the school. Jake's eyes widened at the tracks that had been left behind on the muddy ground.

"Do your teams come into the woods?" Chuck asked, quietly.

Jake shook his head. "No, these aren't ours. My people don't have the training to patrol the forest."

McCain knew the prints were at least a day old but he didn't want to take any chances, silently clicking the selector on his rifle to "Auto." He motioned to Nicholson to follow him and cover their rear. The muddy tracks looked like they had been created by two people wearing boots. Chuck and Jake moved slowly for a hundred and fifty yards, climbing a slight ridge, and stopping at a large downed pine tree.

Chuck saw the indentions where two intruders had lain. He got down on his stomach, peering under the tree. He figured they were a hundred and twenty yards inside the wood line and then another hundred yards from the Admin building. One would not have a commanding view of the campus from here but could observe this area near the entrance completely undetected. I wonder if our visitors have been watching any other parts of the campus? he pondered.

"These are very fresh tracks," McCain told his companion, getting to his feet and pointing to the ground. "I'm guessing whoever they are were here within the last twenty-four hours."

Nicholson nodded, clearly disturbed by this news. "What now?"

"Let's follow the prints back to where they entered the woods and see what we can see."

Twenty minutes later, the two men exited the woods at a gray doublewide trailer with a dirt driveway, noting with alarm the fresh tire tracks and two more sets of boot prints. Nicholson and McCain moved cautiously behind the abandoned residence, where they saw the back door standing open. A quick search of the interior revealed that it was empty except for some old furniture that had been left behind.

Standing next to the fresh tracks on the driveway, Jake looked at Chuck with new respect. "How'd you know?"

McCain shrugged. "I didn't. It's just that the trees on this side of the campus are mostly hardwoods, so the undergrowth isn't very thick. Definitely not where I'd approach from, but the guys that we're dealing with strike me as the type to take the path of least resistance. And if it's the same ones I saw at the kidnappers' house, it's no surprise they'd be doing a little recon if they figured out where we are from the school ID cards."

"You said yesterday you didn't think they'd try anything."

"Who knows how criminals think?" Chuck smiled bitterly. "I can't imagine that small group I saw trying to assault this campus but obviously, someone has been here, seeing what they could see."

Jake led them back to the school property and they continued walking around the campus. The rest of the forest surrounding the college was thick with undergrowth and briars, Chuck noticed. As they completed their loop of the outer perimeter, two members of the campus security team approached them.

One was a tall, slim man in his thirties wearing glasses with a pistol belt over his jeans and web gear over his black coat. The other was a muscular younger man wearing black cargo pants, a cammo jacket, with a large black canvas pouch attached to his belt. The older of the two was carrying a tricked-out AR-15 with a flashlight attached to the front rail and an ACOG scope mounted on top of the gun. His companion cradled a scoped, bolt-action hunting rifle with a black composite stock. Both men had whistles hanging around their necks. They paused as they got to McCain and Nicholson.

"Hey, Jake, Mr. McCain," the senior of the two said. "What brings you way out here?"

"Robert, Todd," Nicholson acknowledged. "I'm just showing our guest around. You guys see or hear anything?"

Both men shook their heads. "All quiet," Robert answered.

Jake told them of their discovery of intruders. The concern was evident on both their faces.

"For now, gentlemen, let's keep this quiet," Nicholson told them. "I don't want to cause a panic. I'll brief the rest of the security team later."

Both men nodded in agreement.

Jake looked at Chuck, his hand on the shoulder of his sentry with the AR-15.

"Robert teaches in our Computer Information Systems Program but he's also a competitive shooter. He's helped me with a lot of the firearms training for our people. He's a really good instructor. Todd's a student in our Emergency Medical Technician Program. It's always good to have an EMT around."

McCain smiled at the men. "Nice to meet you, Robert. Todd and I met briefly yesterday when he let Elizabeth and me in at the roadblock."

"Mr. McCain, I haven't gotten a chance to thank you for what you did out there and for bringing Elizabeth back," Robert said, extending his hand. Todd nodded in agreement.

"Please, call me 'Chuck,'" he smiled, taking the proffered hand. "I'm glad I was there for Elizabeth. I'm sorry about your other friends."

"Thank you, sir," Todd replied.

Robert and Todd continued their patrol while Jake and Chuck walked back across the field towards the inner perimeter. Nicholson motioned at the retreating figures.

"We run two patrols at a time. Those guys will walk the outer circle like you and I did. I have another pair who have the inner ring. Since we don't have any night-vision, once darkness hits, both pairs walk the inner ring."

The secondary perimeter of which Nicholson was speaking was the outer sidewalk encircling the school's buildings. McCain had only been on the interior sidewalks during his short stay at the college. Jake walked him around the walkway and showed him the fighting positions they had set up every hundred and fifty feet. Most of them were three- or four-person foxholes surrounded by sandbags.

"We're limited in the number of people that we have so there are times when I have to pair up a male and a female to patrol the perimeter together. That hasn't worked out so well. I get out and walk all hours of the day or night to check on our teams and I've caught them making out instead of patrolling."

"They have the same problem in the military," McCain chuckled. "I mean, what could possibly go wrong with assigning a nineteen year old guy and a nineteen year old girl to sentry duty out in the middle of nowhere?"

"Call me old-fashioned," Jake admitted. "I just don't feel comfortable pairing up two girls. I think it's safer having at least one male per team, but I've never caught two women making out with each other. I just feel better having some guys out there. Today, Robert and Todd are together and Jessica and Maria are together. One pair works the outer perimeter, the others have the inner one for a while and then they swap."

"Complacency breeds a casual attitude," Chuck commented. "When I was a street cop, a road sergeant, that was one of the few things that earned one of my officers an ass-chewing. If they didn't use good tactics and didn't have their head in the game, I'd be all over them."

Nicholson nodded in agreement. "It was the same with my guys and girls in Iraq. We were in a war zone but because we weren't frontline troops I was always having to adjust somebody's attitude."

"I'm sorry for being nosy," said McCain, after they had almost finished their loop of the sidewalk, "but Tina got kind of emotional last night when I was talking about finding my daughter. I got the feeling that there are some issues with her kids?"

Nicholson looked at his companion, trying to decide what to say. He finally sighed.

"Yeah. You're right. She has a son and a daughter but has no idea what's become of them.

"Her loser of an ex-husband dumped her several years ago and ran off with his secretary. Tina's kids are her life and she's a great mom. Her son, John, joined the army after high school and drives tanks. Guess where he ended up?"

"Iran?"

"You got it. It wasn't a long war but he was over there when the Iranian terrorists launched those last virus attacks here. She feels that he's probably safe at some base in the Middle East somewhere.

"Her daughter, Missy, is another story. She moved to Manhattan a few years ago to pursue her dream of becoming an actress. She's actually had a few roles, both on and off Broadway."

Jake looked across the campus. "Missy texted her mom right after the car bomb went off near the 9/11 Memorial. She was only five or six blocks away, walking to a job interview, and heard the explosion. Tina told her to find some place safe and get off the street. She never heard from her again."

Chuck closed his eyes. "Man, that just sucks. I won't say anything to her unless she brings it up."

The two men ended the tour back at the administration building where Jake pulled out a master key, and opening the front door, motioned for Chuck to go in first. Tina sat at a desk, formerly the domain of the receptionist, with six field telephones in front of her. A large map of the college campus hung on the wall next to her.

"And this is the communications center," Nicholson said, with a laugh. "We have walkie talkies but they're useless since we have no electricity and they have to be recharged. These field phones only need D batteries to work and we have a pretty good stock of those. Anything going on, Beautiful?"

Tina smiled, but saw something in Jake's eyes. "No, all quiet. Did you see anything?"

"We've had people watching us," he answered, telling her what Chuck had found.

She didn't say anything, trying to imagine what it might mean. Jake stepped over, putting his arm around Tina's shoulder.

"Don't worry. It's gonna be OK," he told her, kissing her on the lips. The woman's eyes opened wide in surprise and embarrassment, looking over at Chuck. She gently pushed Jake away.

"Not now, Jake. Sorry, Chuck," she said.

"Don't apologize to him," Nicholson grinned. "I mean, he's in love with a girl half his age."

McCain laughed. "Amazing, huh? A sweet girl like Elizabeth falling for an old guy like me?"

"You're not that old, Chuck," Miles said.

"Sure, he is!" replied Jake. "Of course, I've got my hands full with you." He leaned over and tried to kiss Tina again. She laughed, turning away, and he only managed to get her cheek.

"See, what I mean? Tina's too fast for me, but she's got me wrapped around her little finger."

"After all that Elizabeth's been through, we're glad to see her happy again, thanks to you," Tina said, nodding at Chuck with a warm smile.

Nicholson nodded. "That's true, my dear. Where was I, McCain? The good-looking redhead in the room distracted me. Oh, yeah, the field telephones. We snagged six pairs from that army surplus store.

"There's one at the main entrance roadblock, and another four are divided out among the fighting positions I showed you on the inner perimeter. The sentries are supposed to call in as they walk around the sidewalk. It takes ten to fifteen minutes to get from phone to phone if they aren't rushing or making out. The last phone is in my room so Tina or whoever's working the switchboard can reach me.

"Again, not perfect, but between the phones, whistles, and the sound of gunfire, we should be able to determine pretty quickly where a potential intruder might be. We have a quick response force that is supposed to respond to any alarm within five minutes or less. We've drilled the QRF, but in the middle of the night, in a crisis, who knows how they'll respond?

"So now that you've seen everything and, especially since we know that we've had some intruders, I'd like your feedback. Like you said, sometimes a fresh set of eyes might see something that I've missed and obviously I missed something really big. But, I think that a conversation of that magnitude needs to be handled over a glass or three of that nice bourbon you have."

Chuck laughed. "Sure, Jake. No problem. Let me go check in with Beth and see what she's up to. I also want to use your gym to get a workout in, so let's plan on connecting later this afternoon."

East of Carnesville, Georgia, Saturday, 1500 hours

The three-car convoy turned onto the dirt driveway several miles outside of Carnesville. This was their last stop of the day. None of Carter's other team leaders or gang members wanted to be part of Joey and Wesley's raid on the college campus. They were content to ride out the zombie apocalypse, robbing and looting wherever they could, but a suicide mission? Not so much.

Greg Davis peered out the blinds of his singlewide trailer, clutching his Mossberg .12 gauge pump shotgun. He'd known they'd come for him, he just hadn't known when. Davis watched the nine men exit the two pickups and the passenger car. Surprisingly, he didn't see 5-0 with them. He figured Carter would handle this one himself, or have sent Neil Dodd. Neil was almost as scary as 5-0.

Greg recognized Joey Lester and Wesley Maddox and assumed the rest of the men with them were their gang. They were all armed, which was normal in the current state of affairs, but that fact only heightened Greg's paranoia. While Davis knew who Lester and Maddox were, he had never known 5-0 to use them for his enforcement or disciplinary duties. Maybe 5-0 had promoted them? Or would coming after him be a demotion?

Greg's memory of the previous week's events was a bit hazy, but he hadn't forgotten the fear he'd felt watching that big man, who had called himself "Chuck," gun down Tonya and then threaten to kill him. Thankfully, the murderer had not found all of his drugs. Greg always carried some crystal meth on him in both of his socks. After Chuck had left that day, resuming his own journey, Davis fired up the small metal pipe, already loaded with the drug. The rush was instantaneous and for a few fleeting moments, Greg felt better.

The feeling didn't last, though. It never did, quickly being replaced with anxiety and paranoia. He only had a small amount of meth left and needed to get back home where the rest of his drug stash was hidden. A look across the room at Tonya's dead body and the whimpering baby beside him quickly brought him back to reality.

I can't go home. Tonya's dead and that bastard stole 5-0's drugs. Mike's going to kill me, Greg knew.

"But it wasn't my fault," he said, out loud. "How was I supposed to know that the guy was going to shoot her? He was supposed to just give up his stuff and leave."

After Tonya and Greg had entered the abandoned house, Chuck had stayed outside to deal with the zombies that they had all heard growling nearby. Greg told Tonya that they would rob the stranger as soon as they got a chance. If he resisted, they'd have to kill him, but they sure didn't want to attract any more Zs with gunshots.

Tonya was a good, submissive prostitute who always did exactly what 5-0 and Greg told her to do. Carter had trained her well and the girl knew that her own supply of drugs was dependent on following orders. When Greg had told her to rob Chuck, he'd had no doubt that she would do it.

Davis understood, or thought he understood, that most men would hesitate to shoot a woman, preferring to just comply and give her what she wanted. Why hadn't that Chuck guy just gone with the program and given up his guns and equipment? Instead, Mr. Tough

Guy had to shoot Tonya, hit me in the face, and leave me handcuffed all night. Then, he took our stuff. The big man had even stolen the little bit of food that they'd had for this short trip. Davis put his head in his hands as he sat against the living room wall.

"All you had to do was just leave your guns and then get out," he mumbled, feeling the anger rising inside of him. "But no, you had to be some kind of bad ass. Kill the woman, punch me, and then take our guns, drugs, and food. You better hope I don't ever run across you again, Chuck."

This was supposed to have been an easy job. Greg had been running drugs and girls for 5-0 for the past six years. The corrupt cop had started off paying Davis in cash. As Greg's meth habit grew worse, though, Carter started compensating him in drugs and sexual favors from the hookers.

Carter's instructions for this mission had been simple. Take Tonya and the drugs to an address a few miles south of where they had met Chuck. This was the compound of a biker gang that 5-0 did a lot of business with. Tonya would be their party girl for a week and in return, the bikers would give Greg a bag of weapons to take back to Carter as payment.

Greg and Tonya had left after lunch on Monday in Greg's 2005 Nissan Sentra. Davis should have been back home that afternoon, but whatever money the drug dealer should have spent on maintaining his car had long been smoked up in the form of crystal meth. The thirteen-year old Sentra had sputtered to a stop eight miles north of the abandoned house.

Tonya had been so scared having to take Jeremy out in the cold. What if the baby cried and they got eaten by zombies? Thankfully, they hadn't encountered any people, living or dead, on their walk until Chuck had invited them to share the house for the night.

The reality of his situation hit Greg in the face. What if he comes back? the sudden thought frightening him. Oh, my god, what if that

Chuck guy comes back to kill me? I've got to leave right now!

"But he said not to follow me," Greg mumbled to himself, the meth intensifying his paranoia. He has to be long gone by now. It's time to get outta here, he thought, as he scrambled to get his stuff together, gathering his few possessions. He decided to light his pipe for another quick hit before hitting the road.

"Oh, that feels so good," he murmured.

Baby Jeremy started to get fussy and wanted out of his carrier. Greg glanced at the child and shook his head. Davis suspected that the baby was Carter's son but, really, the list of possible fathers for Jeremy was quite long. He might even be my son, he thought in surprise.

Greg had walked across the room, knelt beside the child and put the pacifier in his mouth. After a moment, he had quickly stood, turned his back on Jeremy, and bolted out the front door.

"Greg? Are you in there?" Joey asked, knocking on the front door of the run-down trailer. "It's me, Joey Lester. Listen, man. We need to talk. 5-0 and a bunch of his guys are dead."

Davis stayed quiet in the dark living room, clutching the shotgun tightly. He'd been smoking meth almost non-stop since Thursday, his mind foggy and his thought processing slow. This could be a trap, he thought. How could Mike be dead? That didn't make any sense. Who could kill 5-0? Something about Joey's words rang true, though. He had always known Lester to be a straight shooter.

The front door opened a crack and Joey saw a pair of sunken eyes peering out at him. The mixture of Greg's body odor, vomit, and raw sewage hit Lester and Maddox in the face.

"Whoa, Greg," said Wesley, "you been crapping inside?"

Without running water, most people did their business in a bucket and carried it outside daily. The odor from inside the mobile home smelled like an outhouse.

"You okay, Greg?" Joey asked.

He knew of Davis' drug habit and proclivity towards binges. Lester had never understood why Carter had kept Greg working for him. One day, Joey had gotten the nerve to ask his boss about it. 5-0 had shrugged and told Lester that Greg was a childhood friend who had been there for him in a moment of need.

A quiet voice came through the partially opened door, "Did you say Mike is dead?"

Joey nodded and told Greg about the scene of death they had found in their safe house. Lester spoke slowly, making sure Davis was digesting what he was telling him. When Joey finished, the front door opened all the way and the gaunt figure of Greg Davis stepped out onto the small wooden front porch, sitting down on the top step, laying his shotgun across his legs.

"I thought 5-0 had sent you guys to kill me," Greg said, looking around at the other men.

Lester knew that meth tended to make its users paranoid. "Why would he send us to kill you, man? You were one of his favorites."

Davis told the group what happened the previous Monday and how Tonya had been killed and the drugs stolen. In Greg's version, though, Chuck had robbed the two of them, gunning down Tonya when she tried to resist. A stunned silence greeted him when he finished.

"He…he killed Tonya?" Hoss Harper finally asked in disbelief. She had been his favorite of Carter's girls and he'd visited her every chance he got.

"What did this guy look like, Greg?" Maddox asked.

"He was big, probably about the same size as Mike. Dark hair. He had on dark clothes and gear like a soldier or something. He had one of those military rifles, an M-16 I think."

Joey and Wesley exchanged surprised looks. "That sounds like the same guy we saw at the college wearing 5-0's NASCAR hoodie," Lester said.

Maddox nodded. "It sure does."

Something occurred to Hoss. "Where's Tonya's baby?"

Greg suddenly looked uncomfortable. "I guess that guy, 'Chuck' was the name he gave us, took the baby with him."

"So this Chuck was walking and he stole a baby to carry around with him? That don't make any sense," Wesley observed. "And he didn't have no baby when Joey and me saw him drive into the college."

"I don't know," stammered Greg. "He must've gotten rid of the kid by then. You'll have to ask him."

"Why didn't he kill you, too?" Don Lester asked. "I mean he was pissed off enough to kill Tonya and took all your stuff, including that kid. Why would he leave you alive?"

"Like I said, you'll have to ask him. I just knew 5-0 was going to be mad. Those bikers are probably pissed, too, 'cuz they didn't get the drugs or the girl."

It was obvious to everyone that Greg Davis was strung out on his drug of choice but it was also clear that he had encountered the man who had probably killed Mike Carter and four of his associates. There were some glaring holes in Greg's story, especially concerning Tonya's baby. For now, though, they needed Davis to help them, if they could keep him off the pipe until tomorrow night when they raided the school.

The Northeast Georgia Technical College, Lavonia, Georgia, Saturday, 1400 hours

McCain had gone back to the dorm to see what Beth was doing. She hadn't been in her room, so he'd walked over to the fitness center and lifted weights for an hour. Chuck had the facility to himself. It had been several weeks since his last gym session and his muscles were enjoying the burning sensation of being worked hard.

After not lifting in a while, McCain knew not to fully exert himself, so he went for about eighty percent of his normal load. He had worked his chest and was just wrapping up training his biceps when he heard the front door open.

"I figured this was where you'd be. It's a good thing none of the other girls on campus know you're in here or this place would be packed out," Elizabeth said, eyeing his bulging muscles as he curled a hundred-pound barbell on the preacher bench.

"You think so?" he asked, breathing hard.

"Oh yeah. So, let's just keep this our little secret. I don't need any competition."

"You have nothing to worry about," Chuck said, grabbing Beth and squeezing her in a sweaty hug. "I think you're probably the only girl on campus who has a thing for older guys."

"Ooh, you're all wet and smelly," she laughed, trying unsuccessfully to pull away. "Yuck, let me go!"

"Never," McCain said, kissing her.

They walked back to the dorm together. Since the plumbing was only turned on three evenings a week, a fifty-gallon drum of water was kept in the large bathroom located on each floor. The one on the second level was designated for women and the first floor's was for men. Chuck took a sponge bath and then joined Elizabeth in her room, having decided, for now at least, not to worry her with the news of people watching the campus.

McCain took Benton through a familiarization of her new Glock pistol. After he got her comfortable with the function of the gun, he had her dry fire it. Chuck saw that there was already a new confidence in the way that Beth handled the firearm. He needed her to focus on developing this skill-set so that he wouldn't have to worry as much about her while they were apart.

When she put her holster on and started practicing her draw, Elizabeth saw Chuck's approving look. She was already beginning to read his face, seeing in his eyes that he was impressed with her improvement, or maybe my figure, she mused. Or more likely, both.

Her thoughts returned to the task at hand as she heard Chuck say that if she could become more proficient, he'd be much less worried about her safety. Something clicked inside of the young woman. She continued to draw and dry fire the Glock more purposefully, every repetition programming Beth's muscle memory. After over an hour of training, though, she needed a break. McCain was standing just behind her, patiently making small adjustments to her stance and grip.

"I know why you're standing behind me," she commented, thinking he was going to give her the technical answer about needing to be in a good position to see what she was doing wrong.

He smiled. "It's the best position to make adjustments to your stance but, I have to admit, the view is pretty nice as well."

Feigning insult but secretly pleased, Elizabeth said, "What kind of firearms instructor are you? Are you trying to take advantage of me?"

"Maybe. The thought has definitely crossed my mind," he acknowledged with a laugh, reaching for her.

A loud knock came from across the hall at Chuck's room. Disappointed, he opened Elizabeth's door to see Jake holding his two glass tumblers. Nicholson turned and saw McCain coming out of Benton's room.

"You ought to just move in with her, McCain," Nicholson said, smiling. "It'd save you a lot of time and energy."

Beth came out into the hallway and saw the glasses Jake was holding. "So is this male-bonding time?" she asked, looking at Chuck.

Nicholson answered for him. "I showed your boyfriend around

the perimeter this morning. Now, he's going to let me know his thoughts and recommendations. Over a glass of bourbon, of course."

Beth smiled and shook her head at the two men.

"You're welcome to join us," Chuck told her, with a twinkle in his eye. "Although, I doubt you want Mr. Nicholson to see you after you've had a little whiskey."

The girl slapped his arm and laughed. "That's mean! Well, you fellas enjoy and I'll see you later."

She reached up and kissed Chuck on the lips, smiled at Jake, and disappeared back into her room.

"I'm telling you, McCain," Nicholson said, as he picked up his glass of bourbon and lightly clinked it against Chuck's, "I've never seen that girl so happy. Even before everything, I mean, I don't know how to say it. I know she's dated some other guys, but she's a different person since you came into her life."

The two men relaxed in McCain's sitting room, sipping their whiskey.

"It's going to be tough to leave her in a couple of days," Chuck replied, solemnly. "Did you talk to your team about the intruders?" he asked, wanting to change the subject.

"I did. We're going to run an extra patrol starting immediately. I think one of our problems is a lack of focus. These kids have never seen combat. Other than the couple of times we've had some zombies show up, there hasn't been too much to be concerned about. When I mentioned the possibility of an imminent attack, it seemed to shock everybody. And that's not a bad thing."

Dining Hall, The Northeast Georgia Technical College, Lavonia, Georgia, Saturday, 1800 hours

Chuck and Jake had spent two hours going over the existing

campus security plan. McCain was impressed with what Nicholson had done with some students and middle-aged faculty members but saw several areas for improvement. Chuck diplomatically went over his observations and suggestions, mostly related to increased training, as they enjoyed a couple of glasses of bourbon in the dorm room.

Dinner was served at 1700 hours on Saturdays as opposed to 1600 hours during the week. Beth explained to Chuck that Saturday nights were designated as Community Night and everyone was encouraged to stick around after they ate to play board games, chat, and have a beer or glass of wine. Mr. Nicholson kept the alcohol locked up because many of the residents were still teen-agers. On Saturday nights, however, he relaxed the rules.

McCain would have much preferred some alone time with Beth, but he had to admit, these were good people and he was enjoying his time on campus. While Elizabeth was making her rounds after dinner, three pretty, young female students cornered Chuck, peppering him with question after question about himself: where he was from, his law enforcement career, and how he had rescued Miss Benton. They were clearly enthralled with the big stranger in their midst. One of the girls asked to feel his bicep. Of course, then they all had to do it, clearly impressed, giggling to each other as they squeezed the bulging muscle.

"Hi, ladies," Karen the nurse said, slipping up behind them.

The three students jumped, realizing they had been caught flirting with the newcomer.

"Thanks so much for keeping Mr. McCain entertained for Miss Benton. I'm sure he really enjoyed talking to you," she told them, putting extra emphasis on 'really.'

Karen handed Chuck a beer, took his arm and steered him away from the laughing girls to a nearby table.

"I would say thanks for rescuing me, but I'm not sure that I needed to be rescued," Chuck laughed.

"Trust me," she smiled, tapping her beer bottle to his, "you needed to be saved. They're sweet girls but being confined to this campus with the same crop of people, and especially the same crop of men, for several months has been tough on all of us. So when a tall, handsome mystery man shows up, look out."

McCain laughed again and took a swallow of his beer. "Beth told me how you helped her start working through her depression. It takes a real friend to confront someone over something as serious as that."

"And she's a good friend," Karen nodded. "We've become very close. She told me that talking to you was what really helped to lift that black cloud off of her."

"Well, we had a lot of time to talk, being snowed in for a couple of days."

"Yeah," Karen gave a knowing smile, raising her eyebrows. "Talking is a good thing to do when you're trapped in a snowstorm in a freezing house. That'll keep you warm." She put air quotes around "talking."

McCain grinned and shook his head, knowing what the nurse was implying.

"I did work with her on her firearms handling, too. But, I'm a pretty good listener and I've been through some similar things. We've both lost people that we love. Really, since the zombie virus was released, who hasn't lost someone?"

"Yeah, you're right," Karen acknowledged, touching Chuck's arm. "And I was just kidding. Elizabeth told me you were the perfect gentleman and really treated her right."

Chuck nodded, taking another drink. Karen acted like she had more to say so McCain waited.

Finally, the woman looked into his eyes, as if measuring him. "May I ask you for a really big favor? If you say 'no,' I'll understand. But I have to ask."

She paused and saw Chuck motion for her to continue. His expression, though, had gone from warm to neutral.

The nurse took a deep breath and continued. "It's my parents. Elizabeth told me that you thought your daughter was in Hendersonville. My mom and dad live between here and there. It wouldn't be that far out of the way if you could check on them and let them know I'm OK.

"I'm sure they're fine. My dad was in the army in Vietnam and he's always been a bit of a prepper. They have a few acres of land and enough food and ammo to weather this thing. I haven't been able to get in touch with them for a couple of months, though, and I know the uncertainty of whether or not I'm still alive is killing them."

Karen hesitated, seeing the blank look on Chuck's face. "Is there any way you could go by and let them know where I'm at and that I'm fine? And for what it's worth, it would be a good rest stop along the way. They'd give you a safe place to stay and my mom is a great cook."

McCain saw the pleading expression in Karen's eyes. He looked around the room and spotted Beth chatting with Alicia and two other women on the far side of the cafeteria. Back behind Elizabeth, in the shadows, McCain glimpsed Bradley Thomas watching her while sipping a beer.

The police officer looked back at the pretty nurse who had just asked him to extend his trip while searching for his daughter. Why couldn't this be a man asking him for a favor? He always had trouble saying "no" to women with puppy-dog eyes. Chuck sighed and shook his head.

"I'm not going to make you any promises. I'll tell you what I need and then we'll see how feasible it looks. I'm also going to ask you to do something for me."

McCain saw hope come alive in the woman's eyes and she grabbed his hand. "Thank you! What can I do?"

"First of all, make me copies of maps for the area. I'm sure you have those in the library here. You and I can go over them together so I can see if it's on my route, and I'll need detailed directions to your parent's house. While you're at it, pull maps for the entire way from Hartwell to Hendersonville. Plus, I want you to write your mom and dad a letter introducing me and let me have some background information on you so that they'll believe you actually sent me."

"That makes sense. What else?"

Chuck leaned in towards Karen and locked eyes with her. "Promise me that you'll stay close to Elizabeth. I don't want her dropping back into depression. There's no telling when I'll be able to get back here, but I will come back for her. While I'm away, I need to know that she has a friend, who just happens to be a nurse, looking out for her."

Karen nodded solemnly. "I promise, Chuck. I'll take care of her."

Elizabeth slid up behind Karen, putting her arm around her friend's shoulders. "Well?" Beth asked her.

"He said he'd try. I'm going to get maps and directions for him and he's going to take a look."

"Didn't I tell you he was wonderful?" Benton exclaimed, throwing her arms around Chuck and kissing him.

After they came up for air, McCain looked around and saw that Bradley had disappeared into the night. Chuck also realized that he hadn't seen Jake and Tina since dinner.

"Any idea where Tina and Jake are?"

The two women looked at each other and laughed. Karen answered, "I can guess what they're doing."

Elizabeth shook her head at her friend and looked at Chuck. "I think they're in the command post. They hung out here for a while and then left to keep an eye on things."

"Okay, I need to go talk to Jake about something. Karen, we'll chat more tomorrow. Maybe in the afternoon we can go over those maps? Beth, I'll see you back at the dorm."

He kissed her again and hurried over to Admin.

Jake responded to the knock at the door, Kimber .45 in hand. When he saw that it was Chuck, he motioned him inside. The windows were covered to keep anyone outside from seeing into the office, which was illuminated with a camp lantern.

"Where's Tina?" McCain asked.

"I love having her here with me but she pushes herself to the point of exhaustion. I sent her to back to get some sleep. She's going to be speaking at the memorial service tomorrow and I want her to be fresh. What's up?"

"Bradley Thomas. He's starting to creep me out. I saw him standing in a dark corner a little while ago, watching Elizabeth. Later, she got excited about something and kissed me. When I looked around again, Bradley was gone. What do you think? Is he harmless?"

Jake took his glasses off and rubbed his eyes. "You've seen him. He's a little skinny, scrawny guy, and he hates guns. I don't think he'd ever harm Elizabeth but he can certainly be a pest."

"It sounds like he has too much time on his hands," Chuck said.

"You have something in mind?"

"I know you said you were going to put him on the looting roster. How about sentry duty, as well? Has he pulled any shifts?"

Jake laughed. "That boy's worthless. I've asked him to pull duty several times before and he had eighteen excuses about why he couldn't do it."

"Maybe you could stroke his ego a little bit and tell him how much you need him since you lost those three people last week. I wouldn't take 'no' for an answer. Maybe if he's a little busier, he'll leave Beth alone."

"I'm good with that. I'm actually a person short on tomorrow night's schedule. I was going to pull it myself, but I think I'll have a little talk with Bradley instead and tell him he's been volunteered."

Elizabeth's dorm room, Saturday, 2045 hours

"Thanks for hanging out after dinner and talking to people. Everybody enjoyed meeting you," Beth commented. She sipped a glass of wine, leaning against Chuck on her small love seat.

Before he could respond, she continued with a smile, "Karen told me she had to rescue you from three of the female students. Were they really squeezing your bicep?"

McCain laughed. "They sure were. They kept saying, 'We've never seen one that big.' But I hated every second of it."

Elizabeth giggled and elbowed him in the side. "Oh, I'm sure you did. It's a good thing Karen showed up or that might've gotten out of hand. They might've kidnapped you and done who-knows-what?"

They sat quietly for a few minutes, holding each other. Elizabeth finally asked, "When do you think you'll be back? I'm already missing you."

"I've been thinking about it. If I get to Hartwell and there's nothing from Melanie, I'll turn around and come right back. If she's left me the location of wherever she's ended up, that's where I'm heading. If I can get by Karen's parent's place, I'll do that, too, but I've got to get to Mel.

"After I've reconnected with my daughter, I'll evaluate again. If she's in a safe environment, I'll stay with them for a week or two and come back for you. I'll have a better idea of what things are like on the outside by then. If the travel situation isn't that bad, I'd love to take you back to wherever Mel's at. If you want to, of course."

There was no hesitation on Elizabeth's part. "I'll follow you wherever you go."

Chapter Seven

The Plan

Outside of Lavonia, Georgia, Sunday, 1500 hours

Neil Dodd's gray Jeep Wrangler pulled down Wesley's driveway and parked behind the other vehicles assembled there. Don Lester and Hoss Harper went out to greet the newcomers and bring them inside. Joey and Wesley had just returned from a trip to another of their safe houses, this one on the west side of Lavonia. They had driven two cars and taken four of their accomplices with them to restock food, guns and ammo.

Dodd entered the house, followed by two other men. Neil looked to be in his mid-thirties and was a little bigger than 5-0 had been, Joey thought. His muscles bulged under his tight long-sleeve t-shirt. I wonder if he was juicing as much as Carter was? Lester wondered. The corrupt deputy had been known as the guy whom serious bodybuilders and power lifters utilized to get a little extra help in building muscle.

The two men with Neil were tall and lean and bore a striking resemblance to each other, Joey noticed. Dodd introduced them as his cousins, Kevin and Mark Anderson.

"They worked for 5-0, too, but in a secret capacity," Neil said.

Joey and Wesley nodded, having no idea what he meant by "secret capacity." Don offered Neil and the brothers a beer and they all moved to the living room.

Hoss and Wesley rounded everyone up and told them it was time to talk. Greg Davis was still asleep. The meth addict had slept almost twenty hours since they had picked him up the day before. Don woke him up and Davis staggered into the living room, shirtless, wearing only blue jeans. The Andersons were visibly surprised to see him.

Kevin leaned over and whispered something to Neil, who nodded.

"You got some guns for us, Greg?" Neil demanded.

Greg suddenly looked like a caged animal, searching for an exit. "The deal didn't happen, Neil. This guy robbed me and killed Tonya."

"Which guy robbed you?" Mark Anderson asked, an edge to his voice.

"The guy we're going after tonight," answered Joey. "Tell 'em the story, Greg."

Davis sat on the edge of the couch and told them about his encounter with Chuck. Dodd and the Anderson brothers looked dubious.

"So, this stranger robs you," Neil queried, "kills Tonya, and then guns down 5-0 and four of his guys? Who is this fella? Rambo or something? Joey, yesterday you told me how you found 5-0 and his guys dead. You saw the bodies at the truck stop and the safe house. What do you think happened, based on what y'all saw?"

Lester took a deep breath. "The back door at the house was kicked in and Larry, Bobby, and Ronnie had all been shot. 5-0 had been shot, too, but the only bullet wound I saw was on his hand.

Somebody beat him to death and then stabbed him in the back of the head. His face was destroyed. I mean his nose was smashed in and his right eye was just a mess. I've never seen anything like it."

"Beaten to death?" Dodd exclaimed, shaking his head, and sitting forward in his seat. "I find that hard to swallow."

"You asked me to tell you what I saw," Joey continued, looking Neil in the eye. "That was what it looked like. When we went over to the truck stop, Jerry and those three people from that vocational school had all been shot. No idea how all that happened. If I had to guess, I'd say that the campus cop killed Jerry. They were lying pretty close together."

"And you told me yesterday something about a girl that was with this mysterious man? Was there a girl with the guy who robbed you, Greg?"

"No, he was by himself, but before he robbed us and killed Tonya, he said something about looking for his daughter."

"The girl me and Joey saw with him at the school was young enough to be his daughter!" Wesley exclaimed.

Neal shook his head again. "There's just a lot of stuff that isn't adding up. Like the part where one guy and his young daughter take out Mike Carter and an entire cell of his gang."

They worked all afternoon developing a plan that they could agree on. Dodd had some great ideas, which made Joey and Wesley both feel better about having him along. He was older and more experienced than all of their gang, and had been close to 5-0. Neil was invested in getting revenge for his friend's death.

Lester found out that Kevin and Mark had both been students at the technical college a couple of years before. They had been enrolled in the Pharmacy Technology program. Carter had recruited the brothers after pulling them over for a traffic violation and finding a large quantity of drugs in their car. They had taught themselves how to cook meth while going to school and 5-0 had brought them on as his main providers of the drug.

In most of the urban areas, the Mexican gangs had moved in, taking over control of the drug trade. At the time of the zombie virus outbreak, however, Carter still held the reins of all criminal activity in his rural county. The Andersons had managed to stay off the radar, cooking up small batches of crystal meth at a time. In return, 5-0 had kept them out of prison and had paid them well. Now, they also wanted some revenge.

Since they had been students there, the Andersons were able to draw a map of the campus. The main building that they were concerned about was the dormitory. Everyone agreed that had to be where all the residents were housed. The big challenge was going to be finding the mystery man and the girl in the big, two-level residence hall.

The Northeast Georgia Technical College, Lavonia, Georgia, Sunday, 1500 hours

The memorial service had been somber and moving. Friends tearfully recounted stories about Jason, Margo, and Lamar. The pastor preached a beautiful message from John 15:13, "There is no greater love than to lay down one's life for one's friends."

As the preacher delivered his message he had nodded at Chuck, sitting next to Elizabeth on the front row, and said, "In these difficult times, it is good to know that there are still men and woman of courage in the world who will do the right thing. People who will risk their lives to help others. People who will put the interests of the weak and helpless above their own. May we all aspire to be those people."

McCain had slipped away to the campus gym after the service.

He found that he always seemed to do his best critical thinking as he exerted himself physically. Chuck ran scenario after scenario through his mind of what might happen after he left the relative safety of the campus.

His straightest route to Hendersonville from Hartwell was right at a hundred miles. And that was only if Melanie had left him her address there. He had been very fortunate to survive this far in a world gone awry. How long would his luck hold out?

While grateful to have a vehicle, he also understood that having it made him a bigger and more noticeable target. McCain had to get to Melanie. He had to know that she was OK. Now, however, he also felt responsible for Elizabeth. Sure, she would be safe here, but she was depending on him to survive and come back for her.

Was this normal? he questioned himself once more. He had known this girl for less than a week and he was deeply in love. It wasn't rational and he couldn't explain it but he knew what he felt. And he was sure that she felt the same way. McCain had not been looking for love but it had surely found him.

Later, Elizabeth sat with Chuck in his sitting room, where she watched him take apart his guns. He field-stripped both the rifle and the pistol, cleaning them thoroughly. The big man lubricated, reassembled, and dry-fired them several times to make sure they were functioning properly. He then meticulously checked and topped off each of his magazines in preparation for the next day's trip.

As he worked, Chuck found himself telling Beth stories about the men he had worked with at the CDC. She felt herself being drawn into the circle of friends McCain was describing. She sensed the depth of the camaraderie of Chuck's team.

"I really hope I get to meet all of them one day," she said.

"You will, whenever this crazy world gets sorted out. But right now, it's time for some pistol training."

Beth groaned and made a face. Chuck had her stand, draw her pistol, and remove the magazine. He walked her through pulling the slide to the rear and ejecting the chambered round. She handed him the loaded mag and the single bullet and he had her visually verify that the gun was unloaded.

After they were positive that the gun was safe, McCain had Benton draw and dry-fire, over and over again. Chuck knew that good, solid repetitions were the key to developing the correct muscle memory. That would ensure that, in a crisis, she would be able to respond without having to think about it. Beth drew, going to a two-handed stance and squeezing the Glock's trigger. She would then pull back the pistol's slide to the rear, resetting the trigger, and holstering the gun to do it again.

Elizabeth saw in Chuck's eyes that he was pleased with her progress. She had even been practicing some on her own, trying to implement all the things that he had taught her. He was right in insisting that she develop her weapon skills. These were dangerous days they were living in and she vowed to herself that she would never be a victim again.

After drilling for almost an hour, Chuck handed Elizabeth her pistol magazine and talked her through chambering a round so the gun was ready to fire, then topping off the magazine with a single bullet so the mag was fully loaded. The Glock went into the holster, which Beth put on the coffee table. She motioned for Chuck to sit down, and crawled onto his lap. They both felt the coming separation and they sat for a long time just holding each other. Beth sensed Chuck had something to say.

"There's something you need to know," McCain finally said. "Yesterday, when Jake and I were walking the perimeter, we found where people have been watching the school."

Chuck heard a slight gasp. "Are you sure?" she asked. "We have patrols out there all the time."

"This was inside the woods about a hundred yards, over across from Admin. Jake told me that the patrols have stayed out of the forest and just walked the inner and outer rings of the campus. There's no doubt there were people there.

"I counted two sets of footprints and they were fresh. If I had to guess, I'd say they were spying on the school sometime on Friday. We found where they'd been lying next to a downed tree where they had a good view of Admin and a few of the other buildings."

Beth was silent for a few minutes and Chuck stroked her hair. "Friday was the day you and I got here," she observed. "We stopped at Admin. They could've been watching us."

"Yeah, they could've." He sighed. "I don't like it. Jake felt bad that his sentries hadn't been more effective but it's not his fault. Now that he knows, though, he's added another patrol and his teams have been alerted to be more observant and to not make out while they are supposed to be patrolling."

Elizabeth laughed. "He told you about that? I think he's found his people in compromising positions a couple of times."

"It happens. But now that they know, hopefully they'll be more focused."

"I've always felt so secure here. We've had zombies show up twice but this has been such a safe haven. Now, I'm worried about what might happen."

"I'm sorry but I wanted you to know, especially since I'm leaving tomorrow. That's why I always want you armed. Wear that pistol when you're out of your room and have it close by when you're in here."

Her head was still pressed against his chest. "Okay," she answered quietly. "I will."

Outside of Lavonia, Georgia, Sunday, 2100 hours

Joey, Wesley, Hoss, and Neil sat around Maddox's kitchen table, smoking and talking quietly. Only a couple more hours. All the others were getting some sleep. They would wake everyone at 11:00pm, planning to be at the school by midnight.

"What do you think, Neil?" asked Joey.

The muscular man looked at him and shrugged, stubbing out his cigarette in an ashtray. "I think we're walking into a hornet's nest. There's just so much we don't know. We don't know how many people are on the campus. We don't know how good their defenses are. The biggest problem is that we don't know where Chuck, if that's his real name, and the girl are going to be.

"But, we have the element of surprise and I doubt these little college kids want to stand up to us. I reckon they'll turn tail and run when the shooting starts. We'll be fine. Stick to the plan and get in and out. Let's get some payback for 5-0 and then come back here and have a few cold ones."

Lester nodded. He had been thinking the exact same thing. Sometimes, though, the smartest thing to do was just walk away from the hornet's nest.

The Northeast Georgia Technical College, Lavonia, Georgia, Sunday, 2100 hours

After dinner, Chuck, Elizabeth, and Karen walked back to the dorm and met in Beth's room. Karen had copies of Google maps and hand-written directions, just as McCain had requested. She also had a letter to her parents identifying Chuck as a friend.

Karen was right. Her parents lived less than ten miles off of

Highway 25, the main route to Hendersonville, before it connected with Interstate 26. Their house was nestled in the forest near the North Saluda Reservoir. They had a great place to ride out a zombie apocalypse, McCain thought, looking at the satellite maps. They were surrounded by trees and their closest neighbors were at least a mile away.

McCain sat between the two girls on the small sofa, carefully studying the maps and comparing them with the directions that Karen had written out. The papers were spread out on Elizabeth's small coffee table, illuminated by several candles. Chuck had not said anything for several minutes and he realized that Elizabeth and Karen had stopped talking and were staring at him, waiting for an answer.

He saw the expectancy and hope in Karen's eyes. Beth's eyes shone with love and with something else. Confidence? She gave him a smile and a slight nod. McCain closed his eyes and took a deep breath. He hated it when beautiful women asked him for something. He opened his eyes and looked at Karen.

"Okay. I'll do it."

The nurse threw her arms around him and Elizabeth hugged him from the other side. Life doesn't get much better than this, Chuck thought, enjoying the embrace of the two lovely ladies. Until I'm out there by myself trying not to get eaten by zombies or killed by robbers, that is.

"Thanks, Chuck," the nurse said, still holding onto him. "My mom and dad will be so relieved and they'll take good care of you, I promise."

"I'm sure, but let me give you my disclaimer. I'm planning on going to see them but there's no way I can predict how my trip is going to play out. I don't know if Highway 25 is passable or if I'll have to find a longer, more round-a-bout route to Hendersonville."

"I know," Karen nodded, "and I understand. Don't force it and please don't get hurt. I appreciate you being willing to try."

She leaned over and kissed Chuck on the cheek, then stood, and stepped over to Elizabeth, giving her a hug.

"I'm sure you two have a lot to talk about," Karen said, smiling, putting air quotes around 'talk.' "I'll see you in the morning. I'm going to ask Jake to have the next team of foragers bring me back a man, too."

There wasn't much talking between Chuck and Beth. They lay together on the couch, kissing and holding each other tightly.

Finally, Beth whispered into his ear, "Spend the night with me."

"I'd love to," he answered, "but let's wait. Let's give ourselves something to look forward to."

"You're a strange man, Chuck McCain," she said, softly. "But I love you so much."

Chapter Eight

Revenge

The Northeast Georgia Technical College, Lavonia, Georgia, Monday, 0025 hours

Bradley Thomas fumed. He had no business sitting at this security barrier in the middle of the night. This was a job much better suited for his partner, Todd, and others like him. Todd Stevens normally worked with his best friend, Jermaine Brown, or Robert Clayton, the faculty member.

Brown had been sick for the last several days with the flu, however, and Mr. Nicholson had ordered Bradley to take a shift at the roadblock. Clayton was on perimeter sentry duty, out there patrolling with his team in the dark. Bradley shuddered at the idea of walking around the unlit campus, not knowing what might be lurking in the shadows.

Thomas shook his head as he sat on top of the tall trailer, his feet dangling over the side, staring into the darkness. Stevens, Brown, and Clayton were all gun nuts with Todd and Jermaine talking about joining the army together before the world fell apart. Todd had already told Bradley more about firearms in the last hour than he had ever wanted to know. It was going to be a long night, the former student body president sighed.

The two young men couldn't have been more different. Todd worked out regularly at the campus gym while Bradley avoided physical exercise. Stevens was a student in the EMT program, Thomas had been studying Cosmetology. Even though he had a crush on Elizabeth, Bradley hoped that a career as a hair stylist would allow him to meet a lot of women. Especially if Elizabeth never came around to liking him.

"Yeah, during the day," Todd explained, "I carry my scoped hunting rifle so I can scan the woods with the scope and make sure no one is trying to sneak through the forest. When I pull a night shift, though, I always carry an AR-15. If something or someone slips up on us in the dark, we need to be able to throw a lot of rounds at them."

The idea of a zombie getting close to them in the middle of the night made Thomas pull his legs up under himself, sitting cross-legged. Mr. Nicholson had handed Bradley a black rifle and given him an hour's instruction on how to use the AR-15. Nicholson also gave the young man three thirty-round magazines of ammunition and showed him how to load the gun.

Jake offered ongoing weapons familiarization classes to everyone on campus but Bradley had always been too busy to attend. He didn't like guns and hoped he wouldn't have to use this one tonight. As Todd continued to drone on, sounding like an advertisement for the NRA, Bradley thought about Elizabeth.

He was relieved that her big savior, Chuck, was leaving. Maybe with him out of the way, Elizabeth will finally want to spend some time with me, he hoped. What could that big knuckle-dragger possibly offer a sophisticated girl like Elizabeth? Plus, he was so much older than her.

So Chuck saves her life, and the young, impressionable woman develops a crush on him. That's probably a normal reaction, Bradley thought. Okay, fine. But now he's leaving, hopefully never to return, and I can go back to trying to woo her. Eventually, she'll realize how much I love her and how great we would be together.

A distant noise made Todd stop talking. The uncommon sound of car engines carried across the silence of the night. Stevens couldn't remember the last time they had heard any vehicles driving on Adams Farm Road, a half-mile away. After a few minutes, the night was quiet again.

"What does that mean?" Bradley asked softly, the nervousness evident in his voice. "Is there someone out there?"

"We both heard the cars," Todd whispered. "We're down in a dip here and the surrounding woods play tricks with sounds. They may've just been passing through or…maybe they stopped. Let me call the CP and let them know we heard something."

Stevens reached behind him on the trailer to where the field telephone had been duct-taped to the metal. He lifted the receiver and waited.

"Officer Miles, this is Todd at the roadblock," he spoke quietly into the handset. "We just heard some cars up on the main road and I wanted to report in."

Bradley heard the concern in his partner's voice. If the gun nut is scared, why am I even here? he wondered. I've already forgotten how to fire this rifle that Nicholson gave me, even after his lesson.

"I'm not sure," Stevens answered the police officer on the other end of the phone in Admin. "It sounded like at least two, but definitely more than one vehicle. Yes, ma'am, I'll let you know if we hear anything else."

The Northeast Georgia Technical College, Lavonia, Georgia, Monday, 0045 hours

The four vehicles stopped on Adams Farm Road at the entrance to the technical college, next to the large sign identifying the school. The thirteen gang members were heavily armed, all carrying rifles or shotguns and pistols, along with plenty of extra ammo. They were surprisingly quiet and disciplined for a change, Joey thought.

All the interior vehicle lights had been deactivated and car doors were gently pushed closed to keep their noise to a minimum. The keys were left in the ignitions in case they had to make a fast escape. Everyone realized how important the element of surprise was going to be tonight. They had gone over the plans before leaving the house but Neil had everyone huddle up one last time, speaking quietly to the group, reminding everyone of their responsibilities.

Dodd opted for the direct approach as they were putting the plan together. Joey and Wesley had suggested entering the campus through the woods, using the same route they had on Friday during their reconnoitering mission. The big enforcer had told them that the easy way in was the best way in, and the easiest way was straight down the driveway.

Neil's logic made sense. The forest was noisy and it would be difficult to move through the underbrush quietly. They couldn't use flashlights for fear of being seen. Entering the school grounds through the woods would also leave the roadblock in their rear, from where an attack could be launched against them. The sentries at the barricade had to be eliminated, preferably without them sounding an alarm.

"Plus, if we can take out the guys at that roadblock quickly enough," Neil said, "we might be able to get some information out of one of them about where the man and the girl are."

Neil, Joey, Wesley, and Mark Anderson walked slowly down the long driveway, the roadblock less then a hundred yards in front of them now. The overcast sky meant no moon or stars to illuminate them. Lester was grateful that they had listened to Dodd. He could not imagine trying to navigate through the forest in this almost pitch-black darkness.

Joey carried his Saiga .12 gauge shotgun and had his 9mm Beretta on his hip. Wesley cradled his AR-15, with the .45 caliber Glock in a shoulder holster. Mark held a Colt AR-15 and wore a .357 Magnum Colt Python revolver on his waist.

Dodd's AK-47 was slung across his back, a massive .44 Magnum Desert Eagle in a hip holster, but for the moment, his weapon of choice was a compound bow with an arrow strung. Neil had explained that he'd been a bow hunter since he was a child. They didn't have any suppressed weapons so the bow might keep their appearance a secret a little longer.

The rest of the criminals waited around the corner from the last bend in the road. They would respond to a whistle from Joey or to gunfire. If things went according to plan, however, the four men would rejoin them with a prisoner whom they could interrogate.

Joey estimated that they were now less than fifty yards from the barricade. His eyes had adjusted enough to make out two figures, barely visible, on top of the big trailer. The four intruders continued to slowly work their way down the narrow road, Lester, Maddox, and Anderson prepared to shoot if Dodd's arrows did not do the trick.

Suddenly, one of the people on the trailer stood, facing them, and raising his rifle. An audible "click" broke the silence of the night as the sentry flicked the safety on their rifle to "Fire." A flashlight illuminated the four men, briefly blinding them, but Neil's bow came up quickly and a "twang" announced the release of the jagged arrow. A gasp came from the standing man and he collapsed backwards onto the trailer, his rifle and flashlight clattering loudly to the pavement almost fifteen feet below, darkness now reinstated.

Bradley and Todd had sat, peering out into the night, unable to see anything. They both thought they could hear the sounds of people out there. Whispers, a metallic clink, someone clearing their throat. But the noises weren't close and they both knew that everything was amplified at night. Including their fears. I'm sure my ears are just playing tricks on me, Bradley tried to reassure himself.

After several minutes, though, Todd whispered, "I think I see people walking out there."

Something behind them started vibrating. "That's the phone," Todd said, softly. "We'll get it in a minute. Get your rifle ready."

Bradley reached to his right for his weapon as Stevens climbed to his feet and clicked the safety off of his rifle, raising it to his shoulder. The sentry activated a flashlight revealing four armed men almost to their position. One of them raised a bow and Bradley heard something hit Todd, who grunted loudly in pain and fell down beside him.

Thomas froze up. Who were those people? What happened?

"Todd! Todd, are you OK?"

Thomas reached over to his companion. His fingers brushed across the arrow protruding from Todd's chest, his hand suddenly wet and sticky.

"Oh, my God!" Bradley exclaimed. "I've got to get out of here."

In the dark, Thomas had forgotten about the vibrating phone that was right beside him. His only thought was: I need to go tell Mr. Nicholson and get some help. He'll know what to do. Thomas had also forgotten about his rifle, leaving it on top of the trailer, scrambling down the backside onto the van and then the wrecked passenger car that they used to climb onto the big trailer.

As Bradley's feet touched the pavement, he was grabbed from

behind, a big hand clamping down over his mouth. A menacing voice whispered in his ear, "Don't resist and don't make any noise and you'll live. Nod your head if you understand."

Thomas vigorously nodded. The hand stayed over his mouth and he was led back to the front of the barricade and up the driveway, away from the school. Where are they taking me? he wondered, panic setting in as he stumbled along. He felt several sets of hands dragging him up the road.

After walking for several minutes, Bradley heard a low whistle from beside him and then the sound of a lot of people whispering at once. He was suddenly thrown to the ground onto his back and a huge man was straddling him, knees pinning Thomas' arms to the ground, the hand still covering his mouth. A flashlight with a red filter came on, illuminating the scene. The light wasn't great but Bradley could see a large group of men holding guns, staring down at him with unconcealed hatred in their eyes.

Something sharp jabbed underneath his chin and Thomas grunted, trying to slide forward, away from the pain. The brute on top of him leaned down, letting Bradley see his face in the red light.

"Stop moving or I'll cut your throat."

Thomas complied and lay still. The pain subsided as the knife was pulled back slightly.

"I'm going to ask you some questions, little man. How well you answer them is going to determine whether or not you die tonight. Do you understand me?"

Bradley nodded, his eyes bulging with fear.

"I'm going to take my hand off of your mouth. If you scream, I'll cut your tongue out. Just tell me what I need to know and everything will be fine. First off, what's your name?"

"B...B...Bradley," he gasped. "Bradley Thomas."

"Alright, Bradley, my friends and I are interested in two people on your campus and we want to know where they're at. They killed some of our friends and stole a lot of our stuff. We just want them and we'll leave everyone else alone. The man's name is 'Chuck,' and he had a girl with him."

Thomas swallowed hard. He wasn't about to protect McCain with a knife pressed against his throat. But Elizabeth? Why Elizabeth? She hadn't killed anyone. It was all Chuck's fault. He'd killed those people and now their friends were seeking revenge.

"He…He's here," Bradley stammered. "He's just visiting but is leaving tomorrow. Chuck's in a guest room down the left hallway of the dorm building on the first floor. Go in the front door, take a left, and he's in the last room on the left."

"That's good, Bradley," the man with the knife said. "Very good. See how easy it is to be helpful? What about the girl?"

Thomas paused a moment before answering. "Chuck showed up by himself. There was no girl with him."

The point of the knife dug into the soft skin of his neck and Bradley cried out in pain, feeling his blood flow out of the cut.

"Bradley, I hate it when people lie to me. I know that there was a girl with him and I want to know where she is. Now, I'm gonna give you another chance to answer that question, but if you lie to me again, I'm gonna start cutting off body parts. In fact, not that a little fella like you would miss them, but I think I'll start by cutting off your balls."

Neil kept the knife against Bradley's throat but said, quietly, to those around him, "Pull his pants down. I've got a feeling he's trying to protect that girl and may need a little motivation."

Thomas felt hands tugging at his jeans. His tormentors snickered as they roughly jerked Bradley's pants down. The former student body president felt the cold air against his skin, letting him know that things were about to get much worse.

"No, no, please!" Bradley was sobbing now. "I'll tell you what I know. Please don't hurt me, I'm begging you. She's staying in

Chuck's room. We don't have that many rooms on campus and they're having to share."

The man was still straddling his chest but Bradley could feel his pants around his ankles, the cold ground freezing his buttocks. Maybe, if they think Elizabeth is in Chuck's room, she'll be safe, he thought. These guys will go after McCain and maybe Elizabeth can stay hidden in her room.

"That's the truth. I swear," cried Bradley, the tears still running down his face. "Please just let me go."

"Okay, Bradley. You've been very helpful," the man with the knife said, lifting his weight off of the young man's arms. Dodd suddenly sliced the razor sharp blade across Bradley's carotid artery and throat, blood spraying into the air. As Neil climbed off of Thomas he thrust the bloody knife under the dying man's sternum and into Bradley's heart. Dodd used the dead man's clothes, wiping the sticky red liquid off of his blade, and re-sheathed it.

"Well, if he was telling the truth," Neil told his companions, "this should be easy."

Admin Building, The Northeast Georgia Technical College, Lavonia, Georgia, Monday, 0050 hours

Tina called Jake and woke him up, giving him the report from Todd about hearing vehicles. She had tried to recontact the roadblock to get an update without any response.

"You want me to walk over there to check on them?" the police officer asked the former Marine.

Nicholson was already moving. He had strapped on his prosthetic leg and was pulling on his cargo pants. His head cradled the receiver against his collarbone as he dressed.

"No. You stay on the phones. I'll be out the door in two minutes to walk over and see what's going on. When the other teams call in, send one to secure the dorm and the other to the roadblock, just to be safe."

Months earlier, Tina had given Jake one of the campus police department's soft ballistic vests. It was only rated to stop handgun rounds but it was better than nothing. He strapped it on, pulled on his pistol belt and web gear, picked up his rifle, and rushed out the door.

Jake's room was on the opposite end of the dorm from McCain's and Benton's. He considered waking Chuck but knew that the federal police officer was planning on leaving early. There's probably nothing to this anyway, he thought. The residence hall had entrances on both ends of the corridor as well as the main doorway in the middle that led into the small lobby. Nicholson turned right out of his room, pushed the exit door open, closed it quietly behind him, and rushed towards the entrance security point.

Robert, Danny, and Maria were patrolling on the south side of the campus. Robert Clayton taught in the Computer Information Systems program but he also had a passion for firearms and the shooting sports. In his late thirties, he had never married, not finding the right woman who was looking for a computer geek who also loved to compete in practical shooting competitions every other weekend. If he was honest, Robert would also admit that he was painfully shy around women.

Patrol leader Clayton had chosen to stay on campus after the zombie outbreak because he knew that he could help protect the students and other faculty members, plus he just liked the idea of being able to use his firearms skills. His Smith & Wesson AR-15 was slung across his chest and he carried a cocked and locked S&W 1911 .45 caliber pistol in a hip holster.

Danny Romero had been enrolled in the Automotive Technology Course. He loved cars and was already an experienced mechanic. Danny had never been around firearms before the crisis but his natural mechanical aptitude made him a quick learner. Romero carried a .12 gauge Remington Model 870 pump shotgun loaded with buckshot.

Maria Morris had been one of Robert's students. She loved computers and intended to find a job in the IT field; at least she had until the power grid crashed and zombies dominated the landscape. Maria's mother was on campus, too. Leslie was an HR Specialist, handling payroll and many of the other administrative tasks for the small college. When the zombies swept through, however, the mother and daughter had sought safety with the other survivors. Maria's dad had abandoned them when she was young and her mother had worked hard to provide for her.

Morris had only had minimal exposure to firearms, but when Mr. Nicholson said they needed sentries, she had volunteered. She really liked Mr. Clayton and he had taught her so much about weapons and tactics over the last couple of months. She wondered if he had given any of the other students all the private instruction that he had given her?

Clayton had never acted improperly towards her, but Maria realized that she had developed a crush on him. Or maybe like one of her friends told her, she just had "daddy issues." Mr. Clayton was a nice man, though, and she appreciated all the time he'd spent with her, developing her proficiency with the AR-15 that she was carrying.

The three sentries stopped at the field telephone, concealed in a weatherproof box attached to a light post next to a sandbagged fighting position. They each had a flashlight and used them intermittently to illuminate the area around them as they walked. Mr. Nicholson had worked with all the sentries on patrol techniques and had taught them to periodically turn their flashlights on and off as they moved.

As Robert checked in with the command post, Danny and Maria

shone their lights as far as the beam of light would go, towards the outer perimeter, looking for threats. A few days before, Danny would have been using this pause to hit on Maria to try and get her to spend some time with him. With the knowledge that intruders had been watching the campus, however, all of the campus security team was much more focused.

Clayton got off of the phone and joined them. "We may have a problem. Officer Miles said the team at the roadblock heard some vehicles a little earlier out near the entrance to the college. Now, there's no answer when she calls back. She needs us to go secure the dorm, just to be safe."

"What about the other patrol?" Maria asked. "Do Gina, Tyrone, and Jessica know what's going on?"

"Officer Miles said she'll send them to check on Todd and Bradley as soon as they check in. We're the closest to the dorm so that's where we're going. If we see anything, though, we can use our whistles to alert them."

The residence hall was just a hundred yards from where they were standing and they moved quickly in that direction. When they were thirty yards away from the building, they heard many footsteps hurrying towards them down the sidewalk. Robert started to turn his flashlight on to let the other patrol see them. Who else could it be? But wasn't Officer Miles going to send that team to the barricade?

Instead, he stopped and whispered to Danny and Maria to get off the sidewalk and find cover. They both dove into a sandbagged fighting position to the left of the walkway. Robert legged it across the sidewalk to the dorm parking lot, where he could get a better angle on the intruders. Several vehicles were there and Clayton leaned against the engine block of a Dodge Ram pickup, aiming his AR-15 over the hood.

Robert couldn't see the approaching group in the dark but it sounded like many more than the three people in the other patrol.

When he estimated that the footsteps were near the entrance to the dorm, Clayton activated the flashlight mounted on the front of his rifle. The sight of so many armed men rushing towards the residence hall made him gasp. The three sentries and the group of strangers were only fifty yards apart.

"Stop! Drop your weapons!" Robert challenged them, flipping the safety switch on his rifle to "Fire," putting the cross hairs of his ACOG optics on the chest of one of the men who was also holding an AR-15 rifle.

Three of the intruders quickly swung their weapons around and let loose with a volley of rounds in the direction of the flashlight beam. Robert fired twice, both rounds striking Wesley Maddox in the chest. Clayton ducked behind the engine block of the pickup as bullets punched into the other side of it.

Danny and Maria were frozen by what was happening around them. Who were these armed men heading towards the dorm? They were shooting at Mr. Clayton and Maria was pretty sure Robert had managed to hit one of them.

She raised her rifle and began firing over the top of the sandbags at the gunmen. The muzzle flashes of fired weapons provided the only light and Maria instinctively aimed towards where she had just seen a flash. The boom of Danny's shotgun added to the fray and the return fire from the attackers momentarily slacked off.

Then all of the attackers' guns were firing towards Clayton and his two patrol members. Robert moved to his right, peeking around the rear of the big pickup. He sighted in on the muzzle flash of someone shooting towards Maria and Danny. Robert fired four shots around where he supposed the shooter to be and was rewarded with a cry of pain.

A loud metal thunk signaled the impact of a round next to Clayton's head on the rear fender of the Ram. He crouch-walked back to the driver's side of the vehicle and peered around the front fender, looking for another target.

One of Maria's shots had struck Kevin Anderson in the abdomen. He had collapsed onto the grass and was slowly bleeding to death. Robert was sure that he had hit two of the gunmen but he was far from comfortable. He guessed there were twelve to fifteen intruders in the group that he had illuminated and had no idea if this was all or if there were other attackers moving towards them, as well.

Gunfire from the strangers slowed down again. "Everybody into the dorm," a loud voice boomed from near the entrance.

The gunmen continued firing towards the security team but backed quickly towards the residence hall.

"Cease fire!" Robert yelled over at Maria and Danny.

They didn't want to shoot wildly towards the dorm for fear of striking a resident. He ran over to where his two team members were, making sure they were OK, but knowing they needed to get into the building before these criminals had a chance to hurt anyone inside. Robert quickly came up with a plan for them to defend the dorm.

The Northeast Georgia Technical College, Lavonia, Georgia, Monday, 0055 hours

It was almost a thousand yards from Jake's room to the roadblock. Nicholson was halfway there when gunfire exploded from the direction of the dormitory. The Marine cursed, quickly reversing direction, running back towards the residence hall. There were several shots, a lull for a couple of seconds, and then another long exchange of fire.

McCain woke up at the sound of people running down the sidewalk. His window was slightly open to let in some fresh air and the footsteps were amplified right outside of his room. He sat up in the bed, trying to get his bearings.

Someone yelled, "Stop! Drop your weapons!" A second later gunfire erupted, shattering the silence.

Chuck threw himself to the floor, grabbing his blue jeans as the firefight raged just outside of the dorm. He got the pants on and grabbed his rifle from where it stood, leaning against the wall for easy access.

A voice McCain did not recognize yelled, "Everybody into the dorm!"

Maybe it was one of the security team leaders ordering their people inside. Or maybe it was people with an evil intent. He rushed towards his door, tripping over his boots in the process and falling to the floor. He didn't land hard but it slowed him down. I need to put my boots on but there's no time, he thought. I'm going to be fighting barefoot.

Alicia's room was on the second floor of the dorm but the gunfire and yelling woke her up. She slipped into the hallway and crept down the stairs, holding her flashlight, wanting to get to Elizabeth's room. Alicia was wearing a black hoodie with the school's logo and sweatpants.

She heard dorm room doors open on the far end of her floor as she started down the stairs. Probably some of the other sentries going to see what's happening. What did Mr. Nicholson call them? A quick reaction force? Hopefully, they would be quick tonight.

In the midst of gunfire and yelling, Alicia's first reaction was that she needed to get to Miss Benton. She always knows what to do and will know what's going on. Alicia knew about the possibility of an attack on the school. She had heard Mr. McCain tell Officer Miles and Mr. Nicholson about how the people who had kidnapped Miss Benton and killed their friends had very likely found their IDs linking them back to the college.

Miss Benton is probably OK, she thought. I didn't even think about the fact that she and Mr. McCain are probably together, since it's their last night with the big man leaving in the morning. That would be embarrassing if I knocked on the door and they were in bed together. But something bad is happening outside and I'd rather be with those two than anyone else right now, she told herself.

As Alicia reached the first floor, several more gunshots just outside the front entrance, directly across the lobby from the staircase caused her to jump. A loud voice carried over the gunfire. Suddenly, the door burst open and armed men, strangers, rushed in, talking all at once.

Flashlight beams lit up the young African-American woman, and she froze wide-eyed at the intruders pointing their weapons at her. She quickly turned and tried to run back up the steps. Alicia heard footsteps running down the stairs and others coming up behind her. Hands grabbed her and the overwhelming smells of bad breath and body odor filled her nostrils.

Alicia started screaming as a hand clamped over her mouth. Her teeth bit down hard, drawing blood. Bo Harris yelled and punched her on the side of the head with his other hand, dragging the now-dazed girl back over to the others.

"Look what I found, guys," Bo announced. He wiped the blood from his hand across Alicia's hoodie, grabbing at her breasts. "She's going home with me. I've always liked these little dark hotties."

Don Lester had heard the other sets of footsteps rushing down the stairs. As Bo was manhandling the black girl, the hefty young man raised his Benelli M4 Tactical shotgun. Two armed students, members of the QRF, came into view on the stairwell and Don blasted them with double 00 buckshot from a distance of ten feet, knocking both of them down. Lester fed two more shells into his gun, keeping watch on the staircase.

"Who'd we lose outside?" Neil asked calmly.

"Where's Wesley?" Joey wondered, the concern evident in his voice.

"Kevin's not here, either," Mark Anderson announced quietly. "Joey, I'm pretty sure I saw Wesley go down right after the shooting started."

"Little Tommy Taylor is missing, too," another voice said.

"So we're down three," Dodd observed, slinging his AK and drawing the Desert Eagle pistol. "Give me that girl, Bo."

"Don't hurt her, Neil," Bo pleaded. "I want keep her."

Even in the dim light, Harris saw the flash of anger in the enforcer's eyes and he handed Alicia over to him. She had recovered from the strike to her head and realized that, for the moment, she needed to stay calm. The muscular thug wrapped his left arm around her neck and put the barrel of a huge pistol against the side of her head.

"What's your name?" the gunman asked the trembling young woman.

"Alicia," she said, her voice shaking.

Neil yelled, his voice projecting through the dorm and to the security team in front of the building. "You people outside and everybody inside, we've got Alicia with us. Stay back and we won't hurt her. If you college pukes try anything, I'm going to splatter her brains all over this building."

Dodd looked back at his hostage and spoke in a lower, but still menacing voice, "Alicia, we're here for Chuck. What's his last name?"

She didn't answer. Why Chuck? How did they even know who he was? The gun jammed viciously into her temple.

Alicia grunted with pain. "McCain," she answered, angry tears streaming down her face. "Chuck McCain."

McCain eased the dorm room door open. He heard voices talking excitedly, a woman scream, and then a man yell near the front entrance. A few seconds later, two loud blasts echoed down the hallway. Chuck didn't want to just rush out into the corridor, guns blazing. He needed to assess the situation first and figure out what he was dealing with. He peered around the doorway, only exposing his left eye.

Flashlights flickered and danced down the hallway near the middle of the dorm. A group of armed attackers were standing in a line, near a large man who was holding someone. That has to be who screamed, Chuck thought. What I'd give to have some night vision.

McCain guessed at least ten intruders, but there could be twenty or more hidden in the shadows for all he knew. Chuck considered trying to climb out one of his windows and slipping up behind the thugs. The windows, however, opened outwards with a crank, and he knew there was no way that he'd fit through the small opening.

The dorm door across the hallway opened and Beth's face peered out, the fear evident in her eyes. He saw that she held her Glock in a low ready stance, standing back from the opening. Good girl, he thought.

Chuck whispered from inside his own doorway, "Get back inside, now!" He waved her back from across the corridor.

"What's happening?" she mouthed, her face a mask of terror.

A loud voice yelled for everyone to stay back and announcing that Alicia was a hostage.

"Chuck McCain!" the same deep voice bellowed a moment later from up the corridor. "Our business is with you. Come out with your hands up and walk down here."

"I don't think we've met," Chuck called out. "You seem to know me but I don't know you."

"You met some friends of mine and killed them. And you stole a bunch of our stuff. We've come to collect. Bring that girl with you.

We want to have a talk with her, too."

There was a smattering of laughter from the other gunmen.

"The only one of 'em I got a name for was some piece-of-crap, dirty cop named Mike Carter," Chuck yelled up the hallway. "Is that who you're talking about?"

An angry buzz of voices came from the intruders. "He's the one, him and his men. I also heard you gunned down a girl named Tonya and stole her baby. She was a friend of ours, too."

"You're half right. I did kill Tonya when she and her doper boyfriend tried to rob me. But the baby? I left that little boy with meth-head Greg."

McCain could hear more murmuring from the group of armed men.

"Enough talking!" the loud voice yelled. "Come out right now or I'm gonna kill this cute little black girl. I might even let a couple of the boys have some fun with her first while you cower down there like a scared dog. You can listen if you want."

"I'll come out, " McCain answered. "Just let me put my gun down."

Chuck pulled the thirty round mag out of his rifle, sliding it across the floor and under the bed. He pulled the charging handle to the rear, ejecting the chambered round to the floor. At least this way, they'd have to take a couple of action steps to use the gun. He tossed the M-4 onto the bed and grabbed the Glock off the night table, slipping it into the waistband of his jeans at the small of his back, pulling the Northeast Georgia Technical School sweatshirt down over it.

"I'm coming out now."

Beth's watched in horror from her doorway. She was mouthing, "No!" and shaking her head. He winked at her, smiling as he exited, walking down the corridor, his hands up.

The Northeast Georgia Technical College, Lavonia, Georgia, Monday, 0105 hours

Jake met the second security patrol converging on the dorm after hearing the gunfire. Tina had instructed them to check the roadblock when their team leader, Gina, had checked in. When the shooting started, however, they all turned and ran toward the dormitory. The four cautiously approached the long building, still not knowing what was happening. A soft whistle came from the parking area, adjacent to the front entrance of the residence hall. Danny and Maria were crouched behind a Nissan Sentra.

"Mr. Nicholson, we're glad to see you," Maria said.

She and Danny quickly recounted what they had seen and their part in the gunfight. Mr. Clayton had sent them to the parking lot to wait for backup. Robert had crawled up to the large front windows of the dorm and was concealed in some bushes next to the door so he could monitor what was happening inside.

"It looked like maybe ten or fifteen people with guns," Danny quietly told Nicholson and the other team. "A lot. We think we hit three of them so there's still a big group. The ones we shot are lying right over there," he pointed to a small grassy area near the front of the dormitory, "but we haven't checked to see if they're dead or wounded because we didn't want to give away our positions with our flashlights."

Jake gave some quick orders and they all prepared to move out. Everyone trusted the Marine's leadership and having a plan gave them something to focus on. They knew that their job was to eliminate or capture the intruders and try to minimize casualties in the dorm, a difficult task in a building packed with so many residents.

Nicholson had cautioned them on fire discipline but also told them that they were going to be the ones to end this crisis. Their rules of engagement were not to shoot into the building until he started shooting and not to let anyone escape. Nicholson told them to fire through the glass windows. They weren't that thick and the bullets would easily penetrate the glass.

A loud voice yelled for everyone to stay back and said that Alicia was their hostage. A minute later the same person inside the dormitory called for Chuck and told him to come out. They could only hear part of the conversation from the parking lot but they understood that things were about to come to a head.

Jake sent Danny, Maria, and the other three sentries to join Robert near the front entrance of the dorm. It was a crawl of about forty yards, mostly in the open, but the darkness would conceal them as they moved. Nicholson wanted all six of the security patrol stationed at the front door.

If and when shooting erupted, he would rather have the inexperienced sentries firing into the area of the building where they had the least chance for collateral damage. He assigned Tyrone, a member of the second team to cover the downed intruders in front of the building. Jake hoped they were dead or completely incapacitated but he sure didn't want bad guys sneaking up behind his people.

Jake left the team members to get into place and rushed towards the end of the dorm from where he had exited earlier. He withdrew a key from his pocket, quietly opening the door.

"I'm coming out now." Jake recognized Chuck's voice from the far end of the building.

Nicholson slipped inside, moving stealthily down the corridor, coming up behind the attackers. From the little bit of illumination their flashlights gave off, the attackers all seemed to be focused on the big man walking towards them with his arms raised.

As Jake moved down the hall, several dorm room doors opened partially, scared faces peering out. The Marine held a forefinger to his lips and kept walking.

McCain had his hands at shoulder level as he approached the lobby of the dorm. Rifles and shotguns were pointed at him and he expected the bullets to rip through him at any moment. He walked slowly, watching the men in the faint light, trying to learn as much as he could about them. Chuck knew that Jake, Tina, and the security teams would be here soon.

Chuck also realized that he was a dead man. His only hope was to save Alicia and to delay their escape until Nicholson got his people into place. And, if I'm lucky, maybe I can kill a few on my way out, he thought.

It had sounded like one of the patrols had stumbled upon the invaders and a gunfight had ensued. He hoped Jake's people were OK. It had been brief but intense, just like some of the firefights he'd been in in Afghanistan. What would the Green Berets do in a situation like this? he wondered.

A tall, powerful-looking man held Alicia, a large Desert Eagle pointed at her head. Nice gun, McCain thought. On either side of him were two monsters. They both looked big enough to play offensive line for a Division I school. Why can't I ever get some little guys to tangle with?

A short, wiry, angry-looking young man stepped in front of the brute holding Alicia. Well, there's my little guy, Chuck almost laughed to himself. The small man raised a full-sized AR-15 and leveled it at Chuck's head.

"You killed my daddy," he hissed. "Now I'm gonna kill you."

"Bo, get behind me until I tell you," Mr. Muscles snapped.

"You told me I could kill him, Neil," Bo whined, lowering the rifle.

"Bo, do what I tell you," Neil ordered, the menace clear in his voice.

“Mike Carter was your daddy?” Chuck taunted. “Are you sure? A scrawny little turd like you coming from that big man?”

The rifle came back up and McCain thought he might have overplayed his hand. The offensive lineman to the right of Muscles clamped a meaty hand on Bo’s shoulder.

“Listen to Neil. You can kill him later.”

“Larry Harris was my daddy,” Bo hissed, through clenched teeth. “He was in that house, too, and you gunned him down.”

McCain nodded. “I probably did. I killed several scumbags that night and I’m sure your daddy was one of them.”

Chuck thought that Bo might actually start crying, he was so angry. He started to raise the rifle again but the offensive lineman put his hand on the barrel and kept it from coming up. Bo glared at Chuck with hatred and unbridled hostility in his eyes.

“Bo, I just want to talk to him for a minute and then you can have him, OK?” Neil asked. It was obviously a command but he needed to keep the angry young man dialed in.

“Sure, Neil, but now I want to kill this bastard nice and slow. I think I’m gonna use my knife.”

Bo stepped out of the way, to the side of the bigger men.

“Where’s the girl?” Dodd asked McCain, the Desert Eagle still pressed against Alicia’s temple.

“You seem more like the type who’d like little boys, Neil.” Chuck replied, looking into Dodd’s eyes.

The offensive lineman on Neil’s left was surprisingly quick, closing the distance, and slamming a vicious right uppercut into Chuck’s midsection. The man was powerful but McCain had been hit harder in sparring. He acted the part, though, and doubled over, giving the appearance that he’d really been hurt.

The knee was a surprise, catching him solidly in the face, sending an electrical shock through his neck, and ripping open his right cheek. The blow stunned McCain and he dropped to one knee to allow his dazed head to clear, even as blood dripped to the floor. The offensive lineman drew back and threw a looping right hand aimed at Chuck's face. McCain lowered his jaw against his chest and the punch connected with the top of his skull. It was a vicious punch, ripping Chuck's scalp open and sending another explosion of pain through his head.

Don Lester gasped after landing the punch to the skull, however, grabbing his right hand with his left, feeling bones break in his hand when he connected with the kneeling man's hard head. McCain felt the blood, now running down the side of his head from his scalp, matching what was pouring out of the cut on his cheek. Thankfully, Chuck knew what it was like to get hit in the head, grateful that he was still conscious.

Neil just shook his head. "It's time to end this. We need to get out of here, boys." Dodd stated. "McCain, I'm gonna shoot this sweet young thing in the head if you don't tell me where the girl is."

Chuck looked into Alicia's eyes and saw the terror. She shook her head at McCain. He knew he really had to sell this.

He looked up at Dodd but spoke loudly. "Please, just let Alicia go. The other girl's hiding in my room, the one I came out of. She's scared. She watched your people kill her friends. Then they kidnapped her and tried to rape her. Please, you've got me," he pleaded. "Just let everybody else go."

"Hoss, Joey, Mark, go get her," Neil commanded.

They rushed down the hallway to the room where they'd seen Chuck exit moments ago. As they went, McCain glanced around at the faces of the other criminals. His gaze paused over a familiar looking gaunt figure with hollow eyes, standing off to the side, holding a pump-action shotgun. Greg realized that he'd been made and stepped back into the shadows.

Gunfire and screams suddenly erupted from the direction of Chuck's room.

Elizabeth stood back from her partially open door, pistol in hand, listening to Chuck taunt their attackers. He's going to get himself killed, she thought, tears streaming down her face. The sight and sounds of the brute striking the man she loved made her sick to her stomach and she wanted to rush into the hallway to try and help him as he collapsed to the floor.

At the same time, she knew that Chuck would not want her to do that. Just wait for an opportunity, she thought. She heard Chuck raise his voice, telling the gunmen that she was hiding in his room. Oh, my God! she thought. He's sending them down here. Loud footsteps rushed her way. She pushed her door until it was only open an inch but still allowed her to see into the passageway.

Chuck told them that I'm in his room, she quickly reasoned. They're not going to find me in there so they'll shoot him and Alicia. As the pounding steps were almost to his quarters, in an instant, it became completely clear. Glancing down at the 9mm Glock she was holding, Beth suddenly understood. He's sending those men down here for me to deal with!

There was no time to think and no time to hesitate. Beth took a deep breath and watched the huge man pause at McCain's door. The tall, thin one was following and the athletic looking, younger man with the mullet was behind him. They all held long guns.

As they pushed open the door and stepped into Chuck's room, Elizabeth quietly pulled hers open, raising the Glock, her finger tightening around the trigger.

Jake was almost close enough to where he could start engaging the intruders. The light in the hallway was so dim, he wanted to make sure that no other residents had gotten dragged out of their rooms. He'd heard the conversation and knew they were holding Alicia as a hostage and now McCain was just in front of them, kneeling on the floor after being pounded by one of the animals. Nicholson raised his rifle, sighting in on the back of the head of the muscular one who held a large pistol to Alicia's head.

Gunfire suddenly exploded from the far end of the building, in the area of Elizabeth and Chuck's rooms. The muzzle flashes lit the hallway as the shooter fired shot after shot. A half second later, the man holding Alicia grunted loudly in pain and jerked out of Jake's sights.

Everything seemed to slow down. Nicholson turned his weapon-mounted flashlight on and tried to acquire another target. All of the intruders were moving, several of them swinging their weapons towards McCain.

A little man with a long AR-15 yelled something towards Chuck, aiming his rifle at the kneeling police officer. Jake fired twice, both shots hitting Bo Harris in the back. Everyone seemed to be shooting now. The front glass shattered as Nicholson's sentries began firing into the building at the attackers. People were yelling and screaming, crying out in both anger and in pain.

Nicholson was looking for another target when his light picked up a gaunt, pockmarked faced man running down the corridor towards him. Jake saw the shotgun coming up and he swung his own muzzle towards this new threat. They both fired at the same time. The Marine saw the skinny man spin and fall but he felt the impact of the shotgun blast, knowing that he'd been hit as well as the floor rushed up to meet him.

Alicia was terrified and angry. She was angry with herself for getting taken hostage. She was really mad at these nasty rednecks, but she was especially angry and hurt at Mr. McCain for telling these evil men where Miss Benton was. Why had he done that? She watched in helplessness as the three intruders rushed down the corridor to Chuck's room.

She cautiously eased her right hand up to feel for the knife that she always carried. It was still in the pocket of her hoodie. The smelly little dude whom she'd bitten was more concerned with feeling her boobs than checking her for weapons. This Neil guy pressing his big gun to her head wasn't worried about a little defenseless female hurting him.

Alicia hadn't had much experience with guns but she admittedly grew up on the wrong side of the tracks in Lavonia and had become very familiar with knives, never leaving home without one. After she'd started working for Elizabeth and making good money, Alicia had decided to treat herself.

She had researched knives online and, armed with that knowledge, had marched into a local gun store asking to see their Benchmade automatic knives. She chose a nice black one with a partially serrated blade. Alicia had never imagined that she would be able to afford a knife that cost almost two hundred and fifty dollars, but being Miss Benton's assistant paid well.

Suddenly gunshots rang out from Miss Benton's room, fire from the muzzle leaping out of Elizabeth's doorway towards Mr. McCain's room. Alicia felt the gun against her head slip away and point outwards towards Chuck. She thrust her hand into the hoodie pocket, grabbing the automatic knife. Withdrawing it, Alicia depressed the small button on the side and the three and a half inch, razor sharp blade flicked open and locked into place.

Without hesitation, she turned slightly and plunged the knife into the outside of her captor's right leg, shoving it in until the entire blade had disappeared into his flesh. The huge handgun fired, jumping in Dodd's hand. Alicia saw Chuck, already scrambling towards the wall to his right, flinch in pain, grunting loudly but quickly drawing a pistol of his own. The lobby of the dorm building was filled with gunfire, people yelling, and the acrid smell of smoke.

The man who had been holding Alicia gasped when he tried to

take a step, the knife protruding out of his thigh. Dodd threw the girl to the side as if she were a rag doll, her back slamming into the wall to her left, the impact knocking the breath out of her and sending her to the floor near McCain. She glanced up, seeing her captor's handgun tracking towards her. Suddenly, he jerked backwards as blood spurted from multiple gunshot wounds low on his torso.

Someone grabbed Alicia's arm, pulling her along the floor and lying on top of her. Even while she was breathless from being thrown, Alicia tried to fight this new attacker off as the gun battle raged all around her.

As soon as the shots erupted behind him, hopefully all being fired by Elizabeth, Chuck dove towards the wall, reaching for his pistol at the small of his back. Neil swung the .44 Magnum Desert Eagle, the muzzle acquiring Chuck. McCain saw the blur of Alicia's hand grabbing the knife, opening it, and then stabbing her captor. The big handgun bucked in Dodd's hand and McCain felt the impact, along with an intense burning, low on his left side.

Neil shoved Alicia into the wall and she collapsed to the floor, gasping for breath. McCain watched the barrel of Dodd's pistol now moving towards Alicia as Chuck starting pulling the trigger of his Glock as fast as he could, lying on his right side, firing upward towards Dodd and into the mass of other criminals. Neil stumbled backwards as 9mm hollow points struck him in the groin and abdomen.

Chuck kept shooting, sweeping the gun from left to right, trying to kill as many of these animals as he could before he died. Heavy shooting erupted from the front entrance, letting him know Jake's people were in place and returning fire.

McCain pushed himself forward towards Alicia as he continued to fire the pistol. She was just in front of him and he grabbed her arm, pulling her towards himself. The stunned woman began fighting him.

"Alicia, it's me, Chuck!" he yelled into her ear over the explosions all around them.

She finally stopped thrashing and he covered her with his battered body, shielding her from the flying lead.

"Cease fire! Cease fire!" Robert Clayton yelled, dropping an empty thirty-round magazine to the ground as he smoothly reloaded with a full one.

Everybody he could see inside the lobby of the dorm was down. Clayton shone his weapon light through the broken windows. A few wounded people were writhing in pain, moaning softly, while others weren't moving at all, but no one seemed to want to fight any more.

"Maria and Danny, on me," Robert commanded. "Gina, keep watch behind us. I don't know if these guys have any friends with them or not. Jessica and Tyrone, go secure those three that we shot earlier. We can use our lights now, just be careful that they aren't playing possum."

Running footsteps came up behind them from across the parking lot. Six rifles and shotguns spun towards the new threat.

"Stop! We will shoot you!" Robert challenged.

The runner stopped. An out-of-breath voice called, "It's me, Tina Miles. I just came from the roadblock. Todd's dead and Bradley's missing."

"Thank God you're here, Officer Miles," Clayton said, relieved, illuminating the police officer with his flashlight as she got closer. "We were just getting ready to go inside and check for our people. None of the intruders got away, at least not out this door. Jake went in through the side entrance," pointing in the direction he had gone.

Tina carried a rifle and was trying to recover from her mad dash, clearly not used to running across campus.

Robert let her catch her breath. "It looks like everybody's down inside the lobby entrance here. You want to go in with us?"

Tina nodded, wondering where Jake was. Robert, Tina, Danny, Maria entered the dorm, shining their lights on the bloody carnage. Six intruders were lying in growing pools of blood in the lobby. The security team kicked the attackers' guns away, covering them with their weapons.

Just inside the hallway to the left, they found a battered McCain rolling off of a dazed Alicia. Footsteps came running down the hall.

"Chuck? Alicia? Are you guys OK?" Elizabeth called out, a fearful tremor in her voice.

Beth's flashlight beam lit up her bloody but living boyfriend and she threw herself onto him.

Loud voices came from the other end of the corridor indicating that they had found an unconscious Jake and a wounded intruder. McCain gently pushed Beth away, motioning with his head at Alicia, weeping at his side. Elizabeth reached for her assistant, wrapping her arms around the young woman.

"Beth, are those three guys down?" McCain asked.

For a moment, Benton didn't respond but then nodded, continuing to hold her sobbing friend.

Chuck looked down at the Glock he was still holding, the slide locked open, the gun now empty. He laid it on the floor and picked up a flashlight one of the attackers had dropped. Someone needed to take charge and it sounded like Jake was hurt.

This might not be over, McCain thought. His left hip throbbed but he needed to get to his feet. A young Hispanic man wearing a green Northeast Georgia Technical College sweatshirt and holding a shotgun stood nearby, looking shocked at the carnage all around them.

"What's your name?" Chuck asked.

He looked down at McCain, his eyes getting big as he took in Chuck's bloody face, scalp, and side. The young man swallowed.

"Danny Romero, sir."

"Nice to meet you, Danny. Can you help me stand up?"

Danny reached down and with some difficulty, was able to help the wounded warrior to his feet.

"Thanks," Chuck nodded, his head pounding and feeling the blood pouring down his left leg. He turned and walked towards the sprawled bodies in the lobby of the dorm.

Residents were now coming out of their rooms, many of them crying. Chuck heard a couple of people say that bullets had come flying into their rooms. There was a shout for someone to find Karen or an EMT. Someone had been struck by a stray bullet. Another resident called out from the stairwell saying they had someone wounded there, as well.

It was quickly turning into agony for McCain to walk, as the pain shot from his hip into his leg and the rest of his body. He didn't know how badly he'd been hit but it really hurt. Chuck shone the Maglite on the six men who had just tried to kill him, all dead or dying from multiple gunshot wounds. He's not here. I hope he didn't get away, McCain thought.

Down the hall, one of the sentries leaned over someone on the floor, jabbing him angrily with the muzzle of his rifle.

"Who are you? Why'd you come here? Answer me!"

The prone man only groaned in response. He uttered a few unintelligible phrases and was quiet again.

Chuck staggered painfully down the corridor to where the intruder was lying next to the left wall. A few feet away, Tina knelt beside a barely conscious Jake, who was seated with his back against the opposite wall, holding his head with both hands. McCain got even with the sentry and recognized him as Robert, the IT professor Nicholson had identified as helping him train the sentries.

Chuck's light illuminated the hollow eyes and pockmarked face of Greg Davis. He had been shot high on the right side of his chest, blood oozing out of the wound below his shoulder. Maybe fatal or maybe not. It doesn't really matter, McCain thought, stumbling over to where Nicholson was. I must've lost a lot of blood, Chuck realized. I'm starting to get a little dizzy.

"You OK, Jake?" he asked.

"Oh, yeah, peachy." The Marine looked up at his friend. "I took a shotgun blast to the leg and tore it up pretty bad. Thankfully, I've got a spare in my room. I knocked myself out when I fell, though. And I think I chipped a tooth. How about you?"

McCain managed to smile when he realized that Nicholson was talking about his prosthetic leg being shot. Things were computing slowly tonight for some reason.

"I got shot, too. Maybe in the ass. I'll check it in a minute. Have you got a knife I can borrow?"

Jake pulled the Marine issue Ka-Bar from its sheath and handed it to Tina, who held it out to Chuck. These just feel good, McCain thought, hefting the knife. This has to be what Glock modeled their knives after, he surmised.

McCain turned and limped the few steps to where Greg lay.

"I've got this, Robert, if you want to go check on the others. There are three more bad guys down the hall near mine or Elizabeth's room. She shot them but I don't know if they're dead or not."

Robert hesitated as Chuck slowly slumped to his knees beside the wounded man, holding a big knife. At this point, though, he realized he didn't care what Mr. McCain did to this piece of human waste.

Clayton shrugged and climbed to his feet, "I'll go check them."

"Hi, Greg, remember me?" Chuck lightly jabbed him under the chin with the point of the blade.

McCain could hear the drug addict struggling to breathe, but his eyes fluttered open. Chuck shone the light on his own face so Greg could see who was talking to him, the fear of recognition coming into the drug addict's eyes.

"What did you do with the baby, Greg?"

The wounded man groaned but didn't answer, shaking his head. Chuck stabbed him in the left shoulder, eliciting a scream of pain and then another as he wiggled the blade around. Tina saw what was happening and started to intervene, but Jake grabbed her arm, pulling her back, shaking his head at her. He had heard the story about Greg and figured he was about to get what he deserved.

"What did you do with the baby, Greg?" Chuck repeated slowly, pulling the knife free, waving it in front of the meth-addict's face, blood dripping onto his nose. "You want me to stick you again? Next time, I'm going to stick you lower, someplace really sensitive. Answer my question."

McCain lightly tapped the knife against Greg's groin.

"Chuck, I told you that wasn't my baby," he groaned. "What was I supposed to do, man? I couldn't take him with me. He's fine. I'm sure some people found him and are taking good care of him."

"You left a little baby, what was his name? Jeremy. Did you leave Jeremy by himself in that cold, abandoned house?"

Greg closed his eyes and didn't say anything. The tip of the Ka-Bar started digging into his testicles.

"I'm sorry, Chuck," he pleaded, his voice getting high. "What else could I have done? I didn't have a car. You took my gun. I didn't have a choice; I had to leave him behind. It was your fault. If you hadn't killed Tonya, he would've still had his momma to take care of him. It was your fault, Chuck."

"I understand," McCain said, the room starting spin. He raised the knife over his head and plunged it into Greg's chest. That exertion did him in, though, and everything went black for Chuck McCain.

Chapter Nine

Recovery

Beth's room, The Northeast Georgia Technical College, Lavonia, Georgia, Monday, 1630 hours

Chuck awoke to the late afternoon sun pouring into the room. Sheets containing Beth's scent covered his aching body. McCain was lying on his right side and he reached down to feel the throbbing wound on his left hip, discovering that he was naked from the waist down.

He touched the long gauze bandage covering the injury on his hip and buttock. Chuck could feel the stitches under the gauze, a lot of stitches, then was suddenly aware of an intense pounding from his head and face. McCain gently probed his bandaged right cheek, his swollen right eye, and then the top of his head, feeling the dressing taped to his scalp.

A cool hand touched his left cheek, startling him, and Elizabeth's beautiful but concerned face was hovering over his own. She sat down next to him on the bed, leaning in and gently kissing him.

"Sorry, I didn't mean to make you jump. How are you feeling?" she asked softly.

"Your face and lips will cure anything," he smiled at her. "Are you OK? What about Alicia and everybody else?"

Chuck tried to push himself up but the pulsating pain in his head intensified and he lay back down. Beth laid her hand on his shoulder.

"Slow down. You need to stay in bed. Alicia's going to be fine. She was banged up a little but you saved another young girl's life," Elizabeth said, proudly.

"What about you? You really shot those three guys? I'm so proud of you."

There was a pause and then she nodded. "I did. I killed all three of them. You trained me well. That's the reason you're in here with me. They took the bodies out of your room but they haven't cleaned the blood off the floor yet."

McCain tried to raise himself up again on his right elbow and saw that his pillow was a mess where he had been lying, the wound on his cheek still seeping blood. Dizziness and pain forced him to lie down again. That big punk must've hit me a lot harder than I thought, he mused. Chuck took Beth's hand in his, looking into her eyes, appraising her.

"How do you feel about killing them?"

Elizabeth looked away and gave a slight shrug. "I don't know. What am I supposed to be feeling? I'm not sorry. They would've raped me and murdered both of us, and probably Alicia, as well.

"I guess I'm kind of surprised that I don't feel more emotional about it. Maybe I will later. I'm just glad you're OK," she said, squeezing his hand.

Chuck nodded. "Don't worry about not feeling anything. We all process things differently and it sounds like you're handling it just fine. How many people did we lose?"

She looked at the floor. "Three dead. Bradley and Todd were killed at the barricade. Kevin and Jermaine were shot as they ran down the stairs. They were part of Mr. Nicholson's quick reaction force. Kevin's dead, Jermaine was wounded.

"He had on body armor and Karen says he's going to make it. His arm is kind of messed up but, thank God, he's OK. Another girl, a student, got hit by a stray bullet in her dorm room. Karen says she'll live but it's still a serious wound."

"I'm so sorry. What about the bad guys? Did any get away?"

"Mr. Nicholson will come talk to you later. He told me that there were thirteen bodies. He didn't think anyone escaped."

"Is he upset with me?"

"Why would he be upset with you?" she asked, surprised. "You saved Alicia and almost got killed doing it. Jake said it would have been a lot worse if the sentry team hadn't confronted the gang before they got inside. But he also thinks you killed at least four or five of them when all the shooting started in the dorm."

"I don't know," McCain said, slowly, closing his eyes. "I guess I feel responsible. Their leader, that Neil guy, asked for me by name. I can't help but think that I should've done more to prevent this from happening. Plus, I murdered Greg. He was wounded and I didn't have to kill him, but I did."

Beth's hand touched his face again as she leaned close to him. "I made sure that everyone heard why you did that. Tina was pretty upset at first, but when she heard about the baby, she said, 'It's a good thing Chuck took him out so I didn't have to!'"

Elizabeth leaned over so she could look into Chuck's eyes. "A wise man told me recently, 'You can't beat yourself up for things you had no control over.' Or something like that. I was still a little out of it myself when he shared his wisdom with me. That same wise man also said that there are some very evil people in the world. I'm just glad there are men like you who are brave enough to stand up to them."

McCain sighed, looking into the beautiful eyes of the beautiful girl seated beside him. Footsteps coming from the sitting room made him look up as Karen walked in, clad in blue scrubs, rubbing the sleep out of her eyes.

"Busy day?" Chuck asked.

"I just caught a little nap on the couch. I haven't had to work this hard since I was an ER nurse at Grady."

Grady Memorial Hospital, in downtown Atlanta, was one of the biggest hospitals in the southeast and was known for its trauma unit. If Karen had worked there, Chuck thought, I'm in really good hands.

"You worked at Grady? You've probably got more experience dealing with traumatic injuries and gunshots than most doctors. I'm feeling a lot better about my chances for recovery now."

The pretty nurse managed a smile. "Oh, you'll recover. You're just gonna have less of that nice butt to carry around with you."

"Karen!" Elizabeth laughed.

"So how bad is it?" Chuck asked with a grin. "It feels like a lot of stitches. Did you get the bullet out?"

Karen walked over to Chuck, pulling the sheet down just far enough to expose the injury on his hip. She pulled a pair of blue rubber gloves out of her side pocket and slipped them on.

"Well, if you had to get shot, you picked a good place for it. Jake said it was a .44 Magnum that got you. I'm no gun expert but I know that's a big bullet.

"Thankfully, it just dug a nasty trench down the side of your hip. If it had been two inches to the right, you would've lost your leg and probably bled out. If it had been five inches to the right, well, you would've lost something else very important.

"Now don't get me wrong. It's a serious injury and we're going to need to keep a close eye on it," she said, winking at Beth, "to make sure it doesn't get infected. The wound's almost six inches long, over an inch wide, and half an inch deep. It took twenty-eight stitches to close it up. You lost a lot of blood so you're going to have to stay in bed for a few days."

Karen used a piece of gauze to wipe the edges of the bandage covering the large wound where blood had seeped out, and then pulled the sheet back up. Chuck felt her touching the top of his head and then she knelt down to examine his right cheek and eye.

"You have a cut on the top of your skull and another on your cheek. I used superglue and butterfly bandages to close those up. I hope that's OK. I think the scar will be smaller on your cheek that way. Looking at your face, though, it'll just be one more for the collection. I don't think you've got any broken facial bones."

"Thanks, Karen. I really appreciate you patching me up."

The nurse shone a small flashlight into his eyes. "Elizabeth told me you used to be a fighter?"

"I was."

"You can add another concussion to your list of injuries, too. I saw the body of that kid who beat you. He was huge!"

"I had wins over bigger guys than him in my career. He didn't hit that hard."

"Okay, Rocky, if you say so," the nurse shrugged, rolling her eyes.

"What about Jermaine and the girl who was hit?"

Karen sighed. "Jermaine's got two broken ribs and a shotgun pellet hit him in the bend of his right arm, shattering his elbow. He needs an orthopedist. I cleaned the wound, bandaged it, and set it, but that's about the extent of what I can do here. When it heals, he'll never be able to flex that arm again.

"Amber's the girl who was wounded. She's in kind of the same boat as Jermaine. She'd come to her door to see what was happening. When all the shooting started inside the dorm, a round caught her in the left shoulder.

"It's a bad wound and she needs a surgeon, too. I don't even know where to start with that one, other than making sure it doesn't get infected. We'll do the best we can."

Karen turned to go. "I need to go check on my other two

patients. Chuck, I know you'd planned on leaving today, but that's not happening."

McCain had already conceded in his own mind that he wasn't going to be able to look for Melanie until he healed up. The two injuries on his head would heal quickly, but the gunshot wound to his nether regions was going to severely limit his mobility and he was going to need enough time to recover.

Chuck smiled and nodded, looking at Elizabeth. "I guess you're stuck with me a little longer."

The nurse turned back to her patient. "Since you're going to be around for a little while, would you mind giving me some weapons training? Mr. Nicholson has offered some over the last few months, but I think I only went once.

"I didn't think I needed to learn since we have a security team here. Now I'm thinking that everyone on this campus needs to be thoroughly trained. The results of your coaching Elizabeth were pretty impressive."

"Sure, Karen. I'll let you know when I'll be working with Beth and you can join us."

The nurse nodded her thanks and left to attend to the other wounded.

A loud rumbling noise came from McCain's stomach. "Any chance of getting something to eat in this hospital?" he asked his pretty girlfriend.

Beth's room, The Northeast Georgia Technical College, Lavonia, Georgia, Monday, 1800 hours

Jake and Chuck consumed the last of the Evan Williams bourbon as Nicolson told him as much as he knew of what had transpired the night before. They were still trying to put all the pieces of the puzzle together. McCain was horrified to hear of the manner in which they had found Bradley's body. Chuck had not been a fan of the young man but felt terrible that Thomas had been murdered in such a brutal way.

"We recovered their four vehicles, parked up at the entrance. The bad guys even left the keys in the ignitions for us and, of course, their guns will come in very handy. The cost was way too high, though," Jake concluded.

"Suggestion?" Chuck asked.

"Of course."

"Let's have a debrief session tomorrow. Bring in everyone who was involved: all your sentries, Tina, you, Alicia, Elizabeth, me, and anyone else who played a role. A group debrief will help us to build the timeline of what happened, clarify where everyone was, what they did, and will allow us to learn together. It'll also be therapeutic."

"That's a great idea, McCain. Are you sure you weren't a Marine?"

"If I was, I'd be missing a big chunk of my brain right now," he laughed, pointing towards his wounded buttocks.

"Ha! There's probably some truth to that. Do you mind leading the debrief? I've never done one of those before."

"Sure, no problem."

After Jake left, there was a quiet knock on Beth's door. Chuck could hear two women talking in the other room. A moment later Elizabeth led Alicia to where he lay.

"I'm sorry to bother you, Mr. McCain. I wanted to check and see how you were doing."

"Hi, Alicia! I'll be fine. I've got some good people taking care of me. I'm so glad you're OK."

The young woman seemed uncomfortable, trying to control her emotions. Chuck could see her eyes watering, as she took a deep breath, crossing the room to McCain's bedside. She bent over, placed a hand on his shoulder, and kissed him softly on his uninjured cheek. Elizabeth guided her to the other bed across from Chuck's and the two girls sat down, Alicia wiping her eyes on the sleeve of her hoodie.

"I'm sorry," she laughed self-consciously. "I wasn't planning on crying. Thank you for what you did, Mr. McCain. I really think I'd be dead if it wasn't for you."

"You were pretty impressive yourself. That was some good blade work. Did you get your knife back?"

"I did. Mr. Nicholson even cleaned it off for me. He said we're having a debriefing tomorrow?"

"That's right," Chuck nodded.

"I don't know if I want to relive it," Alicia said, quietly. "I…I don't really think I need to be there. I didn't do that much. It's too painful and I'd rather just forget about it."

"Do you trust me, Alicia?" McCain asked.

Alicia's default position when it came to men was not to trust any of them. She had been hurt too many times. This man was different, though. He had shielded her with his own body, even after being beaten and shot.

"Yes, sir. I trust you," she answered, looking him in the eye.

"You do need to be there tomorrow," McCain told her. "I promise you that when we're done you'll feel a lot better. I've been through these kinds of meetings before. They're important to help us figure out what happened and what we can learn, so history doesn't repeat itself. These debriefings also end up being kind of like a group therapy session."

Alicia nodded and looked at Elizabeth. "Okay, I'll be there. And I just realized we almost lost you twice this week, Miss B! Maybe we all need some group therapy."

Beth put her arm around her assistant's shoulders. "It's been a rough few days, hasn't it? And poor Mr. McCain, he's been shot twice since he met me a week ago!"

Half an hour later, a weary-looking Nurse Karen came back to check on Chuck before she turned in for the night. The candles that Elizabeth had burning in the room didn't give off enough light, so the nurse used a small flashlight to look at McCain's wounds. Another knock at the door admitted Robert Clayton, also coming by to check on Chuck.

"Oh, hi, Karen, Mr. McCain," he said, shyly. "I can come back later if this isn't a good time. I just wanted see how you were feeling and to say, 'thank you.'"

"Hey, Robert," Chuck greeted the IT professor. "No, stick around. Karen's having way too much fun looking at my wounded ass."

The nurse punched him lightly on the shoulder and shook her head. Clayton didn't know whether McCain was making a joke or not so he just gave a slight smile.

"Karen," Chuck said, smiling at the nurse, "Jake told me that if it weren't for Robert and his team things would have gone much worse. Robert's sentries confronted those intruders before they got into the dorm and shot several of them to even the odds a little bit. Then he positioned his team by the front door and they cut down several of the gangbangers when the shooting started. They saved my life, that's for sure!"

McCain looked over at Clayton and saw that he was blushing. "Really good work, Robert. The only reason any of us survived was because of you and your people. That was great leadership."

Robert finally found his voice. "Thanks, Chuck. It was a team effort and I've learned a lot from Jake."

"I heard you're also a pretty good firearms instructor, Robert."

"I enjoy teaching," Clayton answered. "I like helping people develop a love for shooting. I've worked with Jake, doing a lot of the training for folks here on campus."

"That's great," Chuck nodded. "Karen told me that she wants to learn to handle a gun, right, Karen?"

The pretty nurse shot McCain a dirty look, but smiled up at Robert. "That's right. I hope we never have anything like this happen again, but I know I need to learn to shoot to help protect this place."

Robert smiled. "I'd be happy to help you, Karen. Anytime."

After Clayton took his leave, Karen turned towards McCain, her eyes blazing. "What was that, Chuck?"

The big man winked at her. "Just trying to help a sister out."

Later, Elizabeth came and sat beside Chuck on the small bed, being careful to avoid his injuries, but wanting to be near the man that she'd fallen so hard for. She was ready for sleep, wearing sweat pants, a sweatshirt, and thick socks in the cold dorm.

"I feel bad that you can't leave to find Melanie, but I'm happy we get a little more time together."

Beth's hand gently touched the uninjured side of his face. Chuck was silent in the flickering candlelight, his demeanor sober. After a few minutes he looked at the pretty young woman beside him.

"We need to talk about something," he said.

Seeing Chuck's serious expression, Beth's face fell and she looked troubled. "What? What's wrong?"

"Don't answer me right away, but I want you to think about going with me when I heal up and leave. It'll be…"

Elizabeth's squeal of delight cut him off. "Yes! There's nothing to think about. Of course, I want to go with you. You had me worried, Chuck! I didn't know what you were going to say."

McCain managed a tired smile. "If you're sure…"

Benton leaned down and kissed him on the left cheek, moving

her face around to find his lips. She kissed him hungrily, finally coming up for air.

"What made you change your mind?" she asked, out of breath.

"My whole reason for not wanting you to come was that I thought you'd be safer here. Obviously, that was a bad assumption. At least together, I can try to protect you. Or now that you've become such a deadly weapon, maybe you'll protect me," he grinned.

Elizabeth looked at him, her eyes wide in the soft glow of the candlelight. "Thank you so much for the opportunity to stay together. I do love you, and this makes me very happy."

"You have to promise to keep letting me train you. It's a dangerous world out there and I want to prepare you as much as I can."

"I understand and I'll do whatever you say," she answered, gently laying her head against his shoulder. After a few minutes she started kissing him again. "I'm sure that there are a lot of things you can teach me, Mr. McCain."

Beth's room, The Northeast Georgia Technical College, Lavonia, Georgia, Tuesday, 1100 hours

They all met in Elizabeth's suite since Karen had forbidden Chuck from getting out of bed for a few days. She didn't want to take any chances that the large trench on his hip might open back up. The nurse had checked his wounds, changed the bandages, and then she and Beth had helped their patient get cleaned up and into a fresh pair of sweat pants.

A large dry erase board was brought in and set up where everyone could see it. Chuck designated Elizabeth as the secretary. She would be recording the flowchart of events: what had happened, where and when. On the right side of the board Beth and Tina drew a map of the campus; on the left, McCain had instructed Benton to create a numbered list as people talked, detailing the timeline of yesterday's events.

Tina had arrived early with Jake. She hadn't seen Chuck since the incident. The campus police officer sat down beside him on the bed, putting her arms around the big man, her head against his chest, not saying anything. She started to speak a couple of times but nothing came out and McCain realized she was crying, the emotion of the last few days bubbling to the surface.

Finally, Chuck said, "I'm sorry you had to see me kill that bastard. I heard you were pretty mad at me."

The red-haired woman pulled back, looking into his eyes, tears still dripping out of hers. "I was. I mean I am a cop," she told him, drying her eyes with the back of her sleeve. "You're a cop, too. We just don't do that.

"But when I heard the whole story about how he'd tried to rob you and you let him live because of the baby, I realized there was a lot more to it. I heard him tell you that he'd abandoned that child and that it was your fault. When I realized he let a baby die, I changed my tune.

"Jake and I had a long talk later," she continued. "He said that Greg got what he deserved. I don't know. He probably did. I'm not judging you. I guess I'm still processing everything."

Chuck nodded at her. "You're good people, Tina. I hope that killing never becomes easy. We need folks with character to rebuild after what society's been through. In the meantime, though, the rules have changed. There are no jails to hold criminals and no courts to prosecute them."

Tina stood up, taking a deep breath. "You're right about the rules having changed," she nodded and then smiled. "Thank you for what you did for Alicia. You're her new hero."

McCain smiled back at her. "That's nice. I just wished I could've pulled it off without getting half of my ass shot off."

Everyone who had been involved in the shootout packed into the small room. They either brought a chair or sat on the floor. The six sentries, along with Jake and Tina, Chuck and Beth, Alicia, and even Jermaine, his right arm in bandages and wearing a sling, were all there.

Also present were Karen and her medical team. Even though they had shown up after the shooting had stopped, McCain requested that they be present, as well. Her team of nurses-in-training and EMT students had provided excellent care to the wounded.

"My apologies for having to lead this meeting from bed," Chuck opened, nodding across the room at his nurse, "but when Karen gives an order she's pretty scary."

There was light laughter from everyone.

"Before we do anything else, I'd like to have a moment of silence for our fallen friends."

A minute later, McCain spoke up. "The reason for this debrief is so that we can all get a clearer picture of what happened the other night and to see what we can learn from it. We're not looking to point fingers or to criticize. In fact, I think that we're going to see how well this incident was handled.

"Mr. Nicholson and I are both combat veterans, but none of the rest of you have had any experience dealing with this kind of an attack. Mr. Nicholson and Mr. Clayton have trained you guys," he said, nodding at the sentries, "but you really didn't know how any of that training was going to hold up until the bullets started flying."

Several of the sentry team members nodded their heads.

"We just need to put the pieces of the puzzle that each one of us is holding onto the whiteboard and the only way we can do that is talking it out together. So, let's start at the beginning. Officer Miles took a phone call from the roadblock. Tina, can you please tell us what time that call came in and as close as you can remember what they told you, word for word if at all possible?"

Miles told the group what Todd had reported to her over the phone. Elizabeth wrote down the time and a brief synopsis on the left side of the dry erase board next to the number one. On the map, she placed a number "1" at the roadblock.

After speaking with Todd, Jake was the first person whom Tina had contacted. Nicholson described his actions up until he heard gunshots.

Robert Clayton recounted phoning Tina during their patrol, being given Todd's status, and being ordered to go secure the dorm. He described his confrontation and the initial shootout with the attackers. As Robert talked about the exchange of gunfire, aiming at muzzle flashes, and seeing the intruders whom he had shot falling down, Chuck noticed everyone leaning in, many of them hearing this for the first time. McCain saw that Karen was especially engrossed as Robert told the group what he and his team had done.

The debrief took almost three hours but by the end, everyone was feeling better. Each person detailed their role in the incident, no matter how small. For the first time, Chuck heard Beth describe her part in the drama. She started off by describing the fear she had felt as the three criminals rushed down the hall towards her.

When they started into Chuck's room, however, Elizabeth said she pulled her door open, raised her pistol in the two-handed stance that Chuck had taught her and started firing as the first thug, the biggest one, was silhouetted in McCain's doorway. Beth said she stepped into the hallway as she kept shooting, not hearing the gunshots or feeling the recoil, just seeing the fire leaping out of the end of the barrel.

Beth told the group that she instinctively moved the pistol along the line of the three men, putting bullets into each of them at close range. The light of the muzzle flashes was enough for her to see that her rounds were hitting home as the three intruders jerked in pain, and then collapsed to the floor. Benton said she continued firing as they lay on the floor, wanting to make sure they never got up again.

By the time her Glock was empty and the attackers were down, gunfire had erupted in the lobby, bullets whizzing down the hallway of the dorm. Beth had darted back into her room, getting out of the line of fire. She reloaded her pistol like McCain had shown her and waited for the gunshots to cease.

Chuck was proud of Beth and proud of the group. He saw in everyone's eyes that they were proud, too. Each person had performed well to protect the campus. Sharing the experience together had lifted everyone's spirits. After they had recorded a timeline, McCain took them back through the incident, praising the quick actions and response of everyone involved.

Chuck hadn't realized until now that Jake had saved his life by shooting Bo Harris when he had. McCain thanked him and commended him publicly for his leadership. His people had responded well to the violent assault on what had become their home.

McCain also made a point of thanking Robert for his leadership and decisive actions. His team had definitely tipped the scales in the defender's favor. If Clayton, Danny, and Maria hadn't confronted the attackers when they did, the criminals would have gotten into the dorm undetected, which would have been a terrible scenario with a much different outcome. As Chuck spoke about Robert, he noticed Karen again watching the IT instructor closely.

McCain praised Alicia's courage and told the group that if anyone wanted to learn to use a knife to talk to her. That drew a smile of appreciation from the young woman and nods of approval from her friends.

"Now, as we wrap this up, these last few minutes are for

questions. If you want to know why someone did what they did, let's ask. We're friends here. If there's something we missed in our discussion, bring it up and let's get it on the table."

There were several questions to clarify the chronology. Another questioner wondered if Mr. Nicholson or Mr. McCain anticipated any further attacks.

"We'll need to tighten up our defenses, that's for sure," answered Jake. "But if these intruders had any friends waiting for them to come home, they're going to be waiting a long time. Robert and I will continue to offer firearms training for anyone who might be interested. I'm hoping that we'll have some new people volunteer to be a part of the security force."

Maria, one of sentries on Robert's team, shyly raised her hand.

"Mr. McCain, this debrief has been very helpful for us to see what happened, and to get the 'big picture' that you mentioned earlier. I don't know about everybody else, but talking about it together like this has really helped me to put things in perspective. I'm really thankful we were able to stop those people.

"I have a question for you, though. We were right outside the front door and could hear most of the conversation between you and the bad guys. Can you tell us what you were thinking, why you did what you did, and why, in God's name, did you taunt all those men with guns pointed at you?"

This got a laugh from everyone, including Chuck. "That's a great question. What was I thinking? I'm going to die. That's what I was thinking. In fact, I knew I was as good as dead. When those gangbangers said they were going to kill Alicia if I didn't give myself up, there was no doubt in my mind that when I walked out that doorway and down the hallway, that was it. I was done.

"My second thought was, maybe I can save Alicia's life before they kill me.

"My third thought was, I'm gonna to take as many of these

bastards with me as I can before I die.

"I've been working with Elizabeth on weapons handling and tactics, and I knew she was standing in her doorway, holding her pistol. I hoped that by sending those scumbags to my room, she'd act decisively. And she was amazing, taking them all out.

"Why did I taunt all those armed men? I don't know. I knew they were going to kill me so I really didn't have anything to lose. I was a professional MMA fighter for a while, and there were some guys I could gain an advantage over before a fight by getting under their skin. Plus, I figured if I was going to meet my Maker, I might as well have some fun with those pricks first."

This brought another big laugh from the group and everyone was smiling as they left. As they filed out, each person stopped by to shake McCain's hand or give him a hug. Finally, only Elizabeth, Jake, and Tina were left with the bed-ridden warrior.

"Thanks, Chuck," said Jake. "That was pretty impressive for a cop and a Green Beret."

McCain laughed. "I wasn't really a Green Beret. I just pretended for the entire two years I worked with them."

"Either way, that was a really good meeting, and I think it helped everybody in processing the incident and to get a complete picture of how it all went down. Even Alicia left with a smile on her face."

"I'm glad it helped. Any chance of you coming by sometime tomorrow?" Chuck asked. "I've got something I need to talk to you about."

"Sure, Chuck. It'll be much harder without that bottle of bourbon to share, but I'll be here."

Beth's room, The Northeast Georgia Technical College, Lavonia, Georgia, Wednesday, 1300 hours

Elizabeth had not left Chuck's side for more than a few minutes at a time since he had been wounded. When Jake appeared at her door, though, she welcomed him with a hug, telling him she was going for a run as she left the room. Nicholson carried two bottles of beer, handing one to Chuck and pulling up a chair by the bed.

"This must be serious," Jake commented. "I don't think she's been out of this room for two days."

"Thanks for the beer. It is kind of serious. You're the first one to hear this, Jake. Elizabeth's going with me whenever I heal up and head out."

The Marine grunted and shrugged. "I'm not surprised. What changed your mind?"

"My whole reasoning behind leaving her here was for her protection. No offense, but the other night showed that there is no safe place any more. By my count, we've killed eighteen of that gang but who knows if there are any more of them out there?"

"I understand. You don't think she's safe here."

Chuck shrugged. "Man, I don't think it's safe anywhere anymore. You've done an incredible job in securing this campus, but those guys came in here looking for me and her. If we're together, I think we'll be OK. We can look out for each other. Beth has the makings of a warrior. Did you see how she cut those three guys down? Plus, I'm going to keep training her from here on out."

Nicholson was clearly not thrilled by the news, but understood that it wasn't his decision to make. McCain reached under his pillow and pulled out a piece of notebook paper containing a handwritten list, passing it to his friend.

"Here are a few things that we need. I'll make it worth your while if you can fill that list for me."

Jake reluctantly took the piece of paper and looked it over. He finally glanced back to Chuck, folded the list and put it into his breast pocket.

"What makes you think I have all that stuff?"

McCain grinned. "You were a sergeant in the Marine Corps. I've heard that you guys are the best scroungers on the planet."

Nicholson gave a reluctant laugh. "I'll see what I can do."

Chuck reached back under his pillow and withdrew the unopened bottle of Jack Daniels, handing it to Jake. The Marine's eyes got big as he took the whiskey.

"You've been holding out on me! I'm surprised you're letting this go."

"That one's yours. I've still got a bottle of scotch I recovered from that house where I rescued Beth that I'm keeping. You get me all the stuff that I asked for, and I have another special present for you."

"How long before you're up and about?"

"Karen wants me to stay in bed for a week but I'm going to see how it feels to walk tomorrow. I'd like to be able to leave in three or four weeks, but it doesn't make any sense to leave before I'm mobile again. There are still zombies and bad guys out there, and I won't do us any good if I'm not fit to fight."

Nicholson stood. "Thanks for this," he smiled, holding up the bottle of whiskey. "I'll start working on your list."

Chapter Ten

Preparation

Eleven days after attack, Beth's room, The Northeast Georgia Technical College, Lavonia, Georgia, Friday, 1000 hours

After spending a few days in bed, Chuck's head had finally started to feel normal again. He wasn't walking far for fear of opening his stitches up, just short walks in the hallway. Now, a week and a half later, he was feeling restless. He knew the large wound would take a few more weeks to heal fully, but he hoped to at least get outside for some fresh air.

Karen showed up to check his progress. She looked more rested this morning, McCain noted, having released much of the care of the other two patients to her students. Or maybe there was another reason she had a spring in her step. The nurse smiled at Chuck and Elizabeth, pulling on a pair of rubber gloves.

After checking his face and head, Karen said, "Everything's looking good upstairs. Has anyone ever told you that you have a hard head?"

The big man chuckled. "I have been accused of that."

"Now I think it's time to take out those stitches," she told him, helping McCain pull his sweats down far enough to expose the injury.

"That's healing very nicely," she commented, snipping the sutures and pulling them out with tweezers.

"How's Robert?" Chuck asked, an innocent look on his face.

Karen paused and glanced up. "What makes you think I'd know how Robert is doing?"

"I don't know," he shrugged. "I've just heard that you guys have been spending some time together. Has he been imparting some of his survival skills to you? Or other things?"

The nurse suppressed a laugh. "And where might you have heard those nasty rumors?" she asked, shooting a look at Elizabeth.

Beth held her hands up in surrender. "It must've just slipped out," she laughed.

"Some friend you are!" Karen smiled.

"Well, Chuck," the nurse said, "I'll give you this. He's a great guy. I'm surprised I haven't really noticed him before on this small campus. He does tend to stay in the background and he's really shy.

"I can tell he likes me but I'm going to have to take the initiative. Right now, we're just hanging out a little and he's teaching me how to handle a pistol and a rifle. I was going to ask him over for a drink tonight and talk about something other than guns."

"I'm sure you two will have a lot to talk about," McCain needled, putting air quotes around "talk."

"Oh, aren't you a funny one, Mr. McCain?" Karen grinned, pulling the last of the stitches out and giving his bare behind a swat.

Elizabeth sat on the other bed laughing and thoroughly enjoying her boyfriend giving her best girl friend a taste of her own teasing.

Karen checked Chuck's other injuries and concluded, "It looks like my work here is done. Everything looks good. Just keep an eye on the gunshot wound. I'll give you a tube of anti-biotic ointment to put on it until it's completely healed."

McCain pulled his pants up, pushed himself off of the bed, and grabbed Karen in a bear hug. "You're a great nurse. Thanks for taking such good care of me."

He kissed her on the forehead and noticed a tear running down her cheek. Elizabeth got off the bed and wrapped her arms around Chuck and Karen.

"I'm really going to miss you guys," Karen said. "You take care of her, Chuck."

Twelve days after the attack, The Northeast Georgia Technical College, Lavonia, Georgia, Saturday, 1400 hours

Elizabeth and Chuck walked across campus to Admin. McCain had his pistol belt on for the first time since he was wounded. Beth was also wearing her sidearm, still not used to always having the gun on her. The couple walked arm in arm, the young woman carrying a large purse over her shoulder.

When they got to Nicholson's office, Jake was surprised to see Elizabeth stick around. Not that he minded, she was like the daughter he never had. Normally, however, she had left when Jake and Chuck started talking.

"I asked Beth to stay because I want her to be fully briefed as we plan our trip out of here."

"Good idea," Jake nodded, pulling a familiar piece of notebook paper out of a drawer and laying it in front of him.

"Here's your list," said Nicholson. "Let's run through it, starting at the top. Number one: you wanted a four-door, four-wheel drive pickup or SUV. Would you believe that one of those dead guys left his behind?" he asked with a smile. "It's a nice Toyota Tundra and it fits the specs you asked for. I've had some of the automotive students check it thoroughly from top to bottom, and to make some modifications that I think you'll approve of."

"Modifications?"

Nicholson nodded. "I had them weld some armor plating to the doors, hood, and grill. They also installed a heavy-duty front bumper and a few other odds and ends."

Chuck grinned approvingly. "Very nice. Good thinking."

Elizabeth patted Chuck's arm. "I told you Mr. Nicholson was the best."

"The second thing on the list was a riflc for Elizabeth. Easy. We've got several good ARs to choose from, with most of them having some kind of optics. We'll set her up with some mags and ammo, too.

"Number three: you wanted body armor, web gear, boots, and maybe some tactical clothes for the young lady. The only body armor Tina found in the police supply room was the soft stuff. It'll just stop handgun rounds but it's better than nothing.

Nicholson looked at Benton. "Tina will get with you to try on the clothes, combat boots, and your body armor. I've got an extra set of web gear to hold your mags and stuff.

"Number four: McCain, you asked for a case of MREs. Why would you think that I have MREs?"

"Like I said before, Jake, Marines are good scroungers."

Jake smiled, shaking his head, and pulled a cardboard box of Meals Ready to Eat out from behind his desk and handed it to Chuck. "The only reason I'm giving you those is because I love Elizabeth. They're hard to come by and I don't have many left."

"Thanks, Mr. Nicholson," Beth said, sweetly.

"Next on the list, a backpack for her," Jake read. He reached behind his desk again and withdrew a medium-size backpack and handed it over to the young woman. "That was one of mine and it should take care of you."

"What else?" Jake asked, picking up the piece of paper. "Oh yeah, you needed some ammo, too." He reached into his desk, pulled out several boxes of 9mm and 5.56mm rounds, and slid them over to Chuck.

"I think that's everything on your list, McCain. Of course, we'll give you guys some water and some canned goods for the road, as well."

"That does look like everything, Jake. Much appreciated," Chuck responded, holding his hand out to Elizabeth. She handed him her bag.

Chuck reached in and withdrew a compact Kimber .45 pistol. McCain locked the slide to the rear, verified that it was empty, then laid it on the desk near Nicholson.

"How about that, a compact Kimber! I've always wanted one of those!" Jake exclaimed, grabbing the pistol and looking it over. "Do I even want to know where it came from?"

McCain handed him two loaded magazines for the pistol and shrugged. "Right after I started on my trip, three guys ambushed me for my car. One of them was packing that."

Jake shook his head and stared at the muscular man sitting across from him. "I guess he didn't need it anymore?"

"No," was the only answer Chuck gave.

I'm glad he likes me, the Marine thought. That's one dangerous man.

"I've also got a Bersa .380 that Greg had when he and his girlfriend tried to rob me. It's yours if you want it. I'm keeping the .38 Airweight that the girl had. Beth can use it as her backup gun."

McCain repeated the process of confirming the Bersa pistol was unloaded, handing it to Nicholson along with the magazines. Jake briefly glanced at the .380 and put both pistols in a drawer. He placed his hands on the desk and looked at his two friends.

"Anything else? When are you guys planning on hitting the road?"

Chuck and Beth looked at each other. The young woman answered for them. "We were thinking two more weeks. Chuck wants to give me some more tactical training and the extra time will let him heal more."

Nicholson nodded at McCain. "Any chance of you doing some of that tactical training with our people? Maybe you could include them?"

"Sure, Jake," Chuck answered. "I'd be happy to help out any

way I can."

Beth's room, The Northeast Georgia Technical College, Lavonia, Georgia, Monday, 0800 hours

When Elizabeth awoke, the first thing she noticed was that the extra single bed across from hers was empty. She knew where he was. She had found him in her sitting room every morning for the last week reading a small New Testament. There was something incredibly attractive about his faith. Chuck McCain was attractive on every level, but the quiet strength that he exuded was like nothing she had ever encountered before.

The last few days, though, he had withdrawn into a shell. No, that's not it, she corrected herself. He's just been very quiet. I wonder if he's having second thoughts about taking me with him? Maybe he's even having second thoughts about us?

Am I really that insecure? she wondered. Yeah, I guess I am. Karen's words from the night before played through her mind. "Are you sure you want to do this, Elizabeth? Do you really want to leave your friends and family to be with someone you've known for less than a month? Don't get me wrong, that's a good-looking man and if he asked me to go with him, I'd do it in a heartbeat. Just remember, there's so much you don't know about him and I don't want you to get hurt."

Beth padded quietly to the adjoining room and stopped, leaning against the doorway with her arms wrapped around her chest. Chuck was seated on the couch with the Bible open on his lap, the sunlight streaming in behind him. McCain's eyes were closed, an untroubled, peaceful expression on his face.

"Are you spying on me?" his voice startled her, his eyes now open and twinkling at her.

She gave an embarrassed laugh. "Can I join you?"

He put his arm on the back of the couch. "Please, right here would be good," nodding with his head to the space beside him on the sofa.

Elizabeth sat next to Chuck, tucking her legs up under her for warmth. His big arm wrapped around the young woman, squeezing her tightly in a hug.

"So, how does it work?" she asked.

"How does what work?"

"You know, reading the Bible, praying. What do you do?"

"I'll read a chapter or two. Then I'll think, pray, meditate."

She nodded. "Do you hear God? Does he speak to you?"

McCain shrugged. "Sometimes, but never out loud. It's always a quiet voice down deep inside of me. Sometimes when I'm reading the Bible, I'll feel God speaking and guiding me through what I'm studying. Maybe I'll see something I've never seen before, like the words jump off the page at me. And there are other times when I don't hear anything."

Benton digested this. "Do you really think God listens to us when we pray? I mean there are a lot of people praying about a lot of things. With all the crazy stuff happening in the world, I wonder if he didn't miss a few of those prayers along the way."

Chuck smiled and nodded. "I do believe he hears every prayer. The thing we have to remember, though, is that he gave mankind the most powerful tool in the universe: free will.

"If we believe the Bible, the story from the very beginning was that we have the power to choose to follow God, or we can choose to go our own way in life. We can choose to do good, or we can choose to do evil. There's a tension in how God answers our prayers while working around our own good and bad choices.

"For me, I try to remember that God's nature is love and that he wants to have a relationship with us. Relationships can be kind of messy, though, and they take a lot of work. But both human and divine relationships are why we were created."

Elizabeth closed her eyes, her head laying against the big man's shoulder. He made it sound so easy. He talked about friendship with God like it was the most natural thing in the world.

"Are you OK?" Chuck asked. "It seems like something's bothering you."

"I was wondering the same thing about you," she answered softly. "You've been so quiet the last couple of days. I was wondering if you were rethinking your decision to take me with you. I mean it's not like we've had the most normal start to a relationship. I didn't know if you were, you know, still feeling the same way."

Chuck shifted on the sofa, his arm continuing to hold his girlfriend tightly. He gently stroked her hair, then lifted her chin so that he could look into her eyes.

"I'm sorry, Beth. Nothing's changed. If anything, I'm falling more in love with you every day. I really do want you to come with me. I'm not the most talkative person to begin with, but now we're in operation planning mode.

"When it's time to plan a mission, I get very focused. I apologize for being so distant. Obviously, I've got to work on my relational skills. What about you? Are you having second thoughts about leaving?"

There was a long pause. "I guess, maybe a little. My mind says, 'You've only known him for a few weeks.' My heart says, 'You've known him forever.'

"I don't even have words for it, Chuck. I love you like I've never loved anyone else. I want to be a part of your life. I want to help you find Melanie. But then a voice in the back of my head says that you'll change your mind or you'll realize you don't really like me as much as you thought you did."

"Tell that nasty little voice to be quiet," he said, kissing her on the forehead. "I understand what you're feeling, but I'm not rethinking anything. You're the most beautiful woman on the planet, I love you, and I want to share my life with you. Of course, I'd never try to force you to do something you don't want to do, but after all we've been through, I can't imagine leaving you behind."

Elizabeth's face lit up in a smile. "That's the sweetest thing anyone's ever said to me," she said, wrapping her arms tightly around him. "We're going to be a great team and I trust you. That's a big deal for me. I also want to trust myself, so I'm sorry for being wishy-washy just now. Thanks for talking me off the ledge. You know I love you and want to be with you."

She returned his gaze, their lips met, and all of Beth's doubts vanished.

Two weeks later, The Northeast Georgia Technical College, Lavonia, Georgia, Sunday, 2030 hours

The previous two weeks had been incredibly busy for Elizabeth and Chuck. She was seeing first-hand what he meant about being focused as they prepared for their journey. He had made a point, however, of taking time each evening to sit and talk. When he looks at me, she thought, I get the feeling that everything's going to be OK. She hadn't questioned herself or Chuck any more.

The two of them trained every morning for a minimum of three hours. Beth owned a master key for the campus and Chuck taught her the art of room and building clearing, using the various administrative and classroom buildings. This skill was vital for their safety because they would very likely have to clear houses or businesses as they traveled. Houses for a place to sleep and businesses for the same reason or to find supplies.

McCain was an incredible teacher, patiently helping her master whatever tactic they were working on for the day. Even when

Benton made a mistake, he gently took her back through the scenario, helping her to get it right.

After a couple of days, though, Elizabeth was starting to get the hang of it. She began anticipating what she needed to do as they worked through the buildings. Chuck told her she was starting to think tactically. Her movements became fluid while the rifle and pistol both began to feel natural in her hands.

Their training was conducted using all of their equipment. For Beth, it was another completely different experience wearing the body armor, web gear, combat boots, pistol belt, and rifle across her chest. Chuck had shown her how to put on each piece of gear, their "kit" as he called it.

By far her favorite part of clearing buildings was when Chuck would signal that they had trained enough by gently pressing her against the wall, holding her there, and kissing her passionately. She had never been kissed like that in her life. He's working hard to make sure I don't doubt him again, she smiled to herself.

After five days of working inside, McCain took Benton outside to the vehicle that Mr. Nicholson had prepped for them. They practiced getting out of the Toyota Tundra quickly in the event it became disabled or they were ambushed and unable to drive away. Chuck trained Beth in shooting while driving. He showed her how to position both her Glock and her AR-15 where she could access them easily.

By far the least favorite part of her training was when Chuck took Elizabeth into the thick forest behind the campus. Mr. Nicholson had pointed out where the trip flares were located and Chuck had her maneuvering through the woods. She had never enjoyed camping or being out in nature. The idea of being around so many flying and creeping things made her shudder, but the big man, oblivious to any discomfort, taught her some basic field craft. Fortunately, it was still winter and the mosquitoes and snakes were nowhere to be found.

Beth never complained, however, knowing that they could very well end up in a forest if they lost their vehicle. She thought she detected several looks of approval from Chuck over the course of field training as they hiked through the woods, sweat dripping from their faces.

After dinner, the couple talked about contingencies for their trip. There were so many variables but McCain wanted Benton thinking about every possibility. He asked her to process some uncomfortable topics that they needed to discuss.

What would she do if he was killed? What was their plan if the truck became disabled? Together, they used their evenings to study the maps that Karen had provided. Chuck wanted Beth to be able to see the routes in her mind. Having locational awareness was a vital skill to own.

In the afternoons, McCain had Benton help him train the sentries and security teams. In reality, she thought, he's teaching and I'm his assistant. Teaching the students and faculty what she was also learning, however, solidified her own skill set. Beth marveled at Chuck's amazing ability to break years of tactical knowledge and skills down and make them easy for the uninitiated to master.

Chuck took the campus security teams through building clearing drills, foot patrol techniques, and vehicle tactics, similar to what he was teaching Elizabeth during their morning sessions. McCain had spoken to Nicholson about the importance of sending out more than one vehicle and more than four people on a looting mission. Jake had agreed to release two vehicles and six people for the next trip off campus.

The teams rehearsed exercises simulating one of their vehicles being disabled and everyone having to dive into the second SUV. McCain set up scenarios in which a team member was injured and needed to be rescued. Chuck was patient but relentless, having the student and faculty volunteers run drill after drill until it became second nature.

One afternoon, during a break from practicing vehicle exercises, Chuck and Elizabeth stood off to the side. McCain had just told her what the next scenario was going to be when Robert Clayton walked over, unsure if he should approach them or not.

"Sorry to bother you, Chuck. Hi, Elizabeth."

Beth watched Chuck quickly welcome him, putting him at ease. "Hey, Robert, no bother at all. How's the training? Do you think this is helping anybody?"

Clayton chuckled shyly. "This is some of the best instruction that I've ever had. I've spent some money and gone to several of the big name tactical courses. What you're teaching us beats them all. I just wish we could do some live fire."

Chuck nodded. "I'm glad you're enjoying it. Yeah, you're right, it really does limit us, not being able to actually shoot. We just don't need any zombies interrupting our training!"

Clayton nodded, glancing at Benton and then back at McCain. "I wanted to say thank you for suggesting that Karen train with me. It's been, well, she's a really nice person, and, uh, well, I just…" he stammered, his face turning red.

"What are friends for?" Chuck slapped him on the shoulder, almost knocking the IT professor over. "She's a handful, that's for sure." McCain winked at Beth, who was trying to suppress a smile, and lowered his voice, stepping a little closer to Robert, looking him in the eye. "Karen's a good woman and she needs a good man to look after her. I hope things work out for the two of you."

McCain also found some time every day to use the campus gym, hardening his body back up after being wounded and not exercising for a couple of weeks. Beth accompanied him for a few weight lifting sessions but she'd also been running on the campus track, building her endurance. And, Elizabeth had started saying her goodbyes. She wanted to personally speak to as many people as she could over the next two weeks. Would she ever be back? Would she ever see her friends here again?

Tomorrow was the day, Beth contemplated. There had been no training today, Chuck telling her to rest and visit with her friends. She had kissed him, leaving him fieldstripping and cleaning their weapons, as well as checking out all their equipment in her room.

Later in the day, after visiting with a number of friends and dropping by the command center to have a long chat with Tina and Jake, Benton walked back to the dormitory. The tingle of excitement ran through her entire body as she crossed the beautiful campus that had become her home. She was both excited and scared. A sense of anticipation and fear filled her mind. The fear of the unknown loomed large, but the thrill of being with Chuck almost drowned it out.

What did their future hold? He really wants me with him, she thought. He doesn't have to take me as he continues his quest to find his daughter, but he made it very clear that he loves me and wants me to be part of this journey. More importantly, though, he wants me to be part of his life. This man loves me like I've never been loved before.

As she opened the door to her dorm room, she realized that her life would never be the same.

Chapter Eleven

A New Journey

Hartwell, Georgia, Monday, 0900 hours

The entire campus had turned out to tell them goodbye. The gruff Marine, Jake Nicholson, had grabbed Chuck in a bear hug.

"Make sure you bring me a bottle of something good when you come back for a visit."

"You got it, Jake."

Jake gently hugged Elizabeth as Tina embraced Chuck. "I'm praying for you guys. Y'all take care of each other. I look forward to meeting your daughter when you come to see us."

Robert and Karen, holding hands McCain noted approvingly, made sure they personally told Chuck and Elizabeth goodbye. Clayton shook McCain's hand while Karen and Elizabeth hugged. Chuck expected a wisecrack as Karen grabbed him in a tight embrace. Instead, she just said, softly, "I love you. Please take care of my friend."

The tears were flowing as Elizabeth hugged Alicia, whispering something in her ear. The young woman cried even harder after hearing Benton's words. After a few moments, Alicia walked over to Chuck, wiping her eyes.

She looked into the face of the man who had saved her life and threw herself into his arms, starting to cry again. When she finally regained her composure, Alicia spoke quietly so that only Chuck could hear her words.

"I should be mad at you, taking Miss Benton away and all, but I'm not. You're a good man, Mr. McCain, and you already know how I feel about Miss Benton. I think you two deserve each other. I hope you'll be safe and happy together, and I want you to know that I'll never forget you."

A few miles down the road, Chuck reached over from the backseat and touched Elizabeth's arm. "Are you OK?"

She made eye contact with him in the rear view mirror. She tried to smile but he could see on her face how hard the farewell had been. McCain gave her shoulder a gentle squeeze and returned to looking for threats. He'd let her talk it out or cry it out later. They had so much to discuss, he thought, suddenly feeling butterflies fluttering around in his stomach.

The roads were clear and there was no sign of any zombies or human predators. The houses they passed all appeared to be deserted, many of them boarded up. It was a little over fifteen miles from the college to the outskirts of the small town of Hartwell. According the map, it would then be another five or six miles to Brian's home, located northeast of the city, on Lake Hartwell.

Chuck had Elizabeth stop as the houses got closer together and the trees started thinning out, indicating that they were coming into the city limits. McCain climbed into the bed of the pickup and peered through his binoculars. While Chuck looked through the binos, Beth scanned the area, her rifle up and ready.

McCain knew that this was a small community of around five thousand people, just south of Lake Hartwell, a large man-made lake. Approximately half of the body of water was located in

Georgia while the other half fell across the border in South Carolina. The lake and the area surrounding it had been a popular recreation area featuring boating, fishing, and camping, with plenty of places for families to have picnics. Chuck remembered early in his police career spending time on a fellow police officer's houseboat, fishing and drinking beer. Having access to a boat in the current crisis would not be a bad thing if all the other escape routes were closed off.

The Mitchells, Brian's family, had a home that sat right on the lake, and Brian had taken Mel there after they'd fled the carnage at UGA. The challenge was going to be getting through or around the small town. This was a very rural section of Georgia and the number of roads was limited.

As McCain had studied the maps that Karen had provided, he'd come to the conclusion that they could skirt around the north edge of the city on their way to the Mitchell's home. This gave them a few more options for escape than they would have going through downtown on the narrow city streets. They didn't want a repeat of their trip through Carnesville from several weeks earlier, where their vehicle was almost boxed in by the infected. This entire area looked like it had been evacuated, as the governor had ordered, but a large group of Zs in a confined area could be disastrous.

Chuck got back into the Tundra. "How's it look?" Elizabeth queried.

"Everything looks clear. According to the map, we're going to make a left turn as we come around this curve. That road will put us back onto Highway 51 north. Take a right on that and I'll guide you as we go. With no surprises, we should be able to avoid the downtown area of Hartwell. It's only about a mile to Ridge Road, then it's a straight shot to Brian's house.

"Just remember everything we drilled. You're a great driver," he said, reaching up and patting her shoulder. "Take a deep breath, listen to me, and let's get going."

The city limits really did look deserted. That is, until Beth turned off of Highway 51 onto a pretty, tree-lined residential street. A group of three male and two female infected, all badly decomposed, shuffled slowly towards them from the opposite direction. Their clothes were in tatters and their gray flesh was rotting away.

"No problem," Chuck said, calmly. "Drive towards them and right before you get there, steer around them. I don't think any of that group is going to be moving very fast."

"That's so nasty," Elizabeth shook her head at the Zs coming their way.

Benton followed McCain's directions, accelerating, and then jerking the steering wheel to the left to avoid the zombies. Chuck was right, these Zs looked like they were in slow motion as they turned to follow the fast-moving vehicle. A part of Chuck wanted to stop and put bullets in each of the Zs' heads, but they had to stay focused on their mission. Stopping for every group of infected they saw would only slow them down.

"That wasn't so bad," Beth commented, slowing for a sharp curve to the right. "Maybe all of the…Oh, crap! That one's coming right at us!"

McCain had seen it at the same time she had. A young, twenty-something zombie male had sprinted out from behind a house on their left. In an instant Chuck observed that this Z wasn't decomposed at all, which meant he was very recently infected.

He had been a clean-cut, white male wearing a navy polo shirt and jeans. His throat had a gaping wound, blood covering his neck and chest. McCain saw that the zombie's trajectory was going to bring him directly into the driver's door of the truck. As a southpaw, Chuck's rifle was pointing out the right side of the Tundra. His suppressed Glock, however, was laying next to his left leg.

The pistol came up and McCain fired three fast shots at the

running zombie. Shooting one-handed as the Toyota slowed for the curve, Chuck was happy to see one 9mm hollow point bury itself in the Z's sternum, slowing him down slightly. His first head shot missed, but the next round punched through the infected sprinter's growling mouth and out the back of his skull, sending him to the pavement. Beth accelerated out of the curve, speeding away through the neighborhood.

A T-intersection with a stop sign came up in front of them. "Which way?" Beth asked, her voice surprisingly calm.

"Right, then your first left. You're doing great."

As Elizabeth drove down Reynolds Street, they saw the Hart County Health Department on their right, three figures congregating in front of the building. McCain could see that these zombies had also been infected for a while, the Zs in various stages of decomposition. An obese white woman in a bloody white nurse's uniform started growling and walking slowly towards the road. An infected older African-American couple followed the nurse as the truck quickly left them behind.

The elementary school for the region was also on the right side of the street and appeared deserted, thank God, Chuck thought. There were no more zombies, for the moment anyway. McCain's head continued to turn, left, right, and to the rear, watching their surroundings, rifle in hand.

"Isn't this such a pretty little town?" Beth's voice broke the silence. "Back before, you know, before everything happened, my parents and I would come over here sometimes during the summer and have a picnic on the lake. The downtown area is really cute and has some nice shops. I wonder if it'll ever get back to normal?"

They were approaching another T-intersection. Chuck was amazed at the change in Elizabeth. This was not the same girl who had driven them through a pack of zombies in Carnesville a few weeks before. She seemed to have somehow harnessed her fear and focused it into energy for their mission.

"We'll turn right at that next street," McCain said. "Savannah Street will take us to Ridge. I hope it gets back to normal soon because I'd love to be able to walk around the square of some small town with you.

"In fact, what I'd really like is for the two of us to take a trip to somewhere exotic. What would you think of maybe a thirty-day vacation? You can pick the place, anywhere you want to go."

Benton steered the truck onto Savannah Street and smiled broadly at McCain in the rear view mirror, her eyes big in anticipation. "Anywhere? Could we really do that, Chuck? I haven't traveled very much and that would be so much fun! Where do I turn now?"

"That's Ridge Road just ahead," he pointed. "Turn left and we'll stay on it for maybe seven or eight miles. The Mitchells evidently have a house right on the water."

After less than a mile, however, Beth was forced to brake again, Chuck immediately seeing why. A group of fifteen zombies were standing in the middle of Ridge Road at a four-way intersection, a hundred feet from them. As one, the pack started towards the big pickup, spreading out and covering both lanes. To their right, McCain saw a rundown, low-income apartment complex. Ten more infected were moving their way from one of the stairwells.

"I think it's time to test out that reinforced bumper Jake installed on the front of this thing," Chuck said. "Same drill. Aim for the middle of the pack and when you get close, steer for wherever they look thinner."

These were a mixed bag between recently infected and decomposing. They were also a diverse group of black, white, and Hispanic zombies, the virus playing no favorites.

"Put your windows up," Chuck ordered, reaching over and putting up the two rear windows and the automatic back window, as well. "Don't stop for anything. We're almost there."

Elizabeth nodded. Chuck saw the fear in her eyes, but he also noted a confidence on her face that he had not seen before. The group coming from the apartment complex was almost to them. The group up the street was just fifty feet away.

Benton shoved the accelerator to the floor, throwing McCain backwards against his seat. She drove down the middle of the road, straddling the double-yellow line. The two biggest Zs looked like Mexicans, one still wearing a cowboy hat. They were both in the middle of the zombie horde, reaching for the vehicle and growling.

At the last possible second, Beth steered to the right, slamming into a young black woman and a Hispanic teen male, knocking them both into the air and creating a hole for the Tundra to drive through. Dead hands clawed at the truck as it shot by. A twenty-something white male grabbed at the driver's side rear view mirror, only to be jerked off of his feet and run over by the rear tire of the Toyota pickup.

The road ahead of them appeared to be free of threats as Elizabeth sped away. McCain looked back, noting that the big group was shuffling after them. I wonder how long they'll follow us?

They put their windows back down and for the next five miles all was clear. The closer they got to the lake, the nicer the homes became, all of them also appearing to have been abandoned. It was a strange thing to see these huge houses and no one there to enjoy them. A modern-looking church with a sprawling parking area was ahead of them on their right. A large sign identified it as the Hartwell Community Church.

"Can you pull in over there at that church?" Chuck asked. "Park in the middle of the lot, facing out."

When she stopped, McCain handed her a bottle of water. "Great driving! How you feeling?"

Elizabeth took a long drink and self-evaluated. "I'm actually really good. I've had an amazing teacher." She turned so she could look at her boyfriend. "Working with you over the last couple of weeks has really made a difference in the way I'm thinking. I'm still scared, but there's also a confidence inside me that I've never felt before. We have a plan and we've talked through so many contingencies that I feel prepared.

"It's weird, Chuck," she said, with a shy smile. "I feel this tingle. I don't even know how to describe it, but it's like I'm almost enjoying this. Is that wrong?"

McCain took a swallow of water from his own bottle and chuckled. "A tingle, huh? You're riding the adrenaline. You've heard the term 'adrenaline-junkie?' You just had your first hit of that drug and it can be pretty addicting."

Chuck held the map over the seat so Beth could see it. "I think we're only about 2 miles from the house. The first thing we'll do when we get there is walk around the outside of it, seeing what we can see. Then we'll figure out the best way to get inside. When we do, just remember everything we worked on when we trained room clearing."

"I just remember this big, strong man grabbing me and kissing me inside those classroom buildings," she grinned, looking back over her shoulder. When he didn't smile back, Benton said, "I'm just kidding. I remember and I'll follow your lead."

Hartwell, Georgia, Monday, 1000 hours

As they got closer to the lake, the architecture of the homes became more luxurious, and the homes doubled in size. Many Atlantans or folks from Greenville, South Carolina, had lake homes to go with their big city jobs, since the economy had been booming steadily over the past forty years. According to the map, the Mitchell's lake home was almost at the end of a peninsula that jutted out into the water. McCain didn't like the idea of being on a dead end street, but he had no choice. He just hoped this would not be a wasted trip.

"It looks like we're less than a mile," he told Benton.

As they rounded a sharp curve, however, a roadblock was directly in front of them, fifty yards away. Two SUVs and a Ford F-350 pickup blocked the roadway, end-to-end, preventing anyone from passing. Two men in their forties, one black and one white, and a younger white man in his twenties pointed rifles at them from behind the cover of the vehicles. Out of his peripheral vision, Chuck saw movement and picked out a fourth man behind a tree next to a beautiful two-story brick home to his left, sixty yards away.

Elizabeth slammed on the brakes. "What do I do?" Anxiety filled her voice.

"Be cool. Put your hands up and smile. They've got the drop on us."

The older white man had a gray beard, was wearing an Atlanta Braves ball cap, and was holding an AK-47.

"Turn the vehicle off and put your hands up," Gray Beard commanded, McCain picking up a hint of nervousness in the man's voice. "Step out of the truck without any weapons and walk towards me with your hands up."

"Chuck?" Beth asked.

"Turn it off and keep smiling."

McCain yelled out the open window to his left, "No problem. I'm taking my rifle off and I'm getting out. We don't mean you any harm."

To Beth he said, quietly, "Stay in the truck. I think we're OK but if this goes south, crank it up, get low, and get the hell outta of here."

Chuck pulled his M4 off and angled it down with the muzzle to the floor. He left the Glock on the seat and removed his kevlar helmet, exiting the truck. The big man walked slowly towards the roadblock, smiling the friendliest smile he could muster, his hands even with his shoulders. Didn't I just go through this a few weeks ago, walking towards a bunch of men pointing guns at me? I sure hope I'm reading this one right, he thought.

"My name's Chuck," he stated, stopping twenty feet from the barricade. "We're heading to an address just up the road from here."

McCain saw the man's expression change but the AK was still pointed at his chest.

"What's your last name, Chuck?"

"McCain. Chuck McCain. I'm guessing you gents live around here. I'm on my way to the Mitchell's house. I don't know them but my daughter is dating Brian and I talked to Tommy on the phone a couple of times before the grid went down."

The muzzle of the AK was lowered and the speaker said something to his companions. They lowered their rifles, as well.

"Mr. McCain, what was your last job, before everything went to hell?"

"I'm a federal police officer with the Centers for Disease Control. Can I put my hands down now? I've got ID if you want to see it. I'm just wanting to get to my daughter and I'm hoping the Mitchells left me some clue as to where they were going."

"Who do you have with you in truck, Mr. McCain?"

"That's my girlfriend, Elizabeth. We're traveling together, just the two of us."

Gray Beard spoke to the other two men again. The younger one, probably Gray Beard's son, Chuck realized, moved towards the front vehicle, the Ford pickup.

"Mr. McCain, my son, Travis, is going to move that truck so you can pull through. Would you have the young lady pull your vehicle in and stop next to us? I have some information that I think you'll be interested in."

Chuck nodded, turned, and walked back to their Toyota. "Did

you hear all that?"

"Yeah, but can we trust them?" she whispered.

McCain shrugged. "I hope so."

Travis pulled forward into the front yard of a sprawling single-story home on the right side of the street, creating an opening for Beth to drive the Tundra through. When she parked on the other side of the roadblock, the big Ford was backed into place again.

McCain walked through the barricade, following Benton as she maneuvered their truck off to the right shoulder. Chuck now stood in front of the three armed men. Correction, he thought, four armed men. I forgot the one by the tree over there. A younger version of the black man, this one muscular and fit, approached carrying a camo-painted AR-15.

"Mr. McCain, I'm Ben Thompson," Gray Beard said, sticking out his hand, which Chuck shook. "Let me introduce you to my friends. That's my son, Travis. This is Leroy Roberts," nodding at the older African-American man, "and that's his son, Anthony."

The men all shook hands. Thompson pointed at the two-story home across the street. "That's Leroy's. We live there," nodding at the single-story home. "The Mitchells live just up the street," pointing at a much larger brick home a few hundred feet up on the left. "Most everybody evacuated, but a few of us stuck around. Leroy and me, plus the boys here, we try to keep an eye on things."

"Why didn't you guys leave?" Chuck asked. "There are still plenty of infected out there. We ran into a pack of at least twenty a few miles down the road."

Ben and Leroy looked at each other. "Well, I guess we'll be gettin' a visit, then," Leroy said, with the drawl of someone who had grown up in Hartwell. "Then again, maybe not. They seem to lose interest pretty quick."

Thompson looked back at McCain and shrugged. "I'm a pastor. That's my church back down the road on the left. The Hartwell

Community Church. A lot of my people chose to stay and hunker down to protect their homes. We lost a few folks to the virus, but, by and large, we've all made out pretty well.

"My wife and I want to be here for our people. Tommy and Terri Mitchell were volunteer pastors with us and are some of our best friends. Tommy probably would've stayed, too, but he felt responsible for making sure your daughter was safe."

Chuck felt a wave of relief hearing Thompson's words. Knowing that Melanie had gotten away safely brought a smile to his face.

"Any idea where the Mitchells went?"

"Hang on just a second." Ben walked over to his blue Toyota SUV and pulled a white envelope out from behind the visor.

McCain glanced over at Benton, who was watching everything closely, her hands where he couldn't see them. She's got her Glock pointed at these guys, he realized. He caught her eye, winked, and motioned for her to join them. She slowly exited the Tundra, her pistol now in her holster. Chuck could see that she was still uncomfortable, looking at each man closely.

"This is Elizabeth," McCain told the men. He told her each of the men's names and she nodded at them, not making any move to shake their hands.

"Would you mind showing me your ID, Mr. McCain? I told Tommy I'd give this to you if you showed up but I want to make sure I'm giving it to the right person."

Chuck withdrew his badge and ID card from his jacket pocket, identifying him as a Supervisory Agent with the Centers for Disease Control Enforcement Unit. He handed the badge wallet to the pastor, who studied it carefully.

McCain nodded at Leroy. "Why'd you stick around, Mr. Roberts? Are you part of the pastoral team, too?"

"Lord, no!" Roberts laughed. "I'm Ben's pet heathen. He keeps trying to covert me but I'm a hard case. He's a good neighbor, though, and I'll admit, we've had some good discussions about life, faith and the Bible, sitting out here looking down the road, waitin' on zombies to show up.

"But I can't leave. My wife's bed-ridden. She's dying of cancer and can't be moved." He lowered his voice and said sadly, "I don't think it'll be too much longer. With no way to get her treatments, she's taken a bad turn. We just try and make her comfortable. In fact, Anthony, would you go check on your momma and see if she needs anything?"

"Yes, sir." The younger Roberts turned and left the group.

Satisfied, Ben handed Chuck his ID back and pointed at Anthony's retreating figure. "He's a corporal in the Marines. He was in Iran during the war and happened to be home on leave when those last bad attacks happened a few months ago in Atlanta, Washington, and New York. He never received new orders when the communication grid went down and we're sure glad to have him here with us.

"Tommy told me to give you this if, or when, you showed up," the pastor said, handing the white envelope to McCain. "He expected you'd have been here a lot sooner. I'd pretty much forgotten about you."

"It's been a rough couple of months," Chuck said, glancing at Beth. He tore open the envelope and found a hand-written note and a key. The note contained the address and a hand-drawn map of where the Mitchells were going and leaving him the key to their Lake Hartwell residence. Tommy had written that Chuck was to make himself at home, stay as long as he wanted, and to take whatever he needed.

Something wet dripped onto the paper as he read it. At first he thought it was raining but then the big man realized tears were dripping out of his eyes. Elizabeth put her arm around him as she saw him getting emotional. He handed her the note.

"Sorry, Pastor," Chuck smiled, wiping his eyes on his sleeve and reaching for the pastor's hand, gripping in it in a thankful handshake. "That's the best news I've gotten in a long time. Thank you for this."

"There isn't much good news going around these days so it's nice to be able help out."

"This is wonderful, Chuck," Beth said, quietly, after reading the note.

"If Tommy gave you a key, I sure don't want to hold you up," Ben smiled. "Are you folks going to spend the night or do you plan on hitting the road right away? If you're going to stay over, I'd be honored if you'd have dinner with my wife and I. We'd love to hear what's going on out there," he said, motioning with his hands toward Hartwell and beyond.

Chuck looked at Elizabeth and saw that her defenses had finally come down. "It's up to you," she said. "I know you're ready to get to Melanie, but…"

"I think it'd be better to leave early in the morning," he replied, looking into her eyes, "and give ourselves a full day to travel. Why don't we go settle in, rest a bit, have dinner with the Thompsons, and then leave tomorrow?"

The girl's face lit up and he knew he'd made the right decision.

The Mitchell's home, Hartwell, Georgia, Monday, 1500 hours

Chuck and Elizabeth sat on a leather love seat in the sunroom overlooking Lake Hartwell. The Mitchell's residence was beautiful and spacious but this room quickly became the couple's favorite, as they watched the sun just starting to make it's descent into the west. They had shared a large can of beef stew for lunch. Southern hospitality was alive and well, as several food items had been left behind in the pantry in the hope that Chuck would show up and make use of them.

"So, how did you know those guys at the road block were friendly?" Elizabeth asked, sipping from a bottle of water.

"I don't know. I've gotten pretty good at reading people, I guess. I spent two years in the Middle East working with the Army Special Forces. That's a big part of what they do. They're considered 'force multipliers.'

"The SF guys hook up with local militias and groups, offering to train them to fight a common enemy. You have to be able to get a read on people pretty quickly to figure out if they're friend or foe. Plus, I knew I had you over there watching my back," he said, draping his arm around her shoulders.

"I was pretty scared, I'm not gonna lie," Beth admitted. "But you were Mr. Cool. You were smiling and talking to those guys like they were your best friends. You did the same thing with that gang at the college. They were threatening to kill you, Alicia, and me, but then you started trash-talking them. I wonder about you, Mr. McCain. Does anything scare you?"

"Oh, I get scared. Trust me. I just try to turn it into something else. Fear can suck the energy out of you and I'd rather channel mine in other directions."

This was such a beautiful view, looking out over the water, snuggled up next to Chuck. Life was pretty good at the moment, Elizabeth thought.

"No other fears or phobias?" she asked him, looking into his face and seeing something she hadn't seen before. What is that?

"There is something, isn't there?" she pressed.

He swallowed and took a deep breath. "Yeah, I guess there is something," he answered, quietly, feeling the butterflies again.

"It's OK." She laid her head against his shoulder. "You don't have to talk about it. I'm sorry I asked."

After a few minutes, Chuck kissed her on the forehead and

looked into her eyes. "But I need to talk about it. This is important. Remember when we were in the car and I asked you if you'd like to go on a trip with me?"

Oh, that's it, she realized. He knows that isn't going to happen and he feels bad that he said it.

"Hey, don't worry about it," she whispered. "I'm not holding you to that. We were just talking. I know it's not going to happen with the state that the world is in."

"No, you don't understand." He turned on the small sofa so that he was facing her. "What I was asking was if maybe that big trip could be our honeymoon?"

"Our honeymoon?" she repeated slowly, her eyes widening. "You mean, like a honeymoon after a wedding?"

"I'm sorry," he mumbled, "I'm screwing this up."

Chuck got off of the couch and knelt in front of her. "Beth, I'd like, I mean, would you marry me? You said a while back that we don't know each other that well, so if you want to think about it, I'll understand. I wish this was a more romantic setting but…"

Elizabeth's mouth pressed over Chuck's, muffling anything else he might have said as she threw herself into his arms. The couple ended up on the floor in a tangled heap, Benton crying and laughing.

"Are you serious, Chuck? Do you really want to get married? You want to marry me?"

McCain gently lifted her head so he could look into her eyes. "I've never been more serious about anything. You started asking what I was scared of as we were sitting here, while I was trying to figure out a way to tell you that I want to spend the rest of my life with you."

He stroked her hair as she lay on top of him. "So, you never answered me. Will you marry me, Beth?"

"Yes, I'm sorry. I'd love to become Mrs. Chuck McCain."

"Well, good. Now I can check that off of the list."

"List? What list?"

"You know, the list of things that I'm terrified of doing. Like asking a beautiful girl to marry me."

They eventually climbed back onto the love seat and continued to watch the sun set, arms wrapped around each other. Elizabeth's heart was full. Just a couple of months before, she was mired in deep depression after the death of her parents, struggling with feelings of guilt and hopelessness.

Through another tragedy, the murder of her friends, God had brought this wonderful man into her life. Chuck hadn't only saved her from a terrible death, he had helped her work through her guilt, and had loved her back to life. And now he wanted to marry her. Okay, so the circumstances weren't ideal, with zombies and roving gangs of criminals still ruling the countryside, but she didn't care. As long as she got to be with Chuck, nothing else mattered.

A question suddenly popped up in her mind. An obvious question, but one she needed the answer to. Beth kissed Chuck on the lips, her hands on his face.

"When do you think we can get married? I'm guessing most churches aren't doing a lot of weddings right now."

'That's a good question. I guess we can have a nice long engagement if you'd like. Maybe it's better that way?"

She accepted that and put her head against his chest. "Okay, maybe you're right, but what do you mean by 'long?' I'd marry you right now if I could."

He smiled down at her. "Do you trust me?"

That's an odd thing to ask, she thought. "Of course. I said I'd marry you so, sure, I trust you."

"Well, OK, then."

"What does that even mean?" she asked.

"It means we should probably get cleaned up for dinner."

The Thompson Home, Hartwell, Georgia, Monday, 1800 hours

Pastor Ben opened the front door at their knock, a tall, smiling woman, with long black hair, standing next to him.

"Elizabeth, Chuck, this is my wife, Angela. Thank you so much for accepting our invitation."

"Thanks for asking," McCain smiled.

Angela shook hands with Chuck, put her arm around Beth, and led her towards the kitchen to help her with whatever smelled so good.

"Do you have electricity?" McCain asked, wondering how Mrs. Thompson was able to cook.

"We have a generator that we turn on once a day and for special occasions. This definitely qualifies as a special occasion."

"Do you drink wine, Pastor?" Chuck held out held out a bottle of Napa Valley Merlot.

Thompson's eyes lit up. "Please, call me 'Ben,' and yes, we do enjoy wine. I remember reading where Paul told his young associate, Timothy, to 'have a little wine every now and then for the sake of your stomach.' Unfortunately, this is one of those things that's hard to come by now, so a very welcome treat. Thank you."

Chuck laughed. "You can thank your friend Tommy when you see him. I snagged that from his pantry."

"Ha! And here I thought Tommy was a teetotaler!"

Ben led Chuck into their living room and offered him a seat in a comfortable leather armchair. A framed picture sat on the table between the two men. Ben, Angela, Travis, and a pretty young woman smiled for the camera. The pastor saw his guest gazing at the photo and sighed.

"That's our daughter, Tracey. She and her husband live just outside of Chicago. We haven't had contact with her in almost six months. Have you heard any news about zombies in that area?"

Chuck shook his head. "No, nothing. When the CDC Enforcement Unit was still functioning, I never saw any reports about attacks in Chicago. They had some isolated incidents there in the early days, eight or nine months ago, but nothing like the east coast. I'm sure Tracey's fine."

Ben nodded. "Thanks for saying that. These are definitely days which force us to prayer and show us what our faith is made of."

McCain could hear Elizabeth talking and laughing with Angela in the kitchen, like they had been friends for years. Before long, the former police officer and the pastor were talking about their lives, their faith, and whether or not this was the end of the world, according to Biblical prophecy.

When Elizabeth came into the living room thirty minutes later, Chuck was leaned over and speaking to the pastor in a low voice, a serious look on his face. Pastor Ben looked up at the young woman and smiled.

"Congratulations on your engagement, Elizabeth. You're going to be a beautiful bride!"

Benton blushed brightly. "Oh, thank you, sir. That's sweet of you to say. Miss Angela asked me to come get y'all. It's time to eat."

Travis joined them for dinner, explaining to Chuck and Beth that he had been outside, keeping an eye on the street just in case the group of zombies that McCain had told them about decided to pay them a visit. Anthony had taken his place at the barricade so his friend could eat with their guests. The meal was a fabulous venison roast from a deer that Travis had killed, his father boasted. The Thompson's generator had been turned off after the meal was prepared, the dining room now illuminated by tapered candles of various lengths on the long table.

Ben shared that Travis had been the volunteer youth pastor at their church when they still had a youth group and had also run a successful yard care business, serving Hartwell and the surrounding region. Chuck picked up that Travis and Brian Mitchell were pretty good friends, having grown up together.

Angela and Ben asked Chuck several questions about what was going on in the outside world. Without getting too graphic, he told them of the violent gangs, which were becoming more common and of the packs of infected that were scattered throughout the area.

"I'd really love to hear how you two met," Angela smiled, putting her hand on Elizabeth's.

Beth looked at Chuck, who just shrugged. "It's up to you," he said, softly. "It might do you some good to talk about it."

Ben jumped in. "If you'd rather not, or if it's too personal, it's OK, Elizabeth."

Benton looked into McCain's eyes and drew fresh strength. She took a deep breath and said, "No, it's alright. I'd like to tell you how we met, but it's definitely not your typical boy-meets-girl story."

For the next twenty minutes, Beth told them the unlikely and shocking way that their lives had been thrown together. Ben, Angela, and Travis sat transfixed as they heard about Elizabeth's friends being gunned down and her subsequent beating and kidnapping. As Beth described how she'd made peace with God, Angela dabbed at her eyes with a napkin.

All three of the Thompson's looked at McCain with awe as Beth described how he'd kicked in the door, shot three of the attackers, got shot himself, and then had to go hand-to-hand with the last, and biggest, of the kidnappers, finally killing him with a knife. She put her hand on Chuck's arm, recounting how he'd almost had to carry her to their vehicle, only to find a pack of ten zombies coming right at them. Her rescuer had calmly cut down the entire group and then had taken her to another abandoned house up the street.

Benton smiled as she recalled the two days they were trapped inside the cold house, waiting for the storm to break and the snow to melt, and how she found herself falling in love with the big man who had saved her.

"We spent a month together at the Northeast Georgia Technical College before heading out to find Melanie. That was where I worked before the world fell apart and there's a large group of survivors there. But," she concluded, "that's how we met."

Ben shook his head. "I've never heard anything like that in my life. Chuck, I met Melanie a couple of times when we would visit with the Mitchells or they would come here. You came up in one of the conversations, talking about your job and your part in fighting the terrorists and the zombies. Your daughter looked me in the eye and said, 'Daddy will be fine. He's a real-life action hero.'"

"That's nice," Chuck said, quietly, a little embarrassed at the attention. "I'm just glad I was able to get there in time to save this beautiful girl." He gave Elizabeth's shoulder a gentle squeeze.

Angela stood. "Elizabeth, would you help me take this stuff to the kitchen?"

As the ladies carried the dishes into the kitchen, Ben motioned for Travis to come close. Chuck watched as the father whispered into his son's ear, both smiling as Travis quickly disappeared outside. The pastor looked over at Chuck and nodded.

Ten minutes later, the two couples sat chatting in the living room, sipping the last of the wine. Candles placed in strategic locations illuminated the spacious living area. The front door opened, admitting Travis, Leroy, and Anthony, the three men smiling at some private joke, Beth thought.

"How's Betsy, Leroy?" Angela asked.

"She's sleeping, thankfully, so we were able to slip out for this. Thanks for inviting us."

"Thanks for coming," the pastor's wife said. "I'll be over tomorrow to sit with her."

Ben had gotten up and was standing by the fireplace. He motioned for Chuck to join him. Elizabeth noticed that everyone in the room was now looking at her, suddenly understanding that something was happening, but having no idea what it was.

"Beth," Chuck said, his voice strong and confident, "if you don't have anything better to do tonight, would you marry me? Pastor Ben told me that he hasn't performed a wedding in a while and he needs to stay in practice."

Benton realized that her mouth was hanging open, but no words were coming out. McCain walked over to the couch and held his hand out. She took it, unconsciously getting up, her other hand covering her mouth.

He led her to where the beaming pastor stood. Still stunned, Beth stared at both men. "Oh, my God! Is this real, Chuck?"

"This is as real as it gets, Sweetheart. Unless you still want that long engagement?"

"No! This is great! Thank you, Pastor Ben."

The pastor led the couple through a beautiful set of vows, read some Scripture, and then laid his hands on Chuck and Beth, inviting his wife to join him, as he prayed for their marriage and their journey through life together.

Thirty minutes later, the couple walked arm-in-arm up the driveway to the Mitchell's house.

"If you'd like, we can have a big ceremony and invite all your friends, whenever things return to normal. We could even have it at the college if you want."

"That would be so nice," she answered, squeezing his bicep. "I still can't believe you did that," she laughed. "We're really married."

A sudden realization hit her as they reached the front door.

"Chuck, that means we can…"

"Oh, I know. I hope you weren't planning on sleeping tonight," her husband said, easily scooping her up in his arms and carrying her over the threshold into the house. Beth grinned at him as he gently set her down and then started giggling as Chuck chased her up the stairs to the master suite.

"I guess we're about to find out how well my hip has healed up." He lightly swatted Beth's behind and she let out a huge squeal.

"Yes, we are, Mr. McCain," Elizabeth answered, wrapping her arms around her husband's neck and pulling him into the bedroom.

Coming Soon!

I hope you enjoyed *Running Towards the Abyss*. If you did, would you consider leaving me a review on Amazon? Good reviews help authors move higher in the rankings and let other readers know that a book is worth reading.

Climbing Out of the Ruins- Volume Five of the Zombie Terror War Series will be out later this year. If you haven't read the first three books in the series, please check them out, as well.

When the Future Ended

The Darkest Part of the Night

When the Stars Fell From the Sky

If you know anyone that would enjoy these stories, please tell a friend. They will appreciate it and so will I!

I love staying in touch with my readers. Please check out my blog at DavidSpell.com or if you just want to send me some feedback you can do that at david@davidspell.com.

Made in United States
North Haven, CT
03 September 2022

23595269R00182